The
Savage
River Valley

Pamela De Leon

The
Savage
River Valley

A Story of The Hudson

Tate Publishing & Enterprises

The Savage River Valley
Copyright © 2009 by Pamela De Leon. All rights reserved.

No part of this publication may be reproduced, stored in a retrieval system or transmitted in any way by any means, electronic, mechanical, photocopy, recording or otherwise without the prior permission of the author except as provided by USA copyright law.

This novel is a work of fiction. However, several names, descriptions, entities, and incidents included in the story are based on the lives of real people.

The opinions expressed by the author are not necessarily those of Tate Publishing, LLC.

Published by Tate Publishing & Enterprises, LLC
127 E. Trade Center Terrace | Mustang, Oklahoma 73064 USA
1.888.361.9473 | www.tatepublishing.com

Tate Publishing is committed to excellence in the publishing industry. The company reflects the philosophy established by the founders, based on Psalm 68:11,
"The Lord gave the word and great was the company of those who published it."

Book design copyright © 2009 by Tate Publishing, LLC. All rights reserved.
Cover design by Blake Brasor
Interior design by Stephanie Woloszyn
Edited by Vince Conn

Published in the United States of America

ISBN: 978-1-60799-821-1
Fiction / Historical
09.06.09

DEDICATION

This book is dedicated to the loving memory of
my nephew Seger Downey,
who shall remain "forever in my heart."

With love, Aunt Pamie.

ACKNOWLEDGEMENT

Heartfelt thanks for the unconditional support given to me by my daughter Anya and my best friend and colleague Jody. Without their understanding and patience, this book would have remained a figment of my imagination and an unfulfilled dream. Also, I am grateful to countless others who encouraged me during this incredible journey, in particular my students in New York and Virginia. I have walked the historical spots of the Hudson Valley alone and in all kinds of weather, heard countless docents describe past lives, read volumes, and felt curiously drawn to the longhouses at the Fenimore Museum in Cooperstown and in the State Museum of Albany. I gleaned appreciated tidbits from curator George Hamell. My thanks to Shirley Dunn for her help, encouragement, and editing skills; and I look forward to her next book on the Mohicans. I would especially like to thank Janey Hays who believed in my book from the start and my editor Vince Conn for his incredible insight and help. Any liberties I take with the telling of the past are purely my own. I love the Hudson Valley and know of no other place that is dearer to me and countless others, past and present.

O where are Kings and Empires now,
Of Old that went and came?

But, Lord thy church is praying yet,
A hundred years the same.

Hymn No. 214,
Cornwallville, New York

In the Beginning

5:30 a.m., 2001

The ragged shoreline lies concealed in a bank of heavy clouds whose thickness hovers inches above the river and the land.

It is early morning, just before dawn.

The land lies peacefully quiet and still, for the soft breezes of the night have subsided into a subtle movement of air, scarcely perceptible.

Giant oaks, towering maples, evergreen hemlocks, and spruces populate the river's wooded bank and grow close together. Their treetops peak above the low-lying clouds, clouds that typically lift and quickly dissipate into thin air, encouraged by a gentle momentum of wind; but not today, not this early morning. It is a slow and fanciful dance the clouds engage in, delicately twisting, slightly twirling; white puffs fringed with blue-gray borders, its colors barely concealed in the waning hours of the night.

River water drifts in steady currents against the bank, slapping it lightly in soft monotony.

Shrouds of white mist resemble delicately woven cloaks carefully draped over the dark green forest as if winter had already arrived, deliberately dropping heavy snows that have fallen over the land. Across the valley, the mist lies heavy then suddenly begins to move, drifting over grassy meadows, climbing up the hills and knolls, creeping into gorges.

As you open this story and the worlds you are about to enter, you are gently forewarned not to be fooled or to willingly play the part of the fool, as with eagerness you approach this as a new page turning in your life. Listen and read attentively to all that is said and written cautiously, authoritatively, or pompously, with a degree of certainty or not, and subsequently look up, survey the surrounding scenery, feel the rush of exhilaration and believe you understand it! As if it could be that simple. Has it occurred to you that it is not? As if all you have to do is hope? Believe this with a quiet word: you are not part of this land, a land of mountains and highlands reaching up from the river's banks with a long valley full of lush meadows and sloping hills that will far outlast your temporary presence on Earth. However, with the slightest bit of luck, you as the mortal will hear the message. At that moment, you might begin to understand, to appreciate the longevity and the beauty, never ending, always solidly present.

The beauty called land is the silent observer of history.

Perhaps the true meaning of all of this will reach you. The word, perhaps, lingers in your mind and settles heavy on your tongue. It is a risk you agree to take upon your shoulders and accept as your own, as over time you delve into the countless pages and volumes of time that will follow.

Do not profess to be enticed by this story and what you are about to learn and believe yourself to be one with the land, or it will haunt you. It will call to you; softly whisper to you at all times of the day and awaken you at night, leaving you pensive and yearning. Yearning to see it again and protect it at all costs, to live beneath the swaying treetops in the dancing shadows cast by the mountains. Simply enough, being away, by choice or necessity, from the land and its shadowy spots will gnaw at your body's innards like a festering canker, calmed only by sleep with windows opened to a moonlit backdrop of crickets and other night sounds coupled with the scurrying of animals scavenging in the night. You will long for a glimpse of the valley and of the hills crisscrossed by rushing creeks fed by cold-water streams. You will hear the water before you see it

THE SAVAGE RIVER VALLEY

and feel the fragrance of the woods envelope your senses. Snapped twigs, broken branches, and tracks of larger game will present themselves to you. You will hear the call of animals in the far distance yet not see them. The shadowed forest will catch your eye, pique your curiosity, and entice you to follow along the trails to its innermost recesses. Your body will tingle with deep excitement as you wander the halls of each stone house with windows long gone and doors, precariously hung, that creak in the blowing wind; whispers that carry from one room to another of dwellings that house the ethereal presence of previous owners, owners that you might have known if only vicariously through a history book, a faded letter held together by a frayed ribbon stuffed away in a musky attic, or a delicately lettered journal meticulously archived in the Netherlands; lives and spirits that will bid you to enter but never to leave.

You as the observer, adrift in the silence of the moment, will endlessly search, persistently wait, most often will share in the suffering. You will stumble blindly through the heartache of those lost and forgotten, shed tears and collapse from grief. Perhaps you will not understand it all, but you will endure like the land.

The land that lies quiet and still.

You are kindly asked to quietly step aside for now you are joined by the captive who, for quite some time, has been listening with a cocked ear to the spiritual call that would beckon him from the other world, draped in morning mist, though he has never been far away.

This captive comes from a world of half shadows, but his courage is unwavering, his bold heart even more so. It is a heart that you will learn to understand in its entirety. Love that touched him once will not let go. It has called him into the daylight and captured him as much as the land has. The heavy chains that bind him to this earthbound world are nothing that can be seen with the visible eye. The chains are emotional bindings that wrap themselves around him with great strength. Both this love and love of the land hold him the forever beautiful, forever strong captive.

They hold him back. They will not let go.

But, at some point, all captives must be released from turmoil, injury, darkness, and despair. That, since ages ago, has been the plan. They pass to the next world where darkness does not exist. This world is of stepping-stones and passages of rites and the seeking of the light.

You study him quietly with a practiced eye and thumping heart. You think you recognize him, breathe in his smell, sense his all-so-familiar aura. You hesitate, for you are not quite sure. So much has confused you before.

Yet, as life often takes the manner of a brisk business, so must we. There is a delicate choice he must make, and here it presents itself for the first time, and you, as the observer, will follow each step carefully and begin to understand his choice.

Now is your chance to stop, seize the opportunity to resist, go no further, and simply turn and walk away on a road most frequently taken, back to the land of your everyday confused existence, and the captive back to his land of wild animals and the pursuit of the elusive mountain buck. The captive, striking in his native beauty, does not succumb! Words, that is all, just mere words that are spoken in the air and float about you but settle delicately in his ears. Words that make his heart come alive, pounding in its desire to live.

Now the Captive will hear these words.

Bravo, Captive! You have never in your earthly life turned from your true heart and now, as a spirit, you never will.

Go on then, with permission to look forward, Captive, or come to think of it, backwards, for surely you remember the land that stretched before you, the white drifting snow, the red embers of the continuously burning fire, the smooth rub of your bow, the only woman for you.

How could you forget?

It is not likely that you could. For in this instant, although the Captive is not so easily fooled, you, hushed and awed observer, surely believe it to be winter. Why is that? By the power of sugges-

THE SAVAGE RIVER VALLEY

tion, you believe the land is frozen and unyielding to the plow; the air so crisp and cold as to send sharp tingles deep within the lungs of young and old alike. The hardiest of souls, poor or rich, barren or fertile, gather inside at early darkened hours to pull down the shades, draw the drapes and block out the blackness of the night.

Ah, but the captive is not so easily fooled.

Look closely and listen carefully to all, peer into the realm of mixed emotions encompassing barely contained excitement and great indifference, secrecy, mystery, and hidden deceit to a land that has suffered and endured the ravages of passing years and yet, in all stoicism, continues to be as majestic and timeless as it was thousands of years ago. A land that stands long after the demise of those who inhabited it, long after their earthly remains deteriorated and their flesh withered from the bone, and long after it gradually dissipated to dust and ashes, long after a new generation took hold.

Do you recognize yourself, Captive? That is you: dust and ashes. You linger in a woman's heart aching with agonized desperation that rules her days and haunts her night. Ah yes, observer, now you hear mention of a woman. Her agony prompts the Captive's bold spirit to live on. The memory is powerfully unforgiving.

Step forward now, Captive, and know your destiny.

In order to go forward, we must go backward, momentarily visiting the past before we advance to the present and future. We go to a moment in time beyond your celebrated birth when the white-headed eagle, the sacred seer, flew overhead as you gave your first lusty cry to the world and even further back to the time of your great nomadic ancestors.

Yes, speeding in a flash through time to a much earlier day.

A dawning day whose meager reflection of the sun gave forth no evidence that man had even once walked these lands and a setting sun that glowed only on animal footprints. As you come forward and form once more as part of this world, you must know where you came from in order to know who you are in this instant and who you will become. For that is the essence of life, the essence of a spirit guide.

Your family stories told you much but they did not tell all, for they themselves did not know or remember all. They did the best they could with what their mortal memories were capable of supporting and retaining.

You wonder as you look about you, *Years ago, did the land appear as it does today?*

Not a frequently asked question, but a good one.

Now you turn your head to listen, you are curious to hear the answer, the detailed explanation, for you lived your life constant as one with nature. You were the trees that grew tall. You were the snow that fell heavily on the mountain and over the valley. You were the warm sun and the pale moon, the summer day and the winter night. You were the mighty bear, the courageous wolf, and the fast running rabbit.

Where did you live and eventually grow from a young boy into a man?

An explanation is again offered. A very long time ago, beyond the stories you remember, the present northeast lay in the very center of a giant continent stretching thousands of miles in all directions. A time considerably noted before the moment your ancestors arrived, having traveled great distances over thousands of years to find the one spot where they would settle, build villages and crude shelters and, as best they could, nurture their subsistence.

Monumental, sometimes catastrophic, changes in climate and geographical features left their permanent marks. Entire continents ripped apart in less time than it took to form them with such a force that would seemingly destroy everything in their path.

The northern hemispheric landmass in the course of time shifted with fearsome power. Slowly but persistently breaking into huge pieces over millions of years, leaving this land in a state of constant flux and eruptions.

Valleys with north-south rifts in the land were suddenly emerg-

THE SAVAGE RIVER VALLEY

ing as shallow seas were drying, evaporating into the air, or draining to lower grounds. As it was, over thousands of years, the softer rocks were eroded by powerful, dominant forces of nature: rushing water and heavy wind. The modern day mountain range of this land was formed by an even later, consistent erosion of the softer Devonian sandstone, which was a part of the ancient range of mountains to the east. Further south along the valley, volcanic eruptions and shifting of land plates formed the Palisades cliffs; towering sentinels of layered rock looming to the southwest of the valley, while in the north the landmass of highland ironed rocks were produced at intense heat and increasing pressure from twenty-five miles underground, thereby causing a mighty explosion that shook the land for days. In its anger and terrifying strength, the land spewed forth a great uplift of hot earth, lava, and fire to form the tall imposing mountains of solid rock, one in particular displaying a totally white façade. No living creature survived for miles from the epicenter of the blast.

The timeframe shifted as if in fast forward motion. The seasons began to blend. Summers continued to stay cool. The snow that lay in clumps refused to melt so that eventually over the years it never stopped accumulating. The days became as cold as the nights. Ice formed upon ice, new snow accumulating over old; the sheer weight of the mass caused it to spread outward. Far on the horizon, this great white blur was slowly advancing; the fourth such occurrence and nothing in its path could stop it. Each day it grew inches closer. A natural phenomenon, the mighty glacier approached from the north flattening everything before it, raking in mountains of gravel and boulders and carrying everything it picked up in the ice flow for thousands of years. The heat of the earth's surface is gradually replaced by a perpetual external cold.

Listen carefully. Your body shivers as you think of a bitter cold scene that is blue-gray and icy. The cold will insidiously seep into your bones and settle there permanently. You hear the howl of a lonely wind whistling over a barren land. By then, nearly ten thousand years ago, your ancestors had come to this land, feeling the desolate loneliness loom over them daily as they roamed up and down the windy valley hunting giant elk during the last big change that swept over the land and into the climate.

At times, they were so hungry they ate whatever they, often by pure luck, managed to hunt and quickly kill. The meat often times was raw, because they did not take time to light a fire. Almost always, within minutes, their stomachs revolted and in great pain, worse than the pangs of hunger, they spent the better part of the hour retching up the raw undigested food. But the pain had somewhat, and with a smidgeon of relief, been diminished by the few minutes during which they experienced a great sensation: a full stomach.

The frozen landscape spreads for miles before you, a ceaseless white world. It is the Ice Age. Can you see it? Ah, you must for you are shivering. The frozen earth lay sleeping under tons of packed snow and solid ice, a half-mile thick and three-miles wide. An icy grave for the land where very little grew or flourished.

Who lived here and how?

South along the ridge of the great valley on a late winter's afternoon, at a spot which later would bear the name of Stony Point, a mother mastodon, courageous in a spirit equally matched by her size, displays chipped, discolored, and somewhat cumbersome ivory tusks; gracefully curving out from her cheekbone, reaching an awesome length of six feet. She hovers protectively over her furry calf that huddles underneath his mother's massive body and bleats defenselessly beneath the cloudy gray skies. A bitter wind never ceases howling over the land, the mother and calf's slightest movement flattening brown tufts of grasses mostly hidden by the snow and ice cover. The evergreen branches are heavily laden with bluish-gray snow, and all waterways are completely frozen, sheathed in a thick ice cap. It is very much unlike the land you lived in, yet it is the same land, the land where you stand today, the land that lies quiet and still.

THE SAVAGE RIVER VALLEY

A passage of time and then another feature of the valley developed.

The River Valley.

Sometime after the mountains shifted in close proximity, a wrenching collision of the earth's matter caused the ice cap to shift and begin its slow arduous melting and even slower retreat to the north, causing the waterways to converge and a great river to form in the valley. Its length ranged to the inland mountains off to the north and stretched down to the southern sea, characterized by particular areas profoundly deep balancing others occasionally shallow; wide in some parts with craggy islands and sand reefs and narrow in others.

Activity of human occupation and great hunters is evident years later near the Athens outcropping, by the discovery of the renowned Clovis point and bones of animals abandoned or carelessly discarded. Evidence left behind as testament to your ancestral family.

Their struggle and tenuous hold on life lies deep in your psyche. They lived on the sides of the valley or hilltops giving them the advantage to track the movement of the herds below. Not too far indeed from where you are at this moment. The connection between you and your ancestors remains; their struggle becomes your own.

That is the course of history. The struggle is the same. The only thing that changes is the timeframe.

Now, no need to question what you have been told, since you may take all of it as fact, a given history, a natural raping of the land; displaying both constructive and destructive forces. The land shifts, builds, and rebuilds but never disappears. And that is how you have faced time, by choosing not to disappear, by living on in the mind and spirit of a woman.

For aren't you best remembered by those who remember you? Yes, of course you are, but here is another important question.

Why did you resist leaving this land?

The answer is clear. You know what held you here and now you must begin the journey home.

But let us not advance too quickly. Time endures and so will this story. A story that transports you back to the present moment, back from the past to this spot where you now pause to listen and absorb even more. It is in your best interest to weigh in significance, to wonder, to contemplate that which is put before you. Breathe deeply, for the long stretch of summer is just ending and our story is just beginning. After all, you agreed to this journey and stick with it you shall, but stay close for now and don't wander off. It is a fascinating journey that is long and tiring and oftentimes confusing. There will be times when you will have to hide, Captive, and at times, Observer, when you are terribly inconsolably distraught and confused. In the midst of all that angst and emotion, you will find solace, somehow, somewhere.

In the end, the means of getting there will all come together in perfect unison and make perfect sense. Your struggle, your suffering, your memories will prove to be the building tools for a later challenge, the likes of which are unimaginable.

Indeed the blanketing effect of this year's winter has yet to approach; although there is a gentle breeze making its way down from the north country of moose and wolves, glacial lakes and those iron rocks, that rustles the drying leaves at night, cools the sweat off the brow in the heat of the day, and whispers with tempting desire of cooler weather; perhaps the bracing air of autumn.

In the air, there is a hint of change. This moment will not repeat itself.

Captive, your form is clear, distinct from your surroundings.

Look proudly at yourself!

∿

The white mist with muted tones of gray starts to rise slowly, twirling in almost seductive fashion at your feet. It begins to dissipate

THE SAVAGE RIVER VALLEY

above the waters of this River Valley of the Hudson, this historically important, long expanse of, for the most part, calm waters in what is now the enormous state of New York. This river has defined life for hundreds of years for you and your family; not to mention a long string of ancestors-a river that no longer is the exciting frontier it once was. And a river that, not inconsequentially, brought her to you once and will do so again.

Your heart leaps in anticipation, but patiently you must listen and see what stretches before you. Now, it is as if someone of gargantuan size is lighting up an equally gargantuan pipe, exhaling rings of silky smoke into the air that curl in delicate tendrils ever so slowly up over the bank, mingling with the very mist that had, the evening prior, settled over the sleeping inhabitants of the centuries old village of Catskill, nestled just over the rise of the river's moderately wooded west bank.

It is the very mist that helps to bring you back, back to this spot, back to the land, and back to her. These river lands were once the hunting grounds and fishing camps of the Muhicannau and Munsee tribes, all sub-tribes among the greater league of Indians called the Algonquian.

Later this river town or hamlet was eventually bartered for and settled by a group of Dutch pioneers whose last names often began with Van. And who, for a trifling exchange, were diligently instructed to buy land from the local Indians to increase their new world holdings. The Dutchmen built small cottages of stone, flanked with solid chimneys, whose rooms were partitioned by split doors. The Indians, as well as the Dutch, resided inland on the banks of Wildcat Creek or Kats Kill Creek, as it later came to be known.

This town, as contrary as it appears to you this very morning, had once seen better days of moderate prosperity, all too quickly forgotten in the rush of the last century of westward growth and modern technology.

Life surrounds you, but you don't see it for what it really is.

Now is your chance to see it all, with no illusions. No more rushing. No more clouds. Step from the shadows, lift the veil of illusion, and see everything; everything as it is now and as it was before. It is here, all of it, in front of you; the old land camouflaged by a new society.

The rising mist exposes a harsh reality. Dilapidated buildings line a run-down, partially boarded up stretch of road named Main Street. Surrounding neighborhoods branch out in northerly and southerly directions, middling in economy to downright poor. Slowly crumbling habitat is filled with descendents of long ago: Indians, Dutch, Africans, later the English, and all subsequent newcomers to include the Irish, Italians and Germans. They all settled here on these banks close to the river, and some have never left the comforting confines of small town living and never will. Many could not overcome the compelling need for roots that precluded the entertaining of any idea that centered on moving away.

Here you see a poor, derelict town where regular folk live.

High on a southern plain above the town, Grandview Avenue—this morning a densely populated neighborhood of middle class sprawl—was once a spacious esplanade of stately homes and stables, sending forth daily processions of trotting horses and rolling carriages with an expected element of well-to-do circumstance and flair. The avenue had dramatically changed in character over the course of a hundred years. The avenue was no longer considered the prestigious place to live, one that used to afford its residents and visitors an infamous scenic view. Many had described it as grand! The Catskill Creek sparkled, flowing eastward to the Hudson River. On the opposite bank, all roads led upward to Prospect Avenue where all the features of the Victorian era were embodied in mansions that mirrored the prosperity found on Grandview Avenue.

Barely a few mementos of that time remain. On the avenue, the occasional stepping-stone ladies clothed in long finery needed for that upward climb into a high carriage is seldom noticed. These two step blocks are perched on the edge of a walkway or lawn. How

THE SAVAGE RIVER VALLEY

many of them are left? How many of them have been destroyed by the brutal force of snowplows?

One persistent look and your eye will rest on evidence of the past disguised among the modern buildings. A subtle hint that is reminiscent of an era lost and gone. If you turn and carefully inspect the banks of the creek, snug against the waterway, the four-storied brick building that once was a beehive of daily work and production of bricks now sits forlornly vacant, except for water rodents and the inevitable spiders.

Throughout the years in spurts and then over long spells, the town had steadily lost its vitality. Instead of shining like a bright side of a newly minted penny, it is dull and pitiful in appearance and spirit; at one point no longer staking a claim in preserving the living history of the area.

What had transpired here to create such misery? Why had no one saved what had earlier been a jewel of a town?

The massive buildings had crowded on the creek's banks, at one time churning out manufactured wares and goods from numerous mills. The rising chimneys continually smoked even on a winter's day set against the gray tones of falling snow. A once bustling harbor, where river and inland traders met, offered a safe and deep port to ships that traded goods in far off places. These ships jostled for docking space with daily steamers brimming with passengers up from New York City. Slowly this too disappeared. Year by year less ships came. Buildings were decaying, many abandoned, others left to rot. Many of the structures were simply gone, no longer standing, but rather, razed and swept away; the mills, stables, hotels, and shops included. What remained was a pitiful collection. So many interesting and promising lives lived and are now gone, forever silenced.

But today, all is not forgotten. There is an unmistakable, underlying hum of revitalization as a few come together to bring pride back to Main Street, one building at a time. To bring the decay to a remarkable new, starting with the vision of one and, in time, promises to continue with the hopes of many. It is the last river town where this revitalization can occur.

And this is where our story begins.

Do not step away now that you have found your legs. You move them gingerly, testing them for strength to carry you. Come forward, for you above all others are not forgotten. Resist exploring further. There is someone who desperately needs your help. Eventually many will cry out to you for succor when facing an unconscionable but innocent death by burning or that final fall. But you will not be there alone. Surely not.

Take caution to heed this advice. For now, do not enter the Du Bois stone house at the foot of the hill situated near the mouth of the creek where the Cornwallis surrender of revolutionary times was joyously celebrated with a raised tankard of ale. Nor, you are beseeched, should you stop to read the memorial on Jennet's gravestone at the family plot. Nor wander by the splendidly preserved early Dutch homestead of the Van Vechten clan further up around the bend, located on the same waterway that afforded an ideal shallow crossing both to your ancestors and your people and later the colonists. And most assuredly, which cannot be stated too emphatically, do not go up to the flats that lie beyond Leeds. It would be dangerous to cross the old stone bridge to the plains of Old Catskill.

Ah, yes, the flats! They hold remnants of Native American artifacts, old fire pits and deep holes containing what would have been a winter's stash of food supplies.

All of it came from a hauntingly familiar world: a comb carved from bone, shards of ceramic pottery engraved with faint lines of a pattern, burnt bits of corn kernels, and an elbow-shaped pipe. These remnants of old are camouflaged by new surroundings, but remnants that no doubt will speak to your memory.

To go back now would provoke a familiar tug at your heart. You would recognize the surroundings and instantly hear the voices of ghosts. There on the open flats is where you would feel unwaver-

THE SAVAGE RIVER VALLEY

ingly obliged to stay. You would be caught in a web from which there is no escape, not even for you. There you would keep a vigil that is infinite in time.

No, there is another purpose for your coming back. This is indeed the moment for you to stay close. The story of these buildings and the land call in unison, tearing at you to remember, seek, and relive the past, but something is happening at this moment that will change life forever and you should be, must be, a witness to it. More than that, you will become part of it.

Instead of lingering at these homesteads and settling comfortably near the warm hearth to relive moments gone, climb back up over the rise stretching high above the town, opposite the Grand Avenue. On your journey, step lightly, admire and then climb the stairs of the front wooden veranda of a pretty Victorian house painted a bright yellow that once belonged in another century to the gentleman affectionately dubbed the Father of American Landscape Painting.

Who was this man? folks wonder as they pass by the elegant and obviously old homestead.

A painter he was, a doting father, a generous husband. Originally from England, Thomas Cole dreamt of becoming an artist. In later years, he resided in this very house and would portray the landscape of nineteenth-century America at its best. His creative style was exuberantly revealed in marvelous paintings depicting cascading waterfalls, sunsets dipping behind mountain crests, deer poised to drink water from a stream, and much more; including a famous painting entitled *The Last of the Mohicans,* all of them portrayed on huge spreads of canvas.

The sound of that title frightens you, but see what he would have seen daily, rising to windows facing the west, staring off to blue hued mountains of hemlocks that called to his spirit and talent; the same mountains that once upon a time also called to your restless spirit.

An impressive view no doubt.

He had quite an eye for beauty. With his brush, palette, and talented strokes he opened the world of nature to the human eye. Although not instant, nevertheless he attained long lasting fame.

Alas, you look puzzled and suddenly feel isolated and out of place. It is all too foreign for you; too modern, too confusing. There is worry and a tinge of uncertainty in your dark eyes. You find all this talk of the past unsettling. You sense the disquiet of modern society not in sync with Mother Nature.

You suddenly distrust.

You are beseeched to display a bit more patience, for up to now you have been compliant. All will be revealed. The time for curious exploration is drawing to a close, according to plan.

No more pausing to contemplate the moment, for the sprit of Cole is a vibrant force in the house amongst his possessions. He could never entirely shake the morbid apprehension of his own mortality even in the detached newly built studio that gave him peace from the noise and bustle of the house. He knew he was going to die, perhaps not exactly on that cold February morning that dawned bright, but nevertheless he couldn't face it, nor did he try and, in fact, to the last moment never accepted his own mortality. He refused to step into the rays of light.

A blessed angel will help him, but on another day.

Now is not the right time. For his tormented spirit, twisted and perhaps a bit demented, recognizing your own spirit very well might cause a delay, a certain friction of two distinct worlds overlapping. The static would be sufficient to alert a sleeping dog. You need not call any attention to yourself at the moment. There is much to deal with.

Come now, for you must go on.

Turn to the rear of the house, follow the wide planked porch and silently descend the wooden stairs. Follow the path east, walking directly past the studio and avoiding it altogether, over the sloping lawns that sparkle with a few remaining drops of dew that glisten over botanical delights.

THE SAVAGE RIVER VALLEY

Further now, through the woods just beyond the rise of the last hill.

There now, from this vantage point through a thick strand of trees that borders the riverside of the original property. Do you see it? The long cantilevered span of the Rip Van Winkle Bridge stretches twenty-stories high into the air above the swirls of mist and water. Notice how the western portion is framed in, supporting the towering structure of steel beams. Construction on the bridge began a few years back, a brief moment in the history of this land, in the 1930s, when its height was designed to allow passage of large ships and freighters up and down the river, and its long span was to function as a road bridge, even admitting at one time horse drawn carts.

Do not expect to see them now, for the horses and carts have long ago disappeared. The carts decayed and the horses are long dead, replaced by the more efficient automobile. The earlier clip-clop rumble of hooves that rang out over the cobblestones and crudely paved roads were stifled by the obnoxious drone of the modern engine and the blaring beep of their horns, all in the name of advancement and modernization.

One more thing before edging closer.

The carefully thought out blueprints allowed for a pedestrian walkway facing the long stretches of the river as it wound its way down in a southerly direction past many other towns, villages, and smaller cities on course to its final destination: the cold, gray and powerful Atlantic Ocean. The river passes the Island of Manahata, New York City, where once that mighty glacier dropped its sediments to form the many surrounding islands.

New York City: precisely the kind of town that gives you cause to remember. Do you? A polite question, cautiously posed, of course. Perhaps you remember its earlier name?

Nieuw Amsterdam.

Do you remember a wooden stockade—a walled street acting as a barrier against your own kind with hundreds of criss-cross trails?

Ah, a flicker of recognition, the memory is coming back as these words are spoken! Do you remember the time she spotted you in the crowds? She called out to you first in joy, then in agony when she could not catch up with you. In a city built on a waterway that brought her to you, straight into your arms, your life, and heart.

Your dark eyes flash and you look away. Memories are painful. But there is no escaping the memories this River Valley offers.

Return your focus to the bridge itself, named after a legendary figure of long ago lore who, under the spell of secret charms and magic, fell deeply into a dreamless slumber that went on for twenty years; only to abruptly awaken to a rusted rifle propped at his side and a life and many seasons that had passed him by. He had not died, nor was he embraced by angels; rather, he simply fell asleep. Rip's imaginative creator had once resided many miles south on the banks of this very same river and was as attached to the river and his country environs at Sunnyside as to his writing. He was a writer who could sense many things. Do you see in your memories the candlelit drive as it winds its way down to the quaint cottage, styled after Dutch architecture, by the river? Do you remember she walked there alone in the Christmas crowd? How hard it was to entice her to move on? It must have been the allure of the candles, the singing of Christmas songs, the sounds of the pianoforte, and the smells of hot cider and freshly baked cakes. It could have been that she was reluctant to leave the writer's side; so content she was to be surrounded by his words and books.

You shake your head in confusion.

You feel the pull of ages past. The history of the land is rich, exciting, and hungry, embracing you in its grasp. These are all moments on your journey. You have come far already, but you must go further.

You are needed here.

The gray structure of the bridge, though basic in design, has withstood the tests of time with the continual passage of seasons and its oft debilitating effects of rain, snow, ice, and wind that chip

THE SAVAGE RIVER VALLEY

away at the gray covering. But most significantly, the bridge stands as a silent witness to the comings and goings of different travelers traversing both sides of a river notable both in size and beauty.

Now, in the early morning hours of this warm September dawn, the long lines of steel cables sparkle, reflecting the beginning tints of orange and silver as light persistently arches its way from the eastern reaches of other valleys into this one.

The darkness of night is retreating hastily, slipping over the wide expanse of the Catskill Mountains boldly rising west of the river, the rugged lines of the mountaintops posing as guardians over this stretch of the valley.

The mist continues its upward path, lifting higher, growing thinner, and momentarily looking like the passing shadow of an angel's wing.

The first rays of the morning sun are beginning to penetrate the lingering pools of white pockets of mist that settle obstinately over the water.

Good, for now your view will be unobstructed! What you are about to see is extraordinary and will excite you. It is what you have been waiting for.

Ah, yes, the bridge What do you see?

A lone figure stands on the pedestrian walkway precisely at the mid-way point between both ends of the bridge. Yes, it is she, the one you have been waiting for. Your every fiber senses her even before you catch sight of her. You tremble. As difficult as this may be, resist the immediate urge to rush forward.

She purposely walked in by the east side of the bridge, thus avoiding any contact with toll collectors located on the west side. It is barely dawn, and not a single soul is about.

Despite her loneliness, the less questions the better.

There is no longer the obscure safety she desires in the darkness, but rather with the approaching dawn, she becomes visible to any passerby—however remote the possibility of one at this hour of the morning. She wishes to be neither seen nor spoken to. Given time, minutes perhaps, the traffic will eventually pass by and once spotting her the momentum of slowed vehicles and suspicious stares, speculation, and unsolicited questions will be unavoidable.

Staring out over the river, she spies the not too distant sail of a solitary white boat bobbing up and down in the water. There is no movement on deck, no one raising the dropped anchor and getting underway, no one to look up from its polished deck and see her standing there watching, no one who cares. Just the constant motion up and down, up and down, with the gentle water brushing its hull. A lifeless boat carried along by the currents.

∿

She turns her head curiously, slowly, deliberately to where she had entered the walkway. It is, as expected, empty. The lingering shadows of the night hold no promise of seeing him. She knew this day would be different from all the rest.

Except she was more tired than usual; her body so fatigued, her mind so exhausted and her soul so broken, she couldn't summon up the energy to leave the bridge even if she wanted to.

She does not know that you have come out of the shadows, yet she looks anyway, out of habit and longing to see you.

Beyond the eastern portion of the bridge, the left bank is verdant and lush, abundant with multi-generational growth of apple trees whose branches are heavy with ripening fruit. Apples. Juicy reds and pungent greens fill the orchards with neatly growing rows of trees. Autumnal harvests for the valley, the survival of farms and families alike depend on these seasonal crops. She can't help but silently and instinctively think of the isolated families that once dug at the land and eked out a living on these very banks, surviving from one harsh winter to another; always measuring their lives on the inventory of harvested crops. Survival was a yearly, if not a daily, event. Now their descendents have a new worry, as they gauge their lives and the farms on the inventory of land that is lost to encroaching development, the selling off of highly taxed lots, sprawl, and the blanketing effects of pollution from a neighboring industrial plant.

Different eras. Different worries.

She sighs with familiar pangs of anxiety.

On another day, what fun it would have been to have had a juicy red apple in her hand, feeling the smooth contours of its thick, shiny outer layer and delightedly swishing the juices in her mouth. With skirts pulled high and the sun shining warmly on her legs, she would have hitched a ride on the back of a cart from the fields to the barns, but not today.

High above the orchards on the east bank looms the mountaintop of the famous Olana, built on a high hill facing the river and the distant mountains off to the west. An exquisitely designed castle-like abode of an artist whose name she now cannot recall. She is instantly baffled. She knew this man! This artist, with incredible natural talent, understood the anatomy of nature. He brought a vision to life. Over the span of thirty years, during which he gave direction and worked on plans, his creative energy resulted in Olana.

"This is the center of the world and I own it," he joyfully exclaimed to his adoring wife.

On any given day, Olana was breathtaking. Stepping beyond the massive front door, one entered a vestibule that led into the round court hall. Off to the right of the hall rose a wide, two-tiered staircase. To the left of the hall, behold a spectacular view of the Catskill Mountains! Oh, what glory! But neither right nor left, but rather straight ahead—a path to his destiny—lay a long corridor lined with books, and beyond that a magical room revealed to the amazed eye through an open archway. The intimate world of the painter, full of brushes and canvases, works of art, and artifacts collected on worldly jaunts. The painter's studio was overshadowed by a window outlined in yellow and black stencil. On a summer's evening, precisely when the sun appeared in its last moments of luminance, the window lit up as if it were emitting the fiery rays of the sun itself! Had the artist sat there and reveled in the warmth of the setting sun? She was sure of it. All that was missing was the artist himself.

She suffers a momentary loss of memory, then makes an effort to retrieve the information from somewhere deep inside her brain. She could see his face so clearly, the aquiline nose, the small bones of his face, the drooping mustache that covered a thin upper lip, and the expressive eyes that spoke of a genteel upbringing and a gentle nature.

Temple? No, that was not it. What then?

She was always so good with names and faces. It was a religious sounding surname, but all she could remember were mere words: Isabel the dark-haired beauty, Niagara, and two other images; one of a heart shaped pond, the other of a rolling drive stretching up through thick woods past grassy meadows. *How frustrating,* she thought, *to be incapable of distinctly recalling these memories and yet others instantly coming to mind so vividly.* She did not understand them or the reason they stayed lodged in her head like some unwelcome guest who adamantly refuses to leave. And always the dates. Those God-awful repetitious dates that swirled around and around in her head, bringing back haunting dreams that left her nights virtually sleepless.

Random dates: 1895, 1780, 1657, 1601; exceedingly far back in time and always popping into her mind for no apparent reason. Years, months, days … even down to seconds or moments of time measured on an infinitely huge scale.

History books teach dates as a tribute to something significant in the past.

Often her mind raced with seemingly useless information of dates and names that left her head throbbing from the exertion. The images were a kaleidoscope of papers that, when ruffled, rapidly gave off jerky movements of pictures. Migraine after migraine stalked her days, and even now she could feel the beginning of a headache slightly thumping in the base of her skull.

Popping a handful of pills washed down with cold water or juice did not alleviate the pain, nor reduce her memory, nor bring her peace.

Lately, it had become an embarrassing phenomenon when in the company of others.

Why did she always involuntarily blurt out dates? Everyone, in cafes, bookstores, and on the street, looked puzzled, but she no less than they. She always apologized, but there was no explaining the fact. Were they four random numbers, or did they hold a particular significance for her? "Play the lottery," one dear neighbor joked. But it was not a joke.

There was something else—all the names that drove her near crazy, all coming in a jumble with such mixed emotions, enough to blot out any other thoughts. For instance, she knew of the name Minnah. Was that her grandmother's youngest sister from Europe? But she had spelled her name Mina, so it couldn't be, she reasoned.

And then she thought of the others.

White Feather, Titus, Ann … why in heaven and on earth did these names cause her such heart-wrenching anguish, a swelling of sobs that wouldn't be calmed by other than complete exhaustion followed by sleep?

Always there were the same questions, always new tears.

She frowns in silent thought, her eyes scanning the contours of Olana's mountaintop, its smooth line of trees broken by the towers of the artist's home. How curious! The silent halls and rooms designed in the fashion of Arabian nights and Victorian days, the studio built on the northern side of the mansion and the little pink chair in the family sitting room beckon to her as if to draw her away from the bridge. Her thinking is fuzzy and confused. Suddenly the outlines of each room on the hill begin to dissolve. She remembers arthritic hands attempting to hold a paintbrush and, afterwards, the agonized cry resounding from the studio. She looks down. Her own hands start to cramp and bend.

No!

No more attempting to sort out distant memories. Concentrate on the matter at hand. No more distractions. She must stop looking around! It only confuses her and brings on episodes of self-hate and anger, of failure and hopelessness.

The tranquility of the scenery before her and thoughts of a heart-shaped pond do nothing to quell the disquiet that pervades her body, as she looks away from the east bank and back to her immediate prospects. No doubt she will begin to hear the voices again. Voices that incessantly remind her of everything she longs to forget—a life filled with melancholic despair shadowed by an aura of feeling lost. Where was he? If only she could be with him again, to feel his ardent kiss and strong hugs. The aching loneliness to see him and those she had loved for so long, mere shadows in the background of her life, flitting in and out of her dreams, a sordid jumble that she called her life.

It was not schizophrenia, it was real, and she lived it every insufferable day. The memories she dreams about tear mercilessly at her heart. Enough of this! She had had quite enough. She had come to a decision days before. This time, with a new bout of agonizing grief, there were no more frantic appeals to doctors, no more endless rounds of pills that only masked the real problems, no more diagnosis. All nightmares that pursue her will be gone. She will make them go away for good.

She knows she has to act quickly, for she can endure it no longer. She stares down into the waters far below. It cannot be long now. Sorrow and tears will not dim the mirror of her innermost thoughts.

She is drawn to the little eddies, black pools that seem to form a perfect circle, a target of deep water. The water is compelling. Nymphs beckon to her with an invitation of a watery but soothing grave that will provide an end to all her suffering. It is that simple, and in spite of its simplicity, it is unquestionable to consider any other choice. There is no other choice. She has come to the end of

THE SAVAGE RIVER VALLEY

her road and her choices are limited to this long, tall bridge and the water that flows beneath it.

Not to the land, not to the neighboring mountains, and most definitely not to people.

With a sharp pang of sadness, she glimpses the northern stretch of the mountains and immediately hears those male voices again, each one crystal clear.

The church bell is tolling. The organ is softly playing. How could that be? How could she hear something that happened years ago?

1888, March ..."Blizzard today. Going is hard. Shoveled paths around and visited some. Very cold."

1938, February ..."The day is wonderful and bright, and the air crisp. Let us give thanks ..."

Thanks for what? she wondered. Thanks for living buried under two feet of snow with below zero temperatures? February was the hardest month of the year up there on the mountain.

She knew where the voices were coming from.

Those voices were drifting down from the exact location of the Hamlet of Cornwallville, the last man standing, speaking from the pulpit of the church where it had once stood regally in front of the old cemetery that dated back to the 1700s. And then what came next? A choir composed of eighteen voices. The hymn that spoke of kingdoms and empires and, strangely enough, the one phrase that stuck in her memory, "A hundred years the same."

Yes, she thought. *A hundred years ago, about the time they buried Armenius!*

But who was Armenius?

The church no longer sat on the foundation. They had lifted the old structure from the stones underneath and sent it to the Farmers' Museum in Cooperstown. A relic preserved by the Clark family. Another voice reached her—that of Armenius Smith!

His voice was deep. "Welcome. This is your home now. This is where you belong."

What about Titus Goodfellow and Ann Palmer, from a different cemetery on Bates Church road? There was some mystery surrounding their deaths.

Who else heard those voices? Who else knew the names of every gravesite up there without looking or recording the facts?

No one.

She was able to reconstruct the entire village by its gravesites.

This was precisely why people looked at her strangely. She could match voices, absurdly so, to different locations and to years in the past. Always in the past, merging with her present. She can hear those men quite clearly, as if they stood next to her. It didn't help in the least to firmly press her hands to her head covering her ears. Nothing worked. The voices still reached inside, repeating over and over again messages she did not care to hear.

Tears begin to flow, dripping delicately off her eyelashes. It had taken every last bit of strength she had to come to a decision. He existed only in her memories, somewhere in a time past. Only it was the present, and she had made every attempt to find answers to the memories that plagued her.

"Is there a way to find you? A road I could travel or even a forest path I could walk? A stream I could follow? For a moment without you is a moment lost... morning rain, evening shadows, and the glare of the sun—is this where I look for you?" she said to the dark of each night for the last year.

Only, there had been no answer.

∿

You quiver uncontrollably. You hear her thoughts from where you stand. Yet how will you tell her you are here? You see her not from the shadows but in the approaching light of day. You remember the countless hours she spent in antique stores fingering bits of Limoges china and delicate lace, searching for clues in old books, and sitting on the hillside each night watching the sunset, hoping you would be there. And then there was the museum in Durham.

THE SAVAGE RIVER VALLEY

Remember the day she poured over old photos and brown maps and then looked up to see you standing there? How she fainted at the sight of you? How no one listened to her or believed her when she came to?

"What did she say?" inquired Joann, a kind and gentle inn-keeper from down the road.

"She was incoherent. Couldn't catch her words," the museum keeper whispered.

That was both a happy and sad day for her. She happily caught sight of you, but when she saw you disappear, she knew then that you were not of her world. It shattered her dreams of finding you. Yes, a sad day it was.

Let us edge a bit closer.

Though she cannot see you, your presence must be felt even as a reminder at this point.

She opens her eyes wider. They are framed in dark lashes that are long and lustrous over eyes that once were vibrant and alive, only now they are dull and lifeless, swimming in tears.

The sight of her standing on the bridge stirs you to no end. Your heart is near bursting with the enormous burden of the past and her suffering. You wish to reach out to her and hold her tightly within your arms, never to let her go away from you again.

If you must reach out to her, embrace her in your mind, then you must. But beware; it will not change the course of events. You do not possess that power. At this moment, you are not a spirit of dust and ashes but a heart of solid mass, and you must let her go on.

Suddenly you are beside her.

Your gentle fluttering fills the air around her slight body, caus-ing her to raise her dark eyes and look about, equally surprised and fascinated by the noise, momentarily distracted from her ear-lier thoughts of the water. You notice how alarmingly thin she has grown. She looks sickly and pale, with deep dark circles under her eyes from sleepless nights. Her bones protrude under her thin garment.

She stopped eating weeks ago.

The tears are quelled. She welcomes the noise and smiles for the first time. It reminds her of the arms that hold her close in the darkness of the night hours.

Your fluttering is soft and caressing on her bare arms. She had dreamt of this gentle touch many times, a touch that strokes her skin in an upward fashion, leaving goose bumps in its wake. A touch that slowly, softly, and then lovingly strokes her cheeks, smoothing back her hair and lifting the ends in a tender caress. Do not stand at her back, for she will know it to be you and this will cause disturbance.

You must step away. Now!

She is momentarily exhilarated by your presence, but you vanish as quickly as you appear, shifting beneath her and dropping away, closer to the water far, far below. Since you are the first touch of gentleness she has felt in quite a while, evoking a distant memory tugging at her heart from long ago; standing up on her tiptoes, she leans over the railing straining to see and looks down once more. She searches for the source of the delicious fluttering, hoping to call it back to her. Looking to find comfort, she desires its delicious touch against her skin yet again. but as with all the entreating cries of the past year, this cry goes unheeded as well.

It was of no use. She falters. There is only the sound of the lapping water as it hits the steel pylons over a hundred feet below. The feeling of emptiness returns, and she droops like a wilted flower deprived of water in the glare of a hot summer's sun.

Look upward now! From far below, her figure is etched against the inky sky, a small dot on the horizon. A tiny spot, one human alone in the great scheme of time and all that surrounds her. She is helpless against the course of events, as they would have happened today and even as they are happening now.

The past, the present, and the future will collide at this very spot.

Her demeanor shows a sense of dispiritedness and not even a

THE SAVAGE RIVER VALLEY

faint hint of a will to fight. She is tired from fighting for so long. Now she has given up.

The nondescript clothing she wears belies her inner beauty. Her body loosely covered in a simple cotton dress; her feet encased in slippers, easy to slip off and discard. Her hair hangs loose and full down her back, and the hands that cling to her sides show delicate lines of bluish tint that pulse with life. Her skin is transparent in its paleness and contrasts starkly with her dark hair.

Shush! Don't worry about calling her name right now from where you stand or even where she comes from, hoping to spark a memory. Slow your breathing, calm yourself. There is absolutely nothing you can do however much this disturbs you. Neither can you call out to anyone. It would be in vain, useless against the currents of time.

Your voice is irrelevant, for no one who is stirring in this nearby town knows who she is nor understands her intentions. They do not notice her when she walks on the street, shops on the hill, or stops for coffee. Their day-to-day existence has long replaced the memories of the little girl who grew up on Cauterskill Creek Road and went to school at Grandview Elementary. She was the girl who skipped down country roads and built snowmen. Who skated in bone chilling cold and at five handed a bouquet of wild flowers to her grandmother on the steps of the Cornwallville church. Even if they did remember, no one is there in this instant to save or make a halfhearted attempt at dissuasion.

No argument, regardless how elegantly expressed or earnestly delivered, can change her destiny.

The anticipated moment at length has arrived. Waiting for this moment seems to have gone on forever. Frantic beatings of her heart or quickened gasps of breath are precluded by dull acceptance of her plan. The fluttering is gone and the air is still about her. Only the quiet of the moment prevails under the great expanse of morning sky. She feels utterly alone but does not dread the prospect. She only hopes that somehow, by her actions, things will be better. Yes, better to get the whole affair over with. No more anguish to remind her of the total emptiness in her heart and soul. She wishes to find an end to her suffering.

Then, decisively, the woman grips the gray railing and clumsily swings her leg up and over, onto the steel handrail. She teeters on the other foot and works to steady herself, her hair now blowing in all directions attributed to an unusually sudden gust of air.

You intensely watch her every movement, missing nothing, your heart painfully clutched in an iron grip. Your breath, heavy and fast, is the unexplained puff of air in exactly that spot; bringing your spirit to her, surrounding her, enveloping her as you did years ago in a shaded glen further north.

Poised on the brink of enlightenment, she now hangs momentarily in this awkward position, struggling to bring her other leg into place. It refuses to obey and her dress catches on the steel. She tugs harder. Instead of feeling overcome with exasperation, she reacts automatically, reaching down with one hand to pull the material into place.

By now, she knows there is no turning back, no second thoughts—too late! She does not go entirely unnoticed. Oblivious to the muffled cries behind her coming from the direction of the tollbooth area at the far end of the bridge, she is numb to the cold railing and the precarious perch it affords over the deep waters below, a very long drop from where she shifts to gain a position on the other side of the railing.

Quietly grunting at the effort, she pulls the other leg over.

There is nothing solid between her and the power of nature, only the dizzying freedom of the open air before her.

A sharp intake of breath—she waits.

One moment passes, then another.

She surveys the wide vista of the river and the valley and the sky—and her greatest love, the blue-hued mountain range. It appears unusually close in its glory before her. A startling few inches away. Breathless, she is for the first time that day taken by the timelessness of the moment and the scenery before her. The land is her last comfort and friend in this world. She mouths the word good-bye. She hesitates and lifts her head slowly, holding her breath.

One single moment in time.

You can hear them now but you refuse to look away from her.

Listen! People coming to her rescue are screaming in high-pitched, obviously frightened, tones. Women, no doubt pleading, run toward her, frantic in their appeal and desperate in their attempts to save this woman; they are spurred on by a common link with humanity and survival—a helping hand, a small town instinct. To watch out for each other is typically the order of the day.

Startled by their shouts, growing louder at their approach, she turns slightly to glimpse at the running figures and feels her fingers slipping. Her grasp of the railing is loosening.

Hold your desire! From afar, you've watched her fall before and struggle to rise, only to watch her fall again. Draw deeply on your reserve of patience, bring it forth now! Trust her destiny and yours. Your black eyes are intently watching her, willing her to stop, but she cannot.

She no longer has the strength to hold on; nor does she want to. Her facial expression registers nothing but sorrowful resignation. *I must do this. No one can help me!* Her screams are resoundingly silent in despair.

The spectators gasp and watch in horror when, with one forceful thrust, she frees her entire body from the railing, falling backwards into the air, meeting her destiny in a rush of sound and movement.

They all scream in unison, one startled cry of disbelief.

But the swoosh of air ringing in her ears becomes the most incessant howl of crying, both bitter and sharp, amidst moans of disbelief. Her arms flail in confusion over her head. In mid-air there is nothing to grab onto, no way to hold them still as she continues on a downward course.

In those brief moments, she wishes to cover her ears against the multitudinous cries of distress! Is she imagining this? There is a great chorus of voices, men and women alike, and all of the voices yelling at her lament her choice.

Your voice is the loudest of all. Your grief is unbearable. Go to her now and do what you must.

Hurry! This begins your incredible journey.

Within five unbearably long seconds, her body slams full force into the hard, unyielding surface of the water. Her thoughts continue to be wild and panicked. At such a speed, there is no smooth entry into the water. Her back is snapped in two such as a dry and brittle twig under a stern, unforgiving boot.

This is not what I imagined it to be!

She gulps for air, her mouth wide open and her jaw slackened; her eyes unseeing. She screams out silently, her body pulsing with stinging pain, her conscious thoughts slowly drowning in the deep pool of water, and her lungs filling rapidly.

God—help me! Please, do not forsake me! Take me to him! Have mercy… God?

And suddenly, as fast as it happened, the pain is gone.

Only the darkness prevails.

∿

As you can expect, all is quiet. Those who have raced in vain and have come to an abrupt standstill on the bridge are stunned into silence, their bodies seemingly frozen in abnormally gruesome poses by the shock of what they have just witnessed; as if they too had experienced firsthand the pain of smashing into the water and dying.

The small group gathered, hunched over and huddled; the initial core of witnesses. A few more continue to come to the scene as the news spreads, crowding around. They are horrified, but not as horrified as those who had seen the woman jump. Traumatized better describes their state. The picture of her body falling replayed over and over in their minds and is seared hot in their memory. You

THE SAVAGE RIVER VALLEY

see, the mind is a powerful instrument, not allowing you to forget something painful too easily nor too soon. Years would pass before the sharp image would disappear from their nightmares.

A woman jumped off the bridge and, in all possibility, drowned as a result of the fall.

But the question at this moment remains—why? The very thought of why hangs heavy in the air like the damp mist earlier.

For now, the group huddles in close proximity, subconsciously drawing warmth from the human touch of those around them. Camaraderie in numbers bespeaks comfort.

They continue to scan the water, shading their eyes with trembling hands against the morning sun now rising higher with each second that passes. Against all odds, they hope the woman who jumped off the bridge will bob to the surface, showing the merest sign of life. Then they can point and scream out to her to somehow hold on, stay afloat until help arrives.

It does not happen that way.

The minutes pass slowly as if eternity could be encompassed in that short period of time.

The river, sparkling under the rising sun and lifted mist, continues to flow as before, sedate and constant in movement, but somehow emphatically striking the observers on the bridge as mammoth in its power of the unknown and what lies beneath its surface: the silent deep. The silvery thread of beauty that so often evoked such marvelous sighs of pleasure and joy in the past now frightens them.

Some of them shiver in the morning sun. Others, superstitiously or religiously, make the sign of the cross. They begin to feel uneasy, almost nauseous, looking down so far from such a mind spinning height. Their eyes shift away from the moving water below them, refocusing on each other. They take a half step back from the railing, frightened by the nearness of where the woman had stood just moments before; feeling increasingly jittery by the thought that it could have been any one of them, drowned and gone forever, suffering in those final moments an agonizing death.

None of them speak.

They turn to embrace each other in comfort and in sorrow, warm body pressing against warm body, and partially, but gratefully, in thanks for the life they can still call their own. A few of them delicately make a final sweeping sign of the cross and kiss their finger tips in a silent plea for a blessing-despite the fact that an unknown woman was obviously, from what they could tell, now lost underneath the water's surface, never to take a breath again. They are secretly relieved, as with each meaningful breath they draw borders on miraculous; it wasn't any of them or anyone they knew.

They draw a deep breath of air, filling their lungs. They suddenly are inspired to count their blessings, taking note that life is not so bad after all. They welcome the rushed daily living as their reprieve to what could be a hellish death.

In the distance, a lone jet streaks through the sky, emitting a trailing white line on the northern horizon. Beyond the bank, the rest of the town begins to awaken to the news.

Hovering over a tree top, one blessed angel watches closely. Only the angel could see the dark, evil shapes that flew fast and agitated around the cockpit.

"We will be there waiting " she promised softly, her eyes following the plane as it passed.

∿

The moving water had parted and effortlessly swallowed up the woman's body—water beneath the surface that is black and cold, unlike the warm haven of safety and peace she desired or yearned for. Her body begins a spiral descent down, down, down into the depths of hell.

Her last thought was of the white mist and morning clouds—and of God.

THE SAVAGE RIVER VALLEY

∿

Further south, in the big city of New York, home to fourteen million, only a handful of chosen people specially gifted to see beyond what others could see watched as a gathering of spirits, Keepers of the Sacred Land, appeared in the streets of lower Manhattan. The apparitions, Native American spirit guides, were serene, but the air around them was saturated with static. Those who saw them knew that something big, perhaps a cataclysmic event, was about to happen.

Today was September 11, 2001.

∿

Silence. Her eyelids fluttered and when Clara opened them for the first time, her body, covered in loamy silt, was lying on the earthen bank of the river, shaded by the forest towering over her. The air felt cool and refreshing on her damp face.

How long had she been lying there?

She couldn't tell.

Green leaves hung off protruding branches and formed an extended canopy well above her head, shielding her view of the Rip Van Winkle Bridge, rising up out of the river a few hundred feet from the jutting point of land where she lay. Her eyelids were stiff, too heavy to completely open and hold them as such. She felt overcome with drowsiness and started to close them against the light of day.

The packed dirt with bits of grass, shell, and animal droppings flattened around her provided a hard and dry resting area. A pointed edge of what appeared to be an oyster shell was sharp against her tender cheek. It stung horribly. She slowly dragged her head up, inches away from the ground. The little movement to do so was overwhelmingly exhausting. The shell had pierced her skin. A spot of blood appeared and trickled in a wet path down her cheek. Had she been in a clearer state of mind, she would have wondered as to the origin of the shell, picked it up, and examined it closely. She might even have thought of another time when great beds of pearly oysters surrounded Manhattan Island. Only now, she didn't. She was too tired to care.

What was going on?

She was completely out of the water but didn't remember how she got there. Perhaps it was for the best she not remember, for the torturous struggle, the struggle with a planned death, was best forgotten.

She slowly shook her head, confusion striking her in subtle waves. What had happened to her after she jumped? All that came to mind was the desperate gulping of air, her body's insistent desire to breathe, and how she physically struggled against sinking and, most of all, against dying, even though that had been her plan all along.

Her body felt numb. Instantly terrified, her eyes opened wide in confusion. Her breathing sounded heavy; short indrawn little sips of air, ragged and uneven. But there was something more. She recognized what alarmed her so. It was something she had never heard before.

The unnatural absolute silence of the forest.

She lifted her head a bit higher. Wincing at the effort, she looked around with great foreboding.

She struggled to focus her vision, her eyes resting on the gnarled undergrowth before her. Don't worry. She cannot see you at this moment. No need to step behind the tree out of sight.

River water was streaming from her body in little rivulets around her, fluid pouring from all parts of her body. Her dress a sodden mess, bunched up around her thin childlike thighs. The hard dirt floor beneath her gleaned with wetness, as the murky brown water dribbled out of her mouth, making it appear that she was drooling.

She lifted her hand. With stiff fingers, she attempted to drag

THE SAVAGE RIVER VALLEY

tendrils of heavy wet hair away from her face in order to see clearer, but what she actually saw caused her to gasp.

She was not alone in this quiet spot.

A rather large tree had fallen, its top caught in the crooked branches of a neighboring tree, its trunk opened in splintered shards of wood where the bulk of the tree had broken away from the massive stump. Her eye started at the leafy top, lingered momentarily, and then ran down the long length of the dying tree.

Quite close by, on the rounded edge of the trunk, still rooted deeply in the earth and whose rings numbered well over two hundred, counting it among the primitive forest population, one tiny and apparently very old woman sat, so old, in fact, that she resembled a great crane hunched over, birdlike in her appearance. Her face was long and oval, lined with deep wrinkled crevices. Her skin appeared to be as dry as the packed earth around the tree stump. It was as if the sun has baked her face to a burnished-bronze color, haloed by hair that was long and white, loosely pulled in two braids that lay in thin strands on her chest. Out of the wrinkled folds of skin shone resoundingly blue eyes that even now were focused on the woman lying unceremoniously on the ground in front of her. Her eyes were bright, flashing, and much too youthful, incongruous with the rest of her frail body.

Clara was startled. Yet she made no sound.

For God's sake, what an old decrepit person, she thought. *How old is she? Perhaps as old as the very tree she sits on!* Clara's mind was exceedingly troubled by this woman's presence. She was unsure how she got here. She vaguely remembered the jump from the bridge and even less the struggle in the water. And now she saw this ancient looking relic before her—for all appearances' sake, a woman.

Was this woman from another time? How could this be? Why would this woman be here beneath the cover of trees close to the very river where she chose to die?

This was not a coincidence. Clara's eyes narrowed. She never knew about old people, what they were capable of saying and doing.

45

They just gave her the creeps, especially the ones suffering dementia or approaching death. They could do crazy things. Their talk was unsettling. They saw people in the corners of rooms, when others did not.

The Old One sat patiently, her bony hands demurely folded in her lap, and looked quite expectantly at Clara.

"So," she started, "it is time. You now awaken."

Clara heard the slight tenor of her voice. *Could this be heaven?* God forbid it be hell. People had always warned against suicide, saying it sent one directly to hell. She pushed the thought away. All people deserve the grace of forgiveness, she no less than others. In her heart she knew God to be full of grace.

"Shall we begin?" the Old One said quite knowingly in a patient manner.

Clara, again startled, this time by the clarity and growing strength of the woman's voice, imperceptibly shied away.

Why should this woman be talking to her? Did she deserve it after what she had done? Should anyone be nice to her?

She frowns.

And then she had a strange sensation, the beginning of an anxiety attack with that old familiar sudden jolt of nerves. This just didn't feel right to her. Why should she listen? If her voice was too loud in the silence of the forest and unsettling, her appearance was even more so. This woman looked too old to walk, so incredibly bent over that her bony shoulders practically touched her knees. So how did she climb onto that tall stump? Besides which, was Clara to believe that this frail and feeble woman single-handedly dragged her from the river and saved her life? It didn't seem likely; foolish to consider much less believe. And besides, not a single strand of hair on the old woman's head was wet!

Was there no one with her?

Clara shook her head as if to answer her own questions.

However, for just a moment, a lingering moment that stretched out slowly, the voice seemed vaguely familiar, drifting somewhere in

THE SAVAGE

the deep recesses of her mind,
ago. She searched her memory.
whispered conversation while she
her eyes? Yes, that was it, something
regarding a fork in the road. What tiring
die, she thought wearily.

Once again that same voice broke into her thoughts.

"We have much to discuss. I have been waiting long for you, and our time here is shortening," the woman said, glancing at the sky.

Her lips pursed together in a thin, straight line over teeth that were yellowed and shortened but still functional.

"Your journey in search of sacred wisdom will be long," she promised with a slight lift of the upper lip. "And you must, for your own good, listen to what I have been sent to share. There are rules, you know, and I won't always be there to explain and to guide. Things you must understand and know beforehand, such as talking to past lives. You will, though at the time it will seem unreal, live the lives of others and go forward, even when those lives end, and then travel through the lives of the rest in order to be, as intended, a helper."

In a harmonious and natural way, as if they were the best of friends, she continued.

"In every human being, the unconscious voice calls out in time of need for the highest creative energy of the spirit. You did, you know … call out, I mean," she said quietly, and then kindly added "Your call, as all other calls from people nearing their end, did not go unanswered, as you can see. I am your spirit guide. When worlds are about to collide, there is much to learn and prepare oneself for."

The old woman paused; pleased to bear the message. She had learned this long ago. Now it was time to share.

Clara clamped her lips firmly shut. No reply, curious or friendly, was forthcoming. Stubbornly, she tried her best not to listen, still

LEON

...an came from. It struck a chord

...her bare feet against the bark, the ...avy rotting wood. The movement was ...med in unison: left foot and then right foot and back to left. Thump, thump, thump! Left foot, then right. *Look this way,* the feet seemed to be saying. *Focus on the beat of her heart, the beat of a clock, the rhythm of nature.*

Tiny chunks of dark rotted wood fell to the ground.

Clara was staring, annoyed by the feet so steady in their movement. They disturbed her concentration. Hideous toes! Feet that look liked parched fields after months of no rain. Deep cracks; dry and rough skin, peeling and flaked; brittle yellowed toenails—as if she had lived forever and walked many miles. The old woman shifted her weight and looked outward to the water.

She stilled her swinging feet.

Now she had the young woman's attention.

She tried again, this time louder.

"Do you remember the prayer you learned as a child? Angel of God who is my guardian, enlighten, watch over, support and rule me, who was entrusted to you by the heavenly piety. Amen. Do you?" the old woman gently probed with her voice, even as she looked away.

Puzzled, Clara followed her stare and looked to the shoreline directly in front of her, a few hundred feet away. *What a silly old woman. She knows nothing. She says a-men and not ah-men. Of course, I remember my prayers! I prayed for a Guardian Angel.*

She bit the edge of her lip. The only thing was that in the past years she had forgotten not only to say her prayers but to mean them as well. Naturally, she had felt the usual pangs of guilt. Isn't that what religion was all about, guilt laced with fear? Somehow that didn't seem a persuasive argument. No sense thinking about it now.

THE SAVAGE RIVER VALLEY

uniforms. Some were talking into static radios emitting beeps and strange voices. Others were leaning over to talk to divers in the water, submerging and surfacing at regular intervals. Their dark masks and rubber hoses fitted to their mouths made them look like serpents of the unknown deep. Their lights skimmed over the water's surface and then disappeared as they were pulled down. Each time, they came up to the surface of the river empty handed.

In a flash, Clara realized they were looking for her. It shouldn't be surprising. They searched for a foolish troubled woman who drowned herself out of misery. That's what they all must have been thinking in the back of their minds, all those people in the water and in the boats, and whoever must have been standing gaping on the bridge. Death and suicide were spectator sports, inspired by a morbid curiosity.

Did they hope to find her alive?

No. On the contrary, they were expecting to drag a bloated body from the depths of the river, commiserate at her misfortune, efficiently zip her in a body bag, and take her away from her river's grave and deposit her corpse on a cold metal slab in the mortuary, either in the village of Catskill or nearby Hudson. It is unlikely they would have bothered to take her body further.

Little did they even suspect, for how could they have possibly known, that the woman now miserably watching their futile attempts to recover an unrecoverable body was, in fact, the very same woman they were looking for.

With deepening detachment, as if in another world, she watched the scene before her, silently, reminding herself that she had once again failed in her attempt to find that haven of peace with no haunting memories. Sitting on this bank, Clara had no answers, no more now than before.

There is no stopping this. I am meant to be haunted forever, she silently despaired, shutting her eyes in anguish against the welling tears of hopelessness.

A voice cut through the sobs before they started and cut them to a decisive and final quick.

Clara's eyes flew open.

"Humph ... you have much to learn, and indeed many warm and cold hearths to visit. Forever can be a very long time!" the woman announced with a faint proprietary tone, seemingly unbothered by the lack of attention Clara was paying to her. "There is beauty everywhere, but it requires to be sought. You must seek it, and when you look around upon this earth, you must not forget to look upward to heaven. Listen to the spirit voices! Listen to the message! Living harmoniously does not mean a revolt by impulsively controlling the events that the Great Spirit left to you."

Clara, unsure, although stirred by the words, stared up at her in silence. Was the Great Spirit the God whom she knew as His Holiness and the Trinity?

The old woman closed her eyes, taking a deep breath. She mumbled to herself. Clara heard bits and pieces of what she said.

"She is quite the willful one and not willing to listen to the message. This one will take time. We should consider four hundred years to be long enough." She slowly nodded her head in apparent agreement, as if listening attentively to someone discussing a matter of vital importance. But who was she talking to?

Clara's eyes nervously took in the tree stump, the woman, and the surrounding forest. It was clear to her, as the day was bright, that no one else was present. There were just the two of them in the forest together. Clara nervously began to realize just how alone she was with this woman.

The woman continued in conversation.

"Hmmm ... I understand the heart is troubling you, completely understand. Trust me on this one. You have been most patient, and your patience will win out. Learning is across time, time that includes many different lifetimes. But when it is perfect and winged, it celebrates a journey on high and controls and saves the whole world, and that we will need. However, now is the moment to choose," she continued and then fell silent, as if waiting for an answer.

Choose? Did I miss something? Choose what? Clara inwardly wails. *What the hell is there to choose? Is there anything left after you choose to die? What is wrong with this woman? She makes no sense.*

Clara furtively stole another glance around. The woman sat alone, entirely by herself, yet she carried on this strange conversation, almost as if the woman was speaking to … Clara felt a wary shiver run through her body.

The Old One spoke louder now, "And, it will have to be the hard way, I presume from her willful nature, but it will work." Her voice projected determination, confidence.

Her blue eyes shifted. She now directed her attention back to where Clara lay.

Their eyes met.

"You shall see." She hesitated and then in a lowered voice, as if in quick afterthought, added, "It always does."

At last Clara spoke.

"Who are you?"

Barely a whisper stole from Clara's lips when in reality she wished to yell with great might, hoping to send this woman on her way. Perhaps if she had grabbed her by the shoulders and shook her roughly, despite her apparent age, it would have been enough to get rid of her. Clara needed to make her stop this foolish talk or, at the very least, accuse her of being a lunatic. Clara should know. She had spent plenty of time in places like the Poughkeepsie Crazy House, as local children named it. It was stretched over a great expanse of manicured grounds on which were situated numerous brick buildings with screened windows and padded walls. It was full of lunatics, some raving and restrained; and others who exhibited a calmer disposition who talked to no one in particular and bravely saluted you as you walked by.

The questions came quickly, her anxiety level rising with thoughts of her prior institutions. All those memories that she longed to squelch somehow or another came flooding back in a rush of thoughts accompanied by a sick feeling.

"What are you talking about?" Clara said in a low voice, clenching her jaw and pointing her finger at the woman.

She suddenly remembers that infamous question being asked of her recently; the same question the doctor asked her in the year past. And to exactly the same question, she truthfully replied, "The man in the shadows, the one who lurks in semi-darkness, never speaking, always watching and guarding me." On guard against what she did not know, but there he was, always and obviously present in her dreams. The same one who held her in the dark against her nightmares and screams.

The answer never changed, which inevitably evoked an impatient sigh from the doctor. And then it was on to the next doctor. "Clara," he would start off patiently, "what are you talking about?"

The old woman sat up, straightening her back. She looked impervious. She began to speak. "I was called upon by you to witness the ritual. You must endeavor to find peace with yourself and with the world. Peace needs to be interpreted by the right spirit who prays and looks where no one else thinks of looking. I am mightier than a human, but a god I am not. This you shall see."

It brought to mind all those stupid, useless questions seeking to prove her insane: Clara—the insane woman, Clara—the woman who should be locked away forever. They tried to save the lunatic who knew dates, names, and events and not much else. The lunatic who desperately wanted to see a man no one else saw.

"But I know he is there, I feel him," she explained to them all—the white suited and impressively degreed doctors with folders and clipboards who didn't believe her when she said she didn't understand her memories and cried out for help against those needle-toting nurses clamping her mouth shut with tape. They all made her furious. None of them believed her.

The next whisper was drawn out and ragged.

"See what?" Clara's voice was raspy, her mouth finding it hard to

THE SAVAGE RIVER VALLEY

form the words. She struggled to clear her throat and speak again, this time louder.

"What are you talking about?" Each word dragged out slowly.

The memory was lurking—the white jackets that restrained her arms, stiff and rough, chaffing her skin when she moved, causing sore red spots that drove her into a frenzy of itching that could not be relieved. She was always naked under the jacket; they did it on purpose. There were the forced feedings, the shots, the locked doors, and the bare walls—all of it was supposed to help her, to cure her. All of it was a prison she wanted to forget.

The coiled memory struck like a venomous snake.

"Who unlocked the door, Clara? Who loosened the jacket's strings, Clara? Who drew a picture of the mountains on your wall, Clara?" To which she automatically replied, "The man in the shadows" which drew an angry response from yet another doctor. "That man is part of your insanity," he bellowed.

The old woman turned slightly to her right and stared once more over the stretch of water, completely ignoring Clara's voice, growing increasingly angry but listening carefully to every word.

The Old One began to speak slowly and deliberately. "People who live in anticipation of the end often perceive angels at work. You did not, and you still don't," she said in a soft tone. It was a plain fact.

"Before you, you see a messenger from God, an angel." The old woman leaned forward. "It is of kings and empires," she stated emphatically, "and of old that went and came. Do you feel that which you have felt all your life; the wondering, the inquisitive exploring of lives past, and the constant longing and feeling of loneliness? This is where it has brought you. This is the end of that journey. And now, you must start a new journey. If you do not yield to him, you must go back."

She had heard enough.

"*You*," Clara began slowly in an accusatory tone. "Whoever you are, you don't know me. Why are you here?"

Then she took a deep breath and screamed in agony. "Leave me alone!" All her locked up moments of hysteria came flooding back, while every single one of them, doctors, nurses, and aides, all strangers, just stood there and ignored her pleas.

Her pent up rage started to surface. It wouldn't be long before the stinging tears would start, followed by the shaking of her body. And that damn migraine was threatening again.

The old woman turned her full attention to the damp spot where Clara sat, using her hands as supports against the dusty bank. She smiled benignly; unfastening a long row of buttons down the shimmering silky costume of sorts she was wearing. Her fingers gracefully glided over the buttons as they pulled apart from the fabric. The folds of her long outfit seemed to unravel, spilling out yards of material as feathery light and as voluminous as one could possibly imagine. The material kept coming, more and more of it unfolding. And not one inch of fabric, delicate and flowing, caught in the splintered shards of wood. Clara, in her confused state of mind, had not even noticed before what the woman was wearing.

Now there was no missing it.

Her anger forgotten, Clara stared in horrified fascination as the woman stood with an apparent ease and lightness of being. She stared as the Old One's feet found a solid footing over the rings of the tree trunk. Startled, Clara opened her mouth in great dismay as the folds of the old woman's gown fluttered backwards and unfolded to reveal large but delicate wings that spread in unison up and around the diminutive old woman. What a sight to see! White, diaphanous wings with rounded tips, like those of a glorious angel, almost touched, crowning the old woman's head.

"*Clara! Opus Sanctorum Angelorum!*" Her voice boomed in the silence of the forest, echoing and reechoing through the trees and out over the river, as she lifted her arms skyward. "Work of holy angels!"

Clara never heard the peal of thunder, for she only had one

THE SAVAGE RIVER VALLEY

thought. *"Oh my God, the old woman knows my name! She knows my name?"*

There was only one choice: fight or flight.

Using her feet, Clara instantly pushed out from her seated position in the dust, scrambling away on her hands, dragging herself as fast and as far away as she could. She frantically continued her paralytic slide backwards among the low branches that bounced off her face. The dirt ground her wet skin. She finally pushed up against a rough barked tree. She stopped. The back of her head knocked loudly, momentarily halting her backward flight. The contours of the bark's ridges were rough and pressed into her back.

The river was a few feet away.

She needed to keep moving!

With one eye warily focused on the old woman, she reached upward for support as she climbed to a standing position. If only she could manage calling out to the rescue boats.

Help!

Surely someone would hear her!

Now only if she could yell hard enough over the noise of the engines, radios, and the people yelling down to the divers. She felt stronger; she could stand up and wave her arms wildly to catch their attention. Facing them and their dull questions would be easier than living this current nightmare.

She slipped and came down hard against the earth. The rigid edges of the bark scraped her chin, ripping open the flesh. She groaned in pain and tears filled her eyes.

Oh wicked, wicked hateful world she was in!

The old woman did not move. She was silent, smiling, but sadly shaking her head. *What stubbornness,* she thought!

Clara shot her a look. Damn those wings! They floated around her, illuminating her in a whitish glow offset by the green foliage of the forest and the brown earthen floor of the riverbank. *Why doesn't she go away? What does she want?* Clara had lived with bizarre memories all her life and they had frightened her to no end. This bizarre encounter was not an illusion but one that stood horribly bright in perfect rectangular shafts of sunlight piercing the green foliage and hitting the forest floor.

The old woman lifted her hands and beckoned with her fingers; an invitation for Clara to come closer.

"Step into my arms and feel an embrace that is holy, my child," she whispered. But Clara did not hear her.

As Clara rose for a second time, looking helplessly trapped, her bare feet found a firm footing among the broken tree roots and pine needles. This time her feet did not slip. But suddenly, the ground was filled with thick pulsating roots, moving and pushing up from the earth.

What was this?

She must be imagining again! She faltered and then steadied herself, grabbing a low hanging branch. With trembling hands that quivered and wouldn't be still, she managed to hold on tightly.

She looked ahead, toward the wide expanse of the river. The scene before her, not on the other bank but on the river itself, was not what she expected to see.

She blinked in disbelief.

What in God's name ... ?

Incredibly, she caught sight not of the bridge and the rescue boats, but of a lone wooden canoe striking through the water, coming directly toward her! It had appeared so suddenly. She didn't remember seeing any canoes on the water, especially not one like this.

No, this can't be happening to me! This is not real.

She stared wildly.

So it is true, I am insane! They were all right to think so.

Inside the heavy canoe, which resembled a massive tree trunk sliced in two, stripped of its bark and carved into a half shell, were two male Indians. One seated in front and the other in back, paddled together as one. They paddled swifter now, as if in a desperate pursuit of prey, pulling all their weight into the paddling motion as

THE SAVAGE RIVER VALLEY

they dipped in and out of the water. The canoe was a heavy chunk of wood, dark, thick, and buoyant, sitting low in the water. The older Indian that sat in the back steered the canoe. The younger Indian, of the same size and looks, sat in front. Their shoulder muscles, bulged at the exertion of lifting and pushing the paddle, glistened in the sunlight and strained in an effort to shorten the distance to the shoreline. Both men were noticeably silent in their activity. A primitive sight, their faces, arms, and chests displayed ochre-colored designs in a magnificently painted pattern of strange signs, birds, arrows, and a fish. With every push of the paddle, they cast dark looks at the river's bank.

No shouts, no words, and no grunts.

Just silence and quiet steady dips of water. Long, black tail feathers hung from tufts of hair and lifted with the wind. Neither of them appeared to see her. But she definitely saw them! The canoe continued to lurch forward with each thrust of the paddles, now angling slightly to steer.

Who are these men? Where did they come from?

Within seconds, confusion and terror filled her heart as one thought above all pushed forefront to her mind. The scene unfolding before her could only mean one thing. It was true then. This was a world inhabited by fallen angels from hell, hideous and rejected demons that sought to further evil, to destroy her, to claim her among their ranks as a fallen angel.

But were they demons or Indians? And what about the Old Woman? Could it be that demons returned to earth or perhaps never left?

She was one woman who committed what some would view as a sin.

So, suicide sent you straight to a world of demons? *It must be hell,* she decided, *a fiendish and punishing nightmare, a great and exacting revenge for all the attempted suicides: the pills, the mountain, and now the bridge.* There was no escaping hell; she was now an integral part of it! Oh, she was so very sorry she ever jumped. *Why can't I undo what I did?*

59

Her misery had called for a solution, but not for this. This she wanted to be no part of!

Behind her back, the angel shook her head. "No," she thought, "suicide does not send you straight to the gates of hell, but rather on a long journey to find your spiritual peace. Go find that peace Clara." Clara resolutely stepped away from the shadow of the tree into the open. Desperate to escape for the second time that day, she looked about, opening her mouth to cry out for help.

There was absolutely no one to hear her.

She looked again, up and down the Hudson River. No one!

The entire broad expanse of the river, reflecting the sun's rays, was empty, save for the approaching canoe.

The rescue boats were gone, as were the masked divers. And so was the bridge. The landscape before her was completely devoid of anything she might have recognized from before. There were no houses, no farms, and no orchards on the opposite bank.

She lifted her eyes to the mountaintop. She did not see the spires of Olana. That too has disappeared.

It was no longer the end of the day but morning again, the sun not quite high enough overhead to determine noon. She was aware of the heat of mid morning lying in a shimmering haze over the water, the sounds of river insects and frogs singing out from the bank, these rowing Indians, and no one else.

Was she alone? Of course, there was the old woman behind her.

She knew perfectly well what would face her if she whirled around. She had to get away, far away from that crazy woman. Which was the worse alternative, facing the woman whose blue eyes pierced her soul, or these oncoming men, looking every bit as menacing as the pictures she had seen as a child?

What would it be? She needed to make a choice, desperate or not. It must be here and now.

She had a momentary flashback of detailed, horrid descriptions with gory pictures of savage warriors. The heathens, savages in their own right, would rip the scalp from her head.

THE SAVAGE RIVER VALLEY

Could she imagine worse?

She could.

The pain would linger with no merciful death exactly as the life she had led this past year and apparently was still leading. Only this time it was a worse hell on earth than she could have imagined.

Shaking her head in desperation, she watched the canoe approach the exact spot she was rooted to on the river's bank. It glided to her feet.

It was seconds from hitting the shore.

Move! she screamed to herself.

She gulped some air and whirled around to flee, and in doing so, smacked headlong into the chest of the largest man she had ever seen. He was running toward the riverbank at full speed, his face lined in beads of shiny sweat, his thick, black hair loosely flying with the wind. His angry-looking face had been painted carefully with two long streaks of black across the bridge of his nose and broad cheeks, and in his hair, a braided tuft on the top of his unshaven head, he wore a lone white feather; a feather, although of different color, not unlike those of the men sitting in the oncoming canoe. His swift approach was muffled by feet encased in soft-soled deerskins.

No wonder she hadn't heard him.

He was a young Indian warrior, fleet of foot, armed with a savage-looking weapon poised upward for a downward strike. His chest was bared and he was dressed in a groin cloth with deerskin leggings clinging to his brown, muscular thighs straight down to his tightly laced moccasins. She saw and felt all of him in a split second, as his arms closed about her. He raced through her, and she felt the pull of his massive chest and body, hard and masculine against hers.

He came to a halt.

Clara screamed and then fainted.

Chapter One

1601, the ninth moon

The raging storm lasted through the night, ultimately passing over the land in the early hours of the morning. The downpour, drenching in nature when it came, gave no mercy to anything that happened in its path. No respite for hours while the storm lashed out in destructive fury, pounding the longhouses of coarsely cut bark and sapling and flooding the dirt paths linked to heavily-used foot trails that rose and dipped to lands north and south in the valley. At its peak, the storm saturated the fields beyond the longhouses, soaking crops higher than a man's head, or just about, bending the stalks and whipping the trailing vines of what for centuries had been known as the three sisters: corn or maize, colored beans, and numerous varieties of squash. These village fields, yellowed and ripe, stretched out in all directions, on three sides fronted by the creek. The winds whipped through the nearby tree line, taking down branches and splitting more than one tree in half. Lightning viciously struck in many spots, causing ancient trees to splinter and fall. Thunder ripped across the flashing night sky.

It seemed the world was about to end.

The creek's turgid waters, flowing unfettered from mountaintops to the valley flats, rose steadily. Sometime during the night, the creek had overflowed its banks so that even now, as it receded, a thin sheen of water glistened over the fertile, parched fields; the

THE SAVAGE RIVER VALLEY

dried roots hungrily sucked in the moisture as it seeped into the ground.

The great storm was over.

Puddles blotted the ground as water dripped off saturated leaves. The smell of the rich, damp earth permeated the air, drifting in heavy pockets around the village and over the water.

All was quiet in the pre-dawn moments.

The only remaining evidence of the storm in the dawn sky was the intermittent flickering of flashes of lightning seen off to the north, high above the morning clouds. The storm accomplished one thing; it cleared the air of humidity and broke the hot spell.

Now the air was crisp as dawn approached.

Autumn was on the march.

The past weeks had been stifling hot and seemed to drag on, at a time when, normally, life and daily living space expanded from the winter confines of snug shelters to the summer openness of the outdoors. This particular village was sheltered by the ancient wall of mountains—Onteora, Home to Manito, as the local Indians called it—that formed a crescent shaped barrier to the west of the village. To the east, less than four miles from the village center, flowed the Great River. Despite the generally cool location, it had been an unusually humid summer, the heat held captive in layers of filmy haze that hovered persistently over the land in shimmering waves. The days and nights fused into a pattern of sweat, heavy body odor, and lethargy.

Everyone moved in a slow rhythm matching nature's established pace. They spoke, peacefully and with good intent, in low tones.

On this eleventh morning, in a month when the ninth moon of the year, the harvest moon, rose full in the night sky, twenty-eight healthy native Indians slumbered inside the wooden structure, one that stood in the center of the village; one that sturdily held the storm at bay, one that remained completely dry and water-tight inside, one that belonged to the matriarch of the village. This wooden structure was a noble longhouse extending some sixty feet in length, one of many clustered in villages dotted across the valley. It was built by men to be tight and snug—the home of the people who lived in the shadow of the Onteora, the Algonquian of the late Ceramic Woodland period. The longhouse was a monument to their creative know-how and ingenuity.

∿

The interior, dark and close, was built to accommodate more than one family—several in fact; a long stretch of partitioned compartments with sleeping benches or platforms that gave warmth and shelter to the native people. Here they lay to sleep, revitalize, and procreate.

Within its confines, tucked away in the farthest compartment from the entrance, the twenty-ninth, and incidentally oldest, person lay deathlike still, finally succumbing to a profoundly deep sleep. Some thought she had already passed on to the next world. At noon the day before, she had peacefully closed her tired eyes and had not opened them since.

Who was this sacred woman?

Where did she fit into the scheme of things in this dark dwelling that looked like a giant scooped out log tipped upside down over the brown earth? Why was she so important to the village and to the three women who slept within an arm's reach of her bed?

In short, she was the head of this longhouse and its clan of the Bear, as significant a female leader as could be found. She was the matriarch of one of the Indian tribes of the mountain valley, the tribe of the Catskills, which, by virtue of marriage and intermingling, were direct descendents of the tribes to the near east and north, the ancient tribe of the Mohicans, and near south and further west straight over the mountain range, the Esopus, a branch of the Munsee family, bearing the Unami totem, the turtle.

This matriarch's totem was of her own choosing: the black bear.

THE SAVAGE RIVER VALLEY

She had been the village leader for a very long time. This choice was unusual, since all villages were of the wolf, turkey, or turtle clan.

As the Matriarch, she had been fair in all matters pertaining to the village and a very wise leader—a sachem. She acted as spokeswoman for her own village and for all the villages on the flats; five flats each with its own Indian community. She oversaw the management of her village and was part of a council of elders for all the villages combined.

Her village was Wachachkeek, but there were others nearby.

Pacquiach—signifying clear land or open country—lay the farthest east and closest to the river, on the banks where two large creeks converged. This was the largest of all the villages and closest to the Hop-o-nose village situated along the banks of the river.

Potuck—indicating a waterfall—bordered the rapids in the creek that flowed in the shadow of the Potuck Mountain. For some reason, this was the village that produced the best fishermen, where her youngest son had found a mate and sired five children by the time he had lived through ten winters with his wife's family.

Further west lay the village of Wachachkeek—meaning a place of wigwams or living—where the sachem dwelled with what was left of her immediate family. Beyond that village lay two more filled with hunters and warriors: Assiskowachjkeet and Wichquanach-tekak. All five villages were united by friendship and family ties, yet separated by groves of trees or by gullies and waterways, off shoots of the meandering creek.

All Indian villages were built near streams, creeks, or the river for easy access and transport. These five were no exception.

Men and women in each of the villages had all respectfully called her "the Old One," for so many years no one could remember a time when she had been young. She was the senior person not only in her house but in the entire village as well, having done the almost unheard of feat in those days: reaching an age marked in memory by what would be her sixtieth or seventieth coming winter. No one knew for sure. Even she had lost count. Her life had been spent in remarkably good health. She was never beset with infection or fever or difficult childbirths, but now she lay as still as if she had already passed on to the other world.

The hushed conversations had started weeks before; just talk, nothing certain. Near the creek's banks, whispers passed from one edge of the cornfield to another and beside the fireside of each longhouse. The solemn news greeted the numerous men and few women returning from the fishing camps bearing a summer's worth of dried fish. The dried remnants of a summer's catch offered a hearty and tasty addition to the cooking pots in the months to come, but even this did not distract them from the serious topic of the day.

"We have not seen her in weeks. That is bad," one squaw remarked, rubbing her cheek.

"She is sick. Help from our medicine man can save her," another replied, swiping at a gray fly. The whispers did not stop.

The sachem no longer appeared among the people.

She was unusually weak and, sadly noted, no longer lent her voice to the clan's daily business. Her life, like the ebb of the tide, or a gentle flicker of a candle before it extinguishes, was drawing to an end. Each morning brought that precise moment in time closer and closer, creeping slowly but surely toward that day when she would leave the clan; her voice silenced in the village forever, her spirit traveling off to the west while her body lay facing the east in sacred burial ground.

For now she was alive, although she had had difficulty breathing the night prior, each breath a slow laborious task that shook her frail body and left her limp. Her final journey into the land of the beyond, where all people of the clan traveled to after death, was shortly coming. Final but extraordinary preparations of an elaborate ceremony would begin with the doling out of the white wampum strings that would invite all the surrounding villages to her burial. And as a profound sign of respect, all the five villages comprised of old and young alike, Indian braves and squaws would leave their camps of the valley flats to attend this sad but moving

THE SAVAGE RIVER VALLEY

event. Villages situated miles away yet still related—Hop-o-nose on the banks of the Great Water, Mawignack in the hills of flint, and Castle Height of the great palisades a few miles away—would also be summoned for this ceremony.

The last great sachem of this Catskill tribe was dying.

All knew it was coming, sensed it before they were told, though few would easily accept it, least of all her children and their descendents, those that had surrounded her for decades, those that knew their lives would never be the same once she passed on to her journey, leaving them behind.

Her extended family had retired to separate sleeping compartments the night before, men, women, and children crawling into their compartments where they lay their head for the night, all praying to Manito, the mighty spirit, their great god of nature, to let the Old One live. Before retiring, they heard the rest of the village gathering around the outside fire pit. These villagers, whose ancestors had traveled to this land—so the oral tradition said—led by an ancestor of the Old One, now stood before the village chief.

Inside the longhouse, the family members lay atop their bedding and listened in the early still of the night. At times, they held their breath, listening for the voice of their chief.

"Oh great and mighty Manito, let our mother sachem live," the village chief intoned, passing his hands over the smoke that curled upward. "Great Spirit, who dwells alone, listen to the words of your people gathered here. The smoke of our offering arises."

His voice held steady.

He lifted his open arms to the air above his head as if to help the smoke on its way to the land in the sky and chanted his prayers for little over an hour, bending slowly to the fire then standing erect before falling silent, lost in his own memories of childhood with the Old One, his mother. She had elected him chief, her voice the strongest and most respected among the women elders. He was the oldest son. Now all the responsibility of the clan would fall squarely on his shoulders. Preparation for the chief had been years in the making. He was ready.

All the villagers listened as well. In the far distance, a slight rumble could be heard—thunder.

All those gathered outside bowed their heads as a sign of respect and then retreated to their longhouses standing ten to twenty strides away. Others were located further up the flat.

They had done what they could. The rest was up to Manito. Still, they did not give up hope.

The village was situated on a flat, broad meadow, an alluvial plain, a short up-hill walk from the banks of an ice-cold fresh-water creek that brought respite from the stinging heat on one's tongue and skin. The creek gave life to the fields and to the village.

Water was collected many times throughout the day during hot spells, and even now several bare-chested young girls, ranging in ages from ten to fourteen, were filling large ceramic bowls and various shaped and sized gourds, hollowed out, dried, and polished. Their young bodies were lithe and supple, showing all the signs of having not reached their fifteenth summer, suggesting the easy flexible movements of youth; quick, sprightly, and carefree. Anyone watching them saw that they moved with grace; the future mothers and leaders of distant generations to come. Taking advantage of the moment, they splashed cold water over their sleepy faces, browned from the sun, and their bodies covered in sweat brought on by the close and often stuffy confines of the sleeping platforms. They would have liked to bathe fully, as was the expected daily custom, even in the bitter cold of the winter. The girls thought to let fall the thin layers of skins from their hips, wade into the refreshing depths and shake loose their thick hair from the constraints of braids. Submerged up to their waist in the cool water, they would have playfully splashed each other and talked of the young men in the neighboring villages. But all that would have to wait. Now, much more awaited them on their return; more than the chores of the day, the daily cooking and tending of the fields. Death of a great leader was lurking in the shadows and it cast a pall over their spirited nature.

Kneeling carefully by the creek's edge, balancing on a slippery, bare rock, they gently filled the bowls to the brim, taking into account the sloshing of water lost during the walk back, and began the slow climb to the village, during which they normally chatted and laughed.

Only today was not a normal day. It was a morning quite unlike the other mornings.

Silently, they kept their thoughts to themselves.

They walked one behind the other in a solemn procession, their bare feet leaving footprints on the damp earthen path, hugging the filled vessels to their chests, quiet and subdued. The sounds of the moving water in the gourds were an agreeable companion to the silence of the woods, its coolness fresh against their warm skin.

They were as quiet as the storm had been loud. They walked as softly and sure-footed as only the young do.

Caught off guard, they were not aware they were being watched.

∿

During the night, the ferocious sounds of the storm woke Minnah, youngest daughter of Tah-neh-wa and granddaughter of the Old One, who now lay alone on a pallet of skins on the dirt floor, spread before a shallow fire.

A resounding clap of thunder ripped through the humid night air. It was louder than anything she had ever heard before. She awoke with a start, her heart beating furiously with fear. She trembled, bracing for the next loud crack that was sure to come. Flashes of light appeared in the smoke holes above.

All gratitude to Manito, for she was not alone.

Inside the darkened hut, illuminated by the eerie glow of burning embers heaped in each of the fire pits in the center of the living quarters, she shivered in spite of the heat and drew close to her sister, older by a year, whose body was warm against her own. They both lay under a lightweight cover of skins, more as a protection against insects than the temperature.

"Ssst, did you hear that?" she whispered to her sister. Her sister slept on.

Minnah had slept beside her sister, Saquiskawa, since she could remember, never once passing a night alone, comforted by her sister's gentle breathing often inches from her ear. Given the fact that their mother was never far away, Minnah felt reasonably secure. As a matter of fact, any one of the women—including her sister, Saquiskawa; her mother, Tah-neh-wa; or she—was very seldom alone, and if so, then not far away from the village perimeters and only for short periods of time.

She listened for sounds of others awake.

The men and women lay in close quarters, long used to night storms and the nearness of so many family members. Tired by a day's endless work, they slept on without waking. Many snored, turned in their sleep, grunted, and groaned, but few awoke. From their clothing and bodies came a strong odor that mingled with the smell of the burning wood. It was a body odor that was not totally subdued by the bear grease they habitually rubbed against their skin to ward off the stinging insects and burning effects of the strong sun. It was a body odor they were no longer aware of.

They were related, by blood and by marriage and human bondage. Sasqua, the matriarch, was head of this clan, the clan of the black bear that lived at the foot of the tall imposing mountains that guarded their living and hunting lands in the valley. One daughter, older but not past childbearing years, her husband, in the prime of his hunting years, and their daughters shared the longhouse with Sasqua. Within Sasqua's own compartment lived her youngest daughter and her three children.

Their tradition was matrilineal. Mothers and daughters continued living in the same house even after the daughters married, as Sasqua's daughters did, obediently bringing their new husbands into their mother's house. Sasqua's sons had left their mother's house to join the clan of their new wives. They found a life among the Lenape: the Munsees and the Wappingers. One son traveled

THE SAVAGE RIVER VALLEY

council village nor the great council fire at Shodack, miles north on the eastern banks of the Great Water. Fire meant life. When hunters traveled far in cold weather, they often carried an ember from the home fire in a walnut shell. One could not survive long in this part of the world without a fire—not only in the depths of winter but throughout the year.

The flames reflected tiny points of light in Minnah's eyes as she watched the smoke curl upward. The dancing sparks and flickering flame held her in a mesmerizing grasp, shedding fantastical forms of moving shadows.

The fire. Indian legend has it that the first fire was created when a lightning bolt struck an old dead tree.

∿

Evidence of village fires up and down the valley attests to our strength in numbers.

A square hole, opened and closed by a removable chunk of bark in the roof, consistently gave an assurance to my village, the ancient tribe of our forefathers, that the fire was lit as smoke filtered upwards and out into the sky. Our hunters coming in from the woods, our fishermen returning from summer camps along the banks of the Great Water, and women walking in from the fields and nearby meadows would first spot the smoke from a distance before they could even smell it. Inevitably, they were comforted by an unconscious thought: the village was protection, home, a safe haven, a peaceful domain in a world inhabited by many natural dangers, human and animal, both on and off the trails, and deep in the woods.

The sight of gray smoke rising.
The smell of dry wood burning.
The warmth of the crackling fire.
All three comforting aspects of our life.

There were three such fires in this longhouse, but this particular fire where Tah-neh-wa knelt belonged to the Old One, and it gave off enough light for Minnah to peer into the darkened corners.

A few clay pots, some filled with water, stood upright, wedged between the rounder stones. Their carved edges and delicate design were visible in the dim light and were so close she could almost imagine reaching out and tracing the carved lines with her fingertips. It was a design that was popular throughout the villages of the flats, often depicting the racing form of the wolf, or the stodginess of bear, or even the strong shell of the turtle. Clay pots had been in use for over two hundred years. Many generations of women treasured their pots used in food preparation, cooking, and storage more than they treasured their other earthly possessions.

Wood to feed the fire, their year-round lifeline, was stacked and fitted under each sleeping compartment and within an arm's length, so that without much effort one of the men could, from where he lay, feed the fire during the night. But there was no man in the Old One's compartment, for she had lost her husband years ago and never took another.

Tah-neh-wa, the one who cared for her now, had suffered a similar fate.

Tah-neh-wa was the youngest daughter of twelve children, and the most beautiful.

In keeping with native custom, it fell to her to not only take care of the Old One at night, but tend her fire as well. She would have done it anyway, for the bonds ran deep with her mother and her children, always nurturing each in a moment of need, whether it was expected or not. She had given them her all without a second thought.

For that was the role of the village squaw: uncomplaining, undaunted, and solid. The Indian woman, a squaw in their language, toiled hard, but unfeeling she was not.

THE SAVAGE RIVER VALLEY

Even now, Minnah could hear the gentle sighs escaping her mother's lips while the rain beat heavy against the walls and roof. Minnah was sure her mother felt alone, thinking of the Old One. No one had risen to sit beside the two women. The others in the longhouse slept on in compartments away from their own.

Tah-neh-wa whispered a few more words, familiar to her sleeping mother.

Minnah heard the gentle swoosh of language, but what she didn't hear were the last secrets her mother shared in whispered tones with her dying Sachem. It was almost a confession, a general unburdening of a troubled spirit to one who is close to meeting the Great Manito, their god.

Minnah was not curious. These words were meant for no one else.

Tah-neh-wa knew in her heart that her mother was listening and would agree with her plan.

Minnah had been gently warned before to not speak or reach out and comfort her mother. Though she hated to see Tah-neh-wa grieving, this was the quiet time between the two older women, and no one interrupted the nightly ministering of the healthy daughter to the sick mother. She held a tiny belt of white wampum in her hand. Any oath she made to her mother in the presence of a sacred thing was not to be taken lightly.

"You have been a friend to me, Sachem, my mother. I have long listened to your words and followed your wishes. I obeyed you. I have stayed at your side." It was then that she made her confession, which must be kept a secret. Moments later, the daughter grew silent.

Tah-neh-wa lowered her head, tears falling in succession to her lap. She held them back during the day in front of the others but now the drops flowed. This surge of uncontrollable emotion frightened the beautiful daughter. Normally she was in control of such things.

Women of the tribe were expected to check their emotions. She was no different than the others.

What would her mother's passing do to the village? And how would it shake her resolve?

Minnah shifted, turning away from what the fire's flickering light revealed.

Above her head loomed the upper platforms and roof rafters. She looked up into the darkness. There they stored the goods of the village; dried foods, beans of all sorts and colors, braided husks of Indian corn, bunches of drying tobacco, hollowed out squash, and gourds filled with seeds. These made their collective lifeline for the coming winter and spring. Above that, the Indians stored an assortment of rolled-up animal skins, light wooden bowls, cradleboards, sacred carved bows and arrows that only the men could handle, and dried stiff antlers. On the highest rafters, the smaller canoes and wooden paddles for rowing were hung, used later in the winter when the waterways froze. Anything of value, including bunches of herbs, when not in use or buried in the outside pits was stored, without fail, above every sleeping compartment, including her own, making the space above her head dark and close.

The storm dragged on.

It seemed like it would never end.

Then, finally, it passed; heaving, as if a reminder, one jagged bolt of lightning to the ground. Not far from the village, on the river's banks, a giant tree over two hundred years old took the bolt, splintering from its mighty trunk.

Minnah heard her mother take a deep sigh of relief.

Feeling drowsy, her eyes began to close. She knew the storm was over.

Before she slept, she thought, *The spirits must be displeased to have sent such a mighty storm.*

Then, all was quiet.

THE SAVAGE RIVER VALLEY

∿

At first light, Minnah stole away. She slowly crawled over her sister, careful not to waken her before she left the longhouse.

It was unusual, but she wanted to be alone, if only for a few minutes this morning. If someone had asked her why, she wouldn't have been able to explain. But somehow it made her feel special, almost important, to be up before the others and to claim the quiet world as her own.

She tiptoed past the other sleeping compartments, hers being the farthest from the entrance door. Her mother, fatigued from the night before, slept on. Ducking slightly, she slipped out the doorway, an open space at the end of the longhouse, and then straightened.

Once outside, she paused and listened. She was very good with sights and sounds, often distinguishing things way before the others. She was an unusual child of the clan, with eyes that saw every detail, missed little, and at this moment in front of her, what others might have taken for granted, was a world refreshed by the rain that had brought moisturizing vitality to a drying land—a world that she imagined for just a short time was her very own, a world that was draped in the remnants of the morning fog after a raging night storm.

Not a single soul stirred in the village compound.

She surveyed the scene before her.

The steady drip of water from the bark siding and leaves was the gentle noise about her, as peaceful a sound that ever fell upon her ears. A kaleidoscope of colors, greens and browns in the woods, yellow and ochre from the cornfields, caught her eye amidst the dying chirps of drowning crickets. An occasional bird's call—a high-pitched caw-caw—from the distance filled the air.

Then she heard the morning dove and its gentle call of coo-ah, coo, coo, coo!

That moment, perfectly content, she stood still and forgot everything else but the joy of the view before her. She breathed in deeply with quiet satisfaction. And for a fraction of a second, the world of this Indian girl was perfect and in complete harmony with nature.

∿

Turning, she carefully made her way to the creek's edge, following a well-worn path, her bare feet wading through the puddles and finally coming to a squat on the sloping rock that led down to the water's edge. The ripples and sound of the village creek brought her peace and a sense of calm, no less on this particular morning than the others.

On the way, she had stooped to pick the heads from specially chosen plants that grew unfettered and tangled in massive clumps; weeds and wildflowers all in a great profusion of summer growth. Nature's medicine cabinet! It had come to her when, at last, she dreamt after the storm had passed. A small, ceramic bowl—perhaps the ceremonial one—filled with wonderful smelling plants; the bittersweet darns root of dogbane, boiled and then mixed with crushed yarrow, the color of the sun, wildly pungent, steamed over the hot stones of their precious fire, always, thankfully, burning inside the longhouse. A constant vapor of fragrant air, ensuring an herbal mist that would gently cover her grandmother's still form. Yes, now she understood her need to be solitary in her thoughts this morning!

Today, she would try something new.

The steam couldn't help but relieve the difficult breathing of the Old One. She was sure of it. So sure, that now as she inspected her leaves and budding flowers, spreading them out in front of her, peeling the petals and handling them with soft delicate strokes, she smiled in relief.

They were all there.

Everything she needed.

"These herbs, smelling of the earth, will save your life and chase away the evil spirit," she whispered with elation. As a child, she had spent many hours in the past foraging wild stems, plants, and roots in the forest under her grandmother's watchful eye. Today, without the supervision of a woman knowledgeable in the medicinal and healing value of nature's plants, her instinct guided her choices. Plants, roots, and bark were handled with great care; dried within the lodge and placed in little leather bags or pouches. The magic existed in their cure. The uses were many: ash bark for colds and fevers, elm for stomach ailments, sassafras root for mosquito bites, mandrake for a purge, and blackberry roots acted as an astringent.

Yes, plants and roots were good medicine!

The rejoicing of the village would pale in comparison to the rejoicing that would fill her heart, for she was close to her grandmother. During the day, the two of them were often inseparable. The Old One and Minnah spent many hours in the fields planting, hoeing, and harvesting. Out in the woods they talked in serious tones of the plants that could best serve the village in both health and sickness. In life or in death, today she would be at her grandmother's side.

She began to pray, looking for the rising sun.

Suddenly her thoughts were interrupted by a loud plop of water. Startled out of her reverie, she lifted her head and looked to the creek.

The creek was fast moving, the waters having swelled from the heavy torrents of rain. The earth was saturated and could not absorb another drop of water, so it pushed the excess into streams high up in the hills and mountains. The streams then rushed down hillsides and over rocks to flood the larger creeks. Eventually the fast water emptied into the Great Water. She could feel the coolness flowing down from the mountains as she lifted her face to the dawn sky. The beginning sounds of the small insects, the musical songs of the grasshoppers and crickets, came from the woods all around her and the world, as she knew it, continued to glisten. Anyone else would think nothing of it. But to Minnah, something didn't seem right.

She could feel little shivers run up and down her arms. A slight prickle of danger? So this is what it meant to be afraid?

"*Mind alert, body ready.*" From the back of her mind she heard her mother's firm voice reciting this well-worn phrase, repeating this familiar warning daily if not more than that since she was a child. A phrase that all Indian children learned from the time they could understand the meaning of language. The world they lived in was fraught with many natural dangers that most likely snarled and growled and walked on all fours, waiting to grab a small child in its mouth and drag it away.

She suddenly looked in the direction of the opposite bank of the creek.

For a moment, she thought she saw movement among the dark trees. Was it a prowling animal? She would have to run fast if that were the case, perhaps yelling to wake the others. Maybe it was something else. A village dog, perhaps? Her eyes had never lied to her before. Her senses of smell, sight, and sound were racing. Whatever it was, this was new.

Her heart skipped a beat.

Was someone there? She made as if to call out, raising her hand to her mouth, but halted midway.

Had someone from her village awakened before her? But why would they have crossed the creek so early? Could it be someone from the neighboring village? By custom, no one crossed the boundaries of another village without an invitation, especially at night. The Indians shared land for hunting but they were territorial when it came to the village itself.

She waited for someone to emerge from the tree cover.

Go on, show yourself!

Only no one did.

There were only the gentle sounds of the early morning, a rustling of the leaves in the soft breeze, and the sounds of the fast moving water.

She hunched down a little and peered closer. For some reason, an unusual one at that, she felt uncomfortable, as if something or someone lurked in the protective covering of the trees. Yes, that was

THE SAVAGE RIVER VALLEY

women ancestors, had been born into the world smiling and placid while harboring a special talent.

She could see into the future.

∿

Everyone in the village knew I was different from the rest. They spoke in hushed whispers amongst themselves in small intimate groups and wondered why it was that Manito, our great god, felt compelled to give me special visions that not even our shaman saw or could at best conjure up. Now, after so many years, they shrugged it off and fully accepted me as a special gift to the village, not as a witch, for witches were, when discovered, killed or run off by the fearful and suspicious tribe. My grandmother spoke to them, assured them of the gentleness of my special gift, and even met with the shaman for a long, hushed conversation that left the shaman shaken and pale, yet condoning my presence in the village.

At the age of four, I could sense things before they happened; stand with the wind at my back and feel the vibrations of feet on the ground miles away as the hunters returned home from the hill. I knew when the last frost had come and gone. I could predict a cold winter and a bad year for our crops, though those years were rare, for Manito's great and giving nature allowed us to build solid wooden structures and continue on the flats near the Great Water where we prospered and had an abundance of food, thus eliminating the need to move our village as often as other villages did.

For hours I would stand at the edge of the meadow bordering our fields, within sight of my mother and grandmother, of course; always at the same spot, always staring, beginning and ending at the same time of the day.

I was waiting.

For what, they did not know. I never told them. They would have laughed and not believed me, scoffed at my imaginings. When we were out of earshot of the others, the only one I told was my grandmother, and she neither laughed nor disbelieved me.

"They will come." I always started off this way.
She sighed deeply, but listened well.

"Home, my daughter's child, my little one, my heart ... come with me," my grandmother would say, having stolen away from her work to place her arms gently across my shoulders and, looking quickly around her, scanning the line of trees, and steer me back to our longhouse. Little children were cosseted and I, like my sister, no less than the rest, perhaps even more, though I knew not why.

ᨈ

She was alone.

Minnah sat quietly, enjoying this moment. She thought of the moving water and its track—how it would meander in a big loop around the village, rushing over a wide stone bed around the flat fields. Then it would broaden and narrow, only to later pass through some deep gorges with sheer rock formations and flow into white rapids over shallow areas that lay level with the bank. Eventually the flow of water joined with the flow of the Great Water, the River that stretched far away.

Ah! The Great Water!

For just a moment she smiled wistfully, wishing she could see the openness of the Great Water, glide with the movement of the flowing current before her, and be free to follow the creek, climbing into a canoe that would float and transport her safely. To be free! To lie back and stare up into her very own patch of open blue sky, unhindered from the tree cover, knowing not where she was going nor caring.

She felt a sharp stab of fear. These were unusual thoughts for an Indian girl. What was she thinking?

Away from her family? And, free of what?

Lately, her musings had increased. Her daydreaming became more vivid in her mind, real pictures of what would happen to her, her people, and the land they lived on; often of images she couldn't

THE SAVAGE RIVER VALLEY

comprehend. Some insisted that her visions were the result of a vivid imagination, too much syrup in her corn meal breakfast, too many berries and nuts on an empty stomach; only she knew better. She willfully pushed the thoughts away. Her mother, fearful of what the others would say, always warned her against these wild imaginings, cautiously shushing her in front of everyone. This morning, if her mother had known, would be no different from the rest.

Only her grandmother understood and soon she would be gone.

Who will I turn to then? she wondered.

A raucous bird cried out in the treetops, as if roughly startled. Its shiny black form was visible against the green backdrop of the leafy branch where it perched. The bird screeched and flapped its wings, angrily disturbed. The jarring noise jolted her from her peaceful daydreaming in the quiet setting.

Her eyes clouded over with worry.

Time had elapsed. She had been here longer than she intended.

A sudden twinge of guilt for such carefree thoughts snaked through her young heart. Her thoughts had foolishly led her astray while her grandmother lay sick. Sheepishly she looked over her shoulder beyond the creek's bank to the bark huts. She didn't want anyone to see her dawdling here.

No one was awake yet.

No one had left the longhouse.

All was quiet except for the usual noises of an early morning and this screeching bird overhead. Even the outside fires had yet to be stoked and stacked up with dry logs. The pits were a wet bed of ashes from the night before. Before long they would be scooped out and new fires set. The ashes, acting as a nourishing food to the earth, would be scattered over the fields.

From where she squat, she could barely see the open entryway and recognize her grandmother's long and rounded house among the other longhouses, built in identical fashion. *Kanonh-ses*—the longhouse; there were fifteen in all.

Soon the other young girls her age will come to collect water. *Soon everyone will be awake,* she thought, sighing deeply. She would no longer be alone. But maybe that is not what she wanted anyway. But for just this moment, she had had the world to herself.

She stood and stared and then, only once, did she turn her head to take a last but long studied look at the opposite bank.

Chapter Two

The door to my mother's house and her mother's house is always open as had been for generations before them.

The open door symbolized our lives, and our hearts; open to nature and to each other. If we close our hearts to our surroundings, shut out the call of nature and the earth, and ignored the path to the Great Spirit whom we called Manito, we were as good as dead.

Nature: the earth, trees, sun, moon, water; all of it would turn its back on us and we would perish. The abundant trees would fall; the ripening maize would wither; the squirming fish would die; the water would dry up or sustain no living thing; the deer, moose, and bear would travel far away from our hunting grounds; and the sun would not bring us warmth.

Our plenty would disappear. In our hearts, there always lingered the threat of the cold barren history of our ancestors, long ago but not forgotten, which none of us wanted to experience beyond the story telling that occurred at the family fire side. Winters were six-moons long and caused hardship for our hunters and wood gatherers, piling up mountains of snow high above the children's heads. We didn't want to live it year round.

We believe because our forefathers and their forefathers believed. Our history is long and each one of us in the village carries it deep within our hearts. Our ancestors wisely and knowingly left us important messages that were passed down through the succeeding generations in story form, told and re-told while seated around the family fire pits during winter nights and during council meetings, messages that spoke of good spirits, found in living constant with nature. Spirits that would pro-

tect us, nature's children, and protect our way of life. The spirits entered and resided in our longhouses of poles, bark, and saplings, enjoying the warmth of our fires lit within. We welcomed them through the door, the door that was always open.

The door symbolized an entry into our lives, into our inner circle. An inner circle our people protected at all costs.

I was a daughter of nature, of the earth, and of this longhouse.

Through that door lay my destiny and the destiny of my people.

∿

The bird fell silent, hidden in some treetop.

Within moments, Minnah spied her mother, emerging from the darkened doorway, stepping out into the brightness of the morning air. Her light colored clothing, a fringed skirt and mantle, was framed against the dark wet siding of the longhouse. Behind her, the others filed out all at once. The scantily-clad men and boys, those who had returned from summer fishing camps, disappeared to the other side of the village woods where they would stand and pee, then squat among the undergrowth. The young girls, already on the path to the creek, shouldered their water containers waiting to relieve themselves as well.

The woman did not move. She stood alone, as straight as one of the trees bordering the rim of the village.

Her mother was the quintessential Indian woman. A squaw whose beauty was soft and appealing; dressed in the softest shift of a doe's skin, a light buff color that fitted her rounded but shapely form, straight dark hair that hung in luxurious thickness down her back, reaching her waist in a single braid, which signified widowhood, and which, when loose, covered her face like a veil when she bent. She was gifted with a noble forehead; large, expressive eyes; and a square jaw overshadowed by her smile, which, when bestowed, would dazzle even the toughest of the tribal hunters. More than one argument has been won due to that smile, and more than one argument had been started bec█████ ██ ██. She wore a necklace of rounded antler and bone, signifying the love of a lost hunter, held together by a string of hemp. She had this very season seen the arrival of her thirty-second summer and, although she had given birth to several children, her beauty was nevertheless still as defined as when she was a young girl. ██████e, the hard work an Indian squaw must endure when caring for her family by tending the fields, gathering nuts and berries in the forest, treating skins, making clothes, gathering firewood, cooking, and seeing to her husband and children—none of it detracted from her beauty.

The women of the village were less beautiful, but none were jealous. She was the baby of the family, only a baby no more. "Tah-neh-wa," her sister would tease years ago, "you have been given a gift of great beauty. Every hunter looks to make you his wife!"

Soon she would have her own longhouse, as her daughters took husbands and gave her grandchildren and the number of family members grew beyond what her own mother's longhouse could sustain.

She delayed joining the other women already bending over their cooking pots. Tah-neh-wa stood in silence, looking in the direction of the creek. Perhaps she was seeking her youngest daughter? She seemed to be looking off to the far distance, far from the village confines, far from the rushing creek, her eyes searching beyond the campsites where women were stoking fires and other longhouses where more Indians were exiting.

She looked to where the meadows and woods bega█ ██████████ on the horizon. She was staring off to the north.

This behavior was unusual.

It was not like her mother to stand so still for so long, so dream-like, so unaware of her surroundings, lost in the middle of an active Indian village. Women were slow moving but they always acted with purpose, for there was always much to be done to ensure their survival. And much of it fell to the women, for the men took on the role of protector, facing the dangers of the hunt and war.

Minnah was ████ and continued to watch her mother.

It appeared Tah-neh-wa didn't see her daughter at first.

She stood for a time and seemed lost in her thoughts, deep within another world that did not exist around her on this fine morning. Had the other squaws stopped to see the expression on her face, they might have mistaken it for ████ Eight years was a long time for a woman squaw to be without a man. No one understood why she didn't take another into her bed as her protector and hunter. Was it an expression of sorrow then? Or was it something else?

None would have suspected anything else.

Minnah stayed quiet, mimicking her mother's behavior by not moving.

Waiting. Wondering. Expecting the moment her mother would catch sight of her standing on the creek's bank. She could often tell what people were thinking by just watching them and studying their movements; quick, smooth, jerky, confident, all so telling about a person's character or intentions. More so was the look that lingered in their eyes, but more often than not, her mother confused her and hid her real self from Minnah. She was the only one who could do that.

What was she thinking about? Perhaps if Minnah waited long enough she could figure it out.

After a while, her mother's eyes blinked, took on a new focus, one fairly close to where she stood, and then she saw her daughter in the foreground, standing before the rushing waters. She visibly ████ lifted an arm in recognition, and waved to her to come back to the campsite.

Minnah smiled in return, swung her arm once above her head, and then quickly leaned over, gathered her plants, scooped up a handful of water, splashed her face, and then hastened back to the campsite beside the solid longhouse where her mother was just stoking the outside fire pit fed by embers and dry firewood from within.

THE SAVAGE RIVER VALLEY

During the day, the others left me alone, knowing that if any one of us could stave off the evil spirits, it would be me. Steam rose from hot water mixed with forest plants to ease her breathing, so shallow and broken. It seemed to help a little, but a little was something I could cling to and place my hopes upon.

Days before, I had carefully rubbed small amounts of bear grease on her stiff joints, hoping to ease her pain. The grease was a special gift of nature in our village, running low until the next bear hunt. We relied on the men, our hunters, to replenish our supplies. With gentle hands, I tenderly bathed her skin hanging in loose folds over her bones and dried her carefully with little pats. Only the finest skins of the house would do to cover her, soft against her skin. I ran my hand over their softness. The skins came from the great number of animals Manito put in the unending forest and on the banks of the Great Water; wild in life but soft and tame in death.

Death! What a strange word!

For us it was merely a journey, a journey into the life hereafter; one that existed in our belief system, one that we highly respected and held sacred in our hearts. But I was too young and I could not follow my grandmother on this journey, so I did everything I could think of to save her, to extend her life for a little while longer. I was not ready to let her go. And I knew the others felt the same.

I did not want to say my good-byes to a woman who understood me best. I could not bear the thought of living a life without her. Who would I share my secret thoughts with? Who would want to hear them and not react in fright?

For many of them were frightening.

She groaned ever so slightly at my side. A slight noise that most would have missed, but it immediately drew my attention to her face. I gently smoothed back her hair, white and thin against her forehead, the skin browned and weathered by the sun.

I twined her thin hair in my fingers and plaited each side to the front. It was a little act of love, for I knew that as a young girl she always wore her hair twined together with strips of soft skins. Hair that once had been a thick, black, lustrous mane but now was pure white and delicately thin.

My hands were rough and dry, but I tried to comfort her as best I could. I often cried out in desperation when I thought she no longer was breathing, but was relieved each time she opened her eyes.

I had the time to sit with her all day, this one spot of time in my life. The nights were my mother's, but the days belonged to me and I guarded that time with zealous determination.

Time to wait.

Time for death to come knocking and steal her away, lift her spirit up from her body, and release her from earthly restraints.

I caught a sob threatening to erupt.

Suddenly, I hated the longhouse. I hated the minutes that went by, so tortured and painstakingly slow while she lay there. Minutes I could not control.

I hated everything that would not help to make her well. I even hated myself, so weak and helpless, for the inability to do the impossible.

During the day, I never left her after she fell sick, except to go out for more plants. It seemed natural to me to want to be at her side. I said very little now, having quietly spoken to her for days. Earlier, I spoke of our lives, what had been and what was now. I dared not tell her of the visions that came to me lately, for I did not understand them myself. I could not put names to the strange faces I saw nor to the places or happenings. The visions came fast. She had known that I had these visions and often, when no one else was around, I had shared them with her, but not now. They were not happy visions that told of good hunting land or where the fishing would yield a prime catch, nor the best day to plant the fields. What I had seen lately were things I could not explain; faces of different colors, things I could never have imagined, and things that terrified me while others left my heart cold. I was terrified by a village of dead people, all with great oozing sores spreading over their bodies. But most of all there was one image that frightened me the most: the giant winged bird that walked over the Great River, and, with its white wings flapping loudly in the breeze, that one day would swoop upon us and our river villages. After that I saw many women and children dead, longhouses and camps burned black like the charred trees in our newly cleared fields, faces scarred by pitted skin and withered bodies.

THE SAVAGE RIVER VALLEY

That vision silenced me and brought great anguish to my heart.

Best kept unspoken, those visions of mine, though I knew she was listening for my voice because sometimes when she opened her eyes, the sparkling twinkle of blue would look deep into my eyes. Her eyes reflected her soul and met my soul on some greater plane. For that moment we connected and our two souls became one on a winged journey.

I smiled at the thought and held her hand tightly, as if I were clinging to her soul. Her response was a gentle pressure on mine. We both knew, I was certain she did, that I would stay with her until the very last moment.

Outside it was crisp and dry, but inside the air was hot and tempered by darkness and shadows. The flames licked hungrily at the dry wood and consumed it almost instantly. I felt a chill run through my body, regardless of the fire's heat.

All the platforms were empty with skins tossed aside from when the occupants had risen that morning and the longhouse unusually quiet.

Only the fire made noise. It sputtered and crackled and all the logs had nearly burned down to charred bits and pieces.

I leaned forward and stacked on more wood. I could feel the flames of fire come close to my skin but I cared not.

Then I sat back, very still, like a stone from the creek's bed, thinking and praying; time, like water, rushing over me. Perhaps this morning, if I was quiet and made absolutely no noise, the bad spirits, chased away by Manito, the same spirit that brought the storm that gave water to the earth the night before, would fly high and quickly over the roof and never know we were inside. For just this once I wanted to fool them like never before. For just this once I didn't want them to win and take my grandmother away.

∿

The shadows shifted.

There was movement at the open door. Minnah squinted in the smoky interior and then looked up from where she sat.

Chapter Three

By noon, the sun stood high in the sky and shone brightly in a cloudless sky, although the air remained cool in the shade. The person who stepped into the longhouse was Minnah's sister, the same one with whom she shared a sleeping compartment.

This tall girl, almost a woman, paused inside the doorway, letting her eyes adjust to the smoky darkness. It never failed to amaze her how their eyes could adjust to almost total darkness with no lessening of sight.

Her name was Saquiskawa, named after her grandmother, Sasqua.

Sasqua meant *light of the sun*.

Saquiskawa meant *light of the sun that speaks softly*, a tribute to her warm and gentle nature.

She was statuesque like her mother and delicately thin, and entered with the grace of a young woman who understood that her family lineage was a noble one. Yet she was kind and always happy and lately, more than one young Indian male had vied for her attention, though she had eyes for only one. And that one had eventually won her heart and secured the promise of a mate.

Saquiskawa was just entering her fifteenth autumn, and for her there would be no greater achievement than to marry with the blessing of the council of elders and give birth to a healthy family. She wanted a husband and a family to call her own, and she wanted them soon.

For years she walked with her head slightly bowed, a shy smile on her face, and looked up at everyone with open and accepting

THE SAVAGE RIVER VALLEY

eyes. Everyone in the village loved her humility and gentleness and coddled her, waiting for the day when she would continue the line of descendents that claimed an honorable place in their Indian nation's history.

Since she was a little girl, she had patiently waited for the right young brave. She found him. He came from another village, a two-day walk south along the foot of the mountains. The village was called Esopus, situated on a creek that also emptied out into the Great River. Their lifestyles were identical, their lineages were intertwined. The inhabitants were the Munsees, neighbors and allies of the Catskill tribes. During the yearly council meeting when all elders came together in communal talks and during the subsequent festival of the corn, she gave him her promise to be his. He had stepped close to her, shielding them from view of the others by covering their heads with a blanket. He was tall and strong, with a good eye for hunting, and their union promised to be a fortuitous one.

He was also her brother's partner in the hunt. They had made a pact as young boys: forever friends, forever hunters. His name was Ramco, and he would come to live with them in the longhouse of Wachachkeek, to proudly spread the seed of his own ancestors among the neighboring tribe of Mohicans.

"Our sons will live in the house of the great Sachem!" he boasted to the people of his village.

But then things changed.

The marriage was put off, postponed because of the Old One's illness. Saquiskawa insisted; she no longer smiled but instead lowered her head and cried many times during the course of the day. Lately she had taken to pulling her hair out, thick strands at a time, a sign of grief often displayed among the women.

So, inevitably to still the inner turmoil, she sought out the company of her sister; the quiet one, Minnah, the one who, when she did speak, always found the right thing to say, the one who made her feel safe.

She found comfort in Minnah's presence. Earlier, she eased her basket off her shoulders and turned to face her mother.

No words were needed to tell her mother what lay in her heart. Her eyes said it all. She knew the other women wouldn't mind her absence. Not on a day like today. Much of the harvest had already been gathered. It had been a healthy crop.

Once again, Manito had blessed the Indian people of this village. They would not go hungry this winter.

Her mother nodded thoughtfully, signaling permission for her daughter to leave the billowing fields of maize that moved in unison as soft morning winds blew over the women as they worked in quiet harmony that day. The woods lay in calm repose. Lesser birds were flitting about while a growing flock of crows was perched on the verge of the wood. It fell to the young boys, squatting on platforms built around the fields, to scare them off. The sunlight gave the effect of light and shade skirting the valley.

Saquiskawa left the field. Several women and children looked up and smiled as she passed, while a few seemed not to notice.

While the men hunted and fished, the women, assisted by younger girls and a few elderly men from the village, harvested the ripe vegetables. Some baskets were small, usually tied around the waist, and contained seed corn for planting. On this particular day, as fall was on the brink of rushing over the land and thus changing the color of the landscape and bringing in cooler air, the women toted their harvesting baskets. These were held up by a carrying strap around the forehead or the chest. Ears of corn with silky golden tassels, once pulled from the stalk with a quick snap, were thrown over the shoulder and into the basket. The husks were later to be braided and hung from poles in the longhouses. The excess after a good harvest was piled up to dry outside. Huge mounds of corn were placed on top of mats. These mats were laid out in long rows on the ground as a barrier against the moisture from the soil. Large white and yellow and red kernels were stripped from the cob. After the front teeth of a deer were chiseled out of the lower jawbone, it was an easier task to firmly grasp and scrape off the corn from the cob. The kernels were stored for safekeeping in the ground. Strong corn

THE SAVAGE RIVER VALLEY

stalks that grew tall supported the twirled vines of beans, whose roots were protected from weeds and the harsh glare of the sun by the shadow cast from trailing squash with giant leaves. The three sisters grew together in the same field. Out of the three, corn was the most sacred and had been for three thousand years. The spirit of the corn plant sustained life.

And what greater gift can there be than life?

Tah-neh-wa stopped, shifting the weight of the strap on her forehead, her hip supporting the almost full basket. It was heavy. She did not mind. With winter approaching she preferred a heavy basket to an empty one! She was used to carrying the full baskets, as were all the women in the fields. Collecting the corn was their job.

She watched the figure of her oldest daughter as she walked along the path in the direction of the village.

"Soon my daughter, Saquiskawa, you will have your own family, children running by your side, a husband to protect you and sleep at your fire," she whispered, more to Manito than to herself.

It was the sight of Saquiskawa disappearing into the dark opening of the longhouse that made her smile sadly. Soon, if all went as planned, she would no longer see that sight. Her heart already ached at the thought.

She looked at the plants around her. The green corn stalks grew in little separate mounds of heaped dirt. She heard the other women's gentle movements and soft murmurings close by as they bent to check on babies bundled in snug cradleboards. It didn't seem that long ago when her three children were tightly secured in their own papoose when she would bend and offer them her milk.

She bent close to the dirt and, with her finger, outlined three figures in the dust and thought. Minnah, the youngest and last child, was like the bean vine that grew up in support around her sister, nourishing Saquiskawa who, like the corn, stood tall and straight and gratefully accepted the supporting network of the bean vines, while their grandmother, like the squash, guarded the two sisters, keeping them, like the roots of the plants, nourished, growing, and shaded from the intense sun.

While her son was away, she was surrounded by women.

The three women she loved the most in life were a field away, there in the longhouse where they dwelt. Soon she would join them. But, first, she had to go to the woods. There was something she needed to do.

∿

Minnah smiled in relief, glad to see her sister.

"Welcome, oldest daughter of Tah-neh-wa," she said. The first greetings between family members were always formal, respecting the mother's family ancestors, descendants of mighty chiefs and sachems.

"My sister," Saquiskawa answered. Her eyes and smile told it all; the sadness, the tears that were never far away these days. It was understandable. They both knew the time was coming soon to say their good-byes to the Old One.

"Is it time?" Saquiskawa whispered, taking Minnah's free hand in her own, squatting down to sit cross-legged on the floor, leaning forward to peer into her grandmother's sleeping face. She had not given up hope but Saquiskawa was a thinker, a planner, always logical and very practical—a gift she received from her grandmother.

Minnah glanced at her sister's delicate profile in front of her, so similar to her mother's, and then, touched by her gentleness, looked away, struggling to hold back her tears.

She had no reply.

Saquiskawa looked to her sister's face.

"Our young men, the runners … they are ready." It would not take long for them to dash to the surrounding villages and make the long distance run to those farther away. Running was one of their roles, and they were very good at it, often covering great distances in a matter of hours.

"Shall I send them now or soon to the other villages? Potuck, Pacquiach, Hop-o-nose … they all wait for news. Is it time to call everyone together?" Saquiskawa asked her questions slowly and gently, and then released her sister's hand as a sign of respect and sat back, while patiently waiting for an answer.

Minnah appeared lost in thought, staring into the fire. For so young a girl, she was given much respect.

To send the boys now with the wampum message was too soon. Could it be that their grandmother, with Minnah's prayers, the herbs and steamy air, and the help of Manito, might improve, open her eyes, and become stronger, perhaps to live a few days longer?

Would she smile and speak to them again? Would the village once again view her blue eyes as she proudly walked from one long-house to another, speaking words of solemn wisdom?

The sound of her voice would comfort them all, yet it seemed unlikely, and for some reason Minnah hesitated. Logic won out over hope.

"It will be soon. But, for now we must wait," she answered, and although she whispered, her voice sounded loud in the quiet of the longhouse.

Saquiskawa nodded in serene compliance.

They both sat in silence. The noises of the outside came softly to their ears. People were moving around the village, although much quieter than usual.

∿

It was a morning of great sorrow.

My visions—in the ancient language onoquaam, meaning vision or dream—told me what I didn't want to know. I refused to see them, to let them into my thoughts, but the effort to do so was nearly impossible. They assailed me, picked me up, and flung me into scenes I dared not look at for very long.

Why?

They frightened me.

With my sister at my side and my grandmother lying on the pallet in front of me, I had time to think. Being alone for any one of us in the village did not happen often. We all lived together, shared our longhouse with our hearts, bodies, and souls, following the routines of life: first birth, then growth, followed by old age, and death. The passages of life, our life, that took us on a great journey to the beyond. We did not judge our lives in terms of easy or hard, for we had nothing else to compare it to. We lived with nature. We survived on plenty with the help of Manito, the mighty spirit to whom we prayed in sacred reverence. When we died, our spirits passed out of our body and traveled to a distant land, where we waited for our descendents to follow.

Our village, Wachachkeek, meaning place of living, consisted of several homes built and maintained by the men and women of our clan. Homes for all of us that accommodated nearly as many people as ten of us could lay each finger on; closed in and sheltered from harsh weather, built strong against the prowling wolves, panthers, and shiny black bears that roam at night, coming down from the wild uninhabited mountains in search of food. As long as I can remember, we never had a palisade, a big strong wooden fence that would protect us against our own kind, for we all lived in peace. A palisade, if built, was only to stop the wild animals that approached the perimeter of our village. Inside our longhouses, we were safe. Sometimes at night, we would hear the snarls and growls as they approached the village. One of the men in each house would pull wood from under the platform where he slept and, without rising from where he lay, would place more wood in the fire pit. The sparks would fly, the smoke would drift up to the roof opening and out into the night air, and the animals would sniff a stronger waft than before. The animals hated fire. The fire was our protector, their demon. It scared them away, and we were safe. Little did I know that someday the fire would be a bigger demon than I could ever have imagined. My grandmother would help escort those from its fiery entrails to a safe place. From afar, I would watch with unimaginable grief.

Women and old men tended to the fires during the day. Our men and young boys took on that duty at night. Who were we, the men, women, and children of our village and of the neighboring villages on the great flat meadow that stretched for miles?

THE SAVAGE RIVER VALLEY

We would later become known as the Catskill tribes; a branch of the ancient tribe of Mohicans. In our time, in the time after the terrible cold which our ancestors battled and endured for hundreds of years, when the warm weather returned and the trees grew strong and straight under the warm sun, we were the River Tribes and our lands extended to the Great Water. Our neighboring villages were Potuck, Pacquiach, and others. Five villages coexisted in peace and solidarity.

Our leaders were wise, our people gentle.

We lived near the Great Water, whose depths flowed with an abundance of fish, whose banks, wild in tangled confusion of undergrowth, swarmed with plentiful game.

The Great Water was the Mohicannituk—the river that flows both ways.

And we were the Muh-hee-kan-nuh—the people of that river, the Great Water, which gave us life and sustenance.

All of this I saw in my visions, as if I were a small bird flying overhead. I saw the lands that stretched far in all directions, to the banks of the long river, to the foot and the peaks of the tall mountains, to the valleys north and south where other tribes, both friendly and unfriendly, dwelled.

If only life could be like the river, flowing both ways. I would have been happy if I could turn back the life of my grandmother and bring her back to a day as I knew her long ago, seeing her once again moving among her people, speaking wise words and loving my family.

A map etched of her life.

A map of what was and is.

A map of what will be.

∿

The noises from outside the bark walls came softly to Minnah, gently bombarding her with a reminder, almost an illogical notion at that point, that life and surviving goes on, stopping for no one. The daily routines had become such a set custom that only a catastrophe would interrupt their daily flow: food, housing, wood for the fires gathered, and water as well; thoughts of an approaching winter drove all the villages to harvest and store. Constant movement told Minnah that while one person lay down to die, many were still living, not forgetting that daily routines meant survival.

She sighed deeply.

How would she be able to live, go on, while stumbling through this? Something so extraordinarily different than the other things that happened in her life; something that, for once, was horrifically painful. Every day that would dawn and the idea of living without her grandmother loomed as a dismal thought.

The seemingly endless bleak months of winter were close; a time when all the family stayed, for the most part, in close confines, gathered indoors for unbearably long stretches of time. A time in the past when her grandmother would have recited the tribal history, standing before those seated around the fire and nearby on the platforms listening with rapt attention, each night helping those before her set a different story to memory.

Who would become the family's new storyteller? Who, in their longhouse, would help to distract the people from the bitter cold winds that would howl around them and the icy coldness that would descend upon them very soon? There would be no one to tell the stories, at least no one as descriptive and knowing as her grandmother.

"Look," Saquiskawa whispered, bringing Minnah back to the present. "Her eyes are open!"

Saquiskawa trembled. She couldn't help herself from crying out. "Grandmother, do you hear us?"

Minnah, silent, felt a deep chill wash over her in the hot surroundings. She closed her eyes for a second and then glanced down at the Old One who had not looked upon the world for many hours. The Old One's eyes were open now. They stared at each other for barely a moment when the two sisters noticed an eerie thing. Their grandmother's eyes slowly turned upwards, looking far above Minnah's head.

The Old One smiled.

The sisters exchanged glances, grabbing the hand of the other and squeezing tightly.

"It is cold now," softly stated the youngest sister in wonder. How could that be when the fire, so carefully stacked with wood, was blazing?

It was the moment Minnah knew would come. In the instant her grandmother looked to the upper platforms and roof rafters, she knew what was there. She wasn't sure when they had arrived, for they had soundlessly appeared.

They had come en masse for the Old One, to bear witness to her last day on this earthly realm, to escort and lead her to the world of beyond, coming to collect one of their own. *M'chuch-creek* was the word for soul, spirit, or ghost. All the spirits of her ancestors now appeared.

"Do not be afraid," she warned her sister.

Saquiskawa saw nothing but felt the sudden change in the air, and regardless of the fire, a coolness that felt fresh on her cheeks.

She leaned close to her sister; her lips almost touched her ear.

A trembling whisper was all Saquiskawa could manage.

"Minnah, are they here?" Her eyes were huge with wonder as she looked into the dark interior. "Can you see them?"

Another long moment of silence followed.

Reluctantly, Minnah twisted her body around. She could see beyond the circle of orange flames. High above her head were the shapes and forms in the half shadows as they sat or stood, grim faces, silent and unmoving. They were looking right through her.

She hesitated and then spoke, her body shaking.

"Yes, I can see them. They are here," she answered, her voice wavering so that each word sounded like a singsong melody. "There are many spirits above us. I have never seen so many before, not in one place, and never here. I cannot see faces clearly, only their shapes. There are too many to count; some appear old and yet others are little and young." Suddenly her throat felt dry.

It was the meeting of an old and ancient world with the present.
What she was about to do was daring.

"Psssst! Go from here." She hissed loudly, hoping to scare them away.

The spirits remained steadfast; they would not leave without the Old One.

Minnah swallowed, held steady her gaze, and then continued.

"They will not leave," murmured Minnah.

Saquiskawa, long used to hearing many strange tales from her sister, stared into the darkness of the upper rafters. She waited for several seconds, wondering why she did not have her sister's rare gift. They had been born of the same mother and father. Strange. She saw nothing more than the darkness and the flickering of the firelight. Yet, she had every confidence in her younger sister. Everything Minnah had predicted had come true in the past, right down to the time when both girls could expect their womanly flow. Her sister never lied to her nor tried to scare her with strange stories, but rather was patient in her truth telling.

"I am no longer frightened," she said, almost glad she couldn't see them, even though she was curious, but nevertheless she believed what her sister told her.

"What should we do?"

Minnah felt a sudden calm come over her.

"Follow me."

She rose and led her sister to the open door.

Minnah turned and faced her.

"Go now. Send the young men for all the elders. Tell them in a strong voice that does not quiver to bear with pride the carrying of the wampum strings to all the villages. It will be their invitation to come," she said. She then added softly, "Tonight we say good-bye. It is time to honor the life of Sasqua, daughter of great sachems and mighty chiefs. And our chief, her son, and our mother, her youngest daughter, must stand at ceremony on the meadow's edge and greet each visitor as they come into the village."

THE SAVAGE RIVER VALLEY

Minnah continued on for a few minutes.

Saquiskawa listened carefully and nodded. She understood what needed to be done.

Long standing rituals must be performed. Traditions, good ones, were the enduring ties, a fabric of society that bound a village, a community of longhouses, and a group of people together. She would not let her people down. She would not let her grandmother down. Now she would be a part of a ceremony that was their tradition. Soon they would celebrate the green corn ceremony followed by others in the months to come.

It gave her a certain pride to carry on the traditions of her people. And it momentarily distracted her.

Lifting her chin, pushing back her shoulders and standing a little straighter than Minnah remembered, she stepped out into the dazzling sunlight.

Minnah watched while her sister walked gracefully to the center of the village, passing a few old men on the way who sat together on mats pulled close to small fire pits, scraping the already harvested corn, letting the kernels drop into a hollowed gourd. Their talk was a low murmur. Their days of hunting were over and now they fulfilled what menial duties allowed to them in the village. They had helped to feed the old people in their youth. Now, they looked to the youth of their village to feed them. Their short exchanges, which relived moments of daring and carefree days of long ago, ceased as Saquiskawa passed. Something in the way she walked caught their eye and held their stare. Without a word, they put aside the cornhusks, stood, and waited.

The only sounds came from the shrill insects in the nearby trees, a high piercing noise that traveled over considerable distances. The sun, high in the sky, had dried off any remaining moisture from the night before. The ground, although not dusty, was dry.

Satisfied that her sister would do as she asked, Minnah started to turn and walk back to the fireside, but something caught her eye. She blinked and looked again.

Afterwards she was stunned, but for now, for just a passing moment in her life, she didn't want to believe her eyes. Why, she asked herself, did she see these things at the most unexpected times?

In a flash that blinded her, Minnah saw her sister from afar; an extraordinary vision, as a tribal spokeswoman, an old woman, not unlike her grandmother, moving among the River Tribes, surrounded by men of different names, gray hair pulled sharply back from her face, her frail body hunched over as she walked.

And then, in a distressing vision, different from the first, that almost drove Minnah to her knees, in a distant time measured by the same number of summers her grandmother had lived, Saquiskawa's daughter, who would be named Nipapoa, out of desperation to save the legacy of her people and faced with very few choices, would sell the lands, meadow by meadow, village by village, to strange men whose faces shone like the pale moon in a night sky, dressed in strange suffocating clothes of heavy dark material that clung to them from neck to booted toe.

Selling their lands?

But by then Minnah and her sister, Saquiskawa, would be dead and buried. And she wouldn't be there to witness firsthand what she saw now. The notion of selling land was so foreign to Minnah that she was almost unsure of what she was seeing.

She hesitated. Should she call out to her and bring her back to the dark confines of the lodge? How could she explain it all to her sister? Would it change anything?

Tongue-tied, she couldn't say a thing. It was no use.

Curiously, there was nothing she could do to prevent what invariably would happen. Even the wisest of shamans knew that the future could not be altered by a human hand. It all lay within the powerful hands of Manito, the Great Spirit.

At that exact moment in time, as the visions disappeared and she once more watched her sister continue her slow march to the center of the village, Minnah decided the future, one that was beyond her

THE SAVAGE RIVER VALLEY

control, did not matter. It wasn't that she didn't care. She did. But after all, she wouldn't be alive. She was one young Indian girl who saw strange pictures in her mind. She was one young Indian girl who wanted to die and go hand in hand up over the mountains to the west with her grandmother. She was one young Indian girl who wished that life didn't have to change.

Sighing, she thought of the long day ahead of her. *Take it one moment, one step at a time,* she reminded herself.

All that mattered, she thought dejectedly, was what she had to face next.

Before Minnah spun around and returned to the fireside, she already knew that her grandmother was gone. No word existed in the Mohican language to mean good-bye. "*Kumpanaxen.* See you again," she sobbed, for in the Mohican world, even if one dies, all will see each other in the spirit world. It was only a matter of waiting, but that was no consolation for a grief-stricken heart that could no longer hear the words of a loved one.

Her grandmother was dead.

With the fire to her backside, she lay down on the dirt floor next to her grandmother's still body, took the Old One's small lifeless hand within her own, and, resting her head on her grandmother's thin shoulder, now cold and stiffening, she closed her eyes.

~

In my thirteenth summer, the day after the storm, unlike any other remembered in my lifetime, as a daughter of the bear clan, as part of the Great Spirit's plan of nature, my life changed forever.

All because of that open door.

These things I knew:

First, my wise and much loved grandmother would die and I, helpless and at a loss, with tears streaming down my face, would watch her pass out through the open door and out of my life for the last time.

Secondly, as the elders streamed onto our lands throughout the day, greeted at the edge of the village by my mother and the chief to mark the ceremonies of my grandmother's burial, I took notice, in all of my moments of utter loneliness and grief, of a brave warrior from a brother tribe across the Great Water. He stepped in through the open door to kneel at our fire, to sit behind Monemin, his father, and pay his respects to our village matriarch. When I looked up from where I sat behind my mother, feeling empty and cold, he was staring at me, and there, in his dark and compelling eyes, I felt pity and love and the stirrings of my own passions. In front of me, my mother smiled, as if relieved of a heavy burden.

And then, there was one more thing.

I had always known that one day, Clara, you would appear.

How and when I was not sure but finally that night, when I needed you most, when I thought my life was over, you did.

Chapter Four

Years ago the warmer winds from the west and south swept over the land, thus encouraging the gradual return of summers, longer stretches of warm moist weather lingered and the icy landscape slowly but surely evolved into wide vistas of greenery: this landscape attracted somewhat smaller game and the thundering herds of heavy-antlered caribou. A new layer of forest grew in the River Valley, one dominated by resilient hardwoods. The hard wood of hickory and basswood provided saplings and bark strips for Indian lodges. Along with the new species of fish that multiplied with rapidity in the river came the white-tailed deer and gray elk, the industrious beavers, wild rafters of turkey, stalking panthers, mountain lions, and the rangy black bears. Right behind them, fast on their trail, came the hunters, fishermen, gatherers and harvesters.

The tribes were following their food sources, and what they found in the valley not only met their needs but also satisfied them. One ancient tribe by the name of Mohicanu had found their paradise in the Valley of the Great Water, a river they named the Mohicannituk, a river they came to revere almost as much as Manito himself. Here they would stay. Roaming to survive was a thing of the past.

A new life was just beginning.

So they settled permanently in the northeast, along both banks of the Great Water. This migratory group had found a home at last.

During a time of transition, the sacred bow and arrow, better in speed, accuracy, and distance than the spear, had a significant impact on hunting. It could be argued that it changed their lives for the better. Only the men could touch, carry, or carve bows. The hunter came to rely on his bow and arrow as his first line of defense against enemy tribes from the northwest, against wild animals, and for hunting food. He never went beyond the village perimeters without the arrows stored away in a quiver, a case often made of hairless skins or wood, with the bow slung over his shoulder, fitted against the contour of his body. And if he did, he took the grave risk of never returning to the village alive.

The woods grew to abundant proportions; covering miles of valley floors. Trees grew up the sides of mountains and eventually covered the Palisades, the Highlands, the Shawangunks, the Taghkonics, the Onteora or Catskills, the Helderbergs, and, in turn, the Adirondacks, all of these areas the domain of the Indian man, the hunter, and the explorer.

The land was one of plenty, where the added presence of humus supported abundant fertility for crops of corn, beans, squash, nuts, and berries. Women, the harvesters, gained respectability and the new status as a food provider. And with that newfound status, she finally spoke up; a voice to be heard and reckoned with in village affairs.

Acorns were an early source of starch but were now superseded by more nutritious and digestible corn. And so it was that in the year of 1601, villages up and down the valley relied on the hunter to provide an extra staple to a corn based diet: fresh meat.

∿

The great bear hunt was on. And the shiny black bear, no bigger than a grown man, long accustomed to invading other territories but not having his grounds invaded, knew it. On what had been a misty morning, for some inexplicable reason, the bear stopped running, came to an ambling halt, and turned to face his predator.

The hunter had become the hunted. Now, as he rose up on his haunches, his eyes took on a new look: anger.

THE SAVAGE RIVER VALLEY

He roared into the air, curling back his mouth to show fearsome teeth and stood his ground and swat angrily at the air before him, but in the end it was no use. What he faced was stronger than he.

On the banks of the gently flowing Mohicannituk, the animal could not defend himself. The one-eyed creature, after a long pursuit rambling over miles of hills at the foot of his mountainous domain and tearing through twisted and thick undergrowth of the forest, which tore at his fur and scratched at his one remaining eye and stubby snout, succumbed to this mighty Indian hunter and his bow at the river's edge, as majestic a place to die as any.

And so, he met his demise.

All because of a slight sliver of wood; a speeding flint-tipped arrow that directly pierced his heart and brought him down dead in his tracks—all because he had been born with one eye; a freak of nature. Not too common, but it happened now and then.

It was early in the week of the ninth moon when White Feather spotted the bear for the first time. It was an exhilarating moment, one he would never forget. His heart beat faster and his eyes shone.

He stood on a hillside, hidden behind a glen of trees, feeling his body tingle as the coolness of the shade touched the sweat beading on his skin. He was adorned as a typical Mohican brave, his deerskin breechcloth, a strip of material that wound between his legs from front to back, was tied with a long length of hemp circling his waist. Although Indians usually wore little during the hot months, White Feather knew his best bet at getting through the undergrowth was his leggings pulled up over his sweaty thighs and heavy on his legs. The bush burning, a ritual performed every fall, in which fires were set to rid the ground of crackling leaves and dry twigs making a hunter's stealth-like approach impossible, had not occurred yet. The leggings would ward off the nasty scratches of the thorns and brambles of thick brush.

The sun had burnt off the remnants of fog and moisture from the storm that had passed through the previous night.

Now it was warm and the air crystal clear. A beautiful morning draped in soft hues of color.

He had stepped out of the sun for just a moment, but in that moment, he had a stroke of luck. Something moving in the tangled brush below him caught his attention.

It was the bear.

The animal stopped, lifting his head to sniff the air. It had grown uneasy in the past weeks, unsure of what, if anything, was threatening its very existence.

White Feather took a deep breath, signifying satisfaction. His chest expanded to an even greater proportion than otherwise. Normally, when at rest, his chest was huge, spreading out to very broad shoulders, narrowing down to sturdy hips, a rounded backside with tight muscles supported by strong legs. He was taller than most of the young braves in his village and in superb physical condition.

"When he runs, the earth seems to rumble under his feet," his mother exclaimed proudly. Even though he had been tracking for hours, alone and unafraid, focused on his task, he was not tired. Instead, he felt as alive as ever he thought possible. Every sense was keen to the hunt that lay before him.

He marveled at his ability to feel so vigorous and strong and took another deep breath. He felt waves of excitement building, almost to the point of robbing him of air to breath or the ability to stay focused.

This was how it was supposed to feel, the peak of the hunt.

Up until then, he had risen at the first hint of dawn and was on the trail for hours, running at a steady pace, and then pausing to kneel, one knee to the ground, all the time fastidiously studying the old tracks and following the circuitous route the bear had taken in the previous weeks. He passed by all the usual haunts of the bear: the two creeks of the valley that intersected near his village and then the fallen trees with slimy grubs and crawling insects eating the rotting bark, anywhere where a food source was available. White Feather was, over the course of time, able to understand the pattern of movements of the bear.

THE SAVAGE RIVER VALLEY

Climb high to the mountains during the day and descend to the valley at night.

Along the way, White Feather also spotted other tracks, a veritable map of information. He could count off the different number of animals passed, at what speed and in what direction they were heading. He saw the tracks of deer, wolves that ran in packs, fox, and the small steps of raccoon as they traveled through the timber. His uncles had long ago taught him to read the maps with an expert eye, the eye of a true hunter, mindful not to miss the tiniest of details, to understand his surroundings and become one with nature and one with his prey.

"You are a good learner, a little rough, but good. But, at times, you forget one important thing."

"What is that?" White Feather, though eager, shot back in a serious tone.

"Yourself," his Uncle Creek admonished early on.

∿

His favorite uncle, a blood brother to his father, Creek, a Mohican from across the Great Water near the council village of Shodack, taught him what every brave in the village needed to know.

He started to train at the age of five and soon his childhood was filled with the art of hunting. He would be a man before long and would be responsible for bringing fresh meat to his family. If it were not for the crops of corn, their lives would totally depend on the men hunting and fishing as tribes had hundreds of years past. As it was, the meat provided an additional element to their otherwise vegetarian diet. Following the custom in Algonquian villages, the boys first learned to handle a slingshot made of twigs and leather strips; their little hands fumbling to pull the sling first before the others. But as they grew older and their hands grew agile and the game they hunted bigger, the boys needed the proper accoutrements.

A bow to call their own. And arrows to go with it.

Creek had taken a full winter of early-darkened evenings sitting close to the light of the fire with his knife in hand, peeling off long strips of hickory bark, readying a new bow for his protégée. His dark hair was slung over his shoulder and the flames revealed a long face with huge black eyes that initially, when he had arrived to the village, seemed to hold others with a fixed stare. Now he did not say much, often not speaking to anyone, his wife included, for days on end.

In tribes across the region, from the five nations of the Iroquois to the huge widespread nation of Algonquian, it was customary for an uncle, not the father, to take on the duties of teacher and mentor. Therefore, when a mother saw her son getting hit on the head for wrongdoing, which was not often as hitting children was frowned upon; she only could commiserate with her husband instead of berating him. White Feather saw many couples unable to reproach a favorite brother or brother-in-law for taking the necessary steps to demand discipline and respect from their son. This saved many marriages in all Indian tribes, and it gave added respect to the mentor. It was a well-devised system to keep the peace among married couples, at least where the children were concerned.

Creek had taken a liking to White Feather, the son of his wife's sister, and even more so after the boy turned twelve. In his mind, Creek could pinpoint to the second when he took the boy completely under his wing. It was after the boy had lost his father, one of Creek's blood brothers born in the same village, when Creek had taken to long spells of saying little. There didn't seem to be much to talk about. Silence seemed to hang over him like a heavy blanket, and he kept most of his thoughts to himself. It wasn't that he was sullen or morose. It was just that things had changed.

Sometimes he had a distant, glassy-eyed look about him when he thought of the past.

Other times he appeared angry, his black eyes flashing at everyone in his path; but regardless of his mood, he never said more than a few words, and that was only at the most necessary of times.

THE SAVAGE RIVER VALLEY

In fact, his silence hid his guilt, and he found it hard to look others in the eye and converse.

They might detect something in his eyes that would betray him, especially when it concerned Tah-neh-wa.

"You teach my son well," she complimented and thanked him often, her bright smile seeming to blind him. Even after all these years, her teeth were a brilliant color of white. When she was close, he became uncomfortable. He averted his eyes as he felt the unwanted and uncontrollable warmth slowly spread over his body.

His body would tremble.

No one seemed to notice.

He was careful that way, careful to hide it, especially from his wife. But off to the side, under hooded eyes, he watched Tah-neh-wa closely. The line of her back as she bent to do her chores, how she sat with the other women and worked on skins, how she conversed with and took care of her children. He knew much about her, yet he wanted to know more. How she felt about the cool water she drank, the tasty meat she cooked, the stars she often stared at in a night sky—all this and more. At night, when others were asleep, he could almost hear her breathing from the compartment where he slept less than ten strides away. And every time she went into the woods, his dark eyes followed her. If she tarried too long at gathering in the forest, he made it a point to make sure she was all right. But she never knew. Nor did his wife, to whom he showed no less respect.

He never talked about what he was thinking, except when he was with the boy. Then the conversation seemed to flow, natural and easy. The boy trusted him, just as the boy's father had trusted him. Creek knew what to teach the boy and what not to teach him.

"Let the earth speak to you," he remarked one day looking straight into the boy's eyes. The gesture was sincere. White Feather sat next to him, perched on a fallen log near the longhouse.

Let the earth tell you which way to go, what to do, and how to live your life, to recognize good when you see it and to avoid danger when you don't. Never forget that you must listen carefully. Open your ears and eyes to what great Manito has set before us."

Often at night, when his grandmother stood before the fire holding her fan of turkey feathers and reciting the family history and legends, White Feather would sit near Creek as he diligently worked on the bow, watching his every move. How his fingers grasped the knife, how the muscles stood rigid in his arm as he held the wood securely against the cutting tool, and how the fire played against his face. His presence calmed the young boy, who was eager to learn what it meant to be a man in the village.

"Teach me, show me all," he begged Creek, for he was the youngest of all the cousins and often left out of the inner circle of young men on the verge of becoming hunters.

The boy would look for his favorite uncle returning from a hunt, run to his side, and follow him around the campsite. He was a small boy with a white feather attached to his hair, something he had been given at birth from his father. Eagle feathers were considered to be a symbol of bravery, humility, and a special link between the earth and the next world. An eagle had flown overhead as the little baby was presented to his father.

"Little Eagle will be his name," his father declared. "Eagle moves like the Wind, through all worlds." The mother thought otherwise.

"Wise husband, look to the color of the sacred seer of Manito," whispered Tah-neh-wa, pointing to the emissary from the sky that had come to rest in a rather large tree on the meadow. "See the white tail feather, a gift from the spirit world, for our son. His name will be White Feather." She finished speaking and turned.

And so it was.

The others in the village came to accept that Creek had more than a protégé; he had a shadow, a boy growing into manhood who believed his world rotated on the wisdom of his uncle. No one interfered in this special bonding of two braves. Not the other uncles. Not even the chief who watched the boy with affection and pride as he watched all the children in the village.

THE SAVAGE RIVER VALLEY

"My son has a new father," Tah-neh-wa said gratefully to her older sister one morning as they sat together. She was appreciative of the extra attention paid to her son. When her son was happy, her own heart sang with joy.

"There are important things a boy needs to learn," she continued, her sister nodding in agreement. These were things Tah-neh-wa knew little about; things she could not teach him. Things she knew she could never do if forced to go out into the woods to live alone.

Creek, overhearing the remarks, said nothing. But it was nothing unusual or disrespectful. They were used to his quiet behavior.

His wife, Ontelawnee, looked at her husband from where she worked with her daughters and smiled. She was a good wife, if not a little plain, and a good mother to all the children in the longhouse. She was fond of the boy too, often stooping to hug him when others were not looking. She hoped to still have a son one day, a son that would take after his father Creek, a boy that would grow up to be just like White Feather.

She often looked up to see the two bending heads over a newly made weapon. She let her husband be when it came to the boy.

Secretly, Creek was as fiercely proud of White Feather as if he were his own son. He was painfully aware that coupling with Tah-neh-wa's sister, a ritual that gave him little pleasure, only produced girl after girl and, each time he rolled away from his wife in the dark of the night, he prayed for a son. But even though he longed for a son of his own, he felt that White Feather could not come closer to his heart than if he had been his true son.

That was how the relationship was between Creek and his little shadow, the boy named White Feather. One strong warrior and hunter with one eager young brave always at his feet. One older Indian who had seen thirty-five winters come and go who was willing to die for the young boy, and one young boy who, when asked, would do anything for Creek.

Only now, the boy was turning into a man.

His sisters would learn by working with the earth in their hands as they planted and harvested food supplies. White Feather, on the other hand, was expected to hunt small game around the village, learn the art of warfare and how to protect his family. As part of their early and arduous apprenticeship under his uncle's watchful eyes in the arts of hunting and war, White Feather and other boys in his village, with whom he had close ties, became adept at killing small animals and birds for their households; so after a time there were few chipmunks, squirrels, or woodchucks around the village.

"What will the earth tell me?" the boy had ventured to ask in a curious yet subdued voice.

His uncle looked down on him, knowing that his words would have a profound effect on the boy.

What he was about to say would stay with the boy forever.

"The earth gave you life and the earth, our true mother, will take it away."

∿

White Feather remembered those words now, as he watched the bear moving across the hillside below him. He was diligent in keeping the wind at his back for his human smell would alert the bear, whose nose was magnified a thousand times more than the human nose to enable him to survive by recognizing the scents he needed to confront or avoid.

White Feather hugged to the sides of hills, sometimes crouching low during the brightness of the day, staying downwind from his trail. He let the bright sunlight expose everything but himself. From the shadowy spaces, he caught glimpses of the bear sometimes close, sometimes far away, rummaging for food or slowly pushing through the forest.

He would watch him quietly from the shadows, his face set, his darkly gleaming eyes shifting with the movement of the bear, following its every step, calculating the moment of death. He had thoughts of nothing else.

THE SAVAGE RIVER VALLEY

He waited weeks to kill the bear. His plan had been simple. He would track the location of this mighty animal and then hunt it over time. The bear would feel the anxiety of being hunted, yet not see what hunted him until the very end or close to it.

So intent was White Feather on the path of the bear that he lost all thoughts of his own welfare.

So he couldn't help what happened next.

He didn't look into the shadows behind him.

He forgot about the dangers of the woods, who or what would be lurking there. He forgot to watch his back. That was where Ramco came in. Usually they would hunt for their prospective villages together, sometimes being out in the woods for weeks in a make-shift hunting camp or under a rock out-cropping, then part ways. But all the time, Ramco, future brother to White Feather by marriage to his sister, would watch their backs, alert to any danger, while White Feather went in for the kill.

In his fervor, he forgot one other thing. Ramco was with Creek, staying close to the shore, waiting for White Feather to single-handedly drive the bear down to the river's edge.

White Feather never looked back.

Otherwise, it would have made his blood run cold at what he would have seen.

∿

And, just as his sister Minnah had been watched at dawn that very morning, so too had White Feather, at intervals and for some weeks now. Just as White Feather was tracking his prey, the black bear, he in turn, was being tracked by someone with a far older and more experienced eye, who could, with little effort, pick up White Feather's trail at any given time. One who knew how to move silently through the forest and one who knew how to blend perfectly with the trees.

White Feather, at the age of sixteen, had much to learn.

PAMELA DE LEON

∿

White Feather followed the Indian path. Some called it the Mohican Trail; a familiar dirt path up the mountain, winding through the forest, first going off to the right away from the village Wachachkeek on the flats, then to the left in the direction of the river, up and down and zigzagging through the forest around larger creeks and ravines, and then following a course due south right up to the tallest peak in the chain of Onteora, land in the sky. The mystical mountains where the Indians seldom ventured and never lived, for that was the place of the spirits. Where the vicious, one-eyed bear that had killed his father roamed, dwelled, and slept in deep hibernation.

He picked up his pace. He needed to stay close to the bear.

∿

It was a gruesome sight. The body, what was left of it, lay askew on the bare earth.

White Feather had seen firsthand his father at the river's edge, eyes staring up at the blue cloudless sky. But it was a blank stare, from eyes that could not see, eyes that no longer took in the beauty of the land and river, eyes that could no longer follow the hunt of deer or the path of his son.

Eyes White Feather did not recognize, because the life and sparkle had seeped out of them. His father lay on the ground, flat on his back, his stomach ripped wide open; the blood long since caked and dried.

The dust rose around the body as they approached.

White Feather in his boyhood had never seen anything like it, and the sight of those long red streaks of flesh that hung off the body made him gasp and step back. It seemed as if the color red was splayed in all directions, each way he turned. To the right, to the left; there was no escaping it. He bent, feeling his food from

THE SAVAGE RIVER VALLEY

the morning rushing up through his body. He gagged and coughed, feeling dizzy all at once.

His father's body had been found long after death had taken its toll.

Yes, White Feather remembered that day well.

He made a vow to himself never to forget.

That night, back at camp, kneeling on the creek's banks, White Feather, with a great cry of anguish, cut a long gash in his forearm, searing the painful memories of what he had seen that day in his mind forever. Memories of his dead father were now synonymous with pain, both physical and emotional.

Creek had been the first on the scene and, within moments, pursed his lips and whistled with bird-like similarity to the others who were coming through the brush; a high pitched call to signal caution.

White Feather, a young, fairly inexperienced brave, froze in his tracks at the sound. It was not the first time he had heard the call, but this time it sent shivers along his spine.

What could it mean?

As the youngest in the group, he would follow in their tracks. Experienced hunters always took the lead.

The little band of Indians from Wachachkeek, accompanying Creek in the search, pushed forward into a small clearing. They spotted Creek crouched over a body. They instinctively halted, slowly drew their tomahawks, cautiously knelt, and remained silent, their eyes always on guard, scanning the area for unexpected company or listening for the telltale signs of hidden dangers.

But all was quiet.

The river flowed in gentle currents and the sun shone bright on their faces and bare chests, all gifts of Manito. But there was one thing that Manito had not done.

Manito had not spared the life of White Feather's father.

What they found that day astonished them. As the hunters rose and gathered close, they couldn't help but let out a moan of disbelief.

125

For beside the mangled body lay a round bloody pulp, opaquely shining in the sunlight.

Grimacing, Creek nudged it with his toe. It slowly rolled over on the dusty bank of the river. An eye, bigger than a human's and of a different color, but it was an eye nonetheless.

So White Feather's father had fought to the end, here at this very spot, several feet away from the river that brimmed with a life-line of fish and waterfowl.

They knew that whatever beast had killed their brother had suffered as well.

Their eyes questioned Creek, the oldest among the small search party, who remained silent. He motioned a quick sign to tell them what he had seen. Well, almost the whole story. There was just one part he left out.

As the case with mistaken identity, the bear was wrongfully blamed for the warrior's death. Indians were almost always on the mark when studying the tracks of animals, but not in this case. The panther, snarling from the pain of a gouged eye, limped away with bloodied claws well before the bear arrived, shuffled about in the dust and curiously nosed around the body of the dead man, at one point attempting to turn it over. Both, coincidentally and ironically, now had one eye.

When Creek and the others had gone in search of his father after a prolonged absence, unusual among the men, White Feather tagged along, at times running to keep up with the longer-legged braves. Now he almost wished he hadn't, as he felt tears stinging his eyes. His emotions welled up inside, but he knew better than to take a swipe at the tears with his hand. He could feel the vomit start again, a churning that burned deep.

Creek took no notice of his nephew as he stood up from the body.

His mind was racing, thinking about something extraordinary that had just occurred. And that took precedence over the tears of a young boy.

THE SAVAGE RIVER VALLEY

Bewildered, Creek closed his eyes for a brief moment to recall the vivid picture in his mind.

In one flash of a second, he remembered what he had seen just moments ago. Spooked by Creek's sudden appearance, the bear took off in the opposite direction. Before the others had approached, Creek, staring at the body, had looked up in surprise and saw a figure slipping out of sight, blending instantly into the colors of the forest. Had Creek been any slower, even a fraction of a second, he would have missed it.

Creek saw a warrior, but not one from his village.

Of that he was certain. He could tell by the body paint of the Indian.

For some reason he couldn't explain, certainly not one of cowardice, he had hesitated to follow the figure or to tell the others. Now it was too late. They would never understand his hesitation, for they would have been off in instant pursuit.

He did not understand it himself. Why hadn't he done more?

He had no answer. But at that moment, deciding against pursuit, Creek sealed his fate.

Two things happened as the men wrapped the body in a skin to carry back to the village for a proper burial. They declared the bear to be the culprit and the killer. And then they looked to White Feather, now openly crying, with pity and great sorrow. His father would be missed. All the braves circled round the boy, laying their strong hands upon his shoulders and forearms, lending him support and giving him inner strength.

He did not pull away. Instead, grateful, he looked at them through his tears. Their manly strength seemed to flow through him, bolstering him for the moment when he would face his mother with the news.

That was years ago.

So now, on the banks of the flowing Mohicannituk, this warm, late summer's month when the leaves of the trees had begun the drying process but had not yet begun to turn color, Creek and Ramco, to honor the manhood of the young warrior White Feather, would witness the bear's death. The canoe drifted in the steady currents of the river. They waited each day, paddling up and down the shoreline, keeping a lookout for White Feather and his bear. At night, they were welcomed into the camp of Hop-o-nose but at first light, they pushed off from shore.

Until then, all that mattered, all that White Feather kept in mind, was the tracking of his prey, the killer bear, singled out by virtue of its one remaining eye. This was the only bear he wanted dead. He barely rested, only out of necessity, even during the storm when he sought refuge and crouched in a dry spot under a rock outcropping on the hillside, alone and impatient to keep tracking.

The bear was out there in the night, somewhere ahead of him. The thought consumed him, chipped away at his heart, and appealed to his sense of revenge. If there were one thing he would do well in his life, it would be to destroy the animal that killed his father.

Good hunters were honored by village approval, prestige, and choice marriage. All the villages would now look at him differently than before, but this was of lesser consequence to White Feather.

He had other ideas.

He had dreamt about this day for a long time now, ever since the episode with his father, who, on that westward journey, would see his son from afar and be proud.

White Feather would finally be a man.

Above his head, the leaves swayed easily with the soft winds that carried over the land.

Chapter Five

By the year 1601, the great northeast was inhabited by two dominant Indian groups. The Haudenosaunee lived to the north and northwest of the Hudson River, building heavily fortified villages on the banks of the Mohawk River, a tributary of the Hudson. The Algonquian, the numerous tribes that constituted an often interrelated family, inhabited vast areas north to Maine and south to the Carolinas. Except in cases of roving marauders or war, the Haudenosaunee steered clear of the Mohican land, and the Mohicans, in turn, did likewise.

The Haudenosaunee, people of the longhouse, were called the Five Nations; the tribes were the Seneca, Oneida, Cayuga, Onondaga, and, the most mighty and ferocious of all five, the Mohawk, all allied into one governing body. Later the French called them the Iroquois.

But for now, the Mohicans called them Iriakow.

The meaning of Iriakow? *Rattlesnakes.*

The Mohawk—*Maquas* in the Mohican language—were known as the Kanionkehahak, people of the place of flint. They lived in longhouses that were sometimes surrounded by huge and reliably sturdy palisades, testifying to their warlike nature. Mohawk roots went as far back as the ancient tribe of Mohicans, a certain but never spoken of mingling among ancestors that somehow, somewhere along the way went bad. Bad blood never could be erased from the minds and hands of the descendents of each tribe, haunting and cursing them today as it had years ago. Little did these tribes know that bad blood cursed more than one area of the world, not letting go of its torturous and destructive grip on the human soul for thousands of years.

As was the custom, their leaders were many, as were their warriors.

On the day the bear was to die, a Mohawk warrior had already slipped undetected though the Mohican territory covering miles of wooded lands in a matter of days. On his way, staying clear but not excessively far from the trails, he caught sight of telltale signs cut deep into the trees that told him he was on Mohican hunting grounds. He recognized their markings or symbols, so different from his own tribe's. And although different, one thing was amazingly clear. They were markings that bestowed a warning to trespassers; he was not welcome.

He had been waiting patiently, hidden among the trees, skirting the permanent villages and summer campsites, seeing men and women at work, first tracking the young hunter and then curiously watching the girl. He was adept at staying concealed, for if he were to be discovered it was likely they, in brutal and united force, would kill him.

There were two reasons for killing him.

His uninvited presence on their lands was one. He was of the enemy tribe. Also, he was certain someone would recognize him. And that he wanted to avoid, for he did not come to stir up trouble.

It was easier than he thought.

The only close call was that morning, near the rushing creek. For just a second, he felt cornered, frozen in place, as if the Mohican girl that had crouched on the creek's rocky banks had spotted him. But then, just when he was sure she would alert the sleeping village by crying out, the young girl seemed to think better of it and turned away. She hadn't seen him after all. For only that one time did the risks of being so far from home become real.

He ventured far from his lands for one purpose only.

A woman.

THE SAVAGE RIVER VALLEY

∿

Minnah was a child of the Mohican branch of Indians known as the Catskill Tribe. Her older brother, White Feather, the only son of Tah-neh-wa, who still resided in his grandmother's longhouse, had set out to earn his manhood weeks into the summer, well before his grandmother grew ill. Now, he was ready to earn that manhood.

He ate but a small amount, surviving on light fare. The baked corn bread his mother prepared and stored in a pouch was long gone and the pouch left behind. Now he had to rely on nature's bounty along the trails to sustain him: nuts, berries, and small animals that he could quietly hunt and roast at night over a small hastily prepared fire.

He ran along the trails carrying very little, his bow and quiver slung over his shoulder, his tomahawk hanging from his belt. White Feather was alone. An unbroken solitude with no word from the village as the summer progressed. It was the given plan for any young brave to set out to earn his manhood. Not only did they face the wilderness alone, but also they conquered it. For if not, then it conquered them; which happened seldom since preparation for this time in a young man's life was diligently pursued.

Therefore, it was unlikely that White Feather would meet his death.

No one from the village worried about him. No one tried to find him.

So he had no idea, on this auspicious day, at least for him, when he chose for the bear to die, that his grandmother would die as well. It was purely coincidental that as the dawn brightened and he roughly painted his face with ceremonial streaks of black from the root of the walnut, he knew the day he had been waiting for had arrived. Why that particular day, he didn't know, but what he did know was that he had to kill a bear, the most sacred totem of the clan, and prove that in his approaching sixteenth winter his courage matched his ability.

And to help him do just that, he needed to bring the bear to camp. The bear was considered a prized catch, its fur, when treated, would make a stately robe for White Feather in warm weather and serve as a blanket in the coldest months, its claws a handsome trophy for all to admire and its meat and oils distributed among those relatives who lived in his longhouse. Every bit of the animal would be used, down to the bones, which would be divvied up among the village: hair combs, sewing needles, hide scrapers, and harvesting tools. Nothing was wasted.

White Feather was a seasoned hunter, but like all young men before him, the sacred totem of the village was off limits to hunt and kill, until permission was given by the village elders, his grandmother counting among them.

"Go now, young warrior, with the blessing of Mother Earth and Manito, and hunt our protector the bear. Bring the dead bear to lie at our feet," she had said solemnly.

The black bear was their symbolic animal. Each clan's identity came from their environment. Every village had a totem, the wolf, the turkey, the turtle, representing animals that lived in their area, all gifts of nature. It was just coincidental, as terrible as it seemed to him in his heart, that the sacred totem was also the prey of his dreams.

∿

He approached the shore carefully, stepping slowly through the brush, ducking effortlessly under low hanging tree branches. He already moved with the grace of a seasoned hunter.

He stopped.

The sun shone hot upon his bare back, the muscles tense under the taunt skin of youth, as he lifted his prized bow with his left arm ever so slowly in front of his body.

This was the sacred moment he had been waiting for. He took a deep breath and then, with his right hand, reached backwards to pull an arrow from his quiver. The feel of the slender arrow wedged between his fingers gave him great pleasure.

THE SAVAGE RIVER VALLEY

He held his breath.

The bow and arrow felt a part of him as he positioned himself sideways, his left side leading.

"Careful, don't move too fast." He could hear his uncle's steady voice at his elbow, for there was no reason now to spook the bear that stood before him. By raising himself on his hind legs, the bear unwittingly placed himself in harm's way, a prime target. The bull's eye, the vulnerable spot that would assure White Feather of an instant kill, was the heart.

White Feather raised the bow to eye level and looked down the length of the arrow while resting the tip on the hand that gripped the bow. He began to pull back the string, a long strip of moose sinew that was delicate and flexible and gave his arrow the speed and strength to pierce the tough skin of the bear. He pulled slow and steady until it was stretched as far as it could be.

He let out his breath.

The angry bear was in his sight. Pitch black and snarling, sounds of anger emitting from its throat.

The moment was near.

He was ready.

This is for you, father. I have not forgotten, he thought.

What happened next startled him. As he aimed straight at the bear, letting loose the arrow and watching it fly whizzing through the air with pinpoint accuracy and sink deep within the bear's chest, he caught sight of an Indian warrior, a little behind and to the right of the bear; a tall, dark Mohawk who had stepped in full view. He met White Feather's startled stare and then turned and disappeared in the direction of the river.

∿∿

White Feather shook his head in complete surprise.

How had he not known there was an enemy warrior on his lands?

Only a second passed before the training of his youth kicked in. He slung his arm through the bow and hoisted it over his shoulder and then crouched for the attack position. He slid his tomahawk from his belt and held it high. But the Mohawk was gone.

He took off at a run, passing the dead bear.

It could only mean one thing. The Mohawk, an invader, came on their lands for no good reason from a tribe they had warred against in the past.

The Mohawks bitterly hated the Mohicans. The feeling was mutual. The Mohicans hated the Mohawks with equal intensity. It was a long-standing feud, never to be solved peacefully, going back hundreds of years. The wrongs of years ago could never be fixed; prolonged into the present and lingering as a constant threat. Irrational thought sparked by heated emotions.

As White Feather tore into the dense brush on the banks of the nearby river in hot pursuit of the enemy, pushing past anything in his path, he saw the Mohawk standing not far away, just beyond a little bend in the bank near a huge split tree, half of which lay on its side. The Mohawk warrior, for half his face was blackened in their unique style, made no attempt to neither raise his own warrior's club from his belt nor draw his bow off his shoulder. He just stood there, arms hanging limp at his sides.

Not moving, only silent and staring.

Strangely enough, there was something frighteningly familiar about the way he stood there in silence, as if he had been waiting for White Feather for a very long time. As if there was a purpose to White Feather seeing him in broad daylight, attacking him. Was this a test of the young man's courage?

White Feather knew no fear. In fact, at the same time he saw the Mohawk, he also spotted the canoe with Creek and Ramco making for the shore. He would not wait for them. He plunged forward in a fury, gripping his tomahawk.

It would be his first human kill. He had forgotten about the bear.

Creek and Ramco had spotted him and the Mohawk as well.

THE SAVAGE RIVER VALLEY

From the river, they had a clear view of what was happening. Creek, steering the canoe from the rear, knew that White Feather, his strong-headed protégée, was in danger. For the first time in his life, he felt heart-gripping fear that left him breathless.

His heart was beating furiously.

The boy had never fought to the death before.

In an eerie flashback, Creek saw the Mohawk, the very same one with the dark brooding looks, the same one that slipped furtively away from the body of White Feather's father. Why had he returned? Would this same Mohawk now kill the son?

He paddled faster.

He had lost his blood brother to this Mohawk. It was the same one. He would swear his life on it. Now he would not lose his son.

Faster, he thought.

Ramco, never turning, sensed his urgency. He put all his strength to the oar.

Just as White Feather turned the bend and was within feet of the enemy, the most unexpected thing happened. He suddenly tripped, feeling a heavy weight pull him down.

He lost his footing!

Never before had he been so careless. He was so surprised that he dropped his tomahawk, grunting as his bow slipped from his shoulder. Automatically he stretched out his arms to give him the balance he needed to stay on his feet. When he stood upright once more and pulled his arms in closer to his body, not only had the Mohawk disappeared but also White Feather had the most unusual feeling.

It was as if he were holding someone in his arms. He looked down in a dazed state.

But no one was there.

It was certain.

He could not see the body of a woman named Clara as he crashed into her and as she fainted in his arms.

And he could not see the distant spirit of his father as he smiled, turned for a last time, and headed into the west.

135

Chapter Six

The death ceremony was about to begin. Had there been a bell, surely they would have rung it as a long steady death toll marking the passing of the village sachem, their voice, their spiritual leader, their matriarch; a sound that would match the solemnity in their hearts and minds. As it was, they had a few drums. The dried tight skins of otter or beaver stretched over the hollow of burnt out logs, tightly secured with hemp. The beat was repetitive. Deep resonant thumps penetrated over miles to far corners of the woods. These drums, a ritualistic utensil, were used only during the most special of funerals, births, or ceremonies, so it was not often the Indians heard the long drawn out drumbeats.

The sound, the night air, the special occasion that bespoke of change called to something hidden within their primitive hearts.

They were unsure, unsettled, and a little afraid. They also felt a tremendous loss, such as a young child would feel upon losing its constant and doting mother.

Nightfall was the key. When darkness descended over the valley, when the mountaintops were a distant dark line across the deep-blue horizon, when the heat of the sun abated, when the thoughts of the unknown in the wild lurked in each heart, the sounds began.

The steady beat would continue until dawn. All the men, boys included, gathered around the large fire pit, dug even deeper than normal and located in the center of the longhouse community, chanting and dancing as the old woman's body was prepared for burial. The squaws did not participate in the ritual dancing but instead took a seat or stood in the background, as befitting their

THE SAVAGE RIVER VALLEY

matronly status, leaving the dance of death to the strong, able-bodied men.

As the late summer's day turned to dusk, the mood was somber and heavy over the village of Wachachkeek, situated on the banks of the rushing creek, as friendly Indians from surrounding villages stepped into view at the edge of the meadow, the threshold of this village, waiting to be greeted and invited into the inner circle of this tribe.

The only sound was that of the night peepers in the nearby bushes and the occasional cooing of pigeons roosting in the trees. Even the village dogs had slunk away to the shadows.

The area was filling rapidly with people.

They appeared like lifeless ghosts, wavering in the shifting blue-black shadows between the tree line and the meadows circling the village. And there they stood in silence, nodding quickly to others from the villages around them, speaking only when addressed by the chief of Wachachkeek.

"You have come from afar to honor my mother, Sasqua. You and your people are welcome," the village chief repeated as each group shuffled off to the campsite and another group came into view. He began in the same way. "You who are from Mackawaic, Castle Heights, Quat-a-wich-nach, Island of Pes-squaw-nach-qua, Kaah-hakie, from Esopus, from Sepasco, from …" His voice carried far into the night.

In the palm of his hand, he carried the shaman stone, weighing ten pounds, standing at nine-and-a-half-inches high. The front of the stone was carved in an extraordinarily delicate fashion, resembling the face of the Great Spirit. One ear was that of the village totem, the bear, signifying strength, while the other was that of the panther, signifying grace. The shaman stone was two thousand years old, passed down in a hand-to-hand ceremony for succeeding generations with great religious zeal. It was never to leave the hands of the noble lines of chiefs and sachems of the village or, as believed from long ago, the curse of the evil spirit would swoop down upon them all, descend with one intent only: to destroy them all or scatter them to the far winds.

The sacred stone was their treasure.

The chief held it reverently in his hands, cupping it gently in front of him, feeling the cold stone against his skin.

All eyes rested on the cup, noting the beauty of the unusual carvings.

Not every village had a shaman stone.

Every village had a shaman, the magic medicine man who was known to treat illnesses, bring an errant Indian home from hunting, and bring a listless child to a ravenous appetite. One thing none of them possessed, however desirable, was a magic statue.

It was the envy of every River Tribe that knew of its existence. It was said to hold magical powers, far surpassing what a shaman could even imagine possible. No one had seen the magic. But all believed in it.

As elders from other villages passed the chief and the shaman stone, they handed him a tiny wampum string, beaded in white, which he dropped into the top of the stone, a depression in the head of Manito. White signified peace. The Wampum strings, being of great value, would be presented as an offering to Manito, to be placed in the burial site with the Old One, as she was laid to rest. The wampum strings would go with her to the land in the West.

Wampum—more sacred than human blood—would be her first offering to the Great Spirit.

"Welcome, my kin people," Tah-neh-wa said, standing humbly though strikingly beautiful behind the chief, her brother. Her long blue-black hair shone in the deepening shadows, hanging like a silken covering down her back. For just this once, she had loosened the braid and combed her hair to a high sheen, adding a tiny dab of bear's grease for effect.

"Let us refresh you with food," she added gently. "And let us give thanks to the Creator, the Great Spirit Manito, that we are alive to greet you and see one another again."

THE SAVAGE RIVER VALLEY

The day had been spent preparing great delicacies to offer their guests; wooden plates brimming with beaver tails and bass heads. Bowls were filled with parched corn meal, others were heaped with roasted meats and mushrooms, crunchy nuts and fresh berries, tender sprouts of young plants and wild raspberries, green corn on the cob, red kidney beans, and tubers. Giant spits had been erected to roast succulent meats: rabbits, grouse, and ducks. With each turn, the fat dripped and hissed in the fire. The smell drifted over the village.

"Come, sit at our fire, and eat," she recited over and over. "The Great Spirit of Manito made food that is for all and, like the air, what is for one also must be for all."

Tah-neh-wa had supervised the preparations of the food and the building of the fire pit's stacked bonfire. Her tears at hearing the news of her mother's death had dried. Outwardly, she was the epitome of calm; inwardly, she shook like a fragile leaf hanging on a delicately thin stem in a great wind. She had been right in going to the woods. It was as she suspected; the time had come.

She did not let her facial expression or eyes betray the inner excitement she was feeling.

No one had noticed her slip away and no one had noticed her return.

Mohican Chief Hopp and his party stepped forward, this group from Hop-o-nose, a fishing camp along the Great River. Another greeting came from her lips set in a serene and welcoming smile. Another chief from the high lands approached with his small band of warriors.

The Mohican rituals for greeting visitors to their campsite resembled those of nearly all the villages up and down the valley. Visitors included strangers, traders, kin people, messengers, and ambassadors from other communities of longhouses and wigwams. They all belonged to the family of the Algonquian.

The visitors did not come empty-handed.

This ritual included a return of the invitation they had received that morning: a string or belt of little marine shell beads attached to a notched piece of slender wood. The beads themselves were called wampum. White beads, like those sent out for Sasqua's burial, showed a peaceful intent and were returned in like manner. First, the wampum was delivered; the notches signifying the amount of days intended to pass before the ceremony. The visitor must not enter the inner confines of a village without an official welcome. That welcome came directly from the village chief or sachem. Or he or she, the uninvited intruder, might be considered an enemy. The string of wampum acted like an invisible gateway, at least to friendly tribes.

Not one Mohawk tribe to the north received an invitation. But all the neighboring tribes, Mohican and Munsee alike, did.

∿

Thousands of years ago, they came to this land.

The New York Mohican claimed ancient roots or ancestry to part of a bigger group: the native people. The Indians, the American Indians, the Native Americans.

Who were they? Each tribe had their unique system of nomenclature, based on their sacred totem, their human world that bordered the spiritual world, nature, Mother Earth, and Manito. The totem bridged the two worlds, affording them a blanket of protective blessings.

All these names, used throughout the centuries, signified a great and enduring people. There is no doubt of that. As history marches on, an even greater importance is rightfully given their civilization.

After all, in a land of future newcomers, they were the first to arrive, to build permanent dwellings on the land.

The original Indian came from another continent, amongst a horde of wanderers, huge migratory groups of tribes looking for a special place to call their own, immigrants looking for a place to live, a better life to give themselves and future descendents, follow-

THE SAVAGE RIVER VALLEY

ing for centuries what they believed to be their destiny. The ancient tribes of Indians traveled through primitive forests only to come upon the banks of a wide and glistening river that rippled with currents rushing downstream along each bank, only to be bombarded by the upcoming current of the tide or floodwaters in between. It seemed to be what they were seeking. That pot at the end of their rainbow that sparkled in the sunlight like precious gemstones of pure clarity.

A great river that flowed both ways: north and south.

The Tribes of the Algonquian included the most ancient of all-the Mohicans and their closest neighbors to the south, the Esopus.

These tribes were all family, all friends, and all allies in the event of war.

On any given day in the month of the ninth moon, in any one of these villages, the surrounding fields would be filled with ripening corn. Everyone would be purposefully occupied, a scene of communal activity that would include tending fires, cooking, grinding corn into a powdery meal, chopping trees for new construction or to repair old, hunters bearing long slender bows coming and going, water gatherers fulfilling their task, builders testing the strength of young saplings, boys playing in groups, deer hides stretched and drying on a rack as part of the treatment process, and daughters following in their mothers' footsteps. All the villages were surrounded by long stretches of wooded primeval forest, a heavy, dark green blanket that covered the land, broken only by the river meandering among hills and flatter land.

No task was too small, no detail ignored.

Today the villages came together, as often they did, for an important ceremony. And just for this day, all normal activity, at least in this village, ceased.

I watched from afar.

My mother and my uncle greeted fellow Indians and their squaws, some with a papoose strapped to their back, Not surprising, great numbers of Indians made the trip from across streams and creeks and from as far away as Shodack, across the Great Water. I caught sight of them as they approached our village on foot. Some had traveled all day after receiving the traditional white wampum with one notch, walking for many hours to reach our longhouse. Some had traveled by canoe, up and down the river, dragging their canoes on shore at Hop-o-nose and walking inland four miles. They were tired and hungry. The welcoming fires, glowing in every campsite and in every longhouse, lit the scene before me as if looking through a cloud; the edges of the shifting groups as they moved past me slightly blurry, unable to focus on any one thing or any particular person's features.

Later I would remember every single detail of what I saw, sizzling in my mind like a hot ember from the fire thrown against a wet and steaming stone. But now, all I felt was a feeling of impending dread come over me.

As the afternoon wore on, more representatives of neighboring tribes arrived and the shadows of the tree line lengthened to cover the spot where I stood.

Indians from my village and others milled about as darkness approached.

Gradually, in the semi-darkness, my head cleared and I looked about me.

I stood at the edge of the meadow, in the exact same spot of my childhood. The same spot, facing east, where my grandmother always knew I would be. The exact spot to bring me home from. Now, others shuffled by. Some I recognized and knew by name, others I had never seen before or, at best, had only seen from a distance. They passed me as if I were not there, as if I didn't exist, never once looking in my direction as I stared at

THE SAVAGE RIVER VALLEY

the opening of the trail that led to the river, a trail that disappeared in the darkness of the trees.

I did not think it strange. I knew in my heart why and for whom I was waiting; my brother, White Feather. I wished him home. His comforting presence would bring me solace and once more peace would fill our hearts.

If only he would return.

I closed my eyes and willed him to appear, opening the channels of my mind to his presence. I could feel little tingles run down my arms and legs. I silently called to him.

Then I found my voice.

"White Feather, hear me speak, feel the sadness in my heart, listen to the beat of the village drum summoning you. Present us your prized catch in memory of Sasqua." I called out in sorrow.

My heart beat strong in my body, a steady rhythm inside my chest that matched what I knew to be footsteps coming over the valley trail that led to our village from the Great Water. I knew those vibrations and recognized them at once. Although they seemed heavier than normal, and sluggish, they belonged to him. Perhaps he was dragging the bear behind him. What a glorified end to his hunt that would be!

Satisfied that soon he would sit at our fireside, I turned to walk back to the village and then entered the longhouse to sit beside my sister. Our mat was placed behind our mother as she sat close to the fire that burned brightly; its magnificence illuminating the shrouded figure of my grandmother's small body.

Soon, yes soon, my brother would appear!

ᴧᴜ

Somewhere out in the forest, hungry and pacing, a wild beast with one eye prowled along the banks of the creek. This beast was not a totemic animal, that is to say it did not normally reside in the valley but did from time to time travel great distances over its lifespan. This was one of those times. It sensed increased activity around one of the villages at the foot of the Onteora. The heavy body odor of many humans assailed its nostrils, driving it insanely close to the village perimeters. The animal emerged from the forest, recklessly oblivious to the huge bonfires that burned in the night or the heavy beat of the drums.

The hunt was on.

∿

Everything happened quickly after that.

My tears continued to flow throughout the evening. My sister, Saquiskawa, was silent and withdrawn, morose, but holding tight to the shaman stone the chief has passed to her for safekeeping. She kept her head lowered and looked up at no one. What were her thoughts? It was her own personal time to grieve, so I glanced at her once and knew to leave her alone. The only comfort I could give her was to sit by her side. In time of trouble, we knew what to do; each would eventually turn to the other.

There was constant movement through our longhouse, a steady but orderly movement of all visitors. Only the elders were permitted to sit and stay. Others walked in, nodded with deep respect to us all seated around the body, then turned and gathered outside. It seemed to me like hours had passed when I happened to look up to see the eyes of a young brave looking into my very soul. I felt as if he knew everything about me and had a right to. I held his stare for only a fleeting moment and felt my face flush. The unaccustomed warmth of blood rushing to my face was an entirely new sensation.

Most of the men had gathered outside, circling the fire pit that stretched wider than three braves lying head to foot. Their shouts increased in fervor and pitch, and with a slightest of nods to me, he, Tamaqua, rose and left the circle of elders and went to join the dance.

From outside, the drums began a steady beat and the men took up a long communal wail followed by a sonorous chant as they pulled their legs up high and bent over nearly double. Against a backdrop of flames

THE SAVAGE RIVER VALLEY

that curled upward, the men's shadows danced with them and reflected an even bigger group of actual dancers.

It was a dance of respect for Manito, for our lives, and for my grandmother. It also was a dance of grief. For some inexplicable reason, I knew what many were feeling; that a change was soon to occur. This I could sense clearly, for the others it was only a vague idea that flitted in and out of their minds, a general unease, nothing they could grasp with any facility and something they might attribute to an unusual day. My mind was racing. What I began to see were all the visions I had seen before. Only this time I saw something else I hadn't noticed before; a presence that lingered in the background, a little light that glowed in the darkness.

Something gave me hope and the bit of strength to know that I would live my life with a purpose.

I was filled with excitement. And in that moment of excitement, I wanted to share this vision with my sister, my mother, and the entire group seated around the fire. What better way than to stand up and shout it out loud to everyone inside and outside the longhouse? Even though as a young girl, not yet a squaw in full womanhood, I had no voice to be heard in a fireside circle; surely they would listen.

Even the drums would be silenced.

They would understand what I saw. I would explain it, carefully and slowly, to all of them. All those I loved, grew up with, and was surrounded by would see the hope of the future and the promise of what that westward journey held, for I had seen the vision of death and what lay beyond.

The white light that glowed in the darkness was comforting, warm, and friendly.

But, just as I was gathering my courage to do so, a whisper was heard among the many people lined up at the door. The buzz grew louder. The crowd suddenly backed up, parting on both sides to allow a large open space. Something was outside the longhouse and coming in.

We all looked up.

My mother gasped. She was startled at the sight of my brother White Feather walking heavily through the open doorway with Ramco and

Creek on either side. At first, I did not clearly see what the others saw, my brother unable to support himself, dazed and stumbling, held up by the strong arms of his companions.

I sat still, afraid to move, frozen in place, while my mother automatically rose. The longhouse grew quiet as my brother fell to her feet.

She bent over him as he opened his eyes and looked up at her face. Their eyes met, and she bent to touch his arms. Her look was tender yet questioning.

Creek and Ramco had stepped back out of sight, but not before Ramco shot a quick look at my sister and not before Creek received a look of gratitude from a stunned Tah-neh-wa.

What had happened to my brother, White Feather? Had the bear wounded him in the hunt?

I shifted to get a clearer view. I had never seen him like this.

As he entered, everyone watched him. He had moved slowly, slumped forward, dragging his feet, almost as if he carried a heavy burden on his shoulders, as if he carried the unbearable weight of the huge black bear, slung across his back.

Only he didn't carry the bear.

It only seemed that way, as he moved with apparent difficulty, for, as we found out later, the bear still lay on the banks of the river to be retrieved later.

Out of all those gathered inside, only I alone knew and saw what he carried and, as my mother rose to reach out for her son, it fell from his body with a thud.

I watched in silent fascination. Perhaps I should have been terrified, but I wasn't. Perhaps I should have risen, pointed to what no one saw, and screamed, but I didn't. This was indeed the moment I knew would come. I felt a thrill wash over me and I found myself leaning forward in anticipation of what would happen next.

In an astonishing moment of time, as I watched a curled up, white-faced woman fall from his arms and roll away from his body, my grandmother, at last ready to depart with the spirits, rose up out of her body directly before me, immediately joined by all the spirits who had lingered in the roof rafters the entire day. She drifted toward the open doorway; a doorway illuminated with light, with elegant ease and fluidity, the spirits of her ancestors at her side. Out she went into the darkness. A great file of departing spirits that left me in total but silent awe, for I was the only one to see the great procession, magical, mystical, and inexplicable.

Grandmother, where do you go? I wondered. I thought of her companions.

She would not travel alone. And now I knew the secret of death; that no one did travel alone on that westward journey. There were spirits, summoned for the occasion, to show her the way.

I was certain my mouth had opened in wonder.

Before leaving, she turned at the open doorway and smiled at me; a smile that foretold a future that would include her. She pointed to Clara and nodded her head.

All of this I saw, not as a vision and nothing made up. It was real.

Then she was gone and the drums continued their steady beat.

∿

It had occurred in quick but confusing succession: turning and crashing into the hunter, floating in the canoe; carried along the sheltered paths; entering the teeming village lit by many burning fires; hearing the steady beat of the drums get louder as they approached the village; feeling the intense heat of the bonfire whose flames seemed to lick at her skin before entering the longhouse.

This string of events brought a bewildered and terrified woman to the inner circle around this Mohican funerary fireside. A woman, bedraggled and half insane, unknowingly thrust beyond another lifetime to another dimension, one some four hundred years to the day into the past. A woman who did not, and in most likelihood never would, belong to their group. A woman who dressed differently and smelled differently. A woman that Minnah, smiling in greeting, could see.

The young Indian girl watched her intently. Momentarily, she forgot her brother as he lay where he fell at her mother's feet, and all the others who crowded around him, peering into his face, hoping to hear his story first. There was a rustle of ankle rattles clanking together as they shuffled their feet

She paid them no attention.

Instead, she was curious to see what this strange woman, a female spirit named Clara, would do. Had she dropped from the sky, like the legendary turtle-woman of their own creation, to start a new world? Would this new world include them all? Minnah, barely containing her excitement, was all curiosity, her eager eyes fixed on Clara, thoughts of her departed grandmother temporarily put aside.

Exactly the way Sasqua, the wise Old One, had planned it.

∿∿

Clara blinked in the flickering glare of the firelight.

She saw the distorted features of these strange people with flat, angled faces framed in dark and thick hair, but it appeared, none of them saw her! At least as far as she could tell, for no one met her frightened gaze. They were intent on the young man she has just rolled away from. Not one of them turned in her direction.

She realized that this group had no idea she had just landed in their world! They were not her people. There was nothing familiar about them. Some of them stood with a grimace on their faces, others showed a kinder disposition, smiling in the direction of the young Indian brave lying on the floor. Their hunter had returned! But none of this she knew nor cared about.

For at that very moment she thought of nothing but getting away—a great escape. Then the thought of the dark forest hit her. She knew it would be fruitless to run now. For where would she go? In terror, she looked around the longhouse beyond the multitude of seated and standing Indians, from the fire to the walls and roof.

Then it happened. She spied one young girl apart from the rest,

THE SAVAGE RIVER VALLEY

sitting in the background. The Indian caught and held her horrified stare with big, wide-eyed wonder.

The girl then smiled at her.

Clara gasped.

This Indian youngster, just a slip of a girl, with thick black braids and dressed in worn deerskins stripped of fur, saw her?

Could it be true?

Clara blinked at her several times, and the girl blinked back. Clara shook her head. The girl did the same. Clara noiselessly shrunk back in fright, her presence now validated. Someone in this circle of heathens knew that she, a woman not called or acknowledged as one of their own, existed. She was astonished and horrified.

How close together they were! Such a confined space aroused feelings of claustrophobia.

The fire burned bright, making it much too warm. She found it hard to breathe.

Oh, what a bitter end to my life, what a bitter hell! The girl sees me she thought, her head aching with the piercing agony of a million jabbing throbs. *How could this be a dream then?* For those in front of her seemed to be real.

And therein lay the problem. They, the Indians circled around the longhouse, were real.

The living nightmare that had cruelly started on the banks of the river had continued.

She gulped, feeling her eyes grow wet.

She was surely at the gates of purgatory now, having arrived to this place in the arms of a man who had held her in a strong grip. Was this man the devil? Even from inside, she could hear the steady beat of a deep-thudding drum, drumming in unison with each throb of her head. From somewhere outside, the chants of the men, their voices deep and forceful, filled her with instant dread. She was trapped in a world of Indians. Was it possible to escape? Did she dare stand and run? Would they see her as she tried to flee their presence?

Possibly, but run where? Into the black of night, not seeing, much less knowing, where she was going?

It was completely useless. There was no hope, how desolate a feeling. Her spirit felt utterly crushed. There was nothing she could do.

She crawled her way into a corner where dried goods were piled up next to a tall wooden mortar used to pound corn. Crumbling in a heap, she cried silent tears, shaking uncontrollably.

It was a bitter and nasty hell indeed.

Clara pulled her knees tightly to her chest, grasping them with her arms. After one hasty but frightened glance around her, she lowered her head and wearily closed her eyes. She thought, *If it is a world of heathens I am in, then so be it. I have died and gone to hell.*

The last thing she remembered was the overpowering smell of the fire, the people, and the sound of the drums.

Chapter Seven

The tradition of saying farewell to a tribal leader was conducted out of doors in an open space, one that this evening reflected the white moonlight, a phosphorescent light that shed an eerie glow over the land. A roaring fire of fragrant balsam logs tempered the crisp air of the night but left it sufficiently invigorating to keep the dancers active. The smell of the corn plants drying in heaped mounds, the breath of the pines blown by the summer's night wind that came off the meadows and ridges, and the smoke of the burning wood and roasting food fed the frenzied activity.

Sometime during the night, all those present ceremoniously and respectfully gathered around the largest fire pit in the middle of Wachachkeek. Its flames now reached high into the night sky and warmed their tired faces. White Feather, sufficiently recovered to pay his respects alongside Creek, danced; some chanted; and some, in the shadows or in pools of reflected light, stood close by as spectators.

Minnah, breaking away from the main group, danced alone in the shadows, singing little songs to Manito. She sang reverently to the powers around her, the recognized forces of nature, the aura of so many people close by, opening her heart to their whisperings. The young warrior Tamaqua, arms folded, watched from a few feet away. He already knew with certainty that he, at the proper time, would someday claim this young woman to be his wife, but for now, he was simply curious. Her strange little ritual and movements fascinated him. He smiled but kept his distance.

He was young yet. And so was she. There was plenty of time.

Saquiskawa had disappeared entirely, going to some hidden spot near the rushing stream. She trusted him, so she took Ramco's offered hand. The look in his eye told her he would wait no more. The death of her grandmother had released some primitive instinct inside of her—perhaps the need to hold on to life and embrace it wholeheartedly, perhaps the need to propagate. She threw all restraints to the wind. A smile on her face, the look in her eyes told Ramco all he needed to know. They settled near the rushes, the thick reeds covering their nakedness from the outside world. In their self-imposed isolation shared by two, a world of innocent yet passionate discovery, in the arms of her vigorous mate, her first child would be conceived under the night sky. The last thing she remembered before succumbing to bliss were the white stars that shone bright above her head and how cool the night air felt on her naked body.

Tah-neh-wa, having watched the dancers for hours, retreated step by step to the edge of the circle, until she felt sure no one would notice her leaving the camp. She left Ontelawnee in the care of her daughters. Her own children were scattered. Now was the time, if any, to make good on her promise.

She hurriedly took one last look around. The swallows were flying peculiarly low over the ground and through the foliage of the trees, perhaps preparing to leave, perhaps readying for a journey south.

Would she ever come back here? She held no hope for that. For one thing, she would never be welcomed back again. If it were ever discovered what she was about to do, they would banish her from the Indian village of her youth.

"Uh-ah-meoway," she whispered. *Be well my people.*

Her heart already cried for her children and her people, their nearness, their familiarity; but something else awaited her since years ago.

It was the reason she had loosened her hair from its braid and let it hang down her back. It was the reason she had decided to leave

THE SAVAGE RIVER VALLEY

the village of her birth behind. It was the reason she was willing to embrace the new and unknown. In the whole village of Wachach-keek, she alone knew the reason.

Behind the longhouse, she had hidden a soft deerskin pouch filled with a four-day supply of small corn cakes, her favorite comb carved from the bone of a bear, and a beaded waistband from her mother. She grabbed it firmly and slipped out of sight.

Walking into the woods, staying off the trails, she listened carefully. The night sounds were all around her: crickets, peepers, and the deep-throated croaks of bullfrogs. For a moment, she hesitated. Alone in the woods at night was something she often cautioned her daughters about.

The harvest moon above her seemed to light her path and now she did not feel so alone. "Show me, father moon, show me the way," she called. She took a deep breath and pushed forward.

There was a little glen, a small opening of trees about a mile north of the campsite. She gingerly made her way there.

The moon rose high in the night sky and, when the clouds parted, the soft white rays shone over the land, softly bathing it in mystical light. From far away, she could hear the sounds of the burial ceremony still going on, accompanied by the slow beat of the drums. Toward dawn, the magical time between night and day, they would take her mother to the ancient burial site a few miles east of the camp and there place her in a grave among other graves, in a sitting position that faced the rising sun, surrounded by what little treasures they could bury with her: a pot, spoon, provisions, and some wampum. Afterwards they would surround the body with as much wood as to keep it from touching the earth. Their burial sites resembled a small dwelling and provoked a sacred respect.

Tah-neh-wa knew her children would be at the burial site. They were a strong clan and they would survive. Her sister and Creek, both particularly close to her children, would see to that. Of that she was as sure as the sun rising each day.

With each step, she paused, her ears alert to all kinds of little sounds. Once she thought she had heard something following her. But, she quickly forgot about it as somewhere in the muted light in front of her she heard a low whisper, a gentle voice that called to her. Smiling, Tah-neh-wa stepped into the clearing, the moonlight illuminating her in soft hues of womanly vulnerability. Although she stood alone in the night, open to any danger that might be pacing in the shadows, she was not afraid. She was ready, now more than ever, to face what lay before her.

She remained stationary. Suddenly she heard a subtle movement close by.

∿

Creek crept slowly along the tree line. The trees seemed enormous in the night: huge, dark, and greenish black.

From a distance, he watched Tah-neh-wa. What was she up to? At first, he was not alarmed, just curious. She picked her way carefully through the trees and brush. Even when the moon shone full on her path, she was unaware that he was following her and had been since she left the campsite. Squaws were not as adept in the woods as the hunters. They were never taught to track or to detect someone tracking them. There was no need to. That is what the men were meant to do.

He frowned.

Where was she going?

He had kept his eye on her whereabouts all evening, after bringing White Feather home. It seemed a miracle that when he deposited White Feather at his mother's feet, the young warrior, confused and in an apparent daze, looked up at his mother and seemed to miraculously revive. He was able to sit up and take stock of what had been happening in the village, able to tell them about the bear he had killed, the Mohawk he had seen, and how Creek and Ramco had come to his rescue and brought him home.

The chief had listened attentively, as had his mother, at this marvelous tale; Tah-neh-wa visibly stiffening as the story progressed.

Creek listened for just a moment and then, assured that his

protégée was safe, stepped outside to join the other men partaking in the ritual dance of the burial ceremony of a great sachem. He too would pay his respects to the Old One, he thought, as he laid aside his bow, quiver, and tomahawk. She was the only one who had known his true feelings, could see deep within his heart of secrets, and instead of condemning him, she had taken pity on him and never spoke of it. Ever since the moment the Old One came upon him watching Tah-neh-wa bathing alone in the stream, she had never betrayed him or belittled him or sent him from her long-house. In the forest, from where he crouched and she stood, their eyes had met. She simply turned and walked away, never saying anything to him or her daughter. What Creek did not know was the wonder the Old One felt as she looked upon his face, naked with love and passion for a daughter that was not his wife. It pained her to know that he was a prisoner to his feelings, yet a good husband to her other daughter.

Creek, not knowing exactly how the Old One felt, was nevertheless grateful, for she did not turn him away from the village. Once again he deeply felt the impact of that shared glance from so long ago in the forest. In silence she had honored him as a man beset with unrequited desire.

From the other side of the bonfire, he watched Tah-neh-wa furtively slip out of the village.

His brow furrowed deeper.

Where was she going and why did she leave at a time like this?

She would be alone and unprotected in the woods, especially at night, and the thought of that Mohawk on their lands earlier in the day never left his thoughts.

He knew he had to follow her.

Step by step, he crept along, each movement a light one, perfected from years of hunting. He watched her reach a clearing and step completely into the open, the moonlight shining upon her as if she were a star gently plucked from the sky. He stared at her in amazement, spied her beautiful mantle of hair shimmering in the light, and felt his heart swell with love for her beauty. He had always dreamed of having her in his arms, her face lifted to his, her soft and full lips meeting his and even now his arms ached to hold her close, to hold her so tight that he would never let go. He longed to feel the texture of her hair, the softness of her skin, and the lips that would yield to his as his weight pressed upon her.

The familiar warmth that often hit him in his groins started again. Creek could feel the slow swelling of his manhood. Only this time was different. He could do something about it.

He was prepared to enter the clearing, make his manly wishes known, and take her far away; far from the village, far from disapproving family, perhaps to the mountains where the divine spirits dwelled, to be with her in a divine union. With Tah-neh-wa at his side, he would forget about his wife, his children, and even his village. He could, with her at his side, dare to brave the winters in the higher peaks. She would feed his courage and strength. Surely the risk was great, as he knew no one lived up there when the heavy snows fell over the ground. How could anything be as important as the woman he truly loved? Suddenly he thought of the winter camp some ten miles to the west where he could live with her until their union was accepted.

He would stand before her and make Tah-neh-wa his. If she had deserted her village to come to the wilderness to fight her grief at losing her mother, then she would not object to his company and his protective might.

He smiled and sighed in great relief.

He never imagined this day would come. It was almost a blessing that the Old One had died.

A dream that he long ago deemed impossible, that he had held secretly hidden from the others, would now come true.

He looked to her with glistening eyes, full of emotion he had so long held deep within.

Why didn't she know he would be close by?

All she had to do was to call out to him. But, she didn't.

THE SAVAGE RIVER VALLEY

She was intently looking in the other direction. He wondered why. Her profile showed him that she appeared blissfully serene, childlike and innocent.

How he loved her! He had always watched over her since her husband was killed.

The sad thing was that she didn't see him as he crouched low behind a tree. Instead, she was looking at a different man, one who had stood in the distant shadows watching her approach. Neither Tah-neh-was nor the man who stepped full view into the clearing knew about Creek's presence.

They had eyes only for one another. For the first time in eight summers, in this quiet spot with everyone for miles around occupied at the death ceremony, they both thought they were alone and safe from discovery.

Tah-neh-wa stood still as the man approached her, lifted his hand, and placed it alongside her face, his thumb caressing the soft skin of her cheek that he remembered so well. He knew what this woman was giving up to come to him as he lifted her chin and bent his mouth to hers.

Dazed, Creek held his breath, now afraid to make a false move—one that would betray his hiding spot. He crouched; transfixed on the scene before him, as Tah-neh-wa obediently stepped into the arms of this warrior and together they stood as one for several minutes.

"Filthy squaw," he wished to scream, but instead, ashamed at what he saw, he remained silent.

He shut his eyes, but only momentarily.

His body went cold and a fury began to build, churning from the middle of his chest. His black eyes burned, wet with shame and anger. How could she come to stand at this Mohawk's side and thereby betray her people on the day of her mother's burial? There was something else, an idea, a memory that was gnawing at the back of his mind, threatening to disrupt his rigid focus on the scene before him. He couldn't shake the feeling that he knew this Mohawk somehow. There was little time to figure that out. Instead, he concentrated on what was happening, unbelievably, right before his very eyes, in a clearing that was less than a mile from the village.

The Indian held her tightly.

Tah-neh-wa was being held not as a captive but as a lover, a lover of a man that did not belong to the village of the Mohicans; a lover that belonged to their sworn enemies; an invader, an intruder on their lands and a ruthless murderer.

All Mohawks were murderers in Creek's mind.

This particular Mohawk, now standing as the victor, was the very same one who had crouched over her dead husband's body. The same Mohawk Indian who had stood on the riverbank and challenged her son to a fight. The son who had courageously killed the bear.

It was the very same Mohawk that now held Tah-neh-wa tightly. What Creek didn't know was that he was also the same Mohawk who had pushed Tah-neh-wa out of the path of the approaching panther as her husband, discovering the two together, bravely took the fatal attack head on.

In a split second, Creek no longer loved this Indian squaw. Suddenly he knew what had been bothering him at the sight of this Mohawk. In anger, he knew her secret, what she had kept from the others, and most importantly, from her husband since the birth of her son. This Mohawk was a replica of her son. The same muscular legs that seemed to hold the power of the earth in some mystical way, the set of the shoulders, and the same dark looks.

Creek hated the very sight of Tah-neh-wa. How quickly his feelings changed!

With a clenched jaw, venomous thoughts brought the burn of bile rushing up his throat, nearly causing him to cough. He would rather see her dead than with this Indian. Creek would kill them both. He was more than capable of that physical act though unable to mentally piece together what led up to this meeting. A plan

THE SAVAGE RIVER VALLEY

instantly laid out to satisfy blood vengeance clarified the confusion of the moment—revenge for his blood brother, his children, and betraying the sacred honor of the village and the greater tribe of the Mohicans across the lands. That much he could grasp with certainty.

An injustice had taken place, years before, and now he would set it right by exacting revenge in his own way and in the ways of the Indians. They lived by a strict honor code, and now it was all too clear; Tah-neh-wa had broken that sacred code.

But first, he thought cunningly, as his eyes swept over the glen, he would let them start on their way, for surely the Mohawk had plans to leave the area soon and she would follow him. At some point they had to rest. Creek would swiftly take them by surprise, while they slept in each other's arms far from the village. In a secluded place the sounds of his killing the Mohawk would only be heard by Tah-neh-wa. No one would come to their rescue. With a determined fury, he knew what he must do.

Thick clouds scudded across the sky and blocked the moonlight, but he knew they were still there, within grasp of his fury.

∿

Tah-neh-wa, clutching the few things she had left in the world, willingly followed in the footsteps of the Mohawk.

As any mighty hunter and warrior did in those days, he led the way. They disappeared from the clearing seconds later, stepping into the dense cover of the tree line, darkness washing over them as they walked together in a northerly direction. From there they would travel a few miles to pick up the trail that led north to the Mohawk's territory and beyond, stopping just short of the cold lands of the Huron tribes. There they would be safe from discovery by any search party.

Creek's thoughts came as fast and as furious as the blood pumping through his veins.

159

He had watched as the Mohawk had slipped his hands over the body of the woman that should have always, since he first saw her, belonged to him; the woman he had dreamt of with the passing of many moons. But she had belonged to his blood brother, and he backed away and held his passion prisoner in a scarred heart.

It was all he could do to watch them together and contain his impulse to step into the clearing. And now, as further punishment, he had to watch her as the woman of yet another man, but unlike before, this Indian, this thieving Maquas, was not his brother.

A good thing, because Creek was going to kill him!

Clever fellow, this Mohawk, he thought sardonically, to boldly come on their lands, steal one of their women, and succeed in getting away with it, especially during a time when the village was preoccupied with the burial ceremony. Creek had one comforting thought. The Mohawk was not as clever as Creek.

Mohawk, you thieving murderer, you will not live to see the end of the night, he swore silently.

Kill them and leave them where they fall, he decided. *Yes, kill them both.* And at that thought, half insane at seeing Tah-neh-wa with a Mohawk, he smiled, a twisted curl of his upper lip.

He anticipated that moment with something close to satisfaction.

Tah-neh-wa's naked body would lie on the ground, bruised and broken. Perhaps he would cut off a great handful of her thick, shiny hair, hacking it off with his sharp tomahawk before he slit her throat. Later he would burn her hair in the fire, watch it disintegrate into ash and smoke, and all the while curse her memory.

He almost smiled again at the vengeful thought.

In the absence of love, there was a cold hatred, a slow burning twist of evil, and a quick, unforgiving reversal of sentiment.

He wanted to hurt her. And to her lover, worse would occur. All his pent up anger would be taken out on torturing the Mohawk's body, mutilating his blackened face before and after death, crudely stripping off his scalp with a cry of conquest until he held it bloody and triumphant in his hands; the sign of a revenge-seeking warrior.

Yes, let them die and be found together, he thought. *For then, all would know the truth, that the youngest daughter of the respected village sachem was a traitor, a deceitful, no-good, lying squaw. They would know that she had abandoned her children, her birthright as a daughter of a sachem, and the sacred memory of her husband for a filthy thieving Maquas!*

An unchaste woman was punished by tribal dictates and therefore suffered the indignity of disgrace; to herself, her family and her village. Chastity was the established norm.

That she had abandoned the land of mountains and the River Valley for the lands where the five nations lived was unforgivable. They were her ancestor's enemies; they should be hers as well.

He had no doubts of how the village would react.

It was just reward for such behavior among Indians, and the honor code would permit that her memory would be forever erased from the oral tradition of their village—it would be a dishonor to mention her name again. To continually satisfy his vengeance, he would dutifully remind the others that she was an outcast, scorned and rejected. It would be no small feat, but he would erase her memory from his heart as well. Bitterness from losing her and bittersweet revenge at killing her would make it an easier thing to do. He would righteously return to his wife and his daughters, stay at their side, hope for a son, and never consider this night again.

What about Tah-neh-wa's son?

Still loving the boy, he would say nothing of the Mohawk to White Feather.

They were out of sight now, but his eyes still burned. He wiped them with the back of his hand. The darkness was all around him. They were gone. He could rise now without fear of being seen.

Suddenly the uncanny stillness of the night struck him.

For just a second more, he hesitated and then froze.

He had been so intent on destroying the two Indians, one

familiar and one a stranger, who had stood only feet away from him moments before, that he committed the unforgivable, exactly what he had always warned White Feather not to do.

In the end, the teacher, the mentor, the trainer of the young hunter had forgotten to do one thing. He had forgotten to take note of his surroundings, to look searchingly, not only in front but behind him as well, and to be alert to danger. He forgot to be aware of that danger always lurking, always present in the forest.

He heard the low snarl before he turned.

It barely took a second before it dawned on him that he had left the campsite unarmed, wearing only a breechcloth and his leggings, having never retrieved his weapons from where they lay near the blazing bonfire. Now, bare-chested and empty-handed, Creek was defenseless against an attack—an animal attack.

Directly in back of him crouched a formidable opponent. Ebony in color, sleek, and hungry; there stood the one-eyed panther, older and somewhat gray around the muzzle, but still a deadly enemy.

The panther had been stalking him since Creek surreptitiously left the perimeter of the village, its huge padded paws making deep imprints on the soft ground, its nose breathing deeply of the man's smell.

Darkness and surprise were on its side.

Its feted breath, reeking of rotted carcass wedged tightly in its jawbone, reached the Indian in a foul hiss of air. The panther bared its teeth.

Creek could feel his body run cold. He let the breath ease slowly out of his nostrils. His knees trembled, yet strangely he noted the sleek magnificence of the animal.

The two stared at each other.

The narrowed yellow eye of the carnivore seemed to mock him as he stood there alone and defenseless. The panther could smell, sense, and relish in the Indian's fear.

Now Creek knew how White Feather's father must have felt moments before the big cat pounced. Oh what a mistake to think

THE SAVAGE RIVER VALLEY

it was the bear, when in fact they should have persisted in hunting down the panther and killing it.

He was trapped.

Creek was certain he was about to die, and the irony of the situation struck his heart at the same moment he let out a terrible scream, as he felt the panther's curved claws slice into his chest.

Chapter Eight

By the turn of the century, all tribes in the River Valley were acquainted with the intricacies of living in close confines. Individual villages, such as the Canarsies of the greater Munsee family, lay close to where the Great River met the Great Sea. Their word on the arrival of the white men was reliable when it came to first contact with the Dutch. The news spread fast. The tribes were linked by commonly used trails that would later be paved over as roads.

These tribes and others occupied land from the mouth of the rushing river to the far north where the Abenaki, the bark eaters, dwelled in the tall mountains beside a small lake, Tear of the Clouds. Here, unbelievably, considering its diminutive size, the river originated. All were separated by miles of rugged terrain and wild animals, gorges and steep clefts in the land, as well as thousands of rushing streams, a multitude of fresh-water lakes and one magnificent river of clear water that afforded them an unfettered, fast-going avenue of travel by canoe. Runners and messengers, all of them males in their prime years, kept the villages in contact while their lives moved forward in a daily rhythm of survival. Their existence, planned and dictated by the matriarchs of each clan house and the villages, was ruled by a sachem's word.

Preceding the year 1601, great stretches of the northeast were populated by the large family of Algonquian, who shared the roots of an ancient language. The whole language itself was lost in the succeeding generations. Only remnants remained. The dialects of the day were many. Nevertheless, by means of words they shared in common, by gestures they made, and by the symbols they carved on

THE SAVAGE RIVER VALLEY

their trees to stake out their hunting grounds, the Indians understood who belonged to their large family and who did not.

They knew every rise, every hill, each meadow, and all strips of land that bordered the endless miles of streams that marked the limits of their territory. They knew the land that covered their kingdom, every square foot of it. More important, they also knew the lands that did not belong to their tribe. And they knew better, by way of tradition, respect, and fear, than to step foot on foreign lands. The possible consequences were understood.

Time passed and the century was well on its way.

$\sim\!\!\sim$

The rumors drifted among the valley fields and over the land-a gentle circulation of whispers that went round and round in every Mohican village up and down the river. Rumors, unembellished yet repeated that evolved into a legend, the stuff their stories were made of. The search was on for the strange man-killing cat. At times, everyone, having heard the strange fate of Creek, claimed they spotted the creature, showing its teeth and glaring wickedly while making the most hideous hissing sounds. Some, the old hunters included, thought it sat high on a rocky cliff in the Mountains of Onteora, watching over the expansive valley, looking to pinpoint its next prey. Some even vehemently swore they saw it streaking through villages wearing a mantle of ceremonial feathers. White Feather, angry and bitter at the death of his uncle and disappearance of his mother, Tah-neh-wa, had seen the panther from a distance-its black form slinking over the wooded hillside where he stood. Unlike the bear that gave him his manhood, this big cat proved a futile prey for even the strongest and most able of hunters.

No one could track it, for it left no discernable paw prints on the ground, sodden or dry. No one could kill it for it never appeared directly in the line of a hunter's spear or bow.

This strange and elusive creature was rarely seen in daylight. Surrounding communities were on the lookout. In one village, the nocturnal alarm was raised with a mighty yell. Minutes later, another warning was shouted, arousing those asleep in far off villages. How could the animal have traveled so fast?

Given the state of affairs, such were the rumors that spread like wildfire of the questionable cat. Was it real? Or better yet, was it a figment of all their superstitious imaginings? The nation of Mohicans believed in ghosts and spirits, both good and evil. Was this cat an omen, a warning of bad things to come?

Mothers shivered in the warmth of day and drew their children closer.

The summer months turned into a blaze of cool autumn, and all the hunters took to the trails and woods. The trees, feeling the cool air of the nights, instinctively began to dry up the supply of sap to its leaves. The many hues of green color would soon flame to bright orange and red. Then the leaves would begin to fall, drifting over the lands, the villages, and on the Indians themselves.

Only one time that autumn did Ramco and White Feather, both grim-faced and hunting as a team, spot the panther and follow the animal to the river's edge, near a swampy area where the same creek that passed by Wachachkeek emptied into the running tides of the Great Water, not far from where his father's body had been discovered years ago. There, at the water's edge, the faint though noticeable tracks of the cat ended. Their efforts had been thwarted yet once more.

There, the two hunters stood, shoulder-to-shoulder, staring at the opposite bank.

It was too far for an animal to swim. So, where did it go?

Simultaneously they both grunted in puzzlement and disgust.

The sudden disappearance of the cat proved to be an unsolvable mystery. It was now thought, as time elapsed, that the cat that killed Creek was a phantom, a slight aberration of the powers of nature that Manito bestowed on the land. Amongst the most superstitious, Creek's wife included, there were those who secretly believed that

THE SAVAGE RIVER VALLEY

the cat was Tah-neh-wa herself, seeking revenge for her disappearance. Stranger things were known to happen during the burial of one as sacred as Sasqua, the grand matriarch of the village.

But why, thought Creek's widow to herself, *would my sister kill my husband?* She dared not say the words aloud. But the thought left her feeling dejected nonetheless. She missed them both; her sister's quick laugh, and her husband's brooding silence. She often walked around the village aimlessly, heading for no particular destination. The others would watch her silently, lost in their thoughts.

No one, at least those who talked about it, discovered what happened to Tah-neh-wa, while the fate of Creek was certain. She simply vanished without a trace. Creek did not.

He was laid to rest in the same burial site as the Old One. His suffering wife could attest to that. She held his hand for hours, chanting little prayers with Minnah at her side.

"Go my husband, to the land of eternal hunting and food. Wait there, until I join you," she pleaded.

And so, over time, the rumors became facts, carefully woven into the threads of their stories. They had reverently decided, out of respect for the hunter and for the grieving widow, that the stream that emptied into the Great Water would be named in honor of the mighty hunter. And so it would be. On the day White Feather returned to camp, as pale as the feather that gave him his name, bearing the chewed and savagely clawed body of his uncle; Cat Kill Creek found its beginning, not as a stream, but as a name.

And all honored that name.

∿

Clara had been asleep for a long time.

Unlike the Indians who rose every day, Clara had no sense of time as it drifted over the valley, days turning to nights, and months stretching into years. Her dreams, although vivid, were fragmented, disjointed, at times playing out like a slow motion movie, revisiting the moments before she jumped from the bridge and at other times, something flickering deep within her dreams forced her to relive the tormented confusion before crashing into White Feather and only then, after dreaming in such a fashion, did she then find herself secured in his arms. Her hair did not grow long, her breath did not turn foul, nor did her stomach grumble for food. None of the bodily demands that one expected on a daily basis made themselves known to her. The only urge she felt was the urge to sleep, and in doing so, to dream.

All her dreams ended in exactly the same way, with strong comforting arms that held her tightly. Arms that had secreted her away from the Old Woman and made her feel safe. Arms that were familiar, reminding her of a time and place that she knew long ago, a man that existed in the shadows. She remembered this man. The sweat of his chest had rubbed against her body and had delicately bathed her face. The texture and smell of this Indian gently enveloped her senses, even while she was sleeping.

For while she slept, his body was close.

She felt herself drowning again and struggled to awake.

But when she awoke, for longer stretches of time, she was in a new and strange world, far different than the world of her dreams. Clara absorbed as much of this world as possible; that is to say, when she raised her head, at first in dread and fright and then, as time went on, in reluctant wide-eyed wonder. As the seasons passed, she, along with the Indian men, women, and children of all the longhouses on the flats, endured brutally cold winters with lasting storms of driving snow that piled higher than the walls of the longhouse, only to be followed by the short warm up of a budding spring, and hot summers that dragged into the cool brilliance of autumn. The Indians with whom she lived in close proximity did not notice her squatting there, staying put in the same spot.

Why they were not able to see her she did not know nor did she try to guess. It would be purely speculative, and that required energy, of which she had little. She accepted it as a twisting turn of fate, a fact not to be denied.

THE SAVAGE RIVER VALLEY

All of them were oblivious to her existence.

All but one.

∿

Year after year, Clara bore witness to every facet of their lives. Still in the longhouse of the Old One in Wachachkeek, Clara came to know each person in the village by name and soon recognized each face and yet, for reasons she could not explain, in the midst of people coming and going, one was missing. As the time went on, hesitantly at first and then with greater purpose, her eyes would automatically scan groups of male Indians as they passed by, recognizing the different men by their looks, stride, and clothing design. But she was only looking for one.

She was looking for White Feather. Disappointed each time, she nonetheless looked up again at the approach of another man.

Then he appeared. And when she saw him, her heart skipped a beat. Several years would pass before it dawned on her. Spirits act through their will and it was not an easy thing for the spirit to affect a body. The human soul acted on its body with the grace of God, and it was the same with angels and devils. Was this a miracle of God, she wondered? Was this reincarnation? Did the will, the spirit, the soul choose a body in different lifetimes? Did this happen to her? Had she made a choice to return to the past?

Of that, she was unsure. But one thing she knew. She saw the Indian man and loved him. How ironic to be out of his line of sight. Even in this Indian world, the little bit of hell had lingered. It provided the only source of her tears.

When he came into camp, which was not often, she saw the dangerous looking tomahawk White Feather laid beside him while eating a meal. His weapon was never far away. He made sure of that. The very sight of him sent a tingling sensation throughout her body, and she yearned to see more of him, to beckon him closer, to touch him, to lie beside him and feel the warmth of his body against her own once again. Where these feelings came from, perhaps from her dreams, she did not know. She knew very little about him, only his name, but perhaps it all came down to one word: *savior*. Perhaps it was the newness of this strange world that made him so attractive to her. Perhaps it was the fact that when she stared him in the face, she saw another man, a man of her past, who was identical to the Indian before her. How could it be?

It frightened her to think such a thing was possible. And now, she had lost recollection of the man of the past. All she knew, was that when she saw White Feather she forgot all else.

Regardless, his handsome yet stern face, rugged by spending years alone in the harsh wilderness, unsmiling and stiff, stayed in her mind and flittered in and out of her dreams. She would often awake, slowly but contentedly, wanting to stretch like a purring cat aroused from a deep sleep, all the while knowing, without seeing him, that he had arrived. He was not far away. She would not yield to the gentle coaxing of his sister Minnah, but when White Feather was close by she was curiously excited, breathless, and nervous, a young girl again.

Minnah could see her and knew Clara was there. But White Feather, living his life in a dark mood, did not. He never looked her way. He had no clue Clara even existed.

He lived alone, spreading out miles over the Mohican territory, camping out in makeshift shelters and finding solace in the loneliness of the woods. He preferred to be alone, for he could trust himself and his instincts to survive. The freedom of the forest gave him respite from memories that did little but haunt. Thoughts of his mother made him angry, of his uncle melancholy, and yet, there was something else, something that nagged at his very existence. Something was missing. So, he set out to seek that very thing, so sure that he would recognize it when he found it. He traveled to all villages in the valley. In time, he was accepted as an unofficial ambassador, speaking to chiefs, delivering messages, and making new blood brothers in every valley nook and on every valley flat.

He was not only recognized but also respected. White Feather

THE SAVAGE RIVER VALLEY

had a standing invitation to every village throughout the Algonquian lands and his word, seen as a serious one, was as good as any elected leader amongst them. The Wappingers, often referred to as the Highland Indians, dwelled in villages on the opposite bank of the Great Water, yet still invited him onto their lands. And every time he passed over their territory, he would stoop and lift a stone only to then respectfully place it on one of their mounds marking their territorial boundaries. He grew familiar with the customs of every tribe, every village, and personally sat at many council fires with chiefs and sachems, deliberating matters of great importance.

He came back to Wachachkeek to speak with his sisters, mentor the young braves, and lately, to spend the coldest of winter months.

"Saquiskawa," he would say, his deep voice echoing in the longhouse, all heads turning in his direction. There he stood at the doorway, filling it with his large frame. In his hands, he carried his bear cloak and weapons. One whole deerskin, with the hair intact, fitted his upper body snugly. His limbs were clothed in long leggings. His appearance was that of a furry animal walking on twos.

"I have returned," he stated.

His older sister stood at once and smiled a warm greeting.

"Brother, you are welcome this day to sit at our fire. Tonight we smoke to ward off evil, to heal the sick, and to bring the rains of spring," she said.

His presence brought great joy to her, a deep comfort, a renewed faith that each time he went away he would return. Ramco would be at his shoulder, having traveled out over the trails in search of his friend, finding him before he reached the village. If there was one man White Feather could trust, it was his boyhood friend, now husband to his sister. Without saying a word, Ramco fell into line and together they trotted back to the village of White Feather's birth.

Over the years since their mother had disappeared, White Feather had not failed to watch over his two sisters and came to the

171

village periodically. White Feather was Saquiskawa's only brother, but he was as dear a brother to her as Minnah was a sister.

A solemn agreement existed between the three siblings. There was never to be any outward mention of Tah-neh-wa, who had abandoned her children. Eliminating her name from their conversations united them in familial bonds. Although this was true, Saquiskawa still considered her mother from time to time and loved her secretly. It had been years since her name was mentioned, but Saquiskawa held the memory clear in her heart. It was a memory she would never let go off, regardless of rigid village law. And often, only at night when she thought the others were asleep, Ramco would hear her whisper to their children. She whispered in loving tones, talking about their grandmother and great-grandmother.

"Your grandmother of the earth, daughter of Sasqua long dead, will be remembered. Never let go of her memory, for through your memory she lives," she would say, stroking the dark hair of each of her children in turn. Her tears fell on their chubby round cheeks and, half-asleep, they would lift little fingers to wipe them away.

Minnah, who listened in the stillness of night, would often hear her as well yet never say a word. The heart of this Indian was not as forgiving as that of her sister.

For Minnah had never considered her mother again. Was she wrong to do so? She did not think so.

After the night of Sasqua's funeral, Minnah had finally been able to see her mother in a vision. It was as if a curtain had parted to allow a clear view, and that clear view was as painful as losing her grandmother. She knew where her mother was and with whom she had left. Minnah had gone off to the woods to be alone, crying for the loss of her mother. She had sobbed loudly for her mother, but no one heard her. Miles away, wrapped in the arms of a Mohawk, Ta-neh-wa sat straight up staring into the moonlit sky. She sat that way for a long time.

It was Minnah's first and last vision of her mother. After that, it was darkness. The curtain had fallen back in place.

THE SAVAGE RIVER VALLEY

But Minnah told no one, for she was ashamed. She tried not to think of her mother, for when she did her face grew red, so she dared not mention her vision.

Thankfully, the village was compliant with their traditions.

It was against tribal law, and the secret would go to the grave with her. She would never speak her mother's name again. Not to White Feather. Not to Saquiskawa. Not to her husband. And not to her children.

In the Indian world, there was no sense of prolonging agony.

And although White Feather, approaching his sisters in greeting, would bring back a rush of painful memories that engulfed both Saquiskawa and Minnah, it was both sisters who never regretted the visits, returning his greeting with equal warmth.

For hours at a stretch, Clara watched his every movement as his sisters prepared a sleeping compartment for him, relieving him of his bear cloak and serving him bowls of hot food. They settled down on either side of him, huddled about the fire, as did their husbands, and listened to his stories of the valley.

Clara longed to slide over to sit beside him.

ᘉ

It was the winter of 1608.

In the Old World, the cities were alive with talk of explorers' quest for a northeast passage, particularly of interest to geographers and mariners alike.

On the other side of the world, winter had arrived early. It was only four weeks since the harvest moon had appeared in the sky. Snow lay deep on the ground everywhere, in some places too deep to walk without snowshoes, gnarled bits of leather twisted over a wooden frame, sturdy and reliable for winter travel.

White Feather, arriving after many days snowshoeing over outlying lands and frozen river, would scoop up a calabash full of sweet water, tip back his dark head, and drink heavily. He knew better than to eat the snow. Reducing his body temperature would surely kill him when out there in the elements.

Clara watched in fascination as he lightly brushed the water from his lips. His hair fell well beyond his shoulders and his clothing. Warm and well-fitted skins clung to his thin but muscled body. He was strong, handsome, and, without knowing it, virile.

With deep satisfaction, he contemplated the scene before him: two women, their men, the children fast asleep, the other relatives in the longhouse, and finally the fire. Tonight they all shared a pipe made of copper, filled to the brim with sweet dried tobacco. The aroma filled the air about them and rose from the lodge. The sacred smoke would cleanse their spirits and hearts, and ensure peace, accord, and a friendly feeling around that fire. At least that was the intent.

He took the pipe and put it to his lips. He inhaled deeply and passed the pipe.

This ritual calmed him.

Then, holding his hands to the fire, he spoke.

"The Maquas, our enemy and the enemy of our fathers, encroach on our land to the north. For years, I have watched them come closer, boldly crossing our borders. They hunt our deer, they trap our animals, and they steal our life away." His voice grew harsh.

His thoughts bitterly turned to his mother and her sudden disappearance. But suspicions were all he had. He quickly glanced at Minnah. Had she read his thoughts, he wondered? She gave no indication of having done so. She stared at him solemnly.

The women listened closely. They knew lately that marauding bands of Maquas stole down on villages and exacted tribute in the form of food. So far, Wachachkeek had been spared. The Mohicans, long a peaceful River Tribe accustomed to the great bounty of crops and good hunting, had traditionally not fought back, and the lack of resolve to war was apparent.

Until recently.

"They do not fear us," Ramco said abruptly.

THE SAVAGE RIVER VALLEY

He too shared White Feather's sentiments. He had often seen Indians on the trail and managed to shoot off a few arrows or stay in pursuit until the boundaries of their lands prevented him from going any further. He too resented their presence on Mohican hunting grounds. It was time to take stronger action. It was time to retaliate.

Minnah sat quietly. She heard the bitterness in her brother's voice, echoed by that of the husband of her sister. Often she could see the conflicting emotions flicker across White Feather's face.

The pain was obvious, even to the others.

She knew he was thinking about the nation of Maquas, the hated enemy tribe known for its ferocious men. They came thundering down river in war canoes or traveling over their lands to kill and steal. She knew he harbored suspicions of who had spirited away their mother, taken her far north, many days walking. Only her brother did not know what she knew. He was completely unaware that her bitter feelings toward an enemy they both had in common mirrored his own.

If only White Feather knew, perhaps things would be different between them. Maybe someday she would be tempted to tell him, when it no longer mattered. Until then, it was still her secret, for White Feather never asked her about what she saw in her visions. If he had, she would have told him about their mother and Clara, the Woman Spirit. But even now, he did not ask.

Her sister broke the silence.

"Can we make peace with tribes to the north, not war?" asked Saquiskawa, ever the peacemaker, glancing at her children sleeping on a nearby platform and then back to her husband and brother. She did not care to think of the harm war would bring to her two sons already born and the third child that grew inside of her.

Outside, the night was cold and dark. For a minuscule of a second, even surrounded by her family, she felt the bite of loneliness. If she lived, what must her mother be feeling, out there under the same night sky? Was her mother warm? Did she share the same thoughts? Did she think of her children left behind?

The daughter shivered.

A draft hit the back of her neck. Frigid air poured through the carved smoke hole in the ceiling. She pulled her blanket closer. Saquiskawa could look down the center aisle of the longhouse and see that most of her mother's extended family, those still loyal to the children of Tah-neh-wa, gathered around their own fires. And now, with her brother here, she knew she didn't feel lonely anymore. She wished it could stay that way.

Seeing her face in anguish, White Feather placed his hand on her arm.

Minnah's husband, Tamaqua, came from the north, though still of the Mohican tribe. He, like his father before him, understood the border conflicts better than his wife's sister. His tribe lived not far from the trails that crossed over to the Maquas' land. Land was shared among Indians, a communal sharing, but only amongst those of the same tribe. Otherwise, it was war.

Angrily he stood, the fire playing on one side of his face, the other side in shadow. His nose was bold and pronounced, and his head shaven, save for only a strip of hair at the back of his head, in true Mohican style. Once a month, Minnah gently applied hot stones to his face and scalp to shave off his hair. She did the same to the scalps of her little sons, all of them resembling their brave father.

Tamaqua. Although his anger scared her, Minnah loved him nonetheless.

She looked at him now, her heart filled with wonder. Her husband spoke fervently to White Feather.

Tamaqua greatly admired his wife's brother since the day he met White Feather at the sacred funeral of the Sachem. At times, he had proudly hunted beside White Feather, even taking up bow and arrow in search of the elusive panther, and now he would go to war with him. He would die next to him if need be, but first peace?

"Mahchem," he spat into the fire. "Never!"

THE SAVAGE RIVER VALLEY

"The enemies of our fathers are our enemies," agreed Ramco. "There will never be peace."

Saquiskawa made as if to rise, to gently counteract those warlike feelings with peaceful intent, but a restraining hand on her arm held her.

She sat back, looking carefully at her husband.

He spoke to Tamaqua.

"We must go to the chief and then to the great council where your father Monemin sits," Ramco urged, not looking in his wife's direction. He always chose his words with careful intent. "The Maquas, who dare to come onto our lands, will die. They must be taught with the spilled blood of their warriors to never set foot on Mohican and Munsee lands again," he said in measured tones. "My own father and brothers from Esopus will go at our side. Together, we all speak as one."

"We will take up the hatchet!" cried Tamaqua.

White Feather, carefully watching the only two men he trusted completely and whom he could trust to safeguard his sisters in his absence, nodded in agreement.

"But, first" he added, taking one more puff on the pipe, "I shall do as they do. I shall go to their lands alone, not to hunt but to see what I can see."

He spoke slowly, definitively, and courageously.

With this unexpected announcement, all surprised heads turned in his direction except one. They knew what this proposal meant, yet no one said a word. The chances of White Feather surviving and coming back to tell of his journey were slight, for if he were caught, they would kill him. After running the gauntlet, the methods of torture by the northern tribe were said to be vicious. A man didn't stand a chance of surviving on his own.

The other men knew better than to protest.

From across the fire, Saquiskawa stared into her sister's eyes, wondering what Minnah was thinking. Or better yet; she wondered what her sister was seeing. For the visions had never stopped. Now the vision told her that her mother was still alive.

177

And then the vision turned cruel, wreathed in black; a vision of a death at the hand of her mother's son. Could it be true?

Minnah stared at her brother.

A single tear rolled down her cheek.

∿

There was too much talk of war and revenge. Although quietly said around the fire, the impact was deafening. Clara heard every word and wished they would stop. She wanted to hear of White Feather's extensive travels, his visits to other villages, but more than that, she wanted him to see her. And come closer.

Drained of energy, Clara wearily laid her head down only when White Feather, having said what he came to say, stood, grasped the forearms of the men in farewell, and abruptly left camp. It would be the last time they would see him for the remainder of the winter and well into the spring. And when he returned, which indeed he did, thin and drained of spirit, he never said a word about the trip north to anyone.

Before she slept, Clara, saddened by his departure, exchanged knowing glances with Minnah as the Indian woman stood up and walked to the open doorway; the winter's night a frozen background against her silhouette.

Minnah came to a standstill, her arms folded in front of her.

From where she stood, she could feel the unhappiness of her brother's heart. The weight was almost unbearable for her.

Muted light from a crescent moon shone down on the land, and the white snow turned an unusual blue in the semi-darkness and reflected back up to the sky so that it was possible for Minnah to look out over the land and watch her brother make his way out of the village.

Minnah stood there for a long time. Her prayers to Manito were silent, but she made them nonetheless. She watched her brother until he was out of sight; his body bundled in his bear cloak,

THE SAVAGE RIVER VALLEY

an eerie specter. It was as if the bear, seen from afar, had come back from the dead and now walked the earth once again. The cold didn't seem to bother White Feather, as he departed into the night. No one except he knew where he was headed. He liked it that way. Complete freedom.

Creek's widow, worried by the exchange she overheard between the men, came to stand at Minnah's side. She sighed and placed a comforting arm around the young woman's waist. She had grown feeble and very frightened since Creek's death, and most often on a night like this, she was already curled up in her sleeping compartment wrapped in her warm skins, leaving her daughters and their husbands to tend her fire. A little stooped and hesitant, she had grown old in a short period of time.

"Minnah," she said kindly, her voice shaking slightly, "he must find his way. White Feather, son of my forgotten sister, is a man now. You must not worry. There is nothing you can do, nor should you try to make him stay. It is the way of a man."

Her voice, though soothing, was wistful and sad.

She too stared out into the night, her warm breath blowing cold.

Minnah replied with only a few words.

"His heart is out there far away, and yet it can be found in here as well." She glanced over her shoulder and looked to where Clara slept. "Only he does not know that. Not yet, anyway. First, there must be a mixing of two worlds. Only that mixing will be the end of all of us."

Creek's widow, used to Minnah's riddles and forecasts, said nothing in return. She only listened patiently. Little the girl said worried her, for she loved her as she loved her own daughters, and talk of two worlds was not as disquieting as one would think. She thought of her own sister and the panther and sighed deeply.

Nightfall was upon them and it was time for sleep.

Ontelawnee inclined her gray head close to Minnah's.

In truth, Minnah welcomed her company, for she was the closest thing she had left to a mother.

They stood there at the open doorway, the cold air blowing around their legs. Neither spoke again.

∿

Clara slept and awoke once more.

In White Feather's absence, she noticed things that bespoke of a life she knew nothing about.

Scattered over the ground were mats with intricate weaving that also lined the beds and, even during the bitter cold of winters, the interior walls and the opening to the longhouse. It was necessary to keep warm, for not everyone had a bear cloak as insulation against the cold.

The fires, characteristically small and direct and therefore not dangerous in a longhouse made of wood, were generally stoked in sunken pits, whose woody smoke encircled her and filled her lungs with their smell. The rounded pots of clay were propped upright between gathered stones. Sturdy tripods were placed in front of every longhouse, where the women, sometimes heavily clothed with their breath frosty in the morning air and other times nude from the waist up with glistening faces, cooked the hearty meals. These forked branches tied together held suspended pots hanging low over the fire's flames. The Indian woman had few but simple utensils with which to cook. It was her art, and skillful at it she was. And when she utilized the grease of the bear and deer, it caused the men to praise her good cooking with grunts of pleasure while eating.

Clara caught sight of different kinds of baskets and simple ordinary eating bowls that held hot steaming corn. The corn had been pounded again and again by the women and daughters in a wooden or stone mortar until enough meal could be had. Large pumpkins, at least those bigger than a new babe swaddled on a cradleboard, were rolled into the longhouse and stored. There was the squash whose insides were scooped out and cooked until tender.

THE SAVAGE RIVER VALLEY

The smell of the fire and of the boiled corn stayed with her, even in her dreams; a constant reminder that she was in another world, unlike the one she was familiar with in New York. Pangs of homesickness, overwhelming at times, only made her rest her head once again and sleep.

When she awoke, often with a start, she watched it all with dull eyes, but in that time she came to know all about them, in more detail than she thought possible.

Clara became quite adept at predicting their every step and movement, from their daily routines, from the time they awoke to the time they slept, to their traditions and customs. On many occasions, she had unwillingly lifted her head and opened her eyes begrudgingly, wide and disbelieving, to the world of the Indian, this Mohican branch of the Catskills, who lived all around her, filling her long days and even longer nights with their smells, activities, and sounds. She saw or heard every aspect of their life from listening to the oral traditions at night in the smoky interior, Saquiskawa having taken over that position, to seeing what transpired outside the doorway. Sometimes, beyond her control, she drifted into a deep but comforting sleep, barely noticing the activity around her. At night the young Indian women procreated with their husbands. During the day the incessant activity of daily work was accompanied by the ever present sounds of their language. She watched the women trudge off to the birthing lodge, rarely accompanied by other women, and return hours later hugging Indian babes wrapped in soft pouches. Minnah always brought her babies to Clara for approval, laying them in front of her, waiting for Clara to lift her head.

In the year 1608, Minnah had four thriving sons, strong and healthy like their Uncle White Feather and their father Tamaqua. Clara took a special liking to the baby Metoxem who resembled White Feather.

Clara would never forget the first day Metoxem lifted his head, turned to her, and smiled. He then turned back to his mother. Now Minnah was not the only one who saw her!

Clara gave a silent laugh and clapped her hands.

The Indian woman named Minnah was in her twentieth year of living. She felt comforted by the spirit woman who sat in their longhouse and never spoke, mostly slept. Nevertheless, Minnah knew that one day, although she did not know when, the woman would rise and live.

Clara slept on or watched as a curious spectator.

At times, Clara was well aware of a certain pair of moccasins softly molded around a woman's feet as they crossed in front of her or stopped at her side. And like the gentle spirit of the wind as it came blowing over the mountains, Clara could feel across her cheek the gentle breath of Minnah as she often leaned close to her and spoke to her at length. Others thought Minnah to be odd, whispering in the corner of the longhouse. But all of them grew accustomed to it, thinking perhaps she was communing with spirits or perhaps to Manito himself. So they let her be and said nothing.

"Wake up and look at the sun and its sister the moon, Woman Spirit that dropped from White Feather's arms," she would beg.

It didn't happen every day, but often enough. So often that Clara came to recognize the voice and, astonishingly enough, in time Clara understood the meaning of the words.

Minnah explained many things about their way of life, extending the gentle favor to a woman who was obviously lost. In return, Minnah asked questions that sought meaning to Clara's presence.

"Why have you come to our lands? Is it someone you seek? Do you have a message for us?"

Minnah would sit quietly, waiting for an answer. Only none ever came.

Minnah took a deep breath. She never got angry.

"Huron Indian myth has it that in ancient times, when the land was barren and the people were starving, the Great Spirit sent forth a woman to save humanity. Are you that woman?"

Clara said nothing. Minnah paused and then continued.

"As she traveled over the world, everywhere her right hand

touched the soil, there grew potatoes. And everywhere her left hand touched the soil, there grew corn. And when the world was rich and fertile, she sat down and rested. When she arose ..."

All she wanted was for this Woman Spirit to show her why she was here. So, she sighed and continued talking.

"Woman Spirit whose presence is honored, tell me who you are and why you are here."

Clara peeked out from behind her crossed arms and saw Minnah's kind face, round with huge expressive eyes and a broad smile. She liked her.

Only Clara was not ready to completely join her world. Call it stubborn, if you will, but at times like these, when this young Indian girl peered into her face, when she lifted locks of Clara's hair and tenderly stroked her face, Clara forced her eyes to remain shut. Only when Minnah brought her new babies to Clara's side for recognition did Clara raise her head and smile feebly. For babies, even babies from strange Indians, were special to Clara. They were beautiful and innocent. They found their way into Clara's heart. When Minnah came to kneel at Clara's side and lay soft skins at her feet, a dress and a mantle with moccasins on top, apparently for her, Clara smiled but said nothing.

There simply was nothing to say. Clara was no wiser than before. She still didn't know what strange force brought her there and kept her there, except as a punishment for her suicide. The end of life brought a new life. There was no other way to explain it.

At times, though less consistently, Clara was still terrified of her newfound surroundings. Curiosity was squelched by confusion at her situation, delaying the moment of opening her mouth in any attempt to speak. It was all too hard to believe. She could not face it just yet.

So, she made a decision.

Hearing the sound of her own voice in this strange, primitive world forced her to remain mute, because the second she produced sounds and was heard as well as seen, it would be that moment, somehow, when she would become one of them.

At times, she still expected to wake up from this horrible dream. Only she never did.

Nor did she think she ever would be ready to face the fact that she no longer existed in the old and familiar world of 2001, back to the familiar things in her house, the piles of stacked books she had read incessantly, and her land in Durham—that quaint, little hamlet of New York where agriculture and the Indian village had long since disappeared, but where the little museum on Route 145 and all the old cemeteries gave her much to read and discover about the area. In that time, it was the old ways, an incomprehensible world of the past, that held her prisoner.

Now, she was haunted by this current world of the Indians who ruled this land she once knew as home; a home of farms, unpaved roads, and community churches. But now it was no longer her home. It was their home, and she was all too aware of that fact. She was indeed a stranger in their very strange land.

She knew not the year, although she considered it, but she was only able to guess the month based on the activities of the Indians and the weather. May brought planting, September the harvest, October the hunt, and February the bitterest of winds and snow.

What she never considered, what she could not face and accept, was that maybe she, the Woman Spirit who unceremoniously dropped into the world of the New York Mohicans, was haunting them. The thought never entered her mind.

When was that exact moment that Clara felt the comfort of the Indian world surrounding her? When did she begin to feel as if she were merging into their lifestyle and their way of thinking? When did she listen for the gentle breathing of Minnah as she lay on her sleeping pallet with her husband and youngest baby? When had she realized that the sight of White Feather excited her beyond compare? When did she feel a motherly comfort in seeing Saquiskawa suckle her babies by the fireside and turn to her husband Ramco with deep affection reflected in her gentle smile and eyes?

It did not occur overnight or at any precise moment. But there was one particular day when she woke and experienced no pangs of anxiety to see the familiar surroundings of the longhouse. Her life and the hamlet of Durham, all fused into one distant memory were no longer her reality.

The diffused memories coincided with the diffused light of day, which came in shafts through the doorway. All seemed to be in order.

She began to feel as if they were her family, and it was a shocking realization that left her breathless. It no longer felt like hell, but now, somehow to her human spirit, it was almost home; a place where she should be, and not as threatening as when she first entered the longhouse in the arms of White Feather. She had grown accustomed to the crackle of the fire and she loved the sound of their stories, the gentle noises they made when eating, and the quiet that descended on the longhouse while they slept.

They were humans, not the heathens she initially encountered.

Sometimes while she slept, the braided bunches of corn were carried inside and hung to dry high above her head. The rustling noise of the dry husks stayed in her head, as did their strange words to one another.

And like a child, she felt safe and secure around her family.

∿

The gentle winds of summer brought all their words in a whispering *whoosh* to her ears, along with the sounds of the outdoors; the call of the blue jay and the buzz of the June bugs.

The language of the people was clear. It was her language now.

Minnah spoke of the Great River. *Maugh*, meaning large, and *hikan* meaning ocean or sea. The suffix *-ituk* meaning a river that flows both ways.

"Our Great River, which gives us life," explained Minnah softly, imitating the movement of the water with a gentle motion of her hands. Her fingers, moving like tiny minnows, held Clara mesmerized.

She spoke of the dried corn.

"*Ach-po-em*," she would say in Minnah's ear. "Eat our sweet corn, Woman Spirit, for it sustains life."

Go-han was the word for *yes*. "Go-han, Woman Spirit," she coaxed, while combing then braiding Clara's hair one day. Clara felt the shivers of attention bestowed on her. It had been so long.

Clara listened to their words, feeling the gentle fingers of this Indian woman run through her hair.

Mountain of the bears, mach-k-tschunk. The others spoke, in hushed tones, of White Feather; where he lived when he was not in camp and why he acted so strange, at times so distant, from the tribe. It was as if he had taken on the spirit of the bear that he had bravely sent on to the next world.

Clara's attentive ear grew accustomed to their soft-spoken language and she found herself, silently and with a stubborn determination, repeating the words over and over again in her mind. She would understand these people. She would. And the one phrase that shadowed her desire, the one that played in her mind when she felt the burden of loneliness was: *Ma-tschi-u, Ka-to-nah?* He is gone, why?

At times like these, she would lift her head and look longingly beyond the open doorway. Not so much that she wanted to go out there, for she was afraid of the outside world and content to stay in the protective womb of this longhouse. Rather, she wanted him to appear.

White Feather, come home!

Only he didn't.

Ka-to-nah? She moaned inwardly. *Why?*

The day was serene. There were no sounds of airplanes overhead, no screech of cars, and no motors of distant lawnmowers. Not one mechanical noise reached her ears. Only the sounds of Mother Earth, of the wildlife, and of those of Indians living close to nature: the piling of wood, the scraping of skins, the husking of corn, soft womanly talk around the fire pits as they prepared food or swaddled the papooses.

THE SAVAGE RIVER VALLEY

No harsh noises.

Instead, it was delightful, and Clara's heart was at peace. A square shaft of soft light flowed though the doorway warming her toes where they curled in the dust. She wiggled them, feeling each toe move. She had yet to put on the moccasins and feel their softness against her skin. Perhaps one day she would.

The far-reaching cornfields stretched beyond the village. Here, the slow-walking, elderly males and agile children helped the agriculturally inclined women for six months of the year. They saw to the hard tasks of planting, weeding, and harvesting. And if she leaned far over and stared out into the far distance, almost uprooting herself and tumbling over head first, she saw the edge of the meadow, mysterious yet defined; where the hunters came trudging in from the forest carrying great slabs of drying meat and torn animal hides laid upon sturdy poles that dragged along the ground or strapped to freshly cut branches resting between the shoulders of two men.

The hunt had been a good one. They smiled as they entered the confines of the village. The women and children awaited their return and stood while the meat was dumped at their feet. The squaws would take over from that point, cutting and cleaning the meat further, distributing it to family members of the longhouse. They would cook for hours, with the smells drifting over the village. The patiently waiting men, eating little while hunting, were hungry.

The mighty hunters had come home.

And it was always on this spot Clara's eyes, when opened, rested in hopes of seeing White Feather as he approached camp.

Chapter Nine

The Indian world of ancient times ended.

There had always been traders from some distant spot beyond the horizon, copper bracelets from an unseen land, white faces in the north, knives that exchanged hands many times and found their way south, bringing with them insidious changes to the Indian world of ancient traditions. Now another change, physical and psychological, came over the land.

The white man, pale face, speaking a strange tongue, and wearing strange clothes, arrived and he intended to stay.

∿

It was late in the summer of 1609.

In the south, a band of hardy Englishmen struggled to settle on a lonely spot they would name Jamestown. Few would survive the approaching winter. Those who did, knowing the pain of starvation and the cold, would opt for life and go join the ranks of the living in surrounding Indian villages. Far north, the French had not only explored the Great Lake they would name Champlain in honor of their leader, but they also now had a fulltime presence there. And on the coast, not more than a weeks' walk for the strong and hardy Indian, the presence of some more settlers was felt. They were the Puritans. Life was not the same except in the far West, for there the Indians' way of life remained unchanged a little while longer.

However, for the River Tribes, the biggest change was yet to come.

THE SAVAGE RIVER VALLEY

Although Clara had no knowledge of the year, something quite extraordinary happened. She would never be able to entirely erase it from her mind, for it would, like a jagged piece of glass, remain sharp and crystal clear in her memory and in and of itself, signal an end to the quiet days of the Indian village and to her deep sleeps which afforded her an escape from reality.

Once, when she felt unusually fatigued, she could barely lift her head where it lay on her arms. She heard a disturbing rustling that woke her, even though she tried to block the noise from her sleep. She slowly opened her eyes to a strange and bizarre spectacle; a man who clearly was not an Indian roughly rummaging around the longhouse, throwing things to and fro in haste. He was rather oddly dressed, oddly meaning unlike the Indians, their dress of skins so familiar to her now. He was dressed in cloth alone, and he kept his back to her. Was that intentional? Did he know she was there? What was he looking for? Oh how she wished to know precisely who he was, this stranger on Indian lands, for it bothered her deeply to see him there, a place she had come to consider her home.

"Shast!" he exclaimed, bringing a bruised finger to his mouth. It was then that she realized he had no teeth as he sucked in his breath.

Obviously he didn't belong.

Yet there was nothing she could do but watch in curious hopelessness. So taken aback was she that when he discovered something that made him gasp loudly, nervously shoved it in his long shirt that hung knotted over shortened pants, and then departed in a hurry, racing out the open doorway into the soft autumn day, she was not sure she understood what had just happened. She knew that the Indians sometimes kept their most precious objects in ceramic bowls, buried or covered under their platforms.

What had he stolen?

Where were the Indians?

The lodge was quiet and deserted.

For the first time in eight years she felt completely alone and defenseless, once again reminding her how vulnerable she was in this Indian world; a feeling she had not felt in many years.

What should I do? she wondered with desperation.

Clara wanted to shout for her Indian family to come running. They must be nearby!

But not one Indian was in camp, neither in the longhouse where Clara resided nor in any of the others. Not even a few camp dogs scratched in the dirt.

The entire village was silent. In fact, the whole group, for some reason that escaped her as she slept, had left to go to the banks of the Great Water. It was once again the time of the harvest, so the apparent lack of industrious activity was odd. They never completely deserted the camp, for much had to be done.

They will return, she thought with a little nervous smile. And the comforting thought helped her to relax and close her eyes again. Little did she know that on this day she was in store for an unexpected shock.

She must have dozed a few minutes, but when she awoke a second time that day, there was a great clamor in the longhouse. Skins were in disorderly array, strewn all over the ground. Pots were overturned, beans spilled onto the earthen floor, and the fire had been extinguished, a boot having carelessly kicked dirt over the embers.

Women were crying and men stood solemnly about, leaning against the walls with arms folded against their chest, visibly angered.

Without thinking twice, Clara stood up in fright. Her legs held up incredibly well. She had never seen the Indians act in such a way. Something dreadful had surely provoked this outrage. Clara quickly searched the distraught group for familiar faces: Minnah, Saquiskawa, and their babies. She did not spot them at first. She saw a distressed Ontelawnee with her daughters and their babies. The men stood against the wall and in groups outside, some visibly baffled, some quite angry. But she was not looking for them.

She grew more anxious.

Please God, let them be safe. Let no harm come to them! Minnah! Metoxem, where are you?

She loved all the children, but this baby was undoubtedly her favorite.

A strange and unexpected thing happened next.

Clara recognized her immediately. She saw her standing behind the others, a little offset from her family.

The Old One had returned. She said nothing, staring in Clara's direction. From the doorway, pale and shaken, Minnah clutched her children to her side, holding the littlest baby to her breast, a boy with a shocking patch of black hair. She too had seen the Old One.

And while Clara's mouth dropped open, someone shouted with a wail, "It is gone ... it is gone!"

And indeed it was.

The shaman stone was gone.

Chapter Ten

Modern history attributes it all to the lure of spices. Was it the flavor? Was it the tempting smell? Whatever it was, this undetermined greed stimulated a great demand.

And so they were off to distant lands. The traders went in eager pursuit of exotic flavors, rich and fragrant plants.

Shiploads of those fabulous edibles brought glorious profits exceeding four hundred percent, to the already deep pockets of Dutch merchants in The Netherlands; unheard of profits far overshadowing most other commonly traded items in the world arena. Not even silk from the Orient or tobacco and sugar from the West Indies could top the profit making ability of spices.

How ingenious the Dutch were, and all for the making of revenue.

In the Netherlands, where the majority of citizens lived a good life enveloped within a bustling economy brimming with means, there were no sentiments of reserve, no doubts or hesitation, and no cumbersome weighing of constraints.

It was a simple matter.

They called it business. And business would be better, faster, and economical, if a direct route, incredible to even consider, were to be discovered!

Everyone wanted a piece of it. Thoughts of a possible, magical, yet-to-be-discovered Northwest Passage spurred them into a private frenzy to acquire the rights to this golden avenue of waters; at any cost, at any means. It would be the watery path to riches beyond the imagination!

And so the Dutch were not to be stopped in their unquench-

THE SAVAGE RIVER VALLEY

able thirst for a quick route to the lands that abounded with mace, cloves, and ginger, not to mention pepper and nutmeg. The risks were squelched by the exciting thoughts of coffers full to the point of brimming with guilders, solid pieces of florins, and gold. There was money to be made, and the Dutch were the ones to make it and keep it.

Those fanatical tradesmen, those wizardly businessmen of the world, a selected council of very rich men, clamored in a clandestine rush to sign on the crusty, sea-bitten Englishman with a moderately reputable background as discoverer and explorer extraordinaire. This captain, exuding confidence, at times haughty and driven to succeed, stood before the administrators of the East India Company in Amsterdam. These dark robed men of various ages, bearded and coiffed, speaking in loud tones, left no holds barred and no words unsaid. The agenda of the day was clear. "We want him and he needs us." Merchant Burgh pronounced loudly. It was that plain and that simple. The Englishman, having said little up to this point, now agreed to their terms. They wanted to be recognized as the master traders of the world. In return, Hendrick Hudson, once in their employ, would be the master discoverer, the one who would be assured a place in history as he did what others—Columbus, Cabot, Cortes, De Gama and Magellan—failed to do. In short, he would find the coveted route!

It was quite easy to say it, wish it, and demand it. Doing it was quite another matter.

An important document was signed with ink quill and in turn stamped with a heavy seal on January 8, 1609. This document was a contract with the Dutch in writing; the terms nevertheless undeniably clear. If Hudson were to find the anticipated route, he would remain a fixture in the permanent service of the East India Company.

The salary was carefully doled out and paid well in advance. The company outfitted him with his sailing vessel, a ship they would name de Halve Maen, measuring a full eighty-five feet from bow to stern, weighing a ponderous eighty tons—a crude though solid ship. They supplied him with a crew, more than the normal fifteen, an odd assortment of thirty-two English and Dutch sailors, and an exact itinerary. In April, he was trusted to sail off to the chilly environs of the Northeast, toward Novaya Zemlya, by way of the northern stretches of Russia, with no deviation in course.

Initially, he did sail in that very direction; only to admit defeat, turn the ship back when thwarted by the solidity of ice.

But was it really *defeat?* What would be the end result of this strictly worded itinerary? Hudson had the solution, perhaps the very desire that haunted his mind and heart from the very beginning: disobey company orders and forego an immediate return to the Netherlands. Instead, taking the initiative, he courageously ignored the dissatisfied grumbling of his crew. He set sail for the Northwest, pushed along by a westward blowing gale toward the North American continent. What a genius!

For once, he did what he had always wanted to do; he charted his own course.

More importantly, perhaps, to the modern historian in his most sincere efforts to re-word history and seek truth, it could be said that Henry Hudson, in all of his doings, was overshadowed by one person. His first mate, the crafty Robert Juet, who, for unknown reasons, fastidiously scribbled in a small, leather-bound packet known as the only surviving journal left of that voyage.

Or so they thought.

ᗯᑎ

They came in the early spring of 1611, the summer of 1613, and then again in 1614. They were the ships of Dutch merchants; the holds loaded with blankets, copper, kettles, beads, axes, knives, and bolts of red material—duffel, named after the village where it originated. Ships and cargo belonging to private merchants that sailed on rough ocean waves that reached to the heavens themselves before

THE SAVAGE RIVER VALLEY

crashing downwards bore men of trade and of the sea. They were relatively small ships and few men, compared to the enormity of the ocean and its mysterious depths, not to mention the continent they set foot on. Nevertheless, regardless of the size of these expeditions, the impact would prove tremendously huge, everlasting, and, in many ways, destructive.

However, as in years past, this time it was not in quest of the illusive Northern Passage.

By then, they knew the fantasy didn't exist. Hudson was gone, vanished, and presumably dead.

On a different voyage in a different body of water, yet still seeking that much sought out waterway, far north in the Hudson Bay in 1611, Hudson was ruthlessly set adrift in a rowboat by a mutinied crew, somewhat, although not altogether, different from the previous group of motley crewmen of 1609. With no provisions and stranded in a frozen environment with no hopes of rescue, for once the odds were all in his favor—of dying—and that he did with no doubts.

What was left of the crew returned to England to tell the truth. Simply put, there was no northern passage to be discovered. It was a lost cause.

Well, so the story goes.

Actually, not all the crew returned. Of the mutinied crew, one was missing.

Robert Juet, the dedicated journalist, was dead. Juet, who had signed on for the second voyage with his ill-fated captain, had died after conspiring with his shipmates against the unsuspecting Hudson. He had watched from the upper deck while his bewildered boyhood friend was left with no means to survive. Now Juet, suffering a mysterious illness, was dead, though the cause of death was never discovered. Juet's body was destined for the bottom of the sea, as befitting all sailors. A sailor sewed him up in a cloth covering and, somewhere in the vicinity of the great banks, they pitched his body overboard. All the remaining crew swore to the same version of events, even though not all saw the downing of the body or the sewing up of the cloth.

Initially Captain Hudson, then the first mate Juet. Both needed to be disposed of, but for extraordinarily different reasons.

Now the Dutch merchants no longer thought of that passage. They had finally let go the idea, as had everyone else. Disappointed yes, but not defeated. Not yet.

The little scrawling script in the leather-bound volume written by Juet was studied by all the Dutch councilmen and consequently filed away in the archives, relegated to a dusty shelf. Only one in particular named Rensallear, a merchant who spent an inordinate amount of time scouring the journal, seemed to notice that pages had been carefully torn out. He made no reference of it to the others.

No Northwest Passage, no Henry Hudson, and no Robert Juet—a finished story with a sad but final ending.

But, a new wind was blowing and life was surging forward as it always does.

The Dutch had other things in mind as they set their sights on this new wilderness that Henry Hudson, in his 1609 voyage, had proclaimed, "a virtual paradise with great potential." This paradise was not to be overlooked or ignored. The potential, the Dutch reasonably decided, was the treasure.

Land was everyone's dream. It meant everything to everyone, especially in a shrinking European arena as the population, naturally checked by disease and infection, still continued to increase as available land for agriculture decreased. But, initially it was not land the merchants were after.

Not by a long shot.

At least not at present, but rather, they caught wind of another commodity they greedily planned to acquire and take back to the Old World. In Northern Europe, their Russian market supplying them with mink was drying up. Now they needed a new one. So once again, they sent out their captains and vessels to lay their stakes,

THE SAVAGE RIVER VALLEY

to assure their investments, and to gather their wares-all under the auspices of a private undertaking of a few Dutchmen.

Dutch merchants plotted, strategically planned, and finally, the ensuing voyages came to fruition. The new council at once hired Captains Christian Hendricks, a dour-faced though reliable man; Adrian Block, the itinerant explorer; and Cornelius May, a veteran trader. Their purpose and duty: to explore, map the river, and bring home the goods; a monopoly that would control all the trade from the River Valley in the New World and land all the profits into the pockets of the Dutch.

So they figured it was to be a monopoly, but a monopoly of what?

In the New World, these traders who sailed up and down the banks of the Nordt River, as more and more Dutch referred to it, wanted one thing: fur.

Where was that fur? Why, on the back of the beaver, of course. And who trapped the beavers? The native savages did.

And among them, central players in the scheme of trading, were the Mohicans and the Mohawks.

∿

The hour was late. For several weeks now a cloaked figure had briskly walked the cobbled streets alongside the well-built canals of Amsterdam until the early hour of the morning, when streaks of crimson light first appeared in the dawn sky. He meandered over the darkened city streets and through back alleyways, often pausing to discerningly cock his ear to a new sound. He, for quite expectedly this mysterious figure appeared in a gentleman's garb comprised of cloak, belted breeches, and a fine felted hat, passed row after row of wooden, weather-boarded buildings. The pantile roofs were steep. The streets were narrow and twisted in irregular patterns and were of cobblestone. City houses were closely crowded together, some so old they tilted, many located just off the canals where servants tossed their master's garbage and emptied the household urine buckets by day.

This particular evening was quiet, a balmy April night that brought no biting wind or remnants of winter weather, and the streets lining the canals were uncommonly empty as the city slept.

It had been a busy day, but he was not tired.

So he continued on his way.

Next he passed the nun's house, the oldest wood and brick building in Amsterdam reflecting typical Dutch urbanity; a steep gable-front and high roofs. He need not worry about silhouetting pools of light on the street corners or anyone sitting on the front stoep. The lanterns had earlier been extinguished by the evening watchmen. They had gone home sometime after midnight. And now, no one was out and about except him.

Therefore, he was free to walk in shadows and darkness. This manner he liked best, to hide his true self from others. That was the little game he played and, after months of practice, he played it well.

No one suspected him, at least not yet. No one thought he had the audacity or courage to attempt anything like this. How wrong he would prove them to be!

Soon he reached the commercial buildings on the waterfront. He stopped and listened, his eyes long since accustomed to spotting anything that moved in the darkness. No vigilant guardsmen on the wharfs, for they had fallen asleep; no barking dogs to warn of his approach; and no sound of anyone approaching. *How careless they all are,* he thought. But, it was to his advantage.

All was quiet here too, at this magical hour when most of the city was tucked beneath their bedcovers.

Why so silent, O great trading bustling city? he wondered.

Could it be because he took the statue from safekeeping and held it gingerly in his hands the evening before when no one was about? Had some of its good luck that had blessed the merchant rubbed off on him as well? He had wished for one last night of soli-

THE SAVAGE RIVER VALLEY

tude, one last time to carefully retrace his planned route of escape. One last night before the ship set sail.

He was his own master, no longer a servant under the strong hand of the merchant. That thought made him shiver with pleasure. He couldn't quite imagine the total freedom to come and go at any hour. He didn't know what it was like. But this little taste of it was greatly to his liking.

It gave him strength and the courage to carry forth with the plan.

Merchant Killian was fast asleep, snoring loudly under fluffy down comforters in his huge wooden bed, his fat, penny-pinching wife next to him, and their daughters, elsewhere under the same roof, safe as well. The few servants were in cold rooms in the damp cellar. That cruel and cunning merchant was so unsuspecting within his own home that it made the cloaked figure smile briefly, for he had managed to fool them all.

He should not be so trusting of family and guests, much less servants.

It had been easy, after all, to hide while preparations for bed were made and slip out of the house in stolen clothes. He had done it many times now, but this would be the last.

He looked to the merchant's building on his right and spotted the telltale insignia on the front.

These massive warehouses were built in typical Dutch fashion: cross-framed windows with lower shutters, cranes at the gable peaks designed to hoist goods to upper levels and loft doors. One building alone could easily hold four shiploads of cargo. Barrels and crates of cargo brought riches to the fat merchant who had little compassion or mercy while overseeing his kingdom of wealth.

All the buildings were deserted, some full of wares, others waiting for trading ships to arrive from out on the high seas. *How easy it would be to set fire to such a building he thought.* For some time now, the cloaked figure had hated the merchant. But trading goods could be replaced and a new warehouse built. He had something else in mind, something that was not so easily replaced or built anew.

All this he knew. Everything was proceeding smoothly; too smooth in fact and, for no reason in particular, he suddenly worried about what or who could effectively ruin his well-laid plans. He shook his head; there was no room for self-doubts.

He turned.

What he saw in front of him fascinated him more than any one building.

At the edge of the wooden dock, a ship with three masts was moored; the sails rolled up and bound, the gangplank pulled in for the night. There were no distinguishable pinpoints of light from lanterns on deck or below, though he was sure the captain was on board, most likely sleeping off another drunken night spent in the confines of one of the city's many drinking establishments. The power of rum and an alcoholic captain was a dangerous combination. Most likely he had come onboard with a whore, yellow-haired and young. His drunken stupor would induce him to slap her and often near strangle her. At these moments he thought of his parents: a cursing mother and an angry father.

Do to others as was done to you, he thought savagely.

Before the crew awoke, the young girl would be roughly pushed down the gangplank and brutally thrown off the boat, and, come early morning, none the richer than the night before, bruised, sometimes broken, and oftentimes crudely cut. She never sought justice, for no one would openly side against a captain for the benefit of a whore. Justice seldom existed for those without a voice.

It was a quiet and dark evening. With water everywhere, one would have thought heavy waves would be crashing around Amsterdam. That was not the case. All the water, the brutal force of it, was walled away from the city and farmlands. The land was actually lower than the sea, but the Dutchmen were keen at keeping the mighty power of the sea at bay. They succeeded. The heavy wooden structure a few hundred feet away barely moved. The canal was serene, the water smooth.

"Ah! The ship that was meant to go half-way round the world was a marvel," some had said.

THE SAVAGE RIVER VALLEY

"Look at its solid mast!" one man remarked just that very afternoon.

"And look at the shine of the wood," a true Dutch woman answered.

Its huge dark form rose up before him. He waited and watched closely, his eye running the length of the tall and solid mast and over the rounded ship, noticing over time only a slight keening to the left and then to the right, barely perceptible when securely tied to the dock and anchored, except to the sailor's eye.

He had that innate keen eye, though he was no seaman. Not even a ship maker or a common laborer on the wharfs. The finely clad gentleman stood there for a long time, staring at the ship with fancy lettering that would change his life for the better. At least he hoped so.

"My life will be better once I have escaped," he repeated softly under his breath.

He had relentlessly prayed to a distant God for this day to come. The God, who had ignored him and had never heeded his cries of succor for most of his young life, was surely a mighty and powerful God that must help him now and bring his just revenge.

He smiled in satisfaction, then turned and left.

∿

A thousand miles away, on the other side of the wide and powerful ocean, there was an unknown continent with another way of life. The wish of the finely clad gentleman would indeed come true. A mixing of two worlds would occur.

But the question remains.

Would it be a change for the better?

Chapter Eleven

June 1618

The captain was in a foul mood. The crossing had been the worst so far of his life at sea, and he had wretched up piles of undigested food and sour beer as his ship tossed on the stormy waves.

This was not unusual. He felt like this when he, more often than not, was in a drunken stupor, but now that was not the case. The captain was just plain seasick.

"Cripes, God almighty!" he moaned, clutching at his belly.

He dragged himself from his bunk, the vomit dripping from his shirtfront, and stared at the floor, which seemed to be heaving in the same motion as his stomach.

The aftertaste, mixed with bile, was grossly bitter in his mouth, and he spat ferociously into the dung bucket while he cursed the weather. He raised his head and felt another wave of nausea rising from the pit of his stomach.

"Clean this mess, you stupid bastard!" he yelled over his shoulder in the direction off to his left. There was nothing worse than feeling like this. It killed him to be abed with the ship at sea.

He waited until he heard the wooden slat slide open. Then he lay back down.

He had never been this sick at sea before. Maybe, at the ripe age of forty-four, he was getting too old for this. Maybe he couldn't take the ship tossing about in the storm anymore. Maybe he hadn't a stomach for it any longer. He cursed even louder.

THE SAVAGE RIVER VALLEY

This was no rogue storm. It stayed with the ship, tracked their course, and followed them for days, or so it seemed. Most probably, it was the captain's imagination. Actually, the storm, relentless in its fury, had lasted only two days and then blew further out to sea. Off to the east, while the ship sailed west.

The tumultuous weather had passed. Indeed, it had, for sunny skies now afforded the seamen a clear view. But the captain was still sick.

They were nearing land, coming to the first harbor, the first refuge from the massive waves of the ocean that had, at one point, wiped the decks clean of anything not tied down. Thankfully, no men had been lost, although many had feared they would be as they slid over the wet boards, their bodies slamming into the railing or anything solid that stopped a screaming descent into the black, angry sea. Soon they would enter the narrow passage of water that led to the upper harbor, a place that bespoke of calm.

But the captain's mind was not calm.

There were other things bothering him, a mix of turmoil in his thoughts that troubled him deeply and robbed him of sleep. And for this, he cursed the easiest thing: the storm. And because of the nasty weather, he forbade the doling out of rum beer, a cheap frothy mixture that immediately hit a man's gut and brought on giddiness. A certain giddiness that made them all momentarily forget the hardships of sea life. For just that moment, when the refreshment hit their lips, their lives were transformed.

"Lock it up!" he bellowed from his sick bed, throwing off the dirty covers and sitting up. "And be quick about it, Broeck!"

Better for the crew to have their senses about them, he angrily reasoned. Who knows what could happen if he were not at the wheel? At any rate, the crew would be as sober if not as sick as he was. Misery loved company.

The first mate jumped to do his bidding. Below deck, the order was received in somber silence and dark looks. The first mate gave the order and, with one look around, backed out of the crew's quarters, a large, open area filled with swinging hammocks.

PAMELA DE LEON

The men below were none too happy with the captain's orders, but they knew better than to complain. One word and a whip would slash their backs raw. They held nothing against the first mate. He just followed orders like the rest of the poor bastards. Their thoughts centered on the captain. Now, there was a different sort of man. The captain was a hardnosed, cantankerous, unforgiving taskmaster in charge of a handpicked crew, so particular a combination that only he could lead. He had ordered a severe lashing on the last voyage, and word had got around even as far south as Leiden. The seaman who got the lashing had foolishly, perhaps drunkenly, challenged the captain, only to suffer a back festered with the white pus. He died days later. Now, the men feared the captain, and it lingered in their eyes. So, they stayed mute and as far away from the captain as possible. But miserable and ornery they were, and quick to start a fight and quick to finish one without the captain ever finding out. Normally they quarreled with other seamen, staggering out of taverns onto the city streets, but now the pickings were slim. They took their male aggression out on each other. It was first mate Wessell Ten Broeck who could keep them off each other's backs and, thereby, maintain a relative peace.

Now the ship had finally arrived. The New World appeared before them in the throes of June.

How glorious it was: the weather, the sky, the land before them, and the birds scattering in pairs over the water, dipping and gliding with the breeze. The warmth of a new summer had descended upon the land of this mysterious and, as of yet, fully unexplored continent.

The air was fresh and exhilarating, carrying no mal odors such as those drifting over the canals and dirty streets in the cities of the Old World. Indeed, it felt good to take a deep breath of clean air and hold it inside before exhaling!

The three-masted ship, a Dutch schooner, creaked and groaned gently as the swaying movement of the waves rocked the vessel up and down. From a bird's eye view up high in the sky, the ship

THE SAVAGE RIVER VALLEY

appeared small. From the deck, the ship was sufficient of size to carry all these men across a wide ocean and through a dangerous storm. It had done its job.

Land was all around them and the pleasantly cool breeze off the ocean filled the sails. The smell of salt water was all around them. They had left the storm far behind, but if they had taken the time to look carefully off to the east they could have spotted two things: the tiniest speck of black sky that lingered on the horizon and a glimpse of still another distant speck on the sea, an advancing sail. But no one cared to look in that direction, for that was behind them.

They wanted to forget the storm.

The men were more intent on something else.

Now there were other sights to see—sights that lay ahead of them.

The boat moved forward with each swell, a sound Captain Christian Hendricks had long grown accustomed to hearing, having spent the better part of his adult life aboard one ship or another, and on this particular ship for the last two months, destined for the New World. It was a sound that comforted him, a sound that bespoke of a floating vessel supported by a massive sturdy keel, a massive beam of wood that sheltered him from the sea below. The keel was his rock, his support, and his lifeline. He always fastidiously inspected the heavy timber in minute-detail before each voyage, knocking on it for telltale signs of wet or rot. The sea was a world of the deep, dark, and unknown-a world that he found glorious, but only from the tall deck on the stern that looked down on the confined world of the lower deck, where the crew scrambled to keep the sails full.

Here, in control of such a mighty power, that of man against the sea, he could shove away the nightmares of growing up unloved and beaten until his body showed bruises black and blue. Out on the ocean, he was someone of value.

Yes, it was his wooden ship all right. The true lady of his heart that had not betrayed him yet, nor, he firmly believed, ever would.

"Solid, you are," he proudly said.

The wooden ship, for which every timber, plank, mast, spar, nut, bolt, rope, sail—and more—was handmade and hand fitted. In Amsterdam, as well in the other provinces of the Netherlands, as many as twenty to thirty different kinds of craftsmen—carpenters, cabinetmakers, rope makers, caulkers, coopers, sail makers, and the like—were employed in the building of a ship. The end result was a masterpiece; a well-built vessel that had to ride the waves properly balanced in the water. The ship had gently rounded curves and was firmly hammered and pegged together; correctly rigged so as to resist the powerful push and pull of the sea while the forces of the wind moved her across the watery distances. And it came as no surprise that she had to be watertight. Too much water in her holds could not only spoil the cargo and rot the ship's timbers but could also send her straight to the bottom of the cold and unforgiving sea.

There was a fine line walked when embarking on a voyage. The uncertainly of what or who awaited them upon arrival and the uncertainty of crossing the sea.

Which was worse? Only a seaman could best answer that question.

∿

It was his ship to command and it kept him, up to today, from his greatest fear.

The water was crashing all around the ship, as he breathed deeply of the invigorating sea air. His greatest love was the robustness and freedom of a sea voyage. However, more often than not, this was overshadowed by the power of his greatest nightmare. What was that fear that often left him fearfully waking in the night drenched in sweat? It can be summed up in one word: drowning.

"I am afraid of no one and nothing," he often declared arrogantly from the deck, alert to any suspicious stares. "Nothing can

THE SAVAGE RIVER VALLEY

touch me, I say!" And almost always before resuming his smug stance, he would glance down at the swirling water below.

For there was one thing the crew didn't know.

No one knew exactly how afraid of the water he was, for he could not swim and was never taught. And quite conveniently, he neglected to tell anyone just that. It was none of their damn business. No captain in the history of seafaring admitted such a thing, at least as far as he could guess. He wasn't about to change that now and become the first fool to do so. His obsession with the sea—his feet planted firmly on the deck of a ship, his hand on the captain's wheel, and his ship put out to open water—that was what he was meant for! But finding himself submerged in the murky drink of the sea? That would mean sure death by drowning, at least for him.

He, knowing himself to be above the rest, was not ready to die. On the contrary, in a man-filled, smoky tavern within earshot of his crewmen, half in their cups, he would belligerently repeat the same line: "Hear me now, men. I am no wheres ready to die. Dying young is for fools. Too many seas to sail."

He hesitated, knowing they would all be staring at him, so as he would down a tankard of beer in one gulp to prove some illusive point, he always added, "And too many whores to bugger." A show of manhood meant to impress the others? Perhaps. He would reach out for his favorite serving girl, Aniline, a yellow-haired, big bosomed girl who always caught his eye but who refused to dally with him for she knew his reputation with whores. She had no wish to be beaten up. Word had gotten around. So far, she was brilliant in eluding his grasp—but not that night.

This time, for some reason, she let him get close. He grabbed her round the waist as she passed by and pulled her down on top of him. She wriggled in his lap but coquettishly so, rubbing her bottom over his legs. Oh, how he liked this one! He pulled out a gold piece and nimbly dropped the coin down the front of her blouse, but not before he had a good squeeze of flesh. Her eyes grew wide as she stopped moving. She smiled mischievously and their eyes met. Surely, this captain, headed for the new world, was rich!

"There are riches beyond your imagination waiting for you on your next voyage" she whispered in his ear. His eyes shone at the prospect.

Unbeknownst to many, as far as captains go, he was moderately wealthy. And he was good at keeping it a secret. No telling who would be begging him for money: distant family, street urchins and perhaps this whore right here in his lap!

Trading in the New World had been good to him, allowing him to tuck away a small fortune in an Amsterdam counting house. With just one more voyage to add to his savings, his future was secure and it blatantly showed in his confident swagger and exaggerated bravado, especially on deck of his ship. This was to be his last voyage. So, he had to make it count.

This particular ship's name was emblazoned on the side in elaborate gold lettering.

De Swarte Beer. *The Black Bear.*

∿

The New World was a primitive, seemingly untouched land!

The traders at first had little knowledge of what they would see. All they had to judge by were the accounts from Hudson's voyage.

"The land," Hudson had written, "is the finest for cultivation that I have ever in my life set foot upon. It also abounds in trees of every direction. The natives are a very good people, for when they saw that I would not remain, they supposed that I was afraid of their bows and, taking the arrows, they broke them in pieces and threw them into the fire..."

Dutch merchants and traders, with a discerning eye, called it the land of milk and honey. Not that its waterways flowed white or its banks glowed golden as the hue of honey, but rather, in Old Dutch terminology, it was thought that the land was as rich and promising as a dinner table in Amsterdam, laden with jugs of frothy milk and bowls of thick, sweet honey that, when spread on biscuits,

THE SAVAGE RIVER VALLEY

melted on the tongue. The land was for the taking, all for their greedy consumption.

For surely that was considered rich indeed—a land that was as rich and promising as any, a land that abounded with plenty, a land that was meant to be theirs and soon would belong to them. A land they would rename in their honor.

The Dutch claim would, in time, become a new Netherland.

∿∿

The ship had dropped anchor the night before. In front of them was a new continent, a pointed tip of land that bordered two rivers converging into one huge harbor; the island of the Manahattoes, the indigenous Indians. This tribe was not to be discounted or underestimated. Previous contact with the Dutch gave them the reputation as horrendously savage men, quick to engage in aggressive responses to the white man's arrival. As far as the Manahattoes were concerned, they had not asked Manito, the Great Spirit of the Algonquian tribes, to send these magical birds that sailed on water and carried strange men to their shores.

"Ka-to-nah?" they asked each other before making an offering to the fire.

They were suspicious, and rightfully so.

The ship had thirty-two men aboard. Two of them were Captain Hendricks and First Mate Ten Broeck. The rest were hired hands. A crew as uncouth and rough as any hung at the railing, their faces and arms weather-bitten with rough patches of skin, red and chafed by the sea air and a thin sheen of saltwater spray that coated them. Occasionally they moved, stretching their hands to roughly scratch at their backside, groins, or at the scruff on their heads. Lice crawled in their body hair and, although they itched regularly, they neglected to wash. Their hair was stiff and matted. Their clothes, the standard issue of cotton shirts and three-quarter pants, were filthy. Their bodies, long accustomed to the smell, stank of rotted garbage and human feces.

These were the seamen of the day.

When they finished at the shit drop, a hole at the far end of the ship open to the swirling sea below, they pulled up their breeches, tied a knot, and sauntered off. No one wiped his backside. What of the fresh-water, one might ask? Common knowledge was that fresh water at sea was for drinking, not for washing up. Not even for the captain. It was when they came ashore that the men, fully-clothed, would whoop and holler as they took a flying jump into a freshwater stream or creek, rinsing away months of crawling crud, scrubbing their clothes along with their bodies, ridding the salt spray from their skin and hair. Then they set about shaving to rid themselves of the crawling lice, cracking the little buggers between their thumbnail and palm.

Sighting land was welcomed for more than one reason: fresh water to drink, fresh food, and, more so, fresh water with which to bathe.

"Land ho!" a sailor atop the mast yelled two days ago.

As the ship slowly sailed to the mouth of the river that bordered the land to the west, the crew, away from the accusing eye of Hendricks who had lain abed for most of that morning and who, when he was up on the poop deck, did not suffer the company of lazy men under his command, had time to lean over the rail or against the rope riggings and inspect the land. Most of them squinted, for the sea reflected the sun in a ferocious way and, over time, wreaked havoc with their eyesight. They caught an occasional glimpse of the wild men on shore.

"Look ashore. A heathen there!" they would yell to one another. It became a jovial game to see who gave the first shout.

The images of this strange land awaited many of them for the first time. Hills rose up in the background. Vegetation was already thick and the warm weather had only just begun; a subtle hint of scorching heat to come in the months ahead. The land that greeted them was the summer preserve of the Indians, abounding with a cornucopia of deer, turkey, gazelles, and rabbits; all wild and trek-

THE SAVAGE RIVER VALLEY

king across land or standing at the water's edge of a hilly island that someday would be the greatest city on earth, albeit a flat one.

From little springs of fresh water that eventually would be filled in by mankind, incredibly high buildings of steel and might would rise. But at this moment, none of that existed and the observers, both on land and on shore, were innocently unaware of the destiny this land would have in the next four hundred years.

The full sails of the sea were shortened, and only the main mast held full, enough to push the ship into the river's mouth. But even at this, the large white canvas was huge to the unaccustomed eye.

To those on shore, the spectacle that swam on the water was unfathomable and threatening, and it struck fear in their hearts. To those on ship, this land was savage and primitive, uninhabited by any of their kind. *We don't take kindly to people who don't look like us,* they all thought. Dutch were known as tolerant, at least for those in the Old World. Here, in the New World of which they knew little about, it was not the case.

As they stood at the railing, they remarked on the strength of the native savages.

"Look strong as can be," they dubiously warned each other.

A few Indians, sulky and curious, appeared on the shoreline. They were clothed in skins and mantled in feathers of many diverse colors. Often they just stared and poked their heads above the undergrowth to observe the progress of the ship, but once in a while, when the crew least expected, they would jump out into the open and hurtle screams in their direction. One wild man, perhaps a chieftain of sorts, shook his one foot at them. From the deck, it was clear that the man was grotesquely missing a chunk of his foot. But he managed to get around on his own all right, as far as they could see.

Suddenly, for no apparent reason, since the men on ship had settled into a moment of lethargy, the same Indian thrust a spear in their direction, which fell short and landed in the water. The spear floated away, bobbing on the surface, caught up in the river currents. The men on the ship watched it for a moment and then lost interest.

The Indian scowled, turned, and disappeared into the forest.

"Just like Juet said, they are wild savages. He called them Wilden and said not durst to trust them," remarked the oldest of the crew. Jan Jansen, at fifty-two years old, was ancient for a seaman and quite the surly type. This too was to be his last voyage.

"What say you again?" the other crewmen asked.

Jansen continued, not paying their request any mind, as if he were making himself a sworn promise.

"And someday, yep, someday soon, I am going to kill me a savage," he said softly. What he did not tell them was a clear recollection of memories that brought to mind an unforgettable event in the past. The year was 1611. How horribly Juet suffered on that voyage, and how much Jansen hated the Indians. His mind would never forget the charred body of Juet just before he put the rowboat to the river. There was something the Indians wanted from Juet but he refused to meet their demands. No one knew what had occurred and no one ever would. The journal of Juet, written over two voyages and speaking of a magic treasure, ended on that day. Jansen, stuffing it in his shirt, escaped with only one other person on his heels, Hendricks.

To save their skin, the crew concocted the story. Juet had died on ship and was buried at sea. No one outside the crew ever knew different, except the merchant Rensallear. Since the day the journal had brought him a handsome price, Jansen never set eyes on the merchant again, nor spoke of it to anyone. That was part of the bargain. Why would he, an illiterate sailor and man of the sea, want a bunch of papers anyhow? Although there was one thing he had not forgotten: the gleam in the merchant's eye when he saw the papers. What Jansen did not know was that the merchant entertained a second visitor later that day—a visitor that had been tracked down in a tavern, a visitor by the name of Hendricks, a visitor with another treasure, this time not a bunch of papers but one

THE SAVAGE RIVER VALLEY

made of stone. Jansen had all but forgotten about the stone statue. Rensallear, having read the journal, did not.

The Black Bear was anchored well inside the inner harbor now, the same harbor they had fled to after setting Hudson afloat. The huge ocean waves were reduced to small swells. The storm was far away and the sky shone clear blue, with puffs of intermittent white clouds.

The land before them was beautiful, and even these hardened and somewhat jaded seamen could squint and gaggle at what they saw. The next day, with the wind pushing them along, they would sail upriver. There, the native savages were friendly, or friendlier, for some reason—no one could tell why. Not like the frightful heathens they saw here.

The seamen fell silent, Jansen among them, lulled to a peaceful state by the gentle movement of the ship and the safe distance from the shore that provided a haven from flying spears and errant arrows.

∿

From somewhere further up shore, a lone Indian stood in the shadows. He had come in the full throes of spring to this island at the mouth of the river to hunt with the Top-paun tribe of his uncle, son of Sasqua. He was to teach his uncle's sons the arts of weaponry and war.

"This warrior, traveler, and son of my sister will hunt at my side. My own sons will follow his lead," the chief explained to his own people.

The uncle, third son of Sasqua and himself a proud warrior, displayed his battle scars from a brush with the Mohawks in his youth. He was chief of a small village that lay miles to the north, but on this particular day the visiting Indian separated from the hunting party with a hand signal, mysteriously pulled toward the shore.

What he viewed on the river did not surprise him.

"Great Spirit, Manito, the pale faced men return," he said. "Ka-to-nah?" *Why?*

He had seen ships of this size for several years now. In warm weather, they arrived from the great sea to barter and trade; and the village of his youth, far up the river, now had beads and knives to show for their troubles. The women no longer needed the jaw of a deer to scrape the hides, and the men relied less on their handmade blades.

"How easy our job is now with the white man's blade," they all concurred.

But there was something terribly wrong. The people from all the River Tribes sacrificed the skins from animals that need not be hunted. The furs and skins disappeared into these ships and the great sails went away. For this, the Indian was troubled. Manito would be displeased with excess hunting for the sake of trading purposes. Hunting was a way to attain food, deer providing the juiciest haunches. But this Indian was also of a forgiving heart when it came to his village, and for that alone he showed no discontent when they piled the furs on carriers and dragged them to a spot north on the banks of the river. The annual trading session was soon to begin.

At this moment, there was something else that captivated his attention.

He looked closely.

It was the sight of a lone figure standing apart from the others. Even though he looked hard, he could see only a dark outline, for the sun, on course to set over the west bank of the river, shone directly in his eyes. Nonetheless and inexplicably so, his heart swelled suddenly with an indescribable emotion. It was a special moment. It was nothing he could explain and nothing he had felt before. It was as if he had seen a vision, albeit a blurred one, but one that left him feeling roused. For days afterwards, he would not be able to rid himself or shrug off the impression. Understand it

THE SAVAGE RIVER VALLEY

he did not, nor did he try to. For often enough in recent years, he had extrasensory feelings for predicting weather and instinctively knowing directions, and while he didn't know for sure where this particular magic came from, he accepted it as a gift from Manito. Perhaps he was more like his sister than he realized. Little did he know that these were feelings of a free spirit.

There was nothing else to do but one thing.

He knew he had to keep pace with the ship.

As the ship, a veritable floating house, passed up the river that day, the current steady and the water cascading in ripples in the ship's wake, the Indian, bearing a white feather in his scalp lock, set off on a well-traveled path north.

∿

Abruptly, the men on board heard a rattling noise from behind.

Quietly, all eyes turned and watched the cripple stumble to the rail and slowly tip out the foul-smelling feces, urine, rancid puke, and spittle from the captain's bucket into the water below. The bucket was full and heavy. As the cripple, faltering under the weight, lifted the thin handle and inched it over the railing, a little brown line of it dribbled down his tattered sleeves.

He didn't seem to notice; because sometimes when he stood at the rail, he felt like another person.

But the crew did.

They also noticed the oozing sores on his hands, the backs of which he used to wipe the snot from his runny nose. A disgusting human being well despised. A being that made one's stomach turn. They thought him to be perhaps half human, half animal. They weren't quite sure. Could such a creature be born to a human? They were God-fearing men during a violent storm at sea when they called on his mercy to get them safely to land, but now an entreaty to God was the furthest thing from their minds.

They all had the same thought and it reflected on each of their faces as they hardened with anger: hatred felt by the strong for the weak-a hatred for anything or anyone that threatened them, their manhood, and their apparent invincibility.

After all, they, the ablest and fittest, survived a sea voyage, not an unworthy feat in those days. Watching the cripple stumble about made each of them feel doubly stronger, or perhaps for some strange reason weaker.

None of them wanted to fall ill.

That cripple was better off dead, they thought collectively, and who better than they to put this creature out of its misery and theirs as well. They couldn't stomach the sight of him limping on deck, dragging that heavy lame foot. They were sure that its very presence on board had brought on such a stormy crossing. Daresay it was the devil himself following them: the cold, dark, evil devil. So, they made two desperate decisions.

First, better to get rid of it.

And, second, better to get their beer back.

They conspiratorially looked to each other. Perhaps now, after two months at sea under the captain's watchful eye, was their chance.

"Ugly bastard, son of a whore monger, hear me well," Jansen hissed. "The bottom of the sea is where you belong, you spawn of the devil," he continued in a raspy voice, harsh from yelling over the deafening sounds of the sea. "Dead is where you'll be. Next time, I swear, I will kill you."

His upper lip curled in a sneer. The captain, having stayed in his quarters for days now, was nowhere in sight. Jansen felt bold. He then spat a long line of phlegm in the direction of the cripple. It fell a few feet short on top of the coiled ropes and then slid down to the shiny wooden deck.

Again, the cripple didn't seem to notice. He shook out the bucket and what didn't fall into the water was carried off by the wind. Then he stared at the land, feeling an odd tug on his heartstrings.

But the others heard Jansen and nodded at the remark. Jan Jan-

THE SAVAGE RIVER VALLEY

sen was their unofficially elected leader among the crew. He was the toughest and meanest of them all, and his experience far outweighed those of the other seamen. His hands were the strongest. He could pull the anchor rope on his own. His face, known to scare little children in port, was the cruelest. His eyes shone the coldest lifeless color. When he sneered in a twisted line of thin lips, chills ran down the spine of many a stalwart person as they stared at the black gaping hole where instead of teeth were tiny rotted stumps.

Nearby stood a sailor who did not care to join in as the crew hunched together.

Kurtjie Harmensen whistled softly under his breath, sliding a Dutch sailors knot up and down a short coil of rope; all the while staring darkly at the shore. If he had to use the rope on Jansen, he certainly would, yanking the knot against the bump in his throat and squeezing from behind. He had nothing against the cripple but for the sake of pure survival, namely his own, he needed to go along with the rest of the crew. Or at least appear to. Alienation on a ship meant certain death. And Harmensen had not forgotten the other night. So, he ignored Jansen for now and turned his back on the cripple. No one need connect the two. All he had to do was keep his mouth shut and make sure the cripple was not killed.

Jansen hated the very sight of the cripple. But no one knew exactly why. No one was about to ask Jansen for explanations. They just followed his lead in mute but ignorant conspiracy.

One thing they all knew: there was no room on board for such a despicable creature as that.

The cripple bore no resemblance to any of the other men on the ship. His crooked form seemed to jerk its way across the deck in spasmodic movement, while the other men stood straight and walked on a rolling ship with little difficulty.

"What is he good for?" the men repeated day in and day out.

His principle duty was to clean the captain's quarters, a sparse beamed room toward the back of the ship, located just under the poop deck. The low-ceiling room was dark and close, containing a crude built-in bunk on one side and a table and two chairs on the other. Wick lamps continually swung from the ceiling with the motion of the sea. It was also the cripple's job to keep his eye on the lanterns, making sure they spilled no hot wax. One mistake and it could mean the end of a ship and its crew.

A rather large trunk, placed at the foot of the captain's bed and bound by leather straps, held his clothing. Still another, closer to the far wall, held his rolled up maps.

A narrow row of double-framed windows lined the back wall. The glass was thick and wavy in texture, but when you looked out at the sea, in a blue-green framework, instead of seeing where you were going, you only saw where you had just been.

∿

The cripple knew what was at stake.

But he had nothing to lose. Not even his life was important, for if he died on this journey, he would have already succeeded partly in what he had set out to do.

"Whatever happens, my life will be better," he repeated to himself.

He had been signed on as part of the crew by Hendricks himself. There was no disputing that fact, since not a single soul came on board without the captain's approval.

That morning in Amsterdam, all activity on ship, minutes from departing, came to a complete halt as the men looked up in stultified disbelief and then in disgust as this repulsive and shapeless, bent over, hunchbacked monster stepped aboard at the last moment, dragging one lame foot and a heavy bundle behind him as he advanced in jerky movements up the plank. Every step looked painful and more than once he tripped over his deformed foot. Beneath a mass of bushy hair, his eyes shifted right, and then roamed left. He looked at no one in particular yet seemed to know exactly where to go.

THE SAVAGE RIVER VALLEY

He, at this pivotal moment, was headed for the captain's quarters.

It was so quiet on deck that no one would have believed preparations for sailing were underway. All motion had ceased, all conversation had too.

A growl started to erupt from the crew, who bent over their work, now straightened. Their looks turned ugly. Jan Jansen, closest to the gangplank, hunched his shoulders and menacingly raising his clenched fists waist-high stepped closer, the others creeping up behind him.

Hendricks, standing on the poop deck at the back of the boat, yelled out an order. He had been sullenly waiting for this moment. Out of the corner of his eye, he had bitterly watched the cripple hobble down the alley and turn on to the dock and slowly advance to the plank.

So, his nightmare was true then. He had not imagined it at all. What a damn fool he had been!

"When this voyage is over, I'm going kill him with my bare hands," he angrily swore to himself, gritting his teeth. If the thought were any consolation, he didn't show it.

He took a deep breath. This would be the first of undoubtedly many challenging moments on this journey. But if there was ever a man to handle it, that would be him. Now that idea certainly did much to bolster his usual arrogant self.

He breathed in deeply, puffing out his chest, knowing what the crew's reaction to be.

He knew the simpleminded crew, unaware of the terrible string of events that unfolded in the previous days, would react viciously to what would be viewed as a curse on the ship, so he headed them off. Captain Hendricks was ready. No one, especially a cripple, would get the better of him. He ran a tight ship, with a near stranglehold on each man's neck. They certainly did fear him, more than the dreaded loose bowels and the painful death that it brought. It was necessary to instill fear or, at some point in time, face the same fate as Hudson. Hudson had been a blind fool!

But a fool he was not.

He sharply slapped the captain's eyeglass against his thigh.

"All hands make way," he bellowed abruptly. "Anchor up."

Hendricks held his breath, his eyes roving over the crowd below, ready for a fight. Jansen looked up, his face reddening.

"Back away!" the captain growled down to the men. "Now," he screamed, his voice booming out over the entire ship. Behind the captain, his first mate stood ready with a pistol nestled in the crook of his arm. His job was to follow the captain's order. If the captain said shoot, then he would.

Jansen slowly backed away.

The moment passed.

Casting angry looks, the crew went back to what they were doing. They stood in line, each man pulling heavily on the same rope, heckling the man in front to pull harder.

The ship began to move, drifting away from its mooring. Its anchor lifted up from the muddy bottom of the canal, the wet ropes tossed aboard, then piled in dripping coils. The anchor pulled flush to the deck.

The captain watched it all with narrowed eyes, ready for any man who dared to counter his orders. Now that the cripple was aboard, he wondered how quietly and quickly they could get away.

Suddenly he heard it. A shout!

Damnation!

Busy and angry, the crew was oblivious to a faint cry below, coming from the wharf.

A man on the dock was fitfully trying to get their attention. Hendricks spotted him right away. He stared only for a moment and then, purposefully, looked the other way.

So intent were they on raising the sails that many of them did not notice the shouting drifting over the docks and the wild flailing of hands. A robust man, older and well dressed, had appeared. He stood on the wooden planks with feet planted widely apart to support his wide girth. He shook his fist angrily in the air above his

THE SAVAGE RIVER VALLEY

head. His face, round and normally a ruddy color, was now seething purple from rage, as if his neck had expanded beyond the limits of his tight, ruffled collar and was cutting off his flow of air. His nose, bulbous and huge, was a sign of a big drinker.

The ship floated away. There was no stopping it now.

No one paid him attention, and he grew angrier.

The crew, Hendricks noticed, eventually caught sight of him, but could not catch his words above the cry of seagulls and the hoisting of the sails; and since the captain was ignoring him, they would too. It was none of their business—they weren't in charge.

"Better for them, the poor bastards," Hendricks thought. "Otherwise, I'd have to kill the whole lot of them."

Amused, he contemplated the thought.

The ship had continued to inch away from the docks until the man, still yelling and now stamping his foot in anger, was almost too far away to see. By that time, the crew had forgotten about him and more so had forgotten about the cripple. Out of sight, out of mind; for they were busy putting out to sea.

Moments passed, then minutes, then an hour.

Sails flapped, wood creaked, and the sound of ocean winds began to whistle around the ship. Loud voices were cut off by the jarring wind in their faces and the roaring in their ears. Seagulls flew overhead. The sun was rising from the east and seemed to light a golden path ahead of the ship that led to the water's edge on the western horizon. Follow the golden path, it seemed to say, as far as the eye can see.

Surely a lucky sign that the gods were with them! And such a golden color indeed!

They were leaving the coast behind for the open sea—no man's land where only the ruthless or the lucky survive.

The voyage had begun.

The ship began to dip and rise with each swell.

The men, feeling the sharp spring air, were occupied with different tasks. No one had time nor cared to watch the coastline grow smaller and smaller.

Not exactly right. There was only one, but nevertheless one, who watched from a secluded spot under the stairs that led to the highest deck where the captain could be overheard shouting his orders, overseeing the men scurrying on board and climbing the masts. He was well hidden from a casual eye, but still the wind managed to reach him and ruffled his coarse hair. No one could see him stooping slightly in this secluded little alcove normally reserved for ropes, barrels, or heaped stacks of wooden crates.

The cripple.

He stood there a long time, in the shadows, bent over, gray eyes staring between the cracks, until the docks of Amsterdam were only part of a small city of gabled houses on the distant horizon. And only then, feeling slightly triumphant, did a smile flicker over his face, and then it quickly was gone.

"Suffer, Killian," he thought bitterly yet smugly. "Suffer and know now what it means to have the most precious thing to you taken away."

∿

The night was not over.

First, there was the matter of Harmensen.

He had stood before the captain and tried to explain what he saw. No, that was not quite true. It was what he heard that bothered him the most. It was imperative he tell the captain. Perhaps he would win some token of appreciation and it might come in handy later on back in port or during a sticky moment on this voyage.

Harmensen had been on deck earlier this evening when he saw the cripple emptying his bucket and pausing at the rail to look out over the harbor and to stare at the land. For the cripple, it was a fascinating prospect, but for Jansen, it was the prime opportunity. The hateful Jansen, ever watchful for a chance to attack the cripple, crept silently up on him and raised a huge rod of wood. With all his might and a heartfelt grunt, he sent it crashing down on the

THE SAVAGE RIVER VALLEY

misshapen hump—a bull's-eye! By all accounts, the cripple should have had a broken back from the powerful blow, but instead he fell limply to the deck, the wind brutally knocked out of his chest.

Stunned, the cripple, wretched in life, was unable to breathe for several seconds after the attack.

Harmensen at once hurried closer, as Jansen stepped back.

"Christ, you killed him!" he gasped, watching Jansen reeling backwards. He looked down in horror. Harmensen expected to see a flowing pool of dark blood, but alas, the cripple was not dead! He was sucking in gulps of air. What astonished Harmensen more were the sounds emitting from the cripple as he lay there stunned, moaning and trying to rise. Jansen, dim-witted as he was, never caught on as he stumbled to recover his balance.

But Harmensen was sure of it and now he was off to tell the captain.

As he stood before Hendricks, he caught sight of the cripple in the shadows of the cabin's back wall. The night was pitch black. Not one single star shone in the sky, no moonlight shone through the heavy leaded windows, and the captain's quarters were poorly lit. So, one could say, it was close to a miracle he saw him there, flattened against the wall.

The cripple was prepared, knowing what Harmensen was about to say.

The captain, feeling dizzy with any sudden movement, looked annoyed. He sat in his chair. He hadn't even time to put his boots on; so insistent this sailor had been to see him.

"Get on with the story and be done with it," he mumbled impatiently, feeling the familiar wave of nausea come over him.

Harmensen stuttered. The captain made him nervous. It wasn't often he had the personal attention of so important a man.

"I s. .s. .saw … it … it all. I ju. .ju … just happened to be there. It was Jansen, sir, Jansen who did it," he blurted out, stumbling over his hoarse words.

"Did what?" the captain, now clearly angry, shot back, lifting his eyes to stare the man in the face.

PAMELA DE LEON

"Jansen saw the cripple on d..d ... deck with his ... I mean ... your bucket, sir."

"What of it?" he snarled impatiently, slapping his hand on the table. "God, man, what of it? You spend my time like it was yours!"

"He ... he tried to kill him," Harmensen carried on. He watched the captain's face, angered by his presence, a bothersome stuttering crewman, and more so by any stories that involved the foul smelling cripple. As a pot of soup begins to bubble over heat, so did the captain's anger over Harmensen's words.

His looks turned bitter.

"And?" the captain said in a low voice, secretly hoping to hear that Jansen had succeeded. After all, the man owed him one for saving his rotten life last voyage.

"Ah ..." A bewildered Harmensen stared into the darkness behind the captain, a little unsure of how to proceed. What if he were wrong? What if what he had heard was not what he thought? He caught the glaring eye of the cripple and stopped speaking. The captain, fixated on the man before him, never turned to look behind him.

Holding up one hand, the cripple opened his fingers, and there, sitting in his palm, were sparkling diamonds of not small proportions. They glittered, they glowed, and they grabbed at Harmensen's heart! The cripple looked at Harmensen and ran his other hand over his mouth, as if to say "Shut your mouth and this is yours."

Harmensen gasped, obviously confused.

He lowered his eyes rather quickly and clamped his mouth shut. What did this mean? Was this a ruse? Was this the devil beckoning to him, enticing him to a sparkling future? He had never seen such riches in his entire life! He came from poor, Dutch stock. As a youth with no great prospects, for he had no head for business, the future spent at sea offered him an escape from working the land and reeking of cow dung. Would the captain or spoils of a plundering voyage ever offer him as much? All for keeping his mouth shut?

224

THE SAVAGE RIVER VALLEY

"And?" the captain repeated, this time in a tone that was deadly.

"Nothing," Harmensen, staring at the floor, whispered back.

Obviously he was lying.

Hendricks pushed back his chair savagely. The captain, not knowing what had transpired behind his back, rose unsteadily to his feet and pointed his hand to the door.

Harmensen stumbled back in fright.

"Get out, you low-life bitch's cur, get out and don't bother me again, you old piss in the pants woman! I'll have you lashed for this!" he yelled.

Behind his back, the cripple smiled wickedly.

∿

Then there was the matter of the journal.

The cripple hovered in a little alcove off the captain's quarter, a sack stuffed with straw served as its bed, a wooden crate being the only other object able to fit in the small area. It was a crawl space, more like a low-lying closet, which could be closed off with a wooden slat and a latch that hung on rusty hinges, but it did not afford enough space to do more than crawl in and stretch out. The crate held an assortment of old clothes, rags to be more exact, a jumble of oddly sized men's clothing that were tied in a bundle, from which the cripple would take an assortment and dress himself each dawn, piling on the layers. But no amount of layers hid the protruding bump on its back. The cripple seemed to be weighed down by its sheer size. The face of the cripple was partly concealed by a mass of gray, coarse hair that hung down over his brow, his crown to his ears covered by another rag tied at the back of his head. The head of this freak of nature appeared to be abnormally huge, but not as huge as the obscene hump on his back.

Hendricks never looked directly at him, as the ugly misfit crawled out of his hole each day. The smell was bad enough, looking at him only would add to the pain. And the cripple, willingly enough, did likewise, saying not a word, grabbing the bucket, and making off for the fresh air of the decks above. When no one was about, the cripple would hide out under the stairs, staring out over the wide expanse of ocean, feeling the freedom of the open sea for the first time in his life, feeling his heart thump wildly with exhilaration, but most often than not, he spent his days closed away in the little closet area feeling every wave of the sea as it tossed the ship to and fro toward the new land. During the wild storm from hell, when the ship seemed to go completely over, the cripple felt he would die there in that little hovel with the sounds of the captain cursing, wood wrenching against wood, wood straining against rope and riggings, and wood washed over by the sea. He curled up in a ball and said a prayer.

"God," he whispered, "I do not want to die."

He was certain he would though, that long night. By the grace of God he and the other seamen lived to see the light of day. When he crawled out of his closet the next morning, amazed but grateful to be alive, he considered the next step to be the most important of his life: make it to land alive.

∿

When on deck, for the most part, he kept his head lowered, downcast eyes glued to the floorboards. Hardly any of the men noticed his features. It was nothing they could describe afterwards. And being the close-knit group they were, no one dared separate from the group to seek the cripple. Most of them avoided him like the plague. When they spotted him limping toward them, they moved off, deliberately turning their heads away for it could be poisonous to be so close to the cripple. They were a superstitious bunch.

There was an awful thing about the cripple that evoked nothing short of disgust from the men.

There was a huge mass of oozing red sores breaking out on his

THE SAVAGE RIVER VALLEY

hands. The crusty and swollen sores made him itch and scratch constantly, but that was not the worst of it.

Above all else, it was his smell.

The god-awful smell resembled a filthy privy. But somehow, Hendricks did not object to having a servant such the likes as no one had ever seen on a ship or, even more so, one quartered inside the captain's chamber. The rest were baffled and openly resentful of such an ugly companion on a vessel that deserved better. But, as some smirked and viciously joked beneath decks, maybe the captain had an added interest—an interest that included bedding cripples along with his whores—or perhaps it was a poor relative of his that he wished to humiliate and eventually get rid of with no objections. Whatever the case, the resentment grew.

No one knew for sure why the cripple was on board, and the captain was not a man to mix company with his crew. They eyed him behind his back, but to his face they saluted, they cowed, they obeyed, they knelt; they did whatever they had to do, for Hendricks was more savage than all captains need be. He was a figure feared by the men serving beneath him, including his first mate. No one stepped in his way or spoke contrary to his orders or even dared to raise an objection.

"You'll do as I say," he snarled, threatening each of them in turn. He'd just as soon lift a pistol and shoot a man between the eyes than lose one guilder in business or have any crew disobey him.

So how did it come about that such a vicious captain hire such an ugly cabin boy?

The proposition the cripple had made to him was unlike any he expected to be offered.

One evening, he sat in an Amsterdam tavern alone, a habitual land spot for him, lifting his head in an angry, blurry-eyed silence to note the appearance of this monster; only then to hear a few raspy words uttered by the cripple, shudder uncontrollably, and then reply in his drunkenness, "You're hired."

The cripple shuffled in glee and almost tipped himself over, straightened, and then smiled a crooked grin. For a split second, the captain, taken aback, thought he caught sight of something quite different, almost a luster in the eyes, a spark of handsome youth. He blinked and then looked again, peering closely in the muted light at the cripple. He saw the blackened teeth, the grimy skin, and the dirty clothes. He had had too much to drink, he thought as he watched Aniline lead the cripple away, their heads bent together. *No, it couldn't be,* he chided himself and shook his head. *A whore and a cripple? I must be crazy!*

But why did he have that uneasy and strange feeling that the two of them were in cahoots?

After that night, Captain Hendricks never looked directly into the cripple's face again. He had other plans for the cripple, once they reached the New World, but for now he didn't waste his time. Right now, he was only a nuisance, an ugly and foul smelling nuisance, who could do him no harm away from the Council of Amsterdam. The Council of Nineteen. He would deal with them later.

In the meantime, why not let the cripple clean his shit bucket?

After all, he smelled like one.

But go near him? Nay, not a chance. This got him to thinking about lowering himself over the bucket and taking a shit himself. He felt his stomach tighten with sharp pains and the urge to push.

Hendricks bent over and forced out some fetid gas, then spit viciously onto the floor, and then rubbed it with his boot.

∿

The hump on his back ached.

The blow had been severe and his skin had been badly bruised, but the great protrusion had miraculously saved his life. His right leg, unused to dragging so much weight, cramped with shooting pains that made him wince. He gently massaged his thigh and calf in circular motions and thought ruefully of his journey with this misbegotten group of rough and illiterate men. But here at least he

THE SAVAGE RIVER VALLEY

was alone, squashed into his little resting place, a miserable space he could call his own on the ship and defend. A tiny space where, for once, he didn't have to hide or pretend to be other than what he was. Where he could take a deep breath and stop the delayed shaking from the near deadly encounter with Jansen and the close call with Harmensen.

He needed to stay away from them.

It never failed to amaze him how stupid and dull-witted most men were. None of them elicited his admiration. Not even Hendricks. For all his knowledge of the sea, he was a stupid man.

The captain, tossing and turning for several hours, was finally asleep, having scoffed at Harmensen's visit to his cabin.

"There'll be no more low-life in my quarters," he yelled after the door had closed.

The sails were lowered and the ship stood anchored at the mouth of the river in the inner harbor for the night. By dawn, they would sail up river, passing miles of bays, inlets, and estuaries, wooded banks, swampy marshes with cattails that swayed in the wind, steep cliffs, and mountains that appeared to rise straight up out of the river.

It was a primitive land indeed.

But all of this the cripple had yet to behold.

Sailing up the river was not a certain prospect in a set amount of time. It all depended on the flow of air that filled the sails. If God sent a brisk wind the ship could reach the first trading post Hendricks had established at Rondout-three rough huts built close to the mouth of the Esopus Creek, where the villages of Ramco's tribes were situated. The Indians translated River to Sepu and Small to Es-all this according to a map from a voyage of 1614.

Now it was four years later.

They would sail even further north up river, the closest thing to headquarters in the New World. There, among the shadows of the trees, the Indians would be watching for the ship or would arrive soon after, having brought their valuable pelts from afar to trade with the white men. The Indians had long ago learned the rules of engagement: skins that abounded in the New World for goods delivered from the Old World. A simple exchange that took place just on shore that left both sides temporarily pleased.

"And there, on the banks of this river, finally, this journey will end. My nightmare will be over at last," the cripple said out loud. He was sure the captain could not hear him, and it was the only chance he had to speak. But the sound of his voice did not totally reassure him. On second thought, perhaps his nightmare was just beginning, if the future was to be judged by what had happened earlier.

Tonight had been dangerous.

The secret he had successfully harbored for months had almost been detected. Thanks be to God the ship had reached near proximity to land. The cripple had secreted away a small stub of a candle from the captain's table, and now, lit from the lantern and with the ship in calm water, it shed a tiny glow of steady light.

It was time.

He pulled the journal, more like a sheath of worn papers, from his bedding of straw, carelessly flicking off bedbugs as they crawled out of the dirty hay. It was the first time he had the chance to inspect these faded papers that held a key to the mystery since the last night at the merchant's house.

It was then that he noticed his hands. The sores were beginning to heal. He knew exactly what to do. Pulling some dried leaves, what little were left from his bundle, he rubbed them over the back of his hands and all over his chest and neck. In a matter of hours, the allergic reaction would kick in, as it did at the start of the voyage. It was the same crushed up heap of leaves the cripple slipped in the captain's drink that made him ill. Being in close proximity to the captain made it necessary to keep his mind on things other than the cripple. And besides, it was easy to slip the leaves in his drinks. The captain never noticed.

Aniline, bless her heart, knew her stuff. Her secret knowledge

THE SAVAGE RIVER VALLEY

of plants and their magical qualities had become a personal vendetta for making men suffer if they mistreated her. Gladly, she had passed it along to the cripple.

By morning, he said to himself, *the sores will bloom once again, and the snot will run heavy! Then,* he assured himself, *no one will look twice at the delicate hands with long fingers or the grimy face with high cheekbones and aquiline nose.*

He took up the sheath of papers and began to read.

This day the people of the countrey came aboord of us, seeming very glad of our coming, and brought greene tobacco, and gave us all of it for knives and beads. They go in deere skins loose, well-dressed. They have yellow copper. They desire cloathes and are very civil.

And here the unedited journal of Juet, harboring secrets of deadly mayhem, rested in the cripple's hands, filled with mystery and terror, the complete journal that only a handful had ever seen before. The journal was just one of the precious things the cripple had spirited away from the house of the merchant. But now an ocean separated them, and the cripple, for the first time in years, was free of the evil-hearted merchant and his long-reaching grasp.

The boat rocked back and forth in a gentle manner from the harbor swells. It was almost comforting. The cripple no longer noticed the movement as anything uncommon or unnatural.

Absorbed in the papers, he continued to read. The candle had almost burned out.

But hee which wee had taken, got up and lept over-boord...

The rest of the page was empty, that particular journal entry never completed.

The cripple turned to the next page.

The next entry read:

Only one was remaining on shipe... he wanted to betray us, but we perceived his intent and we cut off his tooes. He yelped like a dogg in heat. That night, we raised our waste boords for defense of our men. So we rode all night, having good regard to our watch.

The night came on and they came in great numbers in canoes, it began to Rayne, so hard that they could not find the ship. We were able to steale away with one of them againe. Hendricks dressed hem in rede coats. Funnie to behold a savage in rede. The next day we made a pact. One secreted himself on board. He was fearsome with a great longe scar running across his chest. We had the deal. I, Hendricks and Jansen would go ashore. The Captain never knew.

As the cripple read on, he knew that one of the captives would show Juet the treasure, the other would be guarded. When the treasure was safe on board, the two would be let free.

So, it was Juet or one of his men, possibly Hendricks himself who toyed with the idea and then stole the statue, the cripple thought. *And Hudson, with his worldly head in the clouds, was oblivious to it all. A most loving people were about to be betrayed.* The journal continued.

The returne downriver was not without bloode. We came under attak the very next daye. Killed several savages, the encounter was bloodie. Muskets saved our lives. Three more shots with our cannon finished our encounters. The ship turned on course to home.

And there the journal ended.

So the exploration did not go as well as some would have thought or wanted to believe.

Now he understood perfectly well why some of the native sav-

THE SAVAGE RIVER VALLEY

ages, the wild men as rumor had it, who screamed from the tree cover and threw spears, hated the big ships that brought the white man to their shores.

The great bird that sailed over the waters had come uninvited and trespassed on their lands.

They were victims, just as the cripple had been back in Amsterdam. Only these Indians had no idea of what was yet to come—a tidal wave of humanity that, in time, would nearly wipe out their nation of peoples.

From inside the cabin, he heard the captain mumble in his sleep, then cough. The cripple listened carefully but heard no more. *Too bad, he didn't choke to death on his spittle,* the cripple thought. Hendricks was more of a monster than the cripple.

The flickering candle went out, submerging him in darkness.

∿

The ship sailed on a slow course for almost three weeks, following the meanderings of the river, sometimes hitting shoals with low tide and sitting adrift on a sand bar at an awkward angle. Then the flood came creeping up along the hull and the ship, righting itself, floated free.

The cripple, shielding himself from the others with ropes and piles of crates, watched from the little alcove with undiminished delight. He bent to peek to the left and then to the right. It was even better than he had thought! He had arrived to a wild and primitive paradise and if he were to die here on the very banks of this river, then he would have gone to a much sweeter place than he came from.

But he had no deliberate intentions of dying, if he could help it. There was still much to do and, right now, to see.

Every turn brought a new vista.

Up from the river's mouth towered the steepest line of cliffs—huge gray faces of bare rock. Beyond that point, the river stretched a mile wide and then narrowed. The ship followed a zigzag pattern as each turn of the river seemed to be blocked by a mountain lying directly in its path. But the river cleverly snaked around those lofty mounds and thus so did the ship.

It was slow but sure going.

Each day was fair weather, and the breeze held. Luck seemed to be on their side.

The captain, refreshed and feeling much the better, stood at the wheel for hours, at times roughly barking out orders, his voice carrying miles over the water. Then he would be silent as the river gave way to a new stretch.

The crew stayed busy, dragging in nets of struggling fish—sturgeon up to nine-feet long, herring, and bass to add to their depleted food supply. Occasionally, at twilight or early dawn, they took the rowboat in search of fresh water. Not once on the way up river did they encounter any wild men. However, it was halfway up the river when they discovered swift currents of fresh water. The salt of the sea was no longer. It was at that point that all the men went overboard into the shallows to bathe. All except the cripple, who stayed hidden from view.

He could hear their shouts and laughter and coarse talk. He was alone but not lonely.

"In time, it will be my turn. In time," he promised himself, scratching at his scalp.

The beginning of the second week on the river dawned gray and misty. There was a bit of a chill in the air.

There had been a storm overnight. Then it cleared. As the clouds lifted off the river, the cripple, seldom leaving his spot, gasped in wonder. Behold! For there, miles to the west off the starboard side of the ship, rose a jagged line of blue hued mountains, the Onteora. Mesmerized, he stared in awe for a long time as the ship inched its way upriver.

Heaven, he thought.

THE SAVAGE RIVER VALLEY

∿

When the ship docked in fairly shallow waters, it had arrived to the designated trading post discovered by Hendricks in 1611. The meeting place for an exchange was located directly in front of an island just off shore, a place they would name three years later, by summer's end of 1614, Fort Nassau. On this remote but accessible spot, the men had, the year before, built a tiny lodge made of crudely cut logs, stone, and mud chinking.

"Dig up the field stones. Only thing they are good for," ordered Hendricks.

The only source of heat was a drafty stone fireplace that never worked well and allowed more of the heat to escape beyond the crude walls than stay inside. That year, Hendricks had been determined to leave behind some men to man the lodging full time, all year round. Giving no thoughts to a harsh winter and the desolate isolation of the site, he made up his mind. Think of the veritable piles of fur pelts they would accumulate! Then, when summer arrived and so did the ship, the trading was already an accomplished feat. The ship would be immediately loaded and less time spent on the river, the haggling of trade taking place months before.

It came down to one thing—money. But money could not have stopped the throes of winter and the ice floes that surged down the river and continually flooded the little hut on Castle Island.

For centuries, the island, carved by the flow of the river, had belonged to nature. Not to man.

Winter excluded any hopes of a continuous occupation, at least for several years to come.

Be it as it may, the tiny dilapidated hut on the island was their only trading post in that part of the New World, a place where the Mohawks and the Mohicans came to barter with the Dutch captains. A place where the likes of beaver, mink, fox, bear, and otter furs by the hundreds were traded for all the goods the Indians thought unique and craved as desirable, especially a fiery liquid named rum. One might think it strange indeed, but there was no word in the Mohican language for drunkenness, for they had never known of such a thing. In their world of living close to nature, tobacco smoked in a pipe was the only pleasurable habit they knew. But this liquid, once swallowed or gulped or swigged, whatever the case may be, left them stunned and staggering on their feet. It forced their squaws to back off in fear and introduced a whole new element of social dysfunction into their society.

Rum was a liquid that drove them near crazy and wanting for more.

All worlds, New and Old—Mohican, Mohawk, and Dutch— converged on this spot in this pivotal month of June. The year was 1618.

$$\sim\!\!\sim$$

It was the start of summer. The hot sticky weather had yet to begin. Each day dawned clear with a little less humidity than in the months to come.

All the tribes north and south were in a state of determined business, almost bordering on frenzy. There were pelts to gather and bundle, and eventually transport to the coastal flat area where they knew the ship or ships, as being the case, would arrive. They traveled in bands of men and several women, leaving, for the most part, the children behind; carrying, dragging, and toting great heaps of fur. And there was plenty more where that came from. It was rough going, and a long journey for most, but over the course of the summer, they would make the trip back to their villages several times, only to return to their temporary camp with even more furs. Manito had been generous. Trapping had far surpassed the previous years! The past winter had yielded a prodigious crop of pelts. Indian men made trip after trip out into the snow-laden countryside and each time returned with armfuls of trapped animal skins.

Mohican and Mohawk alike, though still enemies but bound by a truce for trading with the Dutch, shared in the anticipation,

THE SAVAGE RIVER VALLEY

though from different villages and lands. For once, the Mohawks, not that the Mohicans were happy about it, were allowed to cross their lands to reach the river.

Far north, an elder Mohawk warrior strode ahead of his band. He carried nothing except his weapons. Always ready to confront the dangers of the woods, he left the burden of transporting the furs to others. Mahwah was his name, and his faithful and obedient wife trotted along behind, followed by their son and other young warriors. His thoughts were grim, as they were each year when they left their village and their lands behind in order to trade with the white-skinned men.

Would they all return safely?

It made him uneasy to travel with his family. He preferred to travel alone.

Once they reached the clearing at the river, he would leave his wife behind.

∾

The ship anchored the night before and floated in fairly deep water some five hundred feet off shore, easily reached by a rowboat. Twelve regular sized men could fit in that little boat. But no one would go ashore that night. They slept fitfully, tossing and turning in hammocks strung all throughout the ship, some even on deck under the blazing stars in the night sky. Each not sure what the next day, much less the next few months, would bring, as each year was different from the past.

This land was wild and untamed.

Ten Broeck heard the men questioning one another late that night. "Oh God, be you the life and light of this wondrous place?" Their reliance on faith, like that of many men in similar situations, arose heartily when scared.

Jansen was disgusted with the talk.

"When night overshadows the starry gloom of dark, when ye all shall wake in the morning," he mocked. "Then see for yourselves, you weak kneed bastards, if it be the land of God or not. Now shut your mouths and sleep," he growled.

Ten Broeck made no comment. He was a quiet man, not one to open his mouth to boast and cause others to cast an evil eye his way. He, therefore, came to a simple conclusion. No one could make any assumptions of what would happen.

The next morning came. It was already heating up. It was six o'clock and the sun rose.

The captain stood on deck, sweeping the shore with his eyeglass, the sun, having risen in the east, still at his back giving him a fair view. His dress fitted the occasion; a doublet made of purple silk and black velvet covered his broad chest with pantaloons, belted a little tighter than usual since he lost some weight, that came down to the knee and tucked into tall boots. His plumed hat was left in his quarters. It was too hot for that.

The crew had assembled on deck, each straining to see the first savage emerge from the tree line. So far, there was no sight of them. All was quiet on land, though several sailors, if they listened closely, felt more than heard slight whispering coming to them over the water. Not to appear skittish to the next man, each kept their thoughts to themselves, but more than one had the sudden urge to urinate.

The captain thought long and hard. It was time for him and his men to move to shore before the Indians arrived. He meant to have first advantage. Let them come to him.

He gave the orders.

"We'll be trading into the afternoon each morning." His voice, arrogant and confident, boomed over the deck. "The ship will be loaded twice a day, afternoon and evening, until the hold is full. Then and only then do we set sail." Hendricks gruffly snapped out instructions to all the men gathered before him. "Each one of you men is to do more than your own share of work."

He grimly eyed the assembled group of men before him. Yea, they were a sight to see, but there was work to be done and riches

THE SAVAGE RIVER VALLEY

to be made and this was the crew he had to get it all accomplished. He briefly wondered which ones he and his first mate would have to kill later on when he made his case to them on the return voyage. It didn't matter because he was prepared to do every last one of them in, if necessary. But that would come on a distant day. For now, there were other matters at hand.

He had lowered his eyeglass before speaking and now, satisfied at his own orders, he scanned the shoreline with his naked eye. He saw nothing close or far to disturb him. What lay before him was a primitive forest in tangled disarray.

He cleared his throat, ready to speak again.

The seamen listened.

Some had already been with him on previous voyages to the New World. Others were told what to expect. All of them, hearing the orders of the captain, eyed the shoreline, waiting and watching. After sleeping for a few hours, they had spent half the late night hours bringing up barrels of trading goods from the hold. Rounded wooded barrels filled with beads, clothes, and knives. The heavy barrels lined the deck, all containing mere trinkets in the estimation of the Dutch, but valuable in the eyes of the Indian. The last barrels, the ones filled with Rum, would be saved until last. The power of the strong trader must be guarded until the appropriate time. The rum would bring forth the best pelts saved for last.

For the Dutch, too, had picked up on the ways of the Indians. If you were an Indian trader, or an Indian giver as the Dutch saw it, you sometimes asked for the goods back and saved them to be traded again.

The captain divvied up the duties: who would stand guard, who would haul in the goods, and who would take them below deck. Some were expected to stay on shore once the captain got there, hunting fresh meat and taking on fresh water, but always in the light of day. For who knew what lurked in the forest at night?

Long days of heavy labor awaited the men. After trading with the Indians, they bore heavy piles of skins to the rowboat, stacked them, and then rowed them to the ship, dragging them up by rope and pulley and packing them away. The hold, capable of holding hundreds of barrels, must be dry so as not to wet the furs and bring on the dreaded rot. The Dutch would dock here for more than two months. In that time, business must be completed and they must be on their way back down the river and across the ocean before winter set in and left them stranded in a primitive world, cut off from life on land as they knew it.

When winter came on, this river froze solid and any ship would come to a halt until spring thaw.

Just the thought of it spurred him to action. While he thought nothing of leaving men behind to face the uncertainties and cruelties of a harsh winter, he himself wanted no part of it.

Hendricks pointed to three men.

"You there, and you and you, will be the first crew ashore," he ordered. Jansen was among them. He openly smirked, clearly pleased to have been chosen to go with the captain. It meant the captain favored him. And it gave him a chance to size up the savages and, more importantly, get a glimpse of their women, who remained hesitantly in the background, dragging hefty bundles of skins through the forest into the clearing while their men bartered with grunts and hand signals. Why not go for a little piece of their womanly goods? That was a mighty token that would satisfy his ever-hungry need for the female flesh.

He considered it par for the course on voyages, where plundering was commonplace. It always satisfied him on previous voyages. He thought of last year above the inner harbor, when going ashore during a trading session with the Manahattoes, he had managed to slip away and get hold of one of the black-haired savages in the woods. She squirmed but never screamed. Her silence was a little unsettling, but God, he could still remember her brown breasts and how they shown in the sun! Drove him into a cruel frenzy it did, so used to white skin he was. Unluckily, on the way back to the ship, there was a slight scuffle with what must have been her Indian mate

THE SAVAGE RIVER VALLEY

whom he surprised on the trail. Too bad Jansen hadn't time to kill him. He had barely begun to fight with the savage. He managed to get in two mighty sweeps of the blade, the first missed and the second came into contact low to the ground, when Hendricks came crashing through the brush and fired his gun. The woman, come to stand behind the scuffling men, was dead, shot straight into the heart. Between the two of them, they overcame the savage, put him unconscious to the ground, and fled to the ship. The captain had never spoken of the incident again and did not stop to trade this time around. The Indians might be primitive, but the Dutch had learned there was one thing they did not do: forget.

That Indian had probably lived and, to this day, would have Jansen's features etched in his mind.

Now it had been too long, this voyage. Whenever in a strange new land, he always, by force, took their women in some quiet spot. A sort of conqueror's habit, his faulty logic told him. What was the sense of ever asking, when he could always take what he wanted? It was the struggle that excited him. Gloating with evil thoughts, he wondered what little juicy tidbit awaited him this time. Would he be surprised if he had brats in every land he sailed to? Probably not. But the thought never crossed his brutal and simple mind.

The island was situated near some narrow river flats. From the flats, the land rose in densely wooded hills away from the shore. Up and down the riverbanks, great rushing streams cut those very hills in two and poured into the river. These streams were called a kill.

～

"Move!" the captain ordered.

They hastily scrambled. The rowboat pitched sideways as it was lowered. The small boat thudded dully against the wooden ship and then settled in the water. A rope ladder was thrust over the side.

Satisfied, Hendricks turned. The cripple, head down, had stood behind him the whole time he barked out the orders.

"And you," he said sharply, pointing to the stinking hunchback, "will be in the first boat to shore. Then you disappear for the day. You will remain out of sight. That means *every* day." He emphasized the word *every* with a cutting swing of his hand, slicing the air in front of the cripple's face.

"No one is to lay eyes on your ugliness. Go into the woods and hide. No one cares how you survive. The Indians that come to shore and those who might come on board must not see you."

He understood the Indians were superstitious. They might be spooked, and then he could have an uprising on his hands or an attempted slaughter.

That was the last thing he needed. Defending against an Indian attack would not be easy.

He stood staring down at the cripple, for once hatred clearly marking his features. No need to deny it now. He was almost done. After the business was completed, he would be free to act. Maybe, even before then.

"Bastard!" he whispered just loud enough for the cripple to hear.

His strength had returned in full force, his head cleared and his stomach, relieved of its wrenching pain, no longer bothered him. He had kept food down for days now. He no longer stank of vomit.

"And," he added, his tone derisive, cruel, and deliberately loud, "while you go into the woods, wash! Not only are you damn ugly, but you stink to high heaven."

The men around them guffawed, satisfied that the captain finally shared their sentiments and joined ranks with the men.

The cripple said nothing, gloomily nodding yet looking no one in the eye. The cripple had, just this morning, wiped a soft smear from the slop bucket across his chest and down his arms, ensuring that no one dare get close. Even for him, appreciating the safety this lifeline afforded him, the smell was atrocious.

The captain jerked his head.

"Now get to the boat," he growled to the cripple, pointing to

THE SAVAGE RIVER VALLEY

the side rail where the rowboat was being lowered. The cripple limped to the railing and looked down. It was a long way to the rowboat, now floating alongside the ship even though the water looked refreshing on this hot morning.

This was going to take some doing.

The men were surprised at the Captain's orders. *Was he serious about the Cripple going to shore?*

Their taunting laughter turned silent. *Damn the Captain!*

With savage glee, they eagerly had planned for the death of the cripple. They wanted to wipe it from the earth. Now the disappointment of seeing the cripple headed for the rowboat left them bitterly disturbed.

But they said nothing. Orders were orders, and they came from none other than the captain himself.

$$\sim\!\!\sim$$

The hardest part had been getting down the rope ladder. After slipping and tangling himself more than once, the cripple had finally succeeded in reaching the rocking wooden boat. It creaked and swayed, and until he sat down, the cripple, conscious of his extra weight, felt sure he would dangerously topple over the side and sink with fatal results. He held on tightly with both hands, choosing a spot farthest from the other men. And there he cowered, praying for his life.

The captain lowered himself into the boat and settled in the front.

The morning was now blindingly sunny. The cripple could feel the sweat tingling down his back and beading on his face. But he was too scared to move. He knew, dressed as he was, that if he went overboard into the water, he was finished. His weight would sink him immediately. No one would help to save him. All would be lost!

Jansen scowled in his direction before putting his muscles to the oar.

They were ready to go ashore.

From the ship's rail, Harmensen watched the rowboat. He had to keep an eye on the cripple. *But, how could he? What was he going to do?* He had not been amongst those picked for the first trip to the island. His job was to bring the barrels to the shore, but that would be much later. What about now? Would the cripple be so foolish as to take the diamonds with him? Perhaps, he mused, it was time to pay another visit to the deserted captain's quarters and see just exactly where it was the cripple slept.

Stealthily, he slipped away from the rest and made for the captain's little room. Entering, he paused. The quiet of the quarters spooked him a little. He closed the door. It creaked loudly, and he froze. Had anyone heard him? He thought not and proceeded to inch his way over to the little closet; he peeled back the slatted door on broken hinges and stuck his head and shoulders in the doorway—for that was all of him that would fit. In the semi-darkness, there was no mistaking that horrible smell of the Cripple. Now it seemed worse. It was then that he realized the cripple had no intentions of ever coming back to the ship. For on the wall, which made him grimace and cover his nose, were great smears of human feces. But clearly the design, though crude, was identifiable. It was the faint outline of the ship and, written beneath, the word *death* surrounded by flames of fire.

On shore, Hendricks turned and gave one swift and intentionally vicious kick to the cripple who was cautiously getting out of the boat. The cripple doubled over, wincing in pain.

The captain shrugged in pleasure, a look of sardonic joy spreading over his face.

Soon, Hendricks thought, *soon you will know with whom you are dealing.* No one blackmailed him and got away with it. With a hint of murder gleaming in his eyes, he watched the cripple fall, only to slowly rise and limp away half covered with wet sand. He had the urge to strangle him now and feel the crack of the throat bones as they gave way to his thumbs. But the moment was not right. He

THE SAVAGE RIVER VALLEY

needed to get the cripple alone, out there in the woods, where none of his crew would hear him forcefully beating the monster to death. He would take no chances on anyone getting wind of what the cripple had to say. There would be plenty of time to kill him later, for there was nowhere the cripple would go but a little distance from the ship. It would be easy to find him.

"Now," he ordered to the eight men, watching the cripple stumble and fall again on the damp, sandy bank, "to the island!"

∿

It was two days into June.

Two months ago the heavy snows that came in shifting blankets of whiteout from the west over the Onteoras or, in some instances, blown up from the south, had melted into the streams and river. The sodden ground had dried. The shad, a trustworthy sign of spring's arrival, had run full upstream in the Great Water, so thick that a man could, with his bare hands, lift a squirming handful of them right up out of the water.

In the forest, the green buds were bursting into full leaves. A pale spring sun that drifted coolly over the forest surface now lifted its face to a summer's path.

The cripple, sweating profusely under his assortment of clothing and anxious to be free of them, hobbled off to a lonely spot, far enough from the riverbank, seeking a shaded inlet or cove where no one was about. He found that cove a half mile south of the little island where the Indians would be meeting the Dutch Captain and his men. The ground was solid under his feet, and it took some time to become accustomed to walking without compensating for the swing of the ship. He longed to take off his filthy clothes and bathe, but not just yet. He had to be cautious.

He found what looked like a path. He followed it.

He did not go sadly, however. In fact, he was highly satisfied that he had defied them all; his secret went undetected. He had

245

managed to fool them for the entire voyage! Who but Aniline, ingenious girl that she was, would have guessed it to be so. Even with an unfortunate upbringing, she was smart and crafty and had such foresight that it was almost eerie. Working the streets and then the brothels, she had learned quickly of the nature of man. It was not a pretty lesson. It was the idea of what made men fearful and compliant that intrigued her and gave her power. She had been the one to hatch the plan. And so far, it was working. He smiled in great satisfaction and, after walking a bit more, stopped and took stock of his surroundings.

It was not a bad place after all. It was actually nice indeed, peaceful and solitary.

It spoke of a wild dignity, a proud rank of trees waving their limbs in the higher air. Among the ferns and moss, he wondered how many herds of wild creatures chased each other through this wood. How many bones, bleached now by the sun and passage of years, lay hidden among the brush as the animals, monuments of the past, had been swept away? How many trees were silent spectators of the changes that came over the valley? How many savage men, red-colored as the Dutch explorers claimed, crept cautiously about their roots and passed noiselessly beneath their boughs? How many wounded warriors lay down in shallow graves that also contained seed from the parent tree?

This aspect of the wood appealed to him, a sense of loss, of never to be again—a sense of the past. This somber thought was replaced by the full chorus of crickets and other insects, trilling their summer song in earnest, rejoicing in the hot weather in an unceasing hum.

Birds fluttered high overhead, and their calls and warbles filled the air.

He breathed deeply of the forest air. How fresh it seemed to him. The smell of evergreen pines pervaded the air, their needles providing a cushiony path upon which to walk.

What was the next step, for there was no going back to the ship? Not ever. That was certain. He would rather face the cruelties

THE SAVAGE RIVER VALLEY

or uncertainties of the forest and the savages than the men he had just sailed with half way round the world. He had brought with him what he needed; his papers securely tucked away in a deep pocket along with his secret treasure, and, in addition, he managed to swipe a sharp dagger from the captain's quarters. He also brought one clean nightshirt that hung below his knees, worn underneath a few layers of grime-filled clothes, and there was nothing more he could bring with him without arousing suspicion.

Keep going, he thought with unequal determination, urging himself on to whatever lay ahead. The path and surroundings appeared safe, yet he was at war with each cry of a scolding blue jay overhead, wary with each new tree he rounded.

Eventually the English ship would arrive. He would make his way downriver and keep a look out for their sail and pay the bribe for them to take him back to England. How hard would that be? That was the long-term plan, but for now, there was nothing short of surviving.

He had to stay alive on his own, by his wits and a lot of good luck.

He was one person in this immense forest. He saw no one else.

So, he walked on. However dire and desperate his circumstances were at the moment, the forest was mystical; terribly big, yet encompassing. Great slanting beams of warm sun filtered down through the branches and lit the path among the trees. He never knew there could be so many shades of green and such incredibly tall trees! After what seemed a lifetime of being cooped up in the merchant's house and in the oppressive closet of the ship, this open-aired freedom was exhilarating and awe-inspiring. He dragged his leg through the woods and stayed clear of the riverbank. No sense taking a chance, they might still spot him from the shore or ship.

For now, he had to suffer the limp on his way through the forest.

After a while, he came upon a perfectly shaded cove, a rather idyllic spot, he thought. The air was pleasantly cool, yet inviting. From far off, further over the knolls that rose gently around the cove, he could hear the rush of stronger moving water. He looked about him. This would do nicely to get cleaned up and discard what he no longer needed. He was sweaty and hot and needed to refresh himself. He had seen many wild berries on the way.

Perhaps after bathing, he could fill his stomach with what he hoped to be their sweetness: blue, red, and black berries. Which to choose? He would choose them all, he decided. Then it would be time to move on. To what, he did not know. A real adventure, welcomed or not, awaited him. Of that, he was certain. If there was one thing Aniline taught him, it was that change was constant, and one needed to be prepared.

His thoughts flashed back to Amsterdam.

The cove, oddly enough, reminded him of a scene he viewed many times on a Flemish tapestry in the merchant's house, a bucolic land of harmony and peace. He had stolen up the stairs from the basement from the rickety cot he slept on, only to stand for hours in the late night staring at the scene. He had never seen anything that beautiful before. By daylight, he passed that delicately woven artwork every miserable day of his life, while he carried buckets, scrubbed floors, or endured the beatings of the merchant's wife. He dared not to touch it, yet it was the one thing that gave him hope and a sense that beauty did exist somewhere in the world, only just not in his, at least not for that moment.

Perhaps the angels from the tapestry had followed him to the new world. Perhaps they were here in this cove at this very moment.

When do the angels begin to appear? he wondered, smiling at his thought.

What would happen if he called out loud for them to appear? He shook his head in faint amusement. Angels were for tapestries and dreams of the rich, a made up world that he would never live in, for he had not been born into wealth and a comfortable life. So he could only stare at the tapestry and wonder. But yet, at this moment, something stronger and greater than himself took a hold

THE SAVAGE RIVER VALLEY

of him. Too bad he was not given the second sight, for had he looked about, he indeed might have seen angels, poised above the sparkling waters, hovering close to their protégé.

But he didn't see or hear anyone.

Instead, the cries of the birds flying overhead and in the trees overwhelmed any other noise he could hear as he sat on a flat rock and began to remove his clothing. He started to strip off layers of bulky pants that were held up by twists of frayed twine that functioned as belts. His nimble fingers patiently worked on buttons, the knotted twine, and filthy clothes.

Discarding each layer was equivalent to taking a step closer to heaven. It was a release of his tortured soul from the boundaries set by others in Amsterdam.

Finally, he was free!

The cripple relished in the moment, let his guard down, and, for the first time in months, knowing the men to be busy back at the ship's landing site, completely ignored his surroundings.

∿

When two worlds collide, primitive meeting civilized or vice versa, destinies are met or changed forever.

Early that morning, a Mohican hunter and warrior, long accustomed to stealth and now an expert at it, advanced at a slow pace. White Feather stepped carefully through the brush, avoiding snapping twigs in two, a mistake that would betray his presence to anyone lurking nearby. He had come to learn that the forest had ears. He knew he was within a reasonable distance, certainly within an hour's walk, of the trading post. He used great caution, knowing that Mohawks might be in the vicinity. A single mistake could cost him his life.

He had not traveled here to cross their path.

What he did know was that they typically traveled the trail that led northwest of the trading post. In years past, he had never attended these trading sessions. He had sternly set his heart and mind against the invasion of white men and their intrusive ways. He did not war with them, for White Feather, more than a skilled warrior, was a man of peace.

However, the newcomers arrived to their lands and changed their way of life. He greatly resented their presence on the banks of the river, on land that, for centuries, had been hunted and harvested by his people. He saw what the presence and ways of the white men did to his people, and it was not good.

There was one more reason he steered away from the trading post. He did not wish to stand on the same meadow as the Mohawks.

Years ago, one winter's night, White Feather had left the fireside of his family and trekked north to inspect the lands of the Maquas. He traveled the many arduous miles alone, staying hidden from sight. And when he finally found what he was looking for, he felt his heart turn to stone. What he saw there, as he crouched at the edge of a certain village, after months of searching, burned in his heart forever. He couldn't let the image of the Indian family, mother and son, escape his thoughts, but yet he was never able to tell anyone of what he discovered. It was too shameful.

Therefore, instead of participating in the summer migration to the trading post, he went into the mountains, the great Onteoras, to distant virgin meadows that abounded with game, and set up camp there, far away from the world as he knew it, alone with nothing but nature and his thoughts as companions. He built a small longhouse with one sleeping compartment and a huge fire pit, for the winters started early so high up. Each summer he returned to see how it fared during the most bitter of winter months. Usually it became a refuge for wildlife, but this he didn't mind. Instead, he gave a mighty laugh. Then he set about to making it habitable once more. In the ninth summer, he loved it as much as the first summer, if not more.

But now, for some strange reason, he traveled to the banks of the river far north of his village. He also knew it likely that within days he would find hunters from his village trading pelts. He hoped Ramco and even Tamaqua would be amongst them, accompanied by their sons and their wives, Minnah and Saquiskawa. Yes, he was certain he would see them all, but first, he had to follow his instincts. And he was curious as to where they would lead him.

They led him to this spot near the Great Water and there, having sighted the ship passing the day before, he calmly waited.

He stopped in the dark green shadow of a large oak tree and knelt. It was one of the great trees that inspired him as it rose two hundred feet into the air. He reverently placed his hands on the bark and looked up through the branches to a patch of blue sky. The oak had yet to give off its acorns. It was too early for that. His knees rested on a thick mat of moss that grew between the roots. How tranquil the setting, he thought. He closed his eyes for just a moment and felt the peace of solitude run in his blood.

Then he heard it.

Suddenly he grew alert, tense.

Someone was coming!

Ahead of him, on a little used path, someone was making so much noise he was certain it was not the sleuth of an Indian male, perhaps a squaw then. He waited.

What he saw next, what caught his attention, was unlike anything else he had ever seen in all the years of living in the forest! He looked on in complete surprise.

The cripple, after entering the cove, limped to a rock ledge that stretched out over a pool of water fed by a bubbling spring. He sat down. He was completely unaware of White Feather, a stone's throw away, as he pulled off his many layers of pants and then turned to his cap and gray hair, while peering into the cool refreshing water. He dangled his fingers and splashed the cool water into the air. He shook his head and the wig and battered cap fell, splashing into the water. They bobbed a few seconds on the surface before sinking.

"Ha!" the cripple said out loud. "You served your purpose, now good-bye to you."

PAMELA DE LEON

White Feather looked on in slack jawed amazement.

There was more to see.

Something unexpected was beneath the cripple's disguise. Thick braids wound tightly around his head, so tight they pulled the skin of his forehead taut. Braids that were the color of the sun that shone upon their crops!

White Feather said nothing. For at that point there was nothing to say.

The cripple clearly was getting ready to bathe in the cool waters at his feet, but first he splashed some water over his face. He had not brushed the poison weed on his face and hands for a few days and already they were healing, the scratched areas drying up. With both hands to his face, he rubbed vigorously. The grime seemed to melt away to uncover a layer of youth and beauty.

Feeling refreshed, the cripple scrubbed harder.

White Feather froze, unable to tear his eyes away. Should he steal away or stay? The forest held many secrets, most of them revealed long ago to White Feather, but a sight such as this? Never. He had to see what was happening next. He could not pull away from the strange scene before him.

In the world of the Indian, where survival of the fittest had reigned for thousands of years, there were no deformed or physically weak people: there were no blind, no deaf, no hunchbacked Indians, or crippled ones at that. Physically and mentally, they were a sound group of human specimens. Those that suffered some ailment at birth or later on in life quickly died off, unable to keep up with the strongest and most able.

There, in this spot, he watched a transformation that was unbelievable. The cripple continued on with washing and then turned to the layers of large shirts. One by one, they came off. He threw them off to the side in a growing heap; all except one of white linen that looked to be a loose fitting garment long enough to cover him from head to knee. It was the only clean article of clothing in the heap.

The cripple, finally disrobing to a point of recognition, was not a

252

THE SAVAGE RIVER VALLEY

bulky man but rather a slender female. A white female at that! He saw the curve of her leg, the twist of her back as she leaned forward.

So spooked was White Feather that he backed away, retreating to a quiet lonely spot among the roots of another giant tree so that he might pray to the spirits. Under the ancient oak, he sought answers.

Manito, guide me to know what this sign means? Is this a good or evil spirit?

For surely he had seen two things: a ghost spirit that changed appearances and the woman that was meant for him. And then he thought he heard a voice, distant, deep, and mysterious. Was it the voice of his heart or Manito himself?

He had two conflicting thoughts.

She will bear my child.

But why a woman so ugly? he asked himself.

He crawled even further into the woods.

~

Sometime later, White Feather came back to the little glen with the pool of dark water to crouch quietly and watch the young woman as she unraveled her braids and combed out her hair with her fingers. White Feather had never seen such a color, and it blazed magnificently in his eyes and seemed to brighten up the little cove where she sat. The tendrils reached to her waist, small and rounded, hidden now for some time under the oversized clothes. A waist he had yet to see in its entirety.

He could feel the curiosity increase as she continued on with her ritual. She pulled off a dozen shirts, one by one, and then numerous pairs of pants, all of them too big and filthy save one. All of them somehow held to her body by the huge distorted hump on her back. Finally, she reached for one last cord of material around her body.

What came next astonished him even more. Under the rags most would not call fit to wear, she was heavily bound by long strips of connected fabric, once white and soft, now gray and tattered. One strip wrapped around her shoulders, stretching across her chest and then drawn to fit under the right knee. Hence the bent over stoop!

Why do this to the body? He did not understand. Certainly, he had never witnessed any of the Indian women behaving like this. Something had to be wrong. The sight was so disturbing.

White Feather could not imagine why this woman desired a crooked frame within which to live. For him, the world was a place to stand straight, run freely over hills and through valleys, and feel the vigor of a healthy body. Was this a standard of beauty for the white women? White women were strange, he decided, but even more so the men, if they too thought this desirable.

Again, he did not understand.

As she tugged on a stubborn knot, the grimy though sturdy strips began to fall at her feet, as she unwound them from around her body. Off they came. One dirty rag tied to another. Out came the dagger swathed in a heavy cloth, and then a sheath of papers which were set aside. The bent cripple, no longer bound, stood up straight and was a cripple no more! She was taller than he imagined; tall, slender, and young. Long strips unfolded to reveal a shapely bosom, the roundness of which White Feather found himself compelled to stare at for a long time. The apparent softness and sway made his face feel suddenly hot, as if he sat near the flame of a fire.

She stretched her arms above her head and then sat down once more. The young woman bent to unfasten a metal shoe that fit to the bottom of her right foot! Her whole body seemed to move in one fluid motion as she undid the straps.

He watched her pick up the shoe, tip it, and spill its shiny contents into a pouch.

Hundreds of stones sparkled in this shaded spot. With a snap, she drew the string of the pouch closed and set it on the rock next to her. No need to keep the metal fitting, so she tossed it on the pile of clothing. The tinsmith in Amsterdam had been a genius at perfecting a shoe that could hold her stash and her weight at the

THE SAVAGE RIVER VALLEY

same time. It had been a heavy burden, but the shoe survived and the diamonds as well. She had not dared to release them from the secret compartment during the voyage. But now she was free to do anything she desired.

Free! She smiled and hugged herself in joy.

The warm air felt refreshing on her almost naked body. She felt young again, as if given a chance at a life that had never been her own before. *What if I never put on clothes again?* she thought with a rebellious smile. Ah! But she was not yet finished undressing. There remained one more thing to take off.

Suddenly, she stopped and reached behind her head. That hideous bump, though covered, was still there. White Feather felt pity for the woman before him. To have been born with such an ugly deformity! Her parents must have angered their Manito. And now she had to live with that and suffer a body no man would touch.

His heart felt twisted, struck with an indescribable pain.

What man would want such a woman? How could she support the weight of a papoose, lie upon her back to stare at the heavens, or lie with a man?

He felt a slight revulsion, but no matter. He could not avert his eyes. The rest of this woman intrigued him.

Then she went further, taking off every bit of clothing for the first time since the ship had left port.

The wind suddenly rustled in the leaves and blew over her body. She arched her back in obvious delight.

He watched, sucking in his breath. Every muscle in his body was tense. What could he expect to see? Nothing that Creek, his long-gone mentor and protector, had ever taught him in his youth prepared him for this. He was not sure what would be unveiled under the last covering. He had lain with women before and had afterwards turned an inconsequential eye to their nakedness, but none that looked like this one.

"Come, my beauty," she said, loud enough for White Feather to hear. Her soft voice carried through the forest, although he did not understand her words.

He cocked his head, listening closely. He only knew that the gentle slide and glide of her sonorous voice made him tremble with inquisitiveness and long to hear more.

He was reminded of a female voice of his past.

It was as smooth as a canoe, striking out over the calm water of a mountain lake on a summer's morning, a sound that brought great peace to his bitter heart. But that hump on her back! She reminded him of a pumpkin squash the village women planted which grew large, round bumps on the outside but, when cooked, was sweet and delicious on the inside.

One thing he knew. This woman was going to be his. But why was he punished by such ugliness? How could he stand tall and proud and bring her to the village of his sisters for approval? He could imagine the horrified looks on their faces. He grimaced. We will stay in the lands of the Onteoras he decided.

Then she spoke again.

"Come, and show me your magic, your beautiful bear and panther, your coldness on my hands and how it tingles when pressed to my face, your little cup for my shiny diamonds. Yes, my diamonds, but I share them with you my lovely."

She chanted as if she were praying. In fact, she was singing a poetic and sincere tribute. It was heartfelt, for the statue had become her lifeline, like an angel from the tapestry that had inspired her escape, one that held a chalice high to the heavens in the sky, one that was filled with shiny stones. She was sure it protected her secret during the voyage. Surely, it had saved her life from Jansen's deadly blow. She tenderly lifted the object to her lips and kissed it before placing it in front of her.

White Feather stood upright at once.

The hump had disappeared.

There, in front of this woman, sat the shaman stone.

Chapter Twelve

The island lay offshore.

For eight months of the year, it rose above the waterline. For four months, it came perilously close to being submerged.

A little one-story hut built on the island was surrounded by river water that acted as a moat and provided a somewhat relative sense of security for the Dutch. The walls were of stone, some precariously sticking out at sharp angles. The great workmanship of masons back in Amsterdam was not evidenced here. The simple hut had been built by seamen. This hut was not intended to be a lasting monument. Indeed not. Its purpose was served as a halfway point between ship and land, a point that helped a man to regain or capture a breath if he had to swim back to ship.

The crew of the Black Bear wearily hauled barrel after barrel, dozens so far, from the ship to the island and when the moment was right, when terms were agreed upon and the captain gave the signal, a single shot fired into the air, the buoyant barrels would be floated to the shore, pushed by the seaman in waist-deep water that swirled around their bodies but did not suck them under. Further out in the river, the currents were strong and deadly to a man, easily pulling him to his death. But close to shore, the currents gently glided and swirled in circular patterns.

Everything seemed to be in order.

"Start unloading," signaled the captain, as he basked under the glorious morning sunshine, admiring the sparkling river and, more so, the lack of any other Dutch competition. For not one other ship, with lowered or raised sail, was in sight. He gloated. The barrels could safely be unloaded to the island now.

The first step of getting the barrels to land was underway without a snag.

Crewman came and went, back and forth, and as everyone stayed preoccupied with a given task, no one, save Harmensen on deck, noticed a single man furtively slip into the woods.

"That bastard, where does he go to?" Harmensen swore softly.

Nevertheless, once on land in that immense wilderness, the Dutchmen would crack open the top with a crowbar, tip the heavy barrel, and spill the goods onto the ground, a sandy stretch of land where the Indians walked a path among the white men, each side wary of the other. The Dutch, satisfied, immediately refilled the empty barrels with the traded goods; skins slashed in circular form for a snug fit, one atop another. This time, however, the barrels were loaded onto the rowboat, stored on the island, and then taken to the ship, one by one. It was a slow and lengthy process that lasted for weeks.

In years past, as each barrel disappeared into the ship's hold, the captain, with basic arithmetic skills, mentally stored the number in his head and counted his share. Each barrel, bursting with goods, represented one more year he could finally call his own. No more groveling to the merchant, no more taking his orders, no more faking a politeness that was foreign to him.

His sneer turned into a half-smile.

Why, someday, he might even build himself his own ship!

He was counting on this year bringing him a considerable share of the merchant's fortune. After all the trips, and only a captain's share, he deserved it—and the merchant would never know. He had arranged to dump his load off the coast of England, burn the Black Bear, and let it sink from view. His scheme was to get rich fast! Faster than sailing a ship halfway across the world, a ship that wasn't really his, having to suffer the hardships and danger of the sea, while the merchant sat warm and safe in port! The crew? Each given a fair share, the crew would all agree they had been shipwrecked and, in all likelihood, some wouldn't make it to shore. They knew when to keep their mouths shut if they wanted to live.

THE SAVAGE RIVER VALLEY

This particular crew, a rotten lot, understood the Captain they were sailing under. And for now, that was enough. There was plenty of time to let them in on his plan later.

There was one snag that he knew of. And at this, he grew angry.

The cripple knew. For when he approached the captain in the tavern, he made it clear that he would rat out the plan to the merchants. After that, no one would give him a ship to command, which would spell a sure end to the honorable Captain Hendricks. There was one question. How did that measly cur find out? Did the Englishman open his mouth to someone? Lord only knew. But the captain had still to figure that one out.

∿

Each year from where they stood on the riverbanks, the Dutch captains smiled, spoke in a cajoling fashion, and easily traded the trinkets and cheaply made trifles for something that was valuable in their eyes and in the eyes of the syndicate in Amsterdam-enough furs and pelts to fill the hold of the ship. Nature had given the forest animals a natural barrier against the forces of time and weather, and for now, the lives of men revolved around the acquisition of that natural barrier.

The fever to acquire furs was not to abate in the near future but instead, continue for a long time to come, fueling empires and dynasties along the way.

More than a hundred years would pass and still the sun would rise on the greed for fur.

The fur supply, as can be expected, would continually diminish, as the beaver became extinct, killed off in the eastern portion of this new world, a world of finite boundaries, and in turn, would push the Indian to its limits and, inevitably, the white man on a trek further west.

Suddenly Hendricks heard a deep voice call out from land. He spotted the young warrior standing in the grassy meadow. Sneaky bastards, always catching him by surprise.

He could feel the instant pump of blood through his veins at twice the normal speed.

So, he thought, *now it begins. Yes, let the trading commence, for the savages have arrived!*

∿

Once the trading seasons were established by 1612, the Mohicans, although allowing tribes to transverse their lands, declined to mingle in the same arena or trading sessions with the Mohawks, who milled closely about the Dutch. The Mohican braves preferred, instead, to deal directly with the pale-skinned men who came ashore in small boats from the ships. The Mohican and Maquas were not blood brothers. They would not stand shoulder-to-shoulder, side-by-side, or smoke the same pipe. They would not even go so far as to face the newcomers to their lands as one people. The thought never entered their reasoning process. Instead, they awaited the arrival of the other ships. More men on shore meant it was less likely a confrontation would erupt between the natives.

Although other ships had yet to arrive, more than one was coming upriver that summer. Trading was not exclusive to one ship or one merchant, as long as they all flew under the Dutch flag. In fact, more than one Dutchman was noted for his heated discussions that led to many a quarrel in Amsterdam and outer provinces over the exclusive right to trade in the New World.

"It is our land now, our right by discovery to claim it as our own, name it as our own!" Merchant Coenraeds fervently shouted in private company.

"But what of England?" Samuel Godin asked.

"To hell with England!" someone shouted.

Then there was the river and what to name it. The topic came up during a meeting of merchants.

"We call it the Noordt River," someone exclaimed.

Another piped in, "We hear many names: River of the Sover-

THE SAVAGE RIVER VALLEY

eign Mauritius, Noordt River, Rio de Montagne." At that the crowd laughed. "And finally, the River Hudson. So what shall it be?"

"It was Hudson's River. Let it remain known as such," they declared louder to each other across council tables.

There was no arguing with logic. The discoverer, Hudson, although English, mapped it while sailing under their flag, therefore gave them exclusive rights to trade on the river. So that is all it took to acquire ownership of a river and its valley in the New World. Sail your ship in first, map it, and declare it to the world! It was as simple as that. Well, an easy feat, that is until another country wanted to take it over.

∿

For now, as it appeared, the one-hundred-and-twenty-ton ship, named the Black Bear, sailing out of Amsterdam under the banner of Merchant Van Rensallear, had been the first ship to arrive. It had creaked and groaned throughout the ocean voyage with each gust of wind and swell of wave, but arrive it did, in one piece, no worse for wear. A bright banner bearing the merchant's crest ruffled with the breeze.

An early arrival was not accidental.

Ah, what a cunning and ruthless man he was, for Hendricks planned it that way.

He hoped to get a jump-start over the other traders and establish high stakes for trade! Yes indeed, that was his goal right from the start, in order to outbid the other captains. He knew one if not two ships were close behind, but so far, he had not caught sight of either—so much the better for him. He felt no allegiance to the other captains.

Every man for himself, he thought grimly.

The fate of other traders was not his concern. They didn't pay his keep nor did they fatten his pockets. Why should it matter?

It didn't. He couldn't care less. He had no heart for humanity, much less for those competing in his trade. Seeing his ship floating alone in the river pleased him enormously that morning. Two solid masts arose from the ship, atop of which flew the merchant's banners. His banners, they soon will be; a proud ship and an equally proud captain. He felt impressed by his own self-imposed importance.

I rose up out of scourge, clawed my way through life, and now I am on the top, he reminded himself, as he inspected the island with his men. "This will soon be my world, and I intend to control it. Lord God, but you have been good to me in bringing me here safely. I have much to accomplish," he thought smugly.

What a fortuitous way to start his last summer of trading!

Hell to the others! Damnation to any man, white or heathen, who stands in my way.

They all sailed for a monopoly of merchants, he, in particular, for the syndicate belonging to merchants of Amsterdam. Amongst themselves, all captains sailing for other merchants included, was an unspoken yet commonly understood law: every man looked out for himself, and to the very man his ship and his share mattered the most. Under the auspices of the New Netherland Company, with permission from the Dutch states to trade in the form of a resolution or charter, they were a stiff and unforgiving group of rivals in an often-violent competition.

To the New World, they all thought joyously! Here was where their future lay.

Among the sponsoring merchants was the very powerful and often self-imposed leader: Killian Van Rensallear.

There were other Amsterdam merchants—Lambert Van Tweenhyusen, Arnout Vogels, and Hans Hunger—all desiring a piece of the pie. This was only the beginning of a movement toward the founding of a national monopoly over all trade and colonies to come.

For now, Lambert Van Tweenhyusen was not to be left behind.

His ship, the Fortuyn, sailed that year as well; just a week after

THE SAVAGE RIVER VALLEY

the departure of the Black Bear. But a week had not been the deterrent one might have supposed. For at this moment, it was just hours from catching up to the Black Bear.

∿∿

The Indians, with great stores of pelts in hand, showed up on the first day. It was a summer day, a perfect day for trading. It was no good traveling near the riverbed. Marshes and swamps filled those muddy banks level with the river for miles north and south. When the tide was high, they became floating greens in the silver-gray water. On the banks grew a splendid array of plants: tall reeds, cattails, bamboo shoots, and upward climbing weeds, not to mention a prolific display of ferns, preferring the shade that crept along the base of each waterlogged tree. The banks were sandy and moist, never completely drying out for the flood waters would rise again that day a mere twelve hours later.

So, the Indians stuck to the dry familiar trails through the woods and along the ridges on high ground. One such trail ran all the way clear to the land of the Huron, someday to be named Canada, where even now the white men called Francaise had set up their trading posts before eventually turning their sights on the very river the explorer Hudson had discovered in the name of the Dutch.

From a point northwest of the island, the Mohawks sent an emissary, the son of Mahwah. An hour earlier, accompanied by his father, he split off from the rest of the group, eighty warriors and hunters, and a handful of women traveling together from various villages, settling in a temporary camp.

He snorted as his mother approached his side and cautioned him on the foray. What a stupid squaw she was, always fussing around the family. He was jealous of the lavish attention his father paid to her, always putting her first. It was not the way of the Indians. This made him angry. When his father stooped to carry her

263

heavy bundles, even though she protested, the son grew furious at them both.

She should know her place and stay in the background, he thought angrily.

He dismissed her as he quickly turned away. He looked to where his father stood. Mahwah, his black locks showing signs of gray, though by no means old, was vigorous in body and in mind. He still held great sway with his village, with his son in particular. His son worshipped him. Too bad the son didn't feel the same way about his mother. The father had watched the interchange between son and mother, and then smiled at his wife before he abruptly turned away.

An hour later, his father, staying out of sight in the shadowy grove of tall hemlocks that abounded in the forest and mountain-sides, watched his son enter the clearing. In years past, Mahwah had been the first to stride forcefully into the clearing and initiate the trading. Time and seasons had passed since his daring escapades of past and, although he was not yet prepared to join the other elders in helping around the village, he was willing to give up the lead he had maintained with the white men. Common sense told him he was not as agile as in his youth. Life was moving forward as the seasons do. A new generation must be prepared to step into his shoes. Soon he would hand over that role to his son. Better this way, for he had a clear view of everything happening around the trading post. He liked to keep his eye on what was going on without being the center of attention. Better to guard his family and keep watch on his wife. She had been acting strange lately, forgetful at times. She squatted by the fire as if in a dream world that no one could enter. Apparently, she was oblivious to the other squaws bustling about their chores, for they often called to her without an answer. He wondered what had bothered her in days past, but for now, as the white men came ashore, his son was his priority.

He would put things straight with his wife later.

On the south side, the Mohicans also watched, but across the clearing under the cover of a distant tree line. No sense in showing themselves too early or getting too close. The first day of contact, when the two worlds met face to face, was always a cautious one.

The young brave—solidly built and tall, dressed in a similar fashion as his father—drew closer and carefully approached the shoreline. He waded through knee-high grasses, came to a stand-still, and waited. He felt arrogantly secure in knowing his father was guarding his back. The white men, he noted, were scurrying over the little island on his left, inspecting the misshapen hut, victim to the ravages of the previous winter. He spied their leader instantly. At seventeen, he was astute. Without moving his head, he shifted his penetrating glance toward the river. Straight ahead, he took in the anchored ship and then, off to his right, the southern tree line.

Suddenly he turned to face the woods.

Had he heard something? It wasn't very often he doubted himself. It wasn't an animal sound. It was the sound of a human drawing in a sudden breath.

Yes—he was certain of it! So, they were there, cowering just behind the tree cover. Nothing he could see with his eyes, but his ears always served him well.

He grew even more alert and still. He never knew when a renegade warrior would take it in his head to attack. Even with his father at his back, he now sensed the need for caution, getting ready to thwart an enemy brave intent on killing him. He felt his first pang of uneasiness.

How many Muhicannau eyes were on him now? He knew the other tribes must be in hiding, as was their particular custom on the first day, crouched behind trees and bushes or flattened to the ground. He had to admit they were experts at blending in with the forest and moving among the undergrowth with the wind at their backs. It would appear to an immature eye as if the wind moved the brush and not the human hand or body. He clenched his jaw. Whether he could see them or not, he still knew they were there. And this made him angry.

He simmered with hostility that knew no boundaries. The hair rose on the back of his neck. His father had taught him well. But unlike his father, this son, called Wanaque Wolf, had a mean heart and cold eyes the color of the blue sky. He was not afraid.

Stand tall, he admonished himself.

He straightened his shoulders even more. Warriors stood proud.

And then he saw it.

An omen. It came out of nowhere. His eye tracked the first thing that moved. Overhead, just clear of the tree cover, flew an eagle so large and magnificent that it caught his eye immediately. He watched it soar inland, disappearing from his sight. Most would have watched in awe, but not Wanaque Wolf.

A momentary shiver crawled along his spine. He got the eerie feeling that something more than danger awaited him here. But he knew not what.

Should he turn back?

He listened for a long whistling call. It was his father's practice to whistle softly at the least hint of danger. A call most would have mistaken for a bird. Only he heard nothing.

He could proceed. If he turned back now, he would lose face. There would be no explaining the strange feeling of dread the eagle gave him.

He knew what he had to do.

"Lennowak!" he called out sharply to the men on the island, cupping a hand around his mouth. He crossed his arms over his chest and waited for a response.

Voices, whistles, and especially screams echoed loudly in a quiet forest, over a meadow and across the water.

∿

The Mohican camp was ready.

Hastily built, makeshift lean-tos, put together with forked branches, rose next to campfires already smoking. The camp was

THE SAVAGE RIVER VALLEY

over a half mile away from the trading post, far enough off the main trail and high on the ridge to prevent crossing with the Mohawks, set in clearing that was easy to defend if need be. The few women accompanying their husbands gathered brittle kindling wood to set the fires and then put food to cook. There was a stream close by to fill the gourds with water. The men scouted the perimeter and set some young boys to guard the camp, those loud enough to give a warning call but too young to fight. The Mohicans anticipated no trouble, but it was wise to always stay alert.

Great piles of thick, brown beaver pelts and other furs were stacked near each brave's fire.

Now it was up to the men of the camps, for there were many in the forest, to set off for the trading post. The open clearing was rather narrow and situated on the west bank of the river. It abruptly ended where the forest began. With one step, a person could disappear into the tangle of dark wilderness or step into the open.

One misstep could mean life or death.

The older men approached the trading post, scoping out the lay of the land and the enemy as well. It was the custom for the younger braves to guard the rear of the line. It was how they learned. It was how they became seasoned warriors.

Two minutes later, they all froze.

When they spotted the lone Mohawk—a fierce looking warrior, albeit a young one—as he stepped into the rays of bright sunlight filtering down between drifting clouds over the meadow, the blood automatically rushed to their heads. So, the Maquas had arrived before them! Immediately they felt the urge to raise their tightly held tomahawks and bury the deadly weapons in his skull one at a time, to send forth a united hair-raising cry of attack and feed their need for masculine revenge. When angered, they were a fighting machine, relentless and merciless against an enemy tribe. A few braves coming from Potuck, together with those braves of the village flats, already schemed to wash their hands with the blood from his pulsating heart. It would do much to satisfy their need to avenge the killing of their defenseless village elders who, once in youth, shared fire embers with the village of Sasqua and brought peace to the spirits who haunted their campfires.

They had not forgotten the sporadic war parties that had, over the years, raided their lands; exacting on the spot tribute from any village they overcame. Tribute came in the form of food but most often in the form of something much more valuable; wampum. Several villages on the flats had fallen victim to their raids within the last year. Potuck took a severe blow. It was ruthlessly sacked and then burned to the ground while the younger men, all fishermen, were away at the edge of the Great Water. The women and children had fled into the fields while a few old men, the third son of Sasqua included, courageously faced the attackers and, in doing so, lost their scalp locks still attached to thick chunks of skin.

But Wachachkeek, graciously taking in what was left of its homeless neighbors for the time being, had so far escaped unscathed.

∿

Two villages already had moved, taking their camp away from restless and unavenged spirits.

The River Tribes were generally not a warring people. But times had changed—and so did the tribes.

Every single brave crouching in that wooded line, whether from Potuck or elsewhere, could feel anger course through his veins. They were one nation, blood brothers, and united in heart and soul. Too many villages to count, on both sides of the Great River, as of lately had been attacked, coming under the fatal blows of a marauding band of Maquas. But now was not the time to best their revenge. It would not be wise. They would reluctantly wait their turn, wisely avoiding any unnecessary interaction with the Maquas as long as the white men, with whom they wanted trade, were present. Powerful chiefs of each village—including Tamaqua's father Monemin from Shodack, village of the council fire, now more slow moving

THE SAVAGE RIVER VALLEY

than in his youth yet still a force to be reckoned with in the moment of battle—calmed the braves by remaining still, seeking to ease the anger they too felt. Young men knew the routine through practice. They couldn't move unless he moved. The elder men at his side, many of them in the fiftieth winters, were old and wise. They knew well the heads and hearts of their sons and grandsons, for in their youth they had felt the same stirrings of emotion. They understood completely. And only they could deter the rash action of an unseasoned warrior against a propitious and unworthy attack.

Monemin held up his finger in a decisive gesture of silence, while keeping his eyes focused on the Mohawk warrior.

So, they all stayed quiet. The eyes of the younger men were on the elders, waiting for a signal to attack that never came, and then they switched back to the scene in the meadow.

From a distance, the Mohicans observed every approaching step of the enemy as he waded through tall grasses of the clearing. He had come through a dark opening in the tree line on the far side of the meadow. His legs were long and muscle bound. They watched him come to a halt and then call to the white men who, up till then, were unaware of their arrival. He was the first to appear. The sun reflected across the young warrior's shaved head with a small row of hair that was closely cropped across the top. A slow burning anger once again flashed in their eyes, and more than one anxiously fingered the sharpened edge of the tomahawk in his hand, while keeping his eyes on the scalp that seemed to ceaselessly mock their blades.

The mere sight of any enemy warriors brazenly striding into the open in a seemingly unconcerned manner, especially on their lands, made them seethe with rage. The watchful Mohicans drew a collective inward breath and almost magically exhaled as one. It could almost be said that the trees moved in rhythm with the Mohicans' breath, and anyone not associated with either side would surely have marveled at the peaceful sight of the forest moving as one.

But the Mohicans could not muster up anything close to peaceful feelings.

This arrogant young Mohawk was so sure of himself! Ah, but for the chance to slay him in his tracks! Or so they all thought. They could imagine his body splayed with arrows and stone blades.

All except one, who looked on not in anger but in growing consternation. All morning he had been cautiously glancing across the meadow, hoping to catch first sight of the enemy tribes. Now his body stiffened as the Mohawk walked into view with an uncanny familiar stride, a familiar gait that Ramco had seen for many years in the hunt.

Only this was not the hunt. Where had he seen this young Maquas before? He would rather die than cohort with the enemy, so he was certain it had not been a friendly encounter.

Ha gave a low, unsettling grunt, and the Mohawk, as if hearing the very sound, turned to face that particular spot in the woods. His face was set in hard lines for one so young. There was a dark gleaming in the eyes, a cruel twist of the mouth, and unusual designs of color painted on the cheek.

The Mohican brave looked closely at the Mohawk's face.

Had he seen this warrior in the woods?

He hadn't.

Only it seemed like he had. For just a split second, he had thought to call out to the Mohawk, mistaking him for another, one of his own tribe. But how could that be? Little did he know that, at that moment, he was experiencing the very same unsettling sensation Creek had had over eighteen winters ago as Creek looked upon another older Mohawk warrior. Human events occur in cycles, and it appeared that the cycle had once again begun. The sensation that had once angered Creek now brought on a deep puzzlement and unease for the husband of Saquiskawa.

The village knew him as a seasoned hunter and warrior who feared no man, but Ramco was baffled and, a bit apprehensive.

But he mustn't show it, not in front of the others.

With furrowed brow, Ramco heard the whispers of his two sons at his side. On the trail to the trading post, their voices were deep,

THE SAVAGE RIVER VALLEY

sometimes breaking on a high pitch that caused them to laugh. Now they were restless. Silence was not their forte. Without moving, he glanced their way.

Each son was a perfect blend of both parents in looks and build. They were born exactly twelve months apart.

At sixteen and fifteen, they were as close as two corn kernels that grew side by side on the same cob on the same solid stalk in the same golden field. Traveling beyond their hunting grounds was new to them, and Ramco thought it heartless to let one go forward without the other. Seldom would one find them apart or separated, not only from each other but also from Metoxem, the youngest male cousin in their longhouse. Even now, as Ramco glanced from the corner of his eye, they shared some secret looks between then that not even Ramco was privy to. He had seen that look before. Normally, it meant rescuing them from some foolhardy adventure.

Foolhardy or not, there was danger here. Not time to play. Not time to laugh. Not time to whisper.

Now Ramco experienced second thoughts. He suddenly grew uneasy. Perhaps it hadn't been a good idea to bring his sons with him. Normally they stayed behind at the camp with their mother and younger sister Nipapoa. This year was their first time at trading, and they viewed the scene with eagerness they could barely contain. The boys heard much of the Maquas, and now they had their first sight of one and it seemed to excite them.

Should he send them back to camp?

Would it be wise to let them travel alone back there on the trail?

He turned to Tamaqua who crouched to his left. He too had agreed to let his eldest two sons accompany them on the first day. They both knelt, serious and attentive, their dark eyes awaiting a signal from their father. Ramco opened his mouth to speak but changed his mind when he saw the expression on the other brave's face. He was staring at the young Mohawk. Ramco could see the muscle in his jaw working hard.

So, he had seen it too!

No need to say a word. Ramco hand signaled his sons to retreat back to camp. Without a sound, Tamaqua and his sons turned and followed.

The two men and four boys trotted single file away from the trading post.

But they were the only ones, for the other braves, from Mohican villages up and down the valley from both sides of the Great River, had other things on their minds. Tamaqua's father spied their retreat and watched them out of sight. He then turned his attention back to the meadow.

Trading was about to commence, for the white men had come ashore. He could see a few barrels already floating in the river on their way to the island.

And it looked like a storm, bearing heavy rain, was brewing overhead.

∿

Down river, at the bend where the shallows first appear, a ship, larger than the Black Bear, was heading north along the waterway. The bluish-gray water was moderately calm and a breeze was at their back. A strong sun shone intermittently between gathering clouds. The ship was making good time, gliding almost noiselessly up the river. Somewhere below deck, a fiddler gave off a weakly played tune; a few notes going astray. Every ship sailing the seas usually had a seaman below who could bow a song or two, although in most cases not very well. Nevertheless, music it was and it was generally appreciated, though more often after downed swigs of beer at the end of the day.

But the captain gave no indication he heard the tune, for he stared straight ahead, his facial expression never changing. Sailing this river was a tricky business. Sand bars lay inches under the water.

Here came the competition Hendricks dreaded.

THE SAVAGE RIVER VALLEY

At its helm was a man of dark, good looks with medium build and average height. In character, he was determined and unscrupulous. In personality, he was charmingly deceptive. His name was Captain Adrian Block, the man who, in Amsterdam, was infamously known for slyly introducing heavily brewed Dutch Ale to the Indians.

On previous voyages, he had often looked on with sardonic amusement after trading ceased, when the natives, new to the world of drinking, stumbled about a campfire drunk and senseless. At first, the Indians were reluctant, but it only took one daring savage to partake and subsequently assure his fellow braves of the exquisite euphoria that accompanied the drink.

Block would, without hesitation, retort hotly when the merchants of Amsterdam questioned him on the moral issue of trading for rum. "What's it to you?" he threatened with a dark look. They invariably took one step backward in the face of such viciousness, their pointed black beards quivering. "You all want your money, don't you?"

And that way, through brute force, he silenced his questioners, for the aim to secure wealth stifled any objections to mistreating the Red Men. And then he turned on the charm. The merchants were all too glad to forgive him his trespasses as they forgave their own.

For Block, a captain who had seen it all, it was a never-failing source of entertainment, besides which the savages seemed to take an unbridled liking to the fiery substance. The Indians had grown lazy over time, but with the stimulus of a new trade item, they were more willing to trap an excess of furs in exchange for liquor than for goods they already had grown tired of. The newness of the trinkets of 1611 had already worn off. Attribute it to human nature, even among the savages. Heavy black kettles were a hindrance to easy and fast mobility and, in the end, how many trinkets could they possibly want?

Was it a claim to fame that this particular captain took it one step further, one deadly step further?

Perhaps it was.

For unlike the previous captains who traded with trifles, Captain Block knew that to secure a full load might be difficult, what with increased competition from the other traders. Word had it that a fellow by the name of Juan Rodriguez had jumped another ship and had set up a bristling little trading business near the great harbor. And then there was Eckels, who abandoned Fort Nassau in the dead of winter, walking off with the Mohawks, perhaps setting up a trading spot elsewhere. Block needed something even stronger than rum to entice the Indians to his trading camp. He would need to up the ante.

And so he did.

The hold of his ship, the Fortuyn, fully funded by the Merchant Tweenhyusen, was crammed full of the stacked barrels of the requisite cloth, kettles, and duffel. However, next to the wooden heap, unbeknownst to the merchant, the crew had secretly loaded thirty clamped and watertight wooden boxes. Inside, nestled in woodchips, lay deadly firearms, long muskets, and a smaller selection of shorter pistols. This was his trump card, the one thing that would place him above and beyond the rest as top trader that year and perhaps, if luck had it, for years to come.

This time he would trade the firearms for pelts. And all be damned to the other traders!

On the last voyage the year past, ships had actually exchanged gunfire, forgetting any overtures of peaceful competition, as once trading ships for the same company might have acted under more benign circumstances.

It had turned into an ugly business. Only it was about to get uglier.

Competition could not be silenced nor compromised. It was not the way of man. Instead merchant clashed against merchant, sea captain against sea captain, and on land, nations of Indians against Indians.

All warring with no reserve.

All warring for no good reason.

THE SAVAGE RIVER VALLEY

∿

They say that in anger one learns many things. Even to the point of learning things that are hurtful or untrue. Anger makes one speak without thinking. Anger also makes one act spontaneously.

In his anger, he said nothing. However, throwing all caution to the wind, White Feather jumped out from behind the shelter of the tree. What was this strange woman doing with the shaman stone? What was the meaning of it here, far from the village where it belonged?

Was she a thief? It appeared so.

It had been stolen long ago, nine winters to be exact, and no one had ever learned of its fate. Images of a lost village filtered through his brain. Now, White Feather discovered it in her possession? Who had led him here to this white devil? For that is what she surely must be; changing her appearance and then pulling the shaman stone from her back! She was a powerful witch. And the first he had ever faced. He was no shaman, nor did he know how to ward off evil spirits.

But he was not afraid.

His breathing was rapid, but his thoughts were precise.

He knew, above all else, that he must recover the shaman stone and return it to the village, no matter what. And only a devil, the craftiest of evil spirits, would have snatched it away from its rightful owners, his village of Wachachkeek, from where it had laid for years, out of respect under the sleeping platform of Sasqua!

The wind above the forest began to stir, blowing a path through the trees. Spring's tender green leaves swayed overhead. White Feather could feel the forest cooling down. A mass of dark clouds was building up beyond the Onteoras. The sunny day of the valley was now turning dim—an ominous sign.

The wind was known to bring evil spirits.

She gazed at him intently from where she sat.

She wanted to cry out, turn, and run, but she knew better than

PAMELA DE LEON

to move, even in a feeble attempt to cover her nakedness. But what did that matter now? Surely, he had been watching her for a while from behind that tree, so he had already seen all of her!

She lifted her chin in defiance, continuing to look into his eyes. She would show no fear! Her mind raced back to the ship, to the cold and harsh treatment from the crew and captain and to the brutal loneliness of the crossing without so much as a soul to speak to or turn to for comfort. She remembered the smell of human feces, the dirty clothes, and the bedbugs. She remembered the fierce kick from the captain, a human monster she hated within the depths of her heart. Well, not quite, for Jansen held first place because he had tried to kill her.

Nay, in her estimation, whatever she faced today would not compare or tempt her to go back.

So numerous the thoughts that flashed in her mind she felt her head spin from the sheer impact. There was no sense in running, for by the looks of him, he was more powerful than she and would, without a doubt, quickly overcome her. The journal of that bastard Juet told her much of the Red Man. She would never forget what she had read. She had even felt a sense of pity for their plight against the white man and his guns.

But it was more than that. There was something else.

Something that whirled in her body, flashed in her mind, and struck at her pounding heart as fast whirling as the darkening clouds overhead.

She had seen many a young and vigorous man in Amsterdam, most particularly those that clamored in the darkened tavern after her sister Aniline, clutching at bosom and hoping for free favors, but never one that spurred the blood to pound in her heart so! Up to now, she had only felt a deep disgust for men and their glutinous ways toward women.

But this man was different.

What a fine specimen of the human race! So startling was the stark beauty and primitive masculinity that her eyes roved over his

THE SAVAGE RIVER VALLEY

face and down to his bare chest, his hard muscle-bound body and solid legs, his limbs clothed in leggings of soft deerskin. He wasn't a pasty-colored white man. His skin shimmered beautifully brown. A brown she had never seen before. The pit of her stomach quivered with a pang and fluttered up through her chest. He towered over her, and what she observed should have scared her. Oh indeed, what she saw was terrifying, of that there was little doubt, but unexpectedly thrilling at the same time.

Terrified, warmly thrilled, and yes, strangely excited; the mere sight of him took her breath away.

Seconds passed.

She then made a deliberate move. She slowly lifted her hands outward in front of her, palms up. Her outstretched hands were empty. He could clearly see that. The dagger she had swiped from the ship lay alongside the journal papers and the diamond-filled pouch—not much good it would do her anyway. He would throw himself upon her and easily rob her of the dagger before she could attempt to defend herself. So that was out of the question—an insane move to provoke his anger.

Clearly, she was at his mercy. Better to show him she meant to submit.

He took a step closer.

"Peace," was all she said.

He paused.

Her voice confused him. A moment of uncertainty flickered over his face.

Who are you, white woman, to stare me in the face without fear? he wondered in amazement.

"Ka-to-nah?" he said.

He continued to gaze on the face of the female.

She had not thought to be discovered so soon. She knew it was inevitable but she hadn't totally prepared herself for her first encounter with the wild men. She had thought, foolishly perhaps, to evade detection in this big land that stretched beyond the sea.

There was so much space, how was it they would find her the first day? Now she knew how naïve that sounded. Certainly, she did not plan for them to come upon her naked as she bathed! What would happen to her now? Just a few hours on shore and already she would meet her destiny?

Then so be it, she decided abruptly. Not even the arrival of the English ship could save her now. Little did she know that days before, the English ship that had been streaming toward the Great River, funded by an Englishman who had months before brokered a deal with the Dutchman Hendricks and bedded a Dutch whore who spun a story that held him transfixed, had been turned back by the ferocious Block and his cannon. The ship had left the harbor and set out to sea.

She stared at the Indian. She saw a beautiful and full feather hanging from his scalp lock. The feather was white. She longed to run her fingertips along the tethered edges. She wondered if they would be soft or hard. And his skin, how would that feel beneath her fingertips? Such silly thoughts for such a moment, she chided herself. Yet, she couldn't help it. There was a man in front of her that made her realize, for the first time in her life, she was a woman enabled with parts that might attract such a man.

His eyes shifted from her face to the statue and then darted back to her face. She saw his hand slowly reach for the tomahawk on his belt.

So, that was it! He meant to kill her!

It was then that they heard a woman's blood curdling scream coming from within the forest.

Chapter Thirteen

The Indian boy looked to the sky.

Metoxem was a boy of ten winters entering his eleventh summer, a boy who was in the stages of perfecting his hunting and fishing skills. Each day he awoke meant another day closer to being a man. He was short for his age, a fact that commonly led others to treat him as if he were younger. Whereas his brothers were stout, he was thin. His jet-black hair, had it been let to grow, would have reached to his waist by now and, like most of the other boys, let loose until the hunt. Yet, his head was clean-shaven of hair so in that respect he resembled his brothers and father. His face was round like Minnah's. Today, in spite of the warmth of the day, he wore full leggings, moccasins, and a loose-fitting deerskin shirt bordered around the neck with a finely woven quill stitch, the work of his loving mother who took great pride in how her family looked to others. Besides, they were on the move.

A dark shadow passed over the sun.

He stopped squinting.

He quickly lowered his slingshot, one made of wood and leather, the same one his father helped him carve, one that he had been aiming high at the sky. Its sinew string had been pulled back taut, poised to bring down a bird. In it, he held a medium-sized, gray stone, big enough to kill a sparrow in one blow yet small enough to do a man little harm. The woods were full of sparrows and other small, flying fowl—fun to hunt, delicious to eat. Their noonday meal would be a sweet tasty morsel of roasted bird over the spit. It only took seconds for the boy to bring a flying bird to the ground.

But something of bigger proportions flew over the head of the boy, something that would not be brought down by a small Indian boy's simple slingshot. The bird was directly overhead of the boy, craning its neck in his direction. The bird turned its finely shaped head.

It seemed that the eye glared at him.

The bird swooped down a little closer.

He stared at it for a single second before alerting the others. The message seemed pretty clear to him. In fact, due to the diligent mentoring of his mother, the meaning struck him almost instantly! She taught him to see things no one else could. He was an apt student and willingly followed her lead, whereas his brothers wanted no part of it. They stuck close to their father. Plants, messages, medicine, and visions were the world of their mother. Not that they belittled it, they just didn't care much to be part of it.

"Look," Metoxem cried out to the native women standing close by. "Look now, all of you, to the eagle flying overhead. It is my great-grandmother—a sign that is meant for us. We, the people of her village, look!"

The women dutifully paused and listened to the excited child-like voice, smiled at his enthusiastic nature, and then went back to what they were doing. All the Indians of Wachachkeek were accustomed to the strange words of Metoxem.

"The boy takes after Minnah," they all agreed. He was like his mother in that aspect, and they had long ago accepted him as they had his mother. However, there was one who always paid attention, listening to him when the others did not. His mother's sister, the squaw Saquiskawa, paused and pushed back her shoulders, placing her hands on her aching lower back. The next child to be born grew large within her protruding belly and soon would open its eyes to the world of Manito. The pain had been a persistent annoyance all morning. It was not the way of the Indian woman to mention these things to anyone. When it happened, she would be ready. Her calculations on the arrival of the new baby were counted by the full

THE SAVAGE RIVER VALLEY

moons that shone in the night sky. There still remained one more moon to shine its light. Then the new baby would arrive. But for now, she forgot about it as she turned her attention to the boy.

She had watched the bird soar over the camp, the beauty of its white head vivid against the blue sky. Its wing span was larger than her arms spread their widest. All Mohicans of her village and Munsees of her husband's village took such things in stride. It was part of their living in nature; birds flew overhead while on the ground animals scurried through the forest, each with its own footprint or call of the wild. Signs from the spirit are called Kee-gay-no-lay-woa-gan. Signs come in unending varieties, she recalled. The elders know and can interpret signs, whether in dreams or in life, as if there were writings on the trees or in the dust of the earth. *A crow chattering at us can signal danger, an eagle tells of company coming or may tell us one of our ancestors is trying to reach us,* she thought silently. *Was this eagle a sign?* She wondered.

And sometimes they, the people of her village, did take it as a sign, a message from the Great Spirit. They reacted accordingly.

And sometimes they did not, by ignoring warnings of great importance.

She would remember the eagle and speak to Minnah about it, she decided.

"Yes, my sister's youngest son, I too see in my heart the spirit of Sasqua," she answered back. Her smile bestowed on the boy grew wider. And the pain in her back grew sharper. But she had much to do.

She still had to cover the wooden frames with branches, where the family would sleep that night. Then there was the food to prepare and more wood to gather.

Busy as she was, she also kept a watchful eye on the son of Minnah, her only sister. It would not be unheard of, or surprising, if the boy wandered off into the forest surrounding the flats. His strong little legs carried him to unusual places. Just when the Indian women would think to look for him, he would wander back into the village. No one knew where he had gone nor asked, for he was safe in the forest, or so he said.

But there was one difference.

This was not the golden green forest of their village. This was the forest of the trading post and unknown territory for the boy. This was the forest that was close to the borders of the enemy of the north, the Maquas. It was too close for comfort, and much too close for a young Indian boy to be wandering alone in the woods.

∿

The boy teetered on the brink of leaving his childhood behind as manhood approached. He could feel it every day, so much was his desire to be a man. His spirit was strong, as strong as the eagle that flew overhead. He felt a surge of energy just by watching it slip into a glide, its wings stilled for a moment. His young heart soared with the bird.

It suddenly occurred to him.

"Sasqua has come back. There is something she seeks," he whispered to himself as the large bird circled overhead. He had heard the stories of his great-grandmother and held her to be a god-like spirit. Now he knew it to be true.

He was reverent, yet a child: the youngest of Minnah and Tamaqua's children, and handsomely brown-skinned and clothed in soft deer hides. He was almost as tall as the other boys his age. Metoxem was as mischievous as they come—but not half as mischievous as his two older cousins, the sons of Saquiskawa and Ramco. Those boys, older than Metoxem by a few years, caused a ruckus wherever they went, entering a longhouse in a tumble of arms and legs and howling noise. They kicked up dust wherever they trod, ate the same food together from the same bowls on the same mats. Either crouching or sitting cross-legged, shoulder touching shoulder, the brothers were never apart. All three, including Metoxem, who they took under their wing as if he were a smaller brother and not a cousin, slept together in the same compartment.

THE SAVAGE RIVER VALLEY

Over the years of childhood, they became an inseparable trio.

Metoxem had three brothers, but he made no secret of preferring the company of his cousins to that of his serious and often sobering brothers, who tagged along after their father. His mother understood his bond with his cousins. His father gave him the freedom to grow close to the other boys.

"One day," his father remarked, "you will all be hunters together. You must look out for each other."

Not long after, the three boys made a pact. In all things, they would stay as one forever. Never would one move away. Never would one leave the others behind in hunting, fishing, and in play. To seal that pact, they sliced the tip of their thumbs with a tomahawk and pressed all three together, their blood mixing with blood. They would spend their youth together and their manhood as well. Little did they know, for they were never told, that their fathers, Ramco and Tamaqua, had made the same pact, only much later in life with White Feather.

So it was unusual on this beautiful morning of the planting moon, that his father, Tamaqua, squatting close to the fire, rose and ordered Metoxem, the youngest of his four sons, to stay close to camp.

"You stay here with the women," he said.

But why, his youngest son questioned with his eyes, knowing better than to voice the thought. A father's word ruled, yet he felt hurt by the rejection. This might have been the opportunity he had been waiting for to prove his manhood to the tribe. Metoxem, greatly disappointed, felt his lower lip quiver. His cousins stood silently at his side. There was nothing they could say.

Seeing his son confused, Tamaqua continued, "Wait for your mother. Help her."

And that was it.

It was not manly for Indian men to show emotion.

So, Metoxem turned away.

Tamaqua stood with his back to his sons and looked over the

camp. Minnah was nowhere in sight. This unsettled him, but a glance and nod from Saquiskawa calmed him. She would see to his wife when she arrived.

"She will be here soon," her gentle but confident nod seemed to say.

He nodded in agreement and prepared to leave the campsite.

Metoxem watched in silence as his father, two older brothers, cousins, and their father, Ramco, rose and left camp. All the men of the camp followed suit. The boys kept their heads forward looking, for Ramco brought up the rear.

So, he sighed as he watched the last man out of sight, *it is this camp for me.* There was not much to do.

Then I will hunt he thought, raising his chin and puffing out his chest.

And more importantly, keep a look out for his mother. For while the other women and his Aunt Saquiskawa, with her daughter Nipapoa toddling behind her, shuffled back and forth around the make shift camp, Minnah had yet to appear.

"Where is mother?" he asked suddenly. He turned impatiently to stare at the woods.

"She comes when the forest spirits are appeased," his aunt replied. He looked over to see her sit down heavily on a mat, pulling her only daughter close. The roundness of her body made him think of the great, late summer pumpkins that grew in the village plots. His aunt took a deep breath. The pain had eased only slightly, and she would arise when her sister appeared. By then, it would be time to serve the food, for the men would have returned in small groups to eat and then collect the pelts for trading.

She tried to distract the boy. She felt his disappointment strongly.

"Catch us a sweet-tasting bird to fill our hungry stomachs, little one," she called to him with a nod. She then added, "Our little hunter." She watched him silently then. It never failed to surprise her how much he resembled her mother. It had been years since she had seen her, but the vision of her face appeared in the young-

THE SAVAGE RIVER VALLEY

est member of the family. Metoxem was the spitting image of his grandmother Tah-neh-wa. The same broad face, square jaw, and wide and brilliant smile. Anyone, not knowing, would have mistaken him for Tah-neh-wa's son, so deep was the resemblance.

Only no one spoke of it.

Metoxem had grown tired of playing with his slingshot and stubbornly set it down. He also grew tired of being called little one. It was a nickname they should have let go, even if he were not as tall as the others.

That made no difference to him.

"I grow tired of being with women. It is my turn to prove myself a man," he muttered under his breath, though not so loud as to offend the sister of his mother. There were times when his mother was occupied in the fields that he loved to be drawn in Saquiskawa's arms and feel the comfort of her body against his. She was another mother to him, and he did not wish to be unkind.

Saquiskawa snuggled with her daughter, all the time watching her nephew.

In the village there was always something familiar that caught his attention and kept him occupied. Here, on the other hand, was an unfamiliar place. It was different now that he had to stay behind with the women. He curiously watched the others. Not all the women had traveled to the trading camp in the wake of their husbands. But, he knew all the women that did. Most of the squaws, in fact, had stayed to work in their village, Wachachkeek. Those mothers who were suckling their newborn babies stayed behind. Those mothers, like Ontelawnee, too old to walk the entire trip and be of any use afterwards, stayed behind. They would tend to the fires and the fields.

Minnah was of neither group. But yet, she still had not appeared.

She lagged behind the main group. A usual activity, one during which she knelt near the trail to give thanks to the wood spirits for their safe arrival. For this, her grandmother had taught her well. The burning of a few plants and a sacred pledge would assure their safety on this trip.

She stopped not far from camp but far enough that her son could not call out to her.

Metoxem watched the activity of the women and grew increasingly bored with the scene. Cooking was squaws' work. And just as hunting didn't interest the females, cooking didn't interest him. The women were gentle—content to stay in one spot or shuffle from the stream to the camp all in a small perimeter. He, on the other hand, was restless, as young men often were. His mood grew sulky. How could they all leave him behind? He wanted to join the other men, his brothers included; the two of the three who accompanied his father and the other who patrolled the camp perimeters with other boys. After all, at ten, he thought he was a man or soon to be one. At such a young age and with no help from his father, how could he prove himself? Could he do it alone? For just a moment, he thought what it would be like to disobey his father's wishes, and then immediately his thoughts switched to another.

An Indian he would never disobey—his Uncle White Feather.

How he longed to see him once more. His uncle, he felt certain, would take him along to trade and meet the white man. In the past, White Feather had shown Metoxem how to hunt and pulled him, not unwillingly, into the activities all the men enjoyed back at the village. Metoxem loved his uncle, at times more than his own family. For White Feather gave him a look that told him he was already a man—a wink, a nod, though subtle, and a gentle tap on the shoulder. Just the thought of his uncle lifted his dark mood.

He noticed movement at his feet. It was enough of a distraction to momentarily divert his attention.

He curiously knelt by a mound swarming with tiny black ants, the kind that bite and leave angry red welts. Such quick energy and movement fascinated him. The ants seemed to know where they were going and why as they carried heavy granules of sand on their backs. Unlike Metoxem, who suddenly resented their freedom to scurry about.

What would happen if I kick the mound? he wondered angrily, but

THE SAVAGE RIVER VALLEY

before he could do so, there was a burst of activity at the meadow's edge. He spotted a strange woman running into camp. He had no time to think of her appearance or the look of terror on her face.

Nor did it occur to him that he used to see her as a baby, for at the same moment, he heard another woman screaming in the forest.

With a gasp of anguish, he recognized his mother's voice.

"Mother!" he screamed, and grabbing his slingshot he took off on a run.

∿∿

It all happened too quickly.

Saquiskawa, upon hearing the screams of her sister, awkwardly struggled to rise when a pain, sharper and deeper than before, sliced through her abdomen. She felt a rush of liquid pour down her legs. Unable to move, she fell back on the mat, still holding Nipapoa in her arms.

"Minnah," she moaned. The other squaws gathered close.

Suddenly terrified at being penned in by the women's bodies, she called out "Sasqua!"

And at that moment, she felt her pelvis bones begin to spread apart.

Chapter Fourteen

History, later told, did not accurately reflect the events of the day. Or perhaps it was man himself who confusedly bungled the whole bloody account. The unfolding of history depends on who tells it and why. Most often, there is something to gain in giving a different account of true events, and something to hide.

At times irrelevant to accuracy, the first official account stays in the record as truth for those who readily read, who readily believe, or who readily accept it as gospel truth, meaning word under the auspices of God's sanctity. But there is one, a person not to be easily swayed or convinced, who for compelling reasons, reasons unbeknownst to the common man, will dig relentlessly for truth of long ago. If it is there, it will be found.

There were mangled versions of what went askew. No one would say for certain what caused the world of the Indian to explode and the white man's presence in the New World to collapse, at least for that summer of trading in 1618 in the valley of the Great River. The events that unfolded that day would shut down trading on a huge scale for years to come. Angry Indians? Plundering whites?

No definitive answer.

Perhaps it was the storm as it came streaking across the sky. Perhaps it was something else, a destiny that had been foretold, predetermined, and now come to fruition.

THE SAVAGE RIVER VALLEY

∾

Truly, I had grown into a woman. I had the strength to do what needed to be done. Even though the thought of it frightened me and left a spot deep within yearning for safety. At times, I felt my thoughts overtake me and I wanted to cry out.

It was not too late. Surely, the spirits would release me from my task?

I could still muster the energy to run, manage to get far away from a place that would bring sorrow that day. The thought flickered in my mind and rested on its laurels. Slip into the sheltering forest, down the path toward camp, or hide. If I hid, I could then escape the imminent danger that soon would be upon me. I suddenly longed for the comforting presence of the other women, my sister especially, and the protective might of my husband and sons. Here, in this lonely spot, away from my loved ones, I was alone, except for the woman spirit who sat at my side. But it was no good to consider such actions. I had no other choice.

It was the only way, as best as I understood, to bring White Feather and Clara together. So many years in the making, and I grew impatient.

So, I chose to stay.

Knowing this to be my destiny, I ignored all the visions that warned me of the terrible thing about to happen, for someone would die that day, though I did not know who.

The curtain of surprise was about to lift.

∾

Faithful, Clara sat silently at her side, knowing not of the horror that would soon unfold. She was happy, gleeful as a child out on an adventure with her best friend. She had the urge to sing a song and even attempt to whistle.

She looked about her, innocent and wide-eyed, at the world that existed beyond the open doorway of the longhouse. She felt as if clapping her hands or jumping in joy was justified.

These feelings she had seldom experienced in her new life.

For eighteen years, Clara had spent more time sleeping and drowsy than awake and alert. Nothing about her physical appearance had changed. She looked the same. She had not aged one day. Her past life was slipping from her mind. One thing she did remember was the old woman's words: "Your journey will be long. At times, you will hear more than see. But learn much, you will. Feel much, you will."

Although she had not seen the old woman since the day the shaman stone was stolen, nor heard her since the day she jumped off the bridge, her voice remained clear in Clara's mind.

Ah yes, now Clara remembered! In 1609, the Old One had left the longhouse without saying a word, but all the children followed her outside. Metoxem, a mere child, having learned to walk the year past, stood at the edge of the meadow long after the group of little children around him dispersed. He stood alone. It was precisely the same spot where his mother had stood for years as a child. Standing at that spot was not the strange part of it. It was what he was doing that was eerie.

Staring off to the woods, the little boy was waving good-bye.

So! He could see the spirit of Sasqua! He was gifted with the second sight, as was his mother and his great grandmother before him. So, the gift, for that is what it was, passed through the subsequent generations.

That startling image stayed with Clara.

The Old One was right. So many images stuck in her mind, but more than that were the words and whispers of the Indian people. It was as if they had become entrenched within her spirit, settling within a lodging somewhere deep in her soul. She no longer lived for herself. She lived as part of the Indian village that surrounded her, and she clung to them, in hope and out of love. She thought less of her old world now. The well being and continuance of Indian life along the shores of the Great River brought her a greater satisfaction than she could have imagined.

THE SAVAGE RIVER VALLEY

There was, however, only a slight mar.

Her confidence in the peaceful world of the Mohicans had been shaken, as had the confidence of the Indians at Wachachkeek, after the intruder stole the shaman stone years ago. It was never found nor was the intruder caught. But the idea of stealing stayed with all of them and, over time, became a slight worry that never left them. Then there were the sporadic attacks of the northern tribes that came dangerously close to Wachachkeek. A bit of their peaceful way of living had disappeared.

Of some things, they were uncertain.

What they did know and what they told in their fireside stories and passed on to their children was as such: One day, eighteen harvest moons ago, their sachem of great powers, Sasqua, passed on to the next world. Nine summers ago, when life flowed as gentle as a wide summer stream, a powerful bird, bearing men as mighty as Manito himself, came flapping upon the Great Water and their treasured cup of blessing disappeared.

It was a day of great sadness.

∿

The impending storm had gathered in intensity. Dark clouds appeared on the horizon. The wind now whistled in the trees and whipped the water on the river. Rain, threatening to fall, did not deter the Indians or the white men. A band of Mohawk traders pushed forward into the meadow, numbering well over thirty men. Thirty young and impetuous men held in check only by the hand and will of their leader. They stood waiting.

The rowboat was making its way to a spot on the bank.

Captain Hendricks watched them carefully, sizing them up, as he made to go ashore. His eyes scanned the crowd, looking for a glimpse of the Mohawk leader, the mainstay of the group. He fingered his sword at his side and felt somewhat comforted. It was a bit unnerving to stand so close to the Red Men, to smell them, look to their painted faces, and have to communicate with them. But the end result, a ship's hold brimming with furs, ultimately overrode any apprehension he felt. He shrugged.

There was no room for doubt or misgivings, he concluded.

Suddenly, he spied a young warrior slip away from the main group. This bothered more than puzzled him.

"Faster," he said to the men rowing the boat.

∿

The screams of the woman resounded throughout the forest.

Everyone heard her, as the cries were surprisingly magnified in echo a hundred times over, a miracle to be sure. The woman was on the far side of the Mohican camp. So how was it that her voice, terrified and shrill, reached not only the campsite where Saquiskawa lay moaning but far across the clearing to where Ramco, Tamaqua, and their sons were just coming into view?

Ramco rushed to where his woman lay writhing on the mat, the four young boys on his heels. All the Indian women of the camp crowded about, so it took them a few moments to break through the crowd.

Tamaqua, recognizing the voice of his woman, instantly broke into a run, taking off in a different direction. At the same time, he savagely drew a large knife from a sheath on his belt.

∿

The man, grizzled and dirty, had appeared out of nowhere—a white man who smelled of distant lands. His face, snarling and distorted, shone with wicked anticipation. He had come across the Indian woman by the purest of luck. A ways back, guided by years of sneakiness, he skirted a small group of Indian boys who, young and inexperienced, let him slip by undetected.

Now, as his wildest obsession had foretold, he was about to get his desserts after the long voyage. This one, like the one of the year before, would provide him with a tasty morsel of Indian flesh. He advanced on the woman who had yet to turn to face him.

His excitement grew. He would take her by complete surprise. The thought of it filled him with a crooked sense of happiness. Jan Jansen licked his lips in anticipation of a struggle. It took a struggle for him to become aroused and stay that way.

"God, thanks be to you for putting her here."

How he loved moments like this one!

It was better than tackling the whores in Amsterdam and better than paying for their goods.

The Indian woman, a good two heads shorter than the white man and indeed no match against the strength of his sea-faring muscles, was sheltered by the side of a hill, snuggled close to the bank of earth where she found a few plants to nourish her prayers to Manito. She had plucked them from the ground and passed them over the flame, whispering to herself. The sacred weed that almost no ceremony took place without.

This should be easy, he thought.

He gave one last look around.

A small fire smoked at her feet, burning around a larger branch the Indian woman had thrust into the little heap. She was alone. Or so he thought.

Jansen, a man of primitive character and no intellect, held no special talents for second sight. So, therefore, he did not see Clara jump to her feet. Startled at first by his appearance, then scared, she backed away. Then she ran.

He smiled as the Indian woman slowly turned and faced him. His look was one of exultation.

That was his first mistake.

I knew he was there before he even came close. I could smell his scent, feel the vibration of his footstep, and hear his raspy breathing from far away. I stayed quiet until he was directly behind me. Then I turned to face him, knowing I would not fight him. It was part of my destiny.

Then he smiled. Suddenly I saw the frozen smile of a corpse flash in my mind. A headless corpse that walked aimlessly about, lost with an unredeemed soul. Would he be the one to die today? I had never wished death on anyone, but now, seeing him so close to me, I prayed to Manito to make it happen.

I didn't like his smell or his looks.

My head was lowered, but looking up through my lashes, our eyes met. His eyes shone with a wickedness I had never seen before. I recognized all the human evil of the world in his intense stare. I had never seen anything like it before. I trembled but stood my ground.

For a split second, he hesitated and then, with one hand, reached out and grabbed me roughly around the neck, pulling me close to him. In his other hand, he carried a long, curved knife.

It was at that moment that I heard her screaming from nearby. In his grasp, I managed to turn my head slightly in the direction of the scream and was shocked by whom I saw standing in the shadow of a tree.

It was then that I grew alarmed. I had not seen this coming.

A timid though willing Clara had finally been coaxed out of doors by Minnah. The Indian squaw held the woman spirit's hand. It was a wondrous world Minnah showed her; of leafy plants, edible, medicinal, or poisonous, and trees that stretched high in the air, a width bigger than she could have thought possible; fresh cooked food that hung over the fire; fields filled with a bountiful crop of corn; so many varieties of beans; and much more. Over the months that she walked at this Indian woman's side, Clara, feeling a new

THE SAVAGE RIVER VALLEY

sense of awe, marveled at the bright shining moon that sparkled over a darkened land, and the sun that bestowed its richness and warmth on them all. She marveled at all she witnessed outdoors. And at night, she placed her head upon the musty and dry skins of what used to be the Old One's sleeping compartment, left empty since her death.

"You will be comfortable here," Minnah promised her.

Her life, as she knew it then, took on a simple quality. She finally donned the deerskin dress and moccasins and, in doing so, she discovered the miraculous! She loved life, their life, as if she had been born anew. She smiled throughout the day. She was happy. Her body tingled with satisfaction and a completeness that pleasured her in simple ways. The others still did not see her, but it no longer mattered much. What mattered was there was at least one companion, one woman, who showed her the way of the Indians. And at times, when he was little, she caught Metoxem turning his baby eyes upon her and smiling. This gave her strength. She belonged here with them, her new family.

But nevertheless, she at times felt timid to the newness.

And so she chose safety over daring.

The only way to do that was to become a faithful shadow to Minnah who was not hesitant to strike out on her own. Up until this moment, she had not left Minnah's side. But as the man approached, looking like a scoundrel and out of place in the Indian world, Clara knew at once that he meant to harm Minnah. Glancing at the face she had come to love, she saw that the Indian woman paid no attention to the footsteps at her back. She wanted to shake her. Did she know of evil white men? Clara's world of innocence ended at that moment. The Indian world had its dangers as well.

She felt the urge to scream rise in her throat, but as of yet, her voice had not made itself heard in their midst. She must flee to the others, and do so quickly.

So, she did the natural thing. She ran for help.

PAMELA DE LEON

∿

Jansen had effortlessly wrestled Minnah to the ground, swiping her feet from underneath her, and landed upon her. With one thrust, he ripped through her mantle, tearing at the skins with his knife.

It was easier that way. So far, his luck was holding out. As most Indian women, she wore nothing underneath. It was his for the taking. After grabbing her breasts and aroused by their exquisite plumpness, he fumbled with the buttons on his pants tugging at them to come undone. How impatient he was! The pants refused to slide down. At a time like this what wretched curse had been cast on him to be so clumsy? The voyage had been long, had played on his nerves, and he had much energy. He couldn't wait any longer and threw all caution to the wind. Without thinking clearly, he foolishly threw down his knife, and, tightly squeezing the woman between his legs, tore at his pants with both hands.

That was his second mistake.

Metoxem had run as fast as his little legs could carry him, jumping over fallen logs, ignoring the forest paths but instead tearing through brush in a straight line toward the sounds of his mother screaming. Knowing his father and brothers to be far away at the trading spot, instinct told him that he alone had to save his mother from whatever danger she faced! It wasn't even so much as proving his manhood, for he gave not a thought to that or to his own safety. Instead, he felt no stabs of fear, only the urgency and primeval instinct of protecting his mother; the mother who, up to now, had always protected him. Little did he know that when he made that decision, he had already taken the leap in joining the ranks of men.

He ran faster. So intent was he on reaching his mother that Metoxem was completely unaware that the woman spirit kept up with him, somehow finding a new strength coursing through her legs as she kept abreast of the young Indian boy. Her lungs were not winded and had she not been so terrified of what was happen-

THE SAVAGE RIVER VALLEY

ing to Minnah, the newness of her strength would have caused her great surprise. She felt an incredible resurgence of life, of a greater strength returning to her long unused limbs. Even her mind was racing. She could almost imagine leaving her invisible world behind!

Then it dawned on her as she ran alongside Metoxem-the boy had seen her! As she had broken through the tree line, only the boy had looked up.

Within minutes, chaos seemed to reign.

Just as Jansen tore that gashing hole through Minnah's skirt, Metoxem, having rounded the ridge at full speed, burst into view. He was downwind of the man who was higher up the slope and could see his arched back and the form of his mother underneath him. Hatred for the man ran wild in his heart. The man was hurting his mother. It was all up to him, for no one else was about. He breathed deeply, trying to steady himself. He looked around, hoping to find a good heavy stick. No luck. Then he spied a stone, larger than any he has successfully used in his slingshot, and grabbed it, settled it into the sinew string, and pulled. He sighted his target with narrowed eye. He let it fly at the man's head at a considerable speed.

The aim was perfect! The man flinched back in sudden pain. The dull thud of stone cracking his skull filled Clara with unspeakable joy. The skillfully aimed stone hit the backside of the man's head, ripping the skin, so that, leaning forward over the woman, the gushing blood flowed into his eyes and down his cheeks. "Yes, you got him!" Clara screamed with jubilation.

She stood just behind the boy. Her heart was bursting with pride for such a young boy willing to confront brutality head on. Little did she realize she had just shouted her first words in this Indian world.

Two things happened next.

The man, furious at this interruption, turned halfway to face his threat. If he thought himself to be angry before as he tore at his clothes, there were no limits to his anger now. As hardened and heartless a seaman and criminal that he was, it surprised even him.

Had the moment been different, he might have guffawed. There stood a young savage—an Indian dressed in skins, with a bald scalp. At first, he let out a grunt.

"You savage bastard!" he screamed.

The primitive heathen glared at him-a spindly, skinny boy with a simple slingshot dangling in his hand, hurting him, the invincible man that he was. The sight made Jansen furious beyond comprehension. Eyes blazing, he growled and let loose a string of nasty words.

He would put him to death and then return his attention to the woman. She lay still beneath him. *I'll kill them both, by the time I am done here and leave them to the wolves,* he thought savagely. He wiped at the blood streaming over his face. The taste so sweet and sticky filled his mouth. He spat it out.

He looked back over his shoulder to the boy.

And then he stopped.

Jesus, he thought, *who is that standing behind the boy?*

It was the strangest thing he had ever seen—and it stared right back at him. Gave him the creeps, it did, all shimmery and white. What was it?

He stared, disbelieving.

An apparition, faintly reminiscent of an old woman, raised her hand and pointed at him, and then she slid her finger across her throat in a cutting motion. They say before death, one sees everything, including spirits, possibly demons, and at times, angels. Had he already died? But he had no more time to think, only react.

The boy, taking a flying leap, was sailing through the air toward him.

He automatically raised his fists to catch the boy in mid-air.

It was then that the woman underneath him reacted. She reached up and grabbed him by the hair. Seeing her son in danger had galled her into action. Vision or no vision, she had to protect her son. Thrown off balance, Jansen's arms flailed backwards just as the boy landed on him. Within seconds, and with one swipe of

THE SAVAGE RIVER VALLEY

his large hands, he grabbed the boy by the throat and at the same time knocked the woman alongside her face. Her head snapped backwards. His brute power was too much for the mother and her courageous son. The muscled seaman quickly got the upper hand, throwing the boy to the ground, who, greatly winded by the punch, landed with a thud. When Jansen turned back to the woman, still pinned between his legs, her cheek revealed a gash that ran from the corner of her eye down to the tip of her upper lip. Just the exact size of his knuckled fist, he thought proudly.

She'll wear that scar forever, he thought.

There was no further time to waste. He pried open her legs and saw all of her.

In his mind, thus disposed to having this woman against her will in this howling wilderness, there was no turning back. On the contrary, he would have his way! He made ready to take the plunge, to sear the bloom of this heathen with his manhood.

It was then that he heard the savage screams of Indian men ring out all around him!

And making his third and final mistake, he looked up.

∿

The Mohawk warrior, Mahwah, leader from the north, had stayed hidden from the white men. Even as his band of young braves assembled in the meadow, flanking his son, he remained motionless. Seeing all the younger men grouped together, he was struck with a pang of sadness. For a split second, he saw the future and felt apart from it. He understood that when he was gone from this earth, these young braves would carry on and live as he once did; courageous, agile, and, if need be, ruthless. He felt the solitariness of his position.

Already his role had changed.

He checked the sky. There was no use in going forward into the light of the sun, diminished by the oncoming storm. At least not yet.

299

The terms of trade had yet to be determined.

The Mohicans, hiding in the forest around him, had yet to appear in the open. He almost smiled at their craftiness.

So, he waited.

Within minutes, and without understanding why, he felt a curious breath of cold air at his back. The wind was blowing and clouds passed quickly overhead. But the fresh air of early summer had been, up to that moment, warm. This troubled him. Mahwah, not superstitious like most Indians of the day, for no logical reason turned in his tracks and saw what he was not supposed to see.

Through the jumbled growth of the forest, he caught sight of a lone figure in the far distance, striking out in the direction of the Mohican side of the trading post.

His face darkened. Without turning to alert the others, he took off at a trot through the woods.

∿

The white woman, known as the cripple, so used to guarding that persona and thus resorting to an imaginary limp until she came to her senses, could barely keep up with White Feather. He ran so fast!

Within moments of hearing someone scream, White Feather had taken a last glance at the naked white woman who sat near the pool of glistening water and then turned and raced away.

"Wait," the cripple cried.

Unsure of what was happening and not wanting to remain alone in that shaded cove that now spooked her, the white woman grabbed the only nightshirt not in the pile of filthy clothes and struggled to slip it over her head. At the same time, she jumped up and went in pursuit of the Indian. There was no reason or logic to justify following him.

She just did.

THE SAVAGE RIVER VALLEY

A low rumble of thunder came rolling over the Onteoras and down into the valley.

It all happened so fast. Years later, White Feather would still be confused as to the sequence of events; what happened next? At times, he would be convinced he had been dreaming—a very bad and frightening dream. When he ran up a rather slippery slope, his heels digging into the earth with each sure-footed step, he came onto a flat area, framed by an earthen bank, atop which towered a ridge of solid rock. He came upon a horrific scene.

For him, there was no time to think, just act. He caught sight of Metoxem, son of his sister, moaning, curled up on the ground. He clenched his jaw in anger. Who would do this to a young boy? Then he saw the vile white man. No sooner had he prepared to raise his tomahawk to send it slicing through the air and kill the man who lay squirming atop his sister pinned below, White Feather caught sight of another Indian, rounding the ridge, stomping into view ahead of him. As this Indian came into full view, White Feather's hand stopped in mid-air and he froze. First, because the Indian, even for his apparent age, so powerful and broad, seemed to move the earth when he walked. Secondly, because White Feather recognized this Mohawk! He had seen him long ago, and he now remembered from when and where.

It was as if the years had passed by in a single breath of air. The Mohawk was older, stouter, moved slower, but nevertheless was the very same Mohawk that had watched White Feather stalk and eventually kill the bear! White Feather felt transported back in time, a déjà vu, a real sense of reliving the past. For a brief and fleeting moment, he stood standing on the riverbank looking beyond the carcass of the bear, seeing a warrior who stood in the shadows.

Behind him, the cripple, taking deep breaths of air, came up behind him. Although no longer hampered by the false metal foot, she was, nevertheless, much slower than the Mohican. Her muscles, normally strong, had atrophied somewhat by the cramped closet of the ship.

She hesitated a moment gasping to catch her breath before looking up.

She, too, recognizing the scene before her to be what it was, stopped. It wasn't so much the man who had a squaw pinned between his knees or the bewildered boy that lay on the ground that held her attention. Nor was it the two heathens, one of which stood close at her side, who stared in fury at each other. Rather, in this place that was half in gloomy shadow and half in sunlight, it was another figure, back turned to her, that made her body go cold. This was not fear. Indeed not. This was an extraordinarily different feeling; coming in contact with another dimension—the world of the dead. She had never seen a specter before, but now she did. How did she know this?

She recognized the figure, the manner of standing, and the tilt of the head. It was not real. It could not be real she reasoned.

Seconds passed.

The figure, a woman, turned to face her. The cripple's eyes widened in disbelief.

Clara, the woman spirit, and the cripple, no longer a cripple but instead a young woman named Klarinda, who had stolen away from her master's house with his goods, looked as two people do when completely astonished. For one thing, they saw each other. For another, they were staring into a looking glass, and what each one saw was a reflection, save for the difference of hair color. They were one and the same. The same full lips, the large expressive eyes, the slender nose, and the strong chin. Klarinda, with flowing blond hair, was the young female who had hidden away in a little closet for most of the journey crossing the ocean, who had disguised herself as a human misfit to escape the clutches of the merchant. In another world, four hundred years distant, Clara, with dark flowing hair, had chosen to end her life to escape what had become an unbearable agony. Both sought redemption and salvation.

THE SAVAGE RIVER VALLEY

Now they stared at each other. "No," they each whispered softly.

For the second time that day, two worlds collided: first, the white man's and the Indian's, and now the past with the future.

It was then that a woman screamed in agony. But the scream came not from the woman on the ground, nor the two who continued to remain transfixed on one another.

The woman whose scream had resounded throughout the forest, and even up into the Onteora mountains, was hidden behind a large tree, another oak tree, for the forest was full of them, comparable to the widest tree in the forest. As Metoxem slowly rose, he saw the man atop his mother reach for his knife and in the same instant scrambled to attack the man once again. This monster meant to kill his mother!

But the scream of the woman behind the tree galvanized the white woman to action.

Before Metoxem could move, the woman courageously jumped onto the white man's back, screaming furious words that Metoxem did not understand. One thing he knew—she was livid! He watched in amazement as the white man reached behind and punched the woman square in the chest and threw her off of him.

She came back at him one more time before he hit her savagely enough to send her flying with arms askew.

When Jansen looked up during the last moments of his life, he managed to catch sight of another Indian flying toward him, this time from somewhere before him, high above the earthen bank where he had come upon the woman. The Indian's face was twisted in anger, yet Jansen was struck by the fierce look in his eyes and the hair-raising scream coming from his mouth. The cry was not human!

Tamaqua had run along the path as swift as the deer that run from the wolves, strong and frenzied, taking quick gulps of air through his nose and out his mouth to sustain him. White Feather years back had taught him how to maintain high speed and not lose his breath. But now all his thoughts were on his woman. No one hurt his family. As an Indian hunter and warrior, and as head of his family, he knew no fear. He had to defend them. As he came up on a rise and ran along the ridge, looking down on his left side, he had a clear view. Below him was a scene that made his anger explode. Taking it all in with one glance: a bloody pale face towering over his woman, his son on the ground; White Feather, confronted by a Mohawk warrior; and strangely enough, a white woman who stood one second before she took a running leap and landed on the white man's back, kicking and clawing her way to his face. He knew what he had to do.

The last thing he saw before he took a flying leap off the ledge was the white woman flung backwards in one swift motion. She went crashing down hard. It was a blow that likely killed her. If a white man had stooped so low with his own people, then Tamaqua had no doubts what the man meant to do to his wife.

The Indian let loose an angry scream.

By lifting his head, the throat of the white man was a perfect target for his knife. For the first and only time of his life, Jansen felt fear, the unmistakable feeling was cold, and it slithered over his body in a matter of a second.

The Indian looked Jansen straight in the eye. With one mighty sweep, and wrenching his arm to the side and letting the knife flow in his hands, the man's throat didn't stand a chance. The jugular vein spurted fast and furious under the slicing action of the sharp blade before the angry force of the Indian hit the rest of the man's body.

The villain who so long ago had ruthlessly stolen the Shaman Stone from the village of Wachachkeek was dead.

Chapter Fifteen

Harmensen could barely believe his luck! How easy it was to escape!

How was it that no one stopped him from coming into the woods? He half expected a bullet through his back at any moment, having deserted his ship and duties. It wouldn't have surprised him a bit. The captain was a mean one. A man neglecting his duties deserved to be shot. Was he that inconspicuous, perfect at stealth, that no one noticed him creeping into the woods or was it that no one cared? At any moment, at the very least, he had expected a shout to ring out, calling for his return. Although he wasn't sure how he got away with it, he was mighty glad he did.

Now where did that blasted cripple go off to? he wondered, angry that the lure of riches made him take unnecessary risks. All the riches in the world wouldn't help him if he were dead, now would it? Being off the ship and far from the others was not his choice. The forest was nothing beautiful or enchanting to him, just a spooky place full of moving shadows and strange noises. For him it was a place of dread.

He had managed to escape the ship, wade through the water, and reach the shore unnoticed by the others, the captain included. They were occupied with the savages. Better for him! He had stumbled through the forest and, after a time, had come across the shaded cove. The seaman Harmensen, in search of the cripple and the diamonds, arrived at precisely the moment when White Feather and the female were frantically running up the slope. He spotted the woman, clawing her way up the slippery incline. Her scantily clad body revealed shapely white legs that shone in the muted light of the forest. He watched her grabbing onto trees for support, in pursuit of the Indian.

This was strange. He wondered what a white woman was doing here. Puzzled, he then looked to the water and the encircling rocks. Taking a step closer, he spied the heap of dirty clothes. Harmensen cautiously advanced. The coolness of the cove washed over him and met his sweaty brow. It was then that he saw it. With a squeal of undisguised delight, he reached out his hand for the shaman stone and the pouch. Before he could get close enough to grab it, brutal screams that were human echoed through the forest. He froze. The noise was chilling. Was it meant for him? Did anyone see him? Was someone behind him, ready to attack? Shaking, he realized then what a terrible predicament he could be in. So far from the others with no weapons, he was little more than defenseless, not to mention innocent to the ways of the savages.

The seaman was afraid and bewildered. He dared to timidly glance over his shoulder, trembling at the thought of what he might see.

Nothing was there.

Then he heard it again, and this time he convinced himself it was the sound of an animal tearing through the bush. To hell with the sparkling stones!

He turned and ran off.

As he stumbled through the forest, this time in the general direction of the ship, Harmensen, sweating and panting, came to a rather shady spot where he paused to wearily rest his arm on a tree, lowered his head to catch his breath, and attempted to get his bearings.

Should he go right? He couldn't tell.

Oh God, he thought, *how dark can a forest be?*

Why did the trees look dangerous, the shadows ready to pounce? Everything was moving. The whole scene around him was spinning and colliding into one frightening blur.

THE SAVAGE RIVER VALLEY

Should he go to the left, then? The prospect held no better promise.

The devil take this place, he thought. Minutes later he heard another angry scream coming from the slope ahead. He cringed, flattening himself against the tree.

Good Lord, the savages are everywhere!

"Save me, Father," he yelped out loud to his God.

It was then that something went flying through the air and landed with a thud before rolling a few feet more.

A short distance away, up on the rise, Tamaqua had sliced Jansen's throat and then skimmed a large chunk of his scalp. He then chopped off the head with several forceful whacks of his tomahawk and, with one mighty yell, threw it off into the woods. Let it be a lesson to all white men!

It landed squarely at Harmensen's feet, the startled eyes in Jansen's skull staring from the purplish face.

Along the way, the decapitated head had landed in dirt and leaves that clung to the bloodied mass, still wet and oozing. The gaping hole with no teeth was filled with dirt. A little bug crawled in the soil.

The sailor, shaking from head to toe, took a step backward and leaned over, feeling vomit rushing up his throat and gushing out through his mouth. Vomit even poured through his nose, burning the tender tissues. Surely, the fright was going to kill him. He wiped his face on his sleeve, sweat blending with vomit.

One second the man was alive, and the next dead. Jansen, master at inflicting cruelty, would never hurt anyone again. Was there revenge to be had? Harmensen paused, only hastily contemplating the sentiment. But pure instinct of survival won out. He would be a complete fool if he stood here in this primitive world of the savage that he did not understand and thought out his next move! There was nothing to hold him back. The cripple was on his own! For all he knew, by now the savages had beheaded or scalped the pitiful creature as well. It wouldn't be until days later that he began to think of the mysterious white woman and the heap of dirty clothes and the fate of the cripple. But, at the moment, he was not sticking around to find out.

Horrified that the same lot would befall him if he hesitated one second longer, he turned and fled the scene, but not before he grabbed the sailor's head by its bloody slick hair.

Already distrusting the sailor since the night in his quarters when Harmensen lied, the captain would need proof of a heinous murder. He held the proof in his hand, the hair clutched in his fingers as he ran. Proof—a good enough reason to halt the trading and set sail immediately. Back to Amsterdam, back to sanity, back to a poor but reasonably safe life among his own folk who spoke his language and followed his customs. He'd rather confront the dangers of a city street or even the small pox than the dangers he faced, or rather ran from, here. He didn't belong here. And if he made it out alive, he swore never to return.

"God be with me!" he cried.

And then, as providence would have it, he fell, tripping over his feet. Putting his arms out to break the fall, the bodiless head came within inches of his own. He could feel the eyes of the dead man upon him. He averted his eyes. Instead, he looked up.

Escape from this hell, he thought wildly as he picked himself up. It was then that he spied two Indian boys making their way toward him—running with bows and arrows.

What scared him the most? They were smiling in delight.

Good Lord! More heathens, he thought!

〰

No one near the place of Jansen's murder noticed the seaman tearing through the woods, for they were all too occupied with the scene before them.

Minnah, a full grown woman, mother of four young braves and wife to a warrior and hunter, long known as a medicine woman and vision seeker, watched it all as if it were a dream.

THE SAVAGE RIVER VALLEY

But this was a dream she had not seen coming—a dream that pained her heart and tore at her soul. In one glance, she took it all in from where she lay. White Feather meant to approach the older Mohawk, to forcefully slice the back of his leg muscles and force him down, but instead he hesitated in the solemn face of this man who made no move to attack him. Clara, clenching her hands to her chest and watching it all in horror, had stepped behind Jansen. At the moment she felt she had to do something but couldn't, the young girl with flowing hair ran past her and jumped on his back. Clara stood dumbfounded, in awe of this spirited girl. She was courageous and daring, while Clara was fearful. Oh, she thought, if she could only be like that!

The girl kicked, screamed, and pulled the man's hair. Jansen, feeling cornered, crouched over the body of the squaw and shook her off. As she came at him again, Jansen threw back his hand and solidly belted her across the face, sending her reeling from the blow, smacking right into a surprised Clara, both of them crashing backwards and falling together as one.

Tamaqua had not stopped running and had taken a flying leap from atop the stone ledge, landing squarely on top of Jansen, slashing his throat in one fatal cut. Minnah, hearing a scream of rage, could feel the whoosh of air as her husband flew over her body, yanking the white man off of her. Perhaps she had been foolish for not telling him the truth of her vision, as limited as it had been. But it no longer mattered.

Metoxem crawled to her. She grabbed him tightly, feeling his little body shaking like a small tender babe uncovered in the cold wind of winter.

"Mother," he sobbed, wrapping his arms around her waist, "did he hurt you?"

She wasn't sure.

The world had gone crazy! White Feather, Clara, Tamaqua, and her son Metoxem, and now this strange woman, had all saved her life. No harm had come to her.

And then she looked down to see blood all over her torn mantle.

PAMELA DE LEON

∿

The most incredible thing happened next. As the Mohawk stood unflinching under White Feather's stare, his son, Wanaque Wolf, alerted by the others to his father's disappearance and following him, came upon the scene. He stood at a vantage point where he could see it all—their startled faces and their tense bodies. He could even sense their fear. Immediately, upon spotting the Mohicans, he pulled his bow from his shoulder and drew an arrow. Strangely enough, his father, a mighty warrior already a part of the oral tradition normally reserved for ancestors, stood motionless, his arms hanging askew. He had not drawn a weapon, neither the tomahawk at his belt nor the bow high up on his shoulder. Surely his father needed him now! The Mohican, trained to put down an enemy, tomahawk in hand, would not kill his father! He grew still, ready to take aim.

Wanaque Wolf experienced a new sensation—uncertainty.

At the breaking point, the woman, seeing her son draw his bow, screamed again. The woman who had, crying and terrified, crouched behind the shelter of a tree, now stepped into view.

All eyes turned to her.

It had not been, as everyone thought, Minnah who had screamed, but rather someone who shared the same tones of voice: deep, melodious, and stirring. Someone of the same blood, someone related to them all.

Who was it then? Metoxem, too young, did not recognize or know her, but the rest of them did. He looked up to his mother's face.

"Who is it?" he whispered.

She remained silent. But his father, hand on the boy's shoulder, found his voice.

"Tah-neh-wa, your grandmother," he said.

The Mohican woman turned Mohawk—the mother of the children.

A woman clinging to the notion that she must see her daugh-

THE SAVAGE RIVER VALLEY

ters' faces, hold tight her grandchildren to her breast, and make peace with the men, if only once more in her lifetime. She had slipped into the woods and made for the Mohican camp. She felt, more than knew, that her children were close.

Standing behind a tree, she had crept silently to the spot where Minnah crouched over the little fire. It was heartwarming to see her daughter a grown woman now. Tah-neh-wa was reluctant to make the first move, to show herself in a reversal of roles, humble before her children. She would ask for forgiveness. As she gathered her strength to step into the open, things began to happen. Her spirit was greatly troubled by the appearance of the white man. He was fierce and wild looking and she hated him on sight. When he grabbed Minnah, Tah-neh-wa let out, in a burst of terror, an alarming scream.

Within seconds Metoxem appeared and then she saw her husband approaching through the woods. Suddenly, she felt a new sensation upon seeing him; shame tinged with betrayal. Her face flamed red.

At the same time, her oldest son, White Feather, changed since she last set eyes on him, came running from the other direction. How handsome and so like his father he looked! She marveled at the man that he had become. And then she saw his eyes and tenderly felt their pain, a pain that jabbed her motherly heart. She had never wished to harm him or the others.

What could she do?

Her heart heavy and rooted to the spot, Tah-neh-wa, the spectator, had been unable to move. Now she felt fluidity return to her legs. She stepped into the opening and carefully stared first at her husband, then, in turn, at each of her children.

Was there a way, here in the quiet of the forest, surrounded by the gifts of Manito, to bring her family together in peace? Could she reach them through a mother's love? Was there a way to make all hearts blend as one?

Tears sprang to her eyes, yet she made no further sounds.

Instead, she was startled by the harsh sound of her Mohawk son who had cautiously come closer.

∿

"Father, pay attention to what I am going to say," Wanaque's voice was hard and his eyes angry. But Mahwah was not listening. He was staring at his wife.

The shame she carries will kill her, he thought. *And it is my fault.*

For reasons of foolish pride, he had never admitted this to himself before. Whatever anger rose up at the sight of his wife making her way to the Mohican camp earlier dissipated, and his heart melted in sympathy. She only wanted to see her children. For once, he completely understood the heart and courage of this woman who had given up all for him.

He must never hate her.

Impossible, where true love existed.

∿

An older brother! It had to be!

It was after Wanaque Wolf had stealthily approached, holding his bow and arrow at a downward tilt, the arrow barb, sharp, and deadly, pointed to the ground, did his eyes rest briefly on all of them and then settled on the Mohican Warrior, who stood a head taller than he. All those in the clearing momentarily pausing to take stock of the situation, heard him gasp.

He looked at a mirror image, that is to say a much older version of himself. He saw the same dark eyes with a prominent jaw line, the same broad swath of cheek, and the fullness of the upper lip, all that from their mother. The face he saw reflected in the clear waters of a stream was the same that looked upon him now. But he didn't like what he saw. A bizarre shock, unexpected and unwanted. He looked to the squaw that he thought stupid and pampered, and

THE SAVAGE RIVER VALLEY

now he understood why he had never accepted her, why as a young boy no one would talk about certain, though subtle, differences: the shy way she spoke their language, the hesitation in searching for a word, the way she decorated their skins and the way she cooked their meals apart from the other women.

Nothing unacceptable, just different. But it was precisely this difference that had infuriated him. He had never understood it until today. She had never been a true Mohawk, no matter how hard she tried for the sake of her husband and son to assimilate into the Mohawk village and way of life.

The realization hit him like a bolt of lightning.

His anger knew no limits at that moment. His mother was a Mohican? If anyone had dared to suggest such a thing, he would have cut him where he stood. How could his father, a true-blooded and proud Mohawk, lie with a woman of the enemy tribe? And that could mean only one thing. He too was part Mohican. The thought filled him with an unforgivable fury directed at both his parents.

"Father!" he commanded.

There was no reply.

"Do you hear me? Look at me!" he bellowed, his voice cracking at the end.

But only the Mohican warrior turned to stare at him, his brow furrowed in concentration.

White Feather had known of the son and had seen the cold blue eyes from a distance. From the secluded cover of the bushes, he had seen his mother tending their fire in a Mohawk village, while the son stood close by, berating his mother for a tasteless morning meal. He heard the sharp sounds of the Mohawk language and knew he had a look alike. That had been in 1608, ten winters back, when one night he left the longhouse of his family and headed north. Then, the son was a mere boy, but in front of him today stood a man—a man that stood in shock at seeing White Feather face to face, a man that was armed to the teeth.

What stunned the Mohican was not the boy with whom he

shared the same mother, but rather the father, as he put together all the pieces of a very mysterious puzzle.

He nodded once and then grunted, finally lowering his tomahawk. He would not kill the husband of his mother.

Now it dawned on him. His life spread out before him: his youth, the death of a man whom he thought to be his father, and the disappearance of Creek from the death ceremony. The vanishing of his mother now made sense to him: how the bands of the best hunters could not find her in the forest, supposedly a woman alone. He never could understand how she made her way north to the land of the Maquas. A squaw, never taught the same skills of a man, would leave tracks. He understood. All that time, days, months, and years after the burial of his grandmother, she had not been alone.

The Mohawk, an expert at covering his tracks, had spirited her away.

That day in northern Mohawk lands White Feather had not spied the father of this family. Little did he know that Mahwah, long experienced in protecting his lands and his people and unmatched in hunter instincts, had known of his approach to the village. He had stood at the campfire with bowl in hand, when suddenly he sniffed the air. His body stiffened, and without a word to his wife, he took off.

In less than an hour, he located the young Mohican. The Mohawk stayed hidden in the shadows, out of sight of the young man, observing this Mohican hunter and warrior who was also his first-born. Curiously, he watched the profile of his first son, noting the muscles in his jaw, the line of his scalp, and the fine feather that hung from his hair. No harm would come to his son if he could help it, but Mahwah grimly acknowledged to himself the futility of any relationship with a Mohican brave. Yet he felt a surge of pride at seeing how this young warrior, single handedly and unaccompanied, had come to find them. Even more so, he had come and found his mother.

THE SAVAGE RIVER VALLEY

So, the bond of son and mother had been as strong as Mahwah had suspected that day years back when he tracked White Feather during his bear hunt. Nevertheless, if the Mohican came to destroy, he would have to defend his family. Fortunately, White Feather stayed but a short while in the shadows and then, having seen his fill, turned his back on his mother forever and left. What the father did not see from afar, as the Mohican trotted along the trails, were the tears, unshed and lingering, in White Feather's eyes. Staying out of sight, Mahwah followed the young Mohican from a distance, and turned back only when he was sure the Indian was truly headed home to his village on the flats near the Great Water.

Mahwah was certain of one thing. They would not see him again.

When he went into camp later that day, Mahwah never told his wife. She was better off that way.

And of this, Wanaque Wolf knew nothing. He felt stupid, betrayed by both his parents.

Conflicting emotions flashed over his face. His father, the Mohawk, said nothing. His mother, the woman that stood between him and this Mohican, looked to both of them with pity and tears. She had never meant for this to happen. But she had missed her Mohican children so! The meshing of the Mohican and the Mohawk world had occurred, and yet she still loved all her children, no more one than the other. She understood each son for their strengths and loved each one for their weaknesses, though she prayed extra for Manito to soften the heart of her last child, who treated others badly and who, without remorse, hunted for the sake of killing—animals or humans. Even though she had done a bad thing by abandoning her village, the sentimental heart of this Indian woman was a good one. Yet it was not enough to smooth over the pain. For now the two sons were enemies by virtue of their different birthing places. In the Mohican village of Wachachkeek, Tah-neh-wa had gone to the birthing lodge to squat and push out her first son, and as she looked upon his face for the first time, Sasqua entered, placed her palm over his head, and softly gave a prayer of blessing. In the Mohawk village, there was no one to help her as she squat and screamed in agony. She felt the bones pull, but no baby came out. Only her husband, Mahwah, hearing her, came to her aid; with his help, she pushed with great force on the babe that resisted being squeezed into the world. Both exhausted, the parents forgot to say a prayer of blessing before putting the babe to tit.

White Feather, feeling the probing eyes of his mother upon him, turned to meet her gaze. Her first-born, the child she had looked upon with such delight and love, could feel his features soften as he looked upon the woman who had given him life. Tenderness welled up inside of him, promising a melting of his hard-edged heart. The look they shared at that moment was eternal. Both understood each other.

White Feather found forgiveness once more in his heart. What of his sister?

From a distance, Minnah held tight to her husband, watching her mother with only a flicker of recognition. This woman seemed almost a stranger. Her hair color looked unaffected by time although her face showed a few wrinkles, and when the woman warmly smiled in her direction, Minnah was hesitant, for she knew more was to come. Death had occurred when the white man breathed no more, when his chest fell flat, and his face turned blue. But her vision was not complete. She held tighter to her son and husband and feared what would happen next. It was nothing she could stop.

Tamaqua sensed her fear and whispered in her ear, "La-tech-ka?" *What is it?*

The Mohawk, known as Mahwah—father of White Feather and Wanaque Wolf, husband of Ta-neh-wa—stepped back. This bond of mother and child was stronger than himself, an intangible force that Mother Earth, wife to Manito, understood. He realized that the heart of his woman was not entirely his. She loved others as intently as she loved him. But all in all, this moment belonged to them.

Only Wanaque was not to be deterred, his anger would be sated. His honor had been grievously injured, insulted, and attacked. This

THE SAVAGE RIVER VALLEY

was personal. And it went straight to his heart like an arrowhead heated in a fire.

"I curse this day and the day that woman was born," he bitterly said.

His heart, pounding in his chest, was filled with evil, all the black forces of the spirit world reveled in his whirling emotions, his uncontrollable energy made for a feast for their insatiable greed.

Minnah gasped in fright. She saw it happen. Around this young Mohawk, who raised his bow to chest height, flew dark shapes, fast and agitated. She could feel their darkness of being, the cold and calculating manner in which they fed off the young warrior's hatred and egged him on. For the second time in her life, she met evil in its purest and earthbound form—the son of her mother. Suddenly, a sickening sensation overcame her. The vision she had seen in 1608, sitting at the fireside with Saquiskawa, their husbands, and White Feather, would be fulfilled today. Her heart sank.

The passions of this agitated warrior stimulated his need to commit a barbarous act—a loathsome deed, an act of revenge. These feelings, unchecked, were to return tenfold during his lifetime. No religion, no morality, no guilt of conscious could stay his arrow. His delight would culminate in drawing the blood of the Mohican. No regrets. A vengeance fulfilled.

"Blood vengeance for my Mohawk ancestors," he said softly.

"No!" screamed Minnah.

ᨑᨑ

He raised his arrow and bow to pierce the heart of this Mohican that looked as he looked; the same face, the same hair, and the same color of eyes. Killing him was the only way to wipe the anger from his heart and mind. The dark and evil spirits rejoiced in his decision.

At that moment, Metoxem, having watched the two men and hearing his mother scream, broke away from his father's grip and ran to protect his uncle. When you love someone, you are willing to die to save them. He had proven his manhood that day, and nothing short of death would stop him any longer. He was a man, fighting in a man's world. Fear was not a part of it. From the corner of her eye, Tah-neh-wa saw her son, Wanaque Wolf, his face showing no emotion, raise his bow and aim the deadly arrow. She had seen him this way before and knew what it meant. Without hesitating, she boldly stepped forward, holding up her arms as if to defend her other son and the young boy running to stand by his side.

"No, Wanaque Wolf, my son," she whispered.

As the arrow let loose, all seemed to happen in slow motion. The cripple still lay on the ground, not making a sound. Clara had disappeared. Tamaqua, all the while alert to the possibility of other white men in the vicinity, had started forward, but his wife held him back, grabbing his arms, chest, and then, finally, his neck, pulling her weight against his own. Seconds later, he disentangled himself, going for his son, but it was too late.

White Feather and Mahwah the Mohawk, unflinching, dove for Metoxem and Tah-neh-wa respectfully. But the arrow was faster than the movement of the older Mohawk, for Mahwah could not step in front of Tah-neh-wa as perhaps he could have once before, given a younger day and sprightlier muscles.

"Ahhhh," he moaned in frustration as he fell forward.

The arrow, shot by a steady finger and guided by a sharper eye, sped to its destination. The woman named Tah-neh-wa took it straight into her chest. And there, in this clearing, she instantly fell in a slump, caught only as she reached the ground by her husband of many years, the Mohawk named Mahwah—her rock of the earth, her best friend, her earthly soul mate who had given her joy in life and essentially robbed her of it at the same time.

And as her heart was pierced, so was his. A million unwanted stings, a multitude of arrowheads torched his soul in unbearable agony. He knew, without even thinking that the woman would die.

How could he live without her, without her face, her smile, her touch, her spirit?

He held her gently in his arms, the tears flowing unabated down his face. How he wished he had taken the arrow instead. The anguish settled deep, he struggled to breathe. He knew it was useless to call out to Manito. It was done. For the second time in his life, he was losing his Tah-neh-wa, and this time at the hand of their second-born son. Only this time it was for good. There would be no rescuing her ever again. Something inside of him was dying as well. There was no way to stop it.

He wanted to go with her on the journey she was about to take. Walk with her, hold her hand, and pull her to him to be with her forever. There was only one prayer left.

"Manito," he prayed silently, his lips moving in worship, "na-te-nil." "Take me with her."

White Feather, holding fast to Metoxem and Minnah, recovered from the shock of what she had just seen, slowly came to their fallen mother's side, and knelt, pushing down the boy between them.

Both children reached for her free hand and clasped it within their own. Already they could feel the skin growing cold as the blood slowed its journey through the dying woman's body.

They both spoke in unison. "Ga-ho-wes" they said softly. "Mother."

Their mother softly spoke. "N-ma-tsch" she said. "I will go home."

Tah-neh-wa looked at each of them in turn. She raised her other hand in a feeble attempt to touch each cheek and look deep within their eyes. Only Wanaque Wolf, her last child of the earth, hung back, watching the scene in sulky bitterness, all the anger welling up like a great explosion of agony. It was then that he made a fateful decision and changed the course of his life. Had he stepped closer, he too would have received a look of love, exonerating him from guilt, for never did she wake to a new day and look upon her Mohawk son with contempt or scorn. His pardon in the eyes of Manito would have been granted. As it was, he refused to step forward.

From somewhere high up in the Onteoras, the spirit of Manito grumbled.

"Wanaque Wolf," his father harshly called to him. "Kneel, ask Manito for forgiveness. Speak to this woman, your earth mother," his father angrily continued. Mahwah turned and looked at his son, but not before he glimpsed the compassionate face of White Feather, the good son, the loving son, the son he would never know. He knew both brothers were as different as the spirit of day and the spirit of night.

He yelled once more at his other son. "Come and beg forgiveness." But at those words, Wanaque Wolf lost every sense of humanity he ever experienced. The blood pumped furiously in his veins, his body shook. His anger knew no boundaries. How dare his father take her side once more! Before turning and running at full speed to escape into the woods, he let fly one more piercing and deadly arrow, the strongest from his quiver.

"You both die, together," was his final call.

Then suddenly, as if Tah-neh-wa heard something, a silent summons intended only for her, she looked beyond their heads. Above the spot where she lay in her husband's trembling arms, perched on a thick branch, was the giant eagle, looking proud and vigilant.

She smiled and then closed her eyes for the last time. At that moment, the legendary Mohawk called Mahwah, her husband of many years, fell dead at her side, the last arrow traveled through his body to reach hers; the barb of the arrowhead hooked them both in death.

∿

And so with the passing of Tah-neh-wa and Mahwah went the secrets of the past: the forbidden love before the turn of the century of a young Mohican girl with a young Mohawk brave, the sighs and whispers as time passed that forbade a union, the possible

THE SAVAGE RIVER VALLEY

explanations, the words that could have been spoken to ease the terrible pain for those who were left, and the wonderings of why and how and at what point their mother had decided to leave and join another tribe, another clan, another land, and village. She drew one last breath and went silent. All the pardons of her misdeeds no longer mattered to her broken heart, for her heart beat no more.

Memories would speak of a time when she was a Mohican, memories of a time when she struggled to be a good Mohawk squaw.

At the exact moment she closed her eyes, across the land several lengths away, just as several raindrops fell, there came the lusty cry of a newborn. The sound reached many ears. A miracle—never a surprise to the Indians, for Manito was the Great Spirit—had taken place; a cleansing of ill will. Minnah, now at a calm she had not felt in years, lifted her head and smiled, knowing the baby to be the child of Saquiskawa and grateful to hear the sound of a new member of her family.

The cripple, from where she lay unconscious and close to the brink of death, felt it reach her as a second breath of life, and she breathed in deeply. When the Dutch girl opened her eyes, she felt somehow different, almost as if she were a new person. She awoke to find White Feather's face hovering inches above her own. She stared into his dark eyes.

He who had long resisted the softening of his bitter nature now was drawn to the courageous nature of this woman. Life had changed.

He held out his hand.

"Peace," he said quietly, thinking that to be her name.

She, who had never known the softening of her heart toward a man until now, took it. White Feather helped her to a standing position. This time, caught in his arms, Clara did not scream nor did she faint.

It was at that moment that Metoxem, driven by his second sight, ran to his uncle and grabbed his arm, pulling relentlessly.

"Hurry," he screamed, "the Great Bird has swallowed my cousins!"

321

Further north, the Mohicans accepted it as sign from Manito not to make war against their enemy. The sachem of Shodack, never one to make a hasty decision to attack without council, wisely gave the sign to retreat back to their villages on both sides of the Great River. They backed away from the clearing that was buzzing with angry Mohawks; forgetting about the ships and white men, leaving their furs where they lay, and avoiding an all out massacre. Had fate not played in their favor, they would all have died that day in the clearing.

By following the call of Manito, they were saved. The renewal of life was complete. Saquiskawa's second daughter and her last child of the earth had been born. The life of Saquiskawa's mother, an old Indian squaw, had ended.

And in the little shaded cove where White Feather first laid eyes on a white woman, the shaman stone, emanating a soft glow that shone over the dark rock upon which it rested, finally, after so many years, had come home to the land of its ancestors. The wood fairies and spirits to whom Minnah had lit the fire now gave thanks, dancing in glee about the little fire that still burned. High in the Onteoras a gentle sigh of relief spread across the land. Manito had spoken.

Some thought it to be the sound of wind.

Chapter Sixteen

The men aboard the Fortuyn were agitated, rushing back and forth along the railing, shouting to the men in the water.

"Swim hard! Swim faster, men!" they yelled in encouragement, the sound of their voices buffeted by the rising wind. It was the unspoken agreement to help other sailors in trouble that urged them to cry out.

Captain Adrian Block remained calm.

Christ, the next thing they'll get into their thick heads might involve the guns down below, he thought. It could mean an all out war. The last thing he wanted.

There's no knowing how many savages would be upon us in that case, he thought grimly.

It was no time to lose their heads or to get panicky, regardless of what was happening on land. Besides, it wasn't his men or his ship that were in desperate straits.

Captain Block stayed the men with a wave of his hand. Luckily enough, he had been blessed with a commanding voice and presence. His own father, a sea captain, had spent many an hour teaching him to project his voice. "A captain's voice is everything," he would say. It inspired them to follow orders. Now, more than ever, it served its purpose. Block gave a hearty shout.

"Let the savages war it out amongst themselves! Hold back!"

The Fortuyn's men, knowing it could be them in the water, stopped their noise and listened.

"A few dead Indians never hurt anyone. We'll not get involved. When the dust clears, when the day is over and all is calm, we will return. Yea, we'll not give up."

Block had grimly watched the events on land unfold without immediately understanding any of it or what had preceded this seeming skirmish. But he was astute enough to know he wanted to become no part of it.

Just a short while back, his ship had sailed into view of the trading post. From afar, on the Fortyun's poop deck, he had spotted the tip of the Black Bear's mast and crow's nest, big enough for one man but only now empty. The little banner atop was full, signifying an increasing breeze. He glanced at the sky and saw the oncoming clouds. So, he thought, the fool Hendricks had arrived early. As they came closer, there appeared to be absolute bedlam everywhere, on shore, in the murky water of the river, and on the Black Bear—where the astonished look of the remaining crew on board told him things were happening fast—too fast for the effects of reason to set in. There was no time to think, only react. To every action, there is a reaction, oftentimes an adverse one.

On shore, a group of savages were locked in a standoff, two different bands of painted warriors facing each other, shifting their weight from foot to foot, passing their tomahawks from one hand to another, all overtures for battle, yet making no move to attack. Block estimated the number of savages to be far above what he considered manageable.

Block felt his body go tense.

"Be Jesus himself, what is going on?"

Where was the ship's leader? He looked for the recognizable lanky form of Hendricks in his plumed hat.

The captain, normally decked out in his velvety and feathery finery that served more to impress himself than the heathens, was nowhere to be seen. No feather bouncing at a cocky angle from what Block could see. It was then that he spotted the rowboat making its way to the Black Bear. Block blinked and took a second look to be certain of what he saw. Inside he caught sight of Hendricks, muddied, wet, and bareheaded. He was standing over a few men, rowing as hard as they could.

THE SAVAGE RIVER VALLEY

And there was more. Block's heart skipped a beat.

The man was out of his mind or brazenly stupid.

Two Indian youths, their bald heads shining in the glare of the sun, huddled under the stare of the white men. Captives? No wonder the heathens were mad!

"To the ship and hurry, you bastard swine, or I'll kill you all myself."

He heard the captain's voice clearly across the waterway, even though the two ships were still a distance apart.

What was the fool thinking?

If only Block could read the man's mind. But, he didn't have to. The scene was playing out before his eyes.

In his haste, without waiting for the rowboat to come to shore and wading out to it, Hendricks relived the moment Harmensen, trailed by two Indian boys in hot pursuit, had raced into the clearing and skidded to a stop at Hendricks's side, throwing Jansen's head onto the sandy bank. The decapitated head lolled to the side, face up. The dead man's eyes stared cruelly at the captain, almost accusingly. Hendricks had recoiled in horror. The Mohicans, too many to count, were directly behind him, finally emerging into the open meadow. Hendricks froze, recalling the murder of Juet—murder, if one counts deserting a Juet surrounded by heathens while he, second mate and privy to the murder of Hudson, turned his back and made for the ship. He could still hear the captured man's screams as they tied him over a heap of branches and set it afire.

"You dirty swine. Don't leave me!" he begged and then angrily screamed at the backs of the retreating men. Scared shitless, Hendricks had been. The urine had poured in a steady hot stream down his leg, soaking his trousers. Even as he ran, he caught a whiff of its strong odor as it seeped through his clothes.

And next to him, exhibiting an equal if not greater amount of fear and running just as fast, was the man whose head now lay on the beach at his feet. Jansen had always been a fool. Now, he was dead. No telling what he had been up to in the woods and how he had gotten away unnoticed by the others, though Hendricks could make a good guess: the Indian man whose squaw Jansen was intent on raping found him and killed him. Finally, his penchant for brutality did him in; he probably deserved it, though the horror of Jansen's death did not escape Hendricks.

He could hear a steady hum of voices from the Indians around him. Suddenly, a piercing war cry spilled over all of them.

It was happening again, a repeat in history.

"God, help us all," he almost cried out in torment. Would they all lose their heads? It was then that he pulled his knife and grabbed one of the Indian youths by the hair. The youth howled and squirmed in his grasp. Hendricks pulled harder, and the boy yelped in pain. Harmensen, following his lead, did the same. They turned their backs on the pressing Mohicans and Mohawks and shoved the boys onto the floor of the rowboat. Hendricks put a hand of each boy under his boot and leaned his full weight forward when they struggled to escape. Soon they grew quiet, their hands throbbing in agony. Once still, the white man shifted his weight and the pain eased.

But Block knew nothing of what had transpired before his ship had sailed into view. He had teamed up with Hendricks years ago as a trader in the New World on the Great River, but had since, after a bitter fall out that left each filled with hatred, parted ways. He trusted the man like he trusted the savages—not at all.

His mind was racing, looking for answers. Putting together the pieces of a complex yet disturbing puzzle.

The captain is fleeing the scene of trading? Was that what he saw?

Heaped on the beach lay shattered barrels, their prized contents spilled out in profusion, spread haphazardly all over the sand.

Is Hendricks giving up on the furs to be traded? Is he giving up the profits to be made that year? No, it couldn't be, he told himself, shaking his head in confusion. Or could it? Unless he was mistaken, Block began to believe his eyes.

THE SAVAGE RIVER VALLEY

He saw the rowboat reach the ship and the frightened men, dragging the squirming boys by the hair, scramble up the rope after the captain. Directly behind them, floundering in the water, was the rest of his crew, swimming fast as if the deserting traders were about to leave them.

So, it was as it seemed! The captain and his men were escaping!

Ah, so the puzzle fits together, a multitude of pieces.

"For God's pity," Block said out loud, feeling moderately safe on board his ship. "What have we here?"

For while the Black Bear made ready to sail, its frightened captain frantically screaming orders as if he had completely lost his nerve, the Indians, still watching each other, turned their sights on the two ships. There must have been over a hundred of them, perhaps more. It was hard to tell.

All of them seemed to be staring directly at Block. Or was it his imagination? He almost stepped back but caught himself.

It was then, at that propitious moment, the kind where God interjects, that they heard it. It was the cry of a baby from somewhere in the southern stretch of woods. All heads, white and Indian alike, went up instantaneously, hearing the miraculous little cry. How magnified was the sound carried over the treetops! How strange that the fragile little cry would touch them so! An innocent beginning in a land that was primitive and vicious. Stranger was the fact that the larger group of Indians, oddly forgetting about the two captive youths on board the ship, turned their backs and slipped into the forest, which seemed to gobble them up in seconds—almost as if they had never been there! If he had not seen the huge band of Indians only seconds before, he never would have believed it could happen in so little time. Canoes full of the tribes that lived on the distant shore streamed across the river. They ignored the big ships that dwarfed their small floating craft. Rowing swiftly past the vessel, the Mohicans posed no threat.

Once on the other side, the Indians pulled their canoes out of the water, hoisted them to their shoulders, and disappeared into the foliage of green.

Block turned his attention back to the beach and the clearing. Someone had set fire to the wooden roof of the little hut the Dutch called Fort Nassau. It marked the end of the white man's fort. The stones would remain, a bit blackened. But all that was wood would burn.

And then he heard the cries for help and saw the smoke at the same time, drawing his attention back to the shore. A cry of anger went up around him. Two of Hendricks's men, no telling which ones, dressed as they were in the short pants and loose shirts all the seamen wore in warm weather, had been captured, their hands and feet tied and bound to a heavy branch. The branch, sloping with the weight of the men, was propped up by several Indians over a fire. Then it dawned on Block and his men—it was a roasting spit for humans.

Block felt his stomach give a heaving jolt. He gripped the railing in white-knuckled fury.

If only he could get the guns up top!

"Get control of yourself," he mumbled.

He shuddered and glanced around, conscious of his men watching him. But Block was smarter than succumbing to horror. Nothing could be gained by seeing their captain overcome by a weak stomach. Burning the men was sickening, but did this act merit starting a war in which the likelihood of all of them perishing would be a certainty? They had a small cannon, but the timing necessary to reload would give an advantage to the savages and they would be swarming his decks. The futility of the captured men's situation dawned on all of them. No one could save them. Fate had dealt the poor bastards an ungodly hand.

Block detested the savagery. It was abominable. Those two men were going to die far from their homelands, far from their families, and for no good reason other than the apparent fact that their captain was a coward. Their bones would lie in a deadly part of this world, uninhabited, for all he knew, by kindred whites for a long time to come, if ever.

Guns or no guns, there were simply too many Indians to fight.

THE SAVAGE RIVER VALLEY

He felt a fleeting sense of hopelessness. His shoulders, so used to carrying the weight of responsibility, sagged.

It was then that the memory of a few years came back to him.

In that year, the promising year during which he traded as a team with Hendricks, each looking out for the other, he had lost his first ship, the Tijger, set ablaze by some hostiles in the lower reaches of the river, quite close to shore. How they did it, he never found out. Ship and cargo were lost. Miraculously, he and a few others had survived. One would have thought his partner would have come quickly and unerringly to his rescue. It was not to be. Hendricks, his ship already with a full crew, deserted him, leaving him and a few others to fend for themselves until word reached Amsterdam and a new ship was sent from the Old World.

This decision would impact their lives for months to come. It could mean their death.

Block remembered the silent fury he felt as Hendricks sailed away. In anger, he watched the sail until he could see it no more. The horizon swallowed the ship from sight. At that desperate moment, he swore he would stay alive, if only to someday exact revenge on Hendricks.

Shortly after that, as he took a harsh look around him, he saw his only chance of survival: befriend the Indians.

In time, Block gained their respect by a few offerings that washed ashore from his ship. The Canarsies, wary though friendly to the white men, helped Block and a few remaining sailors to do one thing. Survive. The Indians bestowed gifts upon the shipwrecked men, dumping heaps of corn and beans at their feet before backing away. The chief sent a few hunters to show them the ways of the hunt. Otherwise, the strange-speaking, pale-faced men from across the sea would have died that winter. With time on their hands, Block and his men set to work. They labored to construct another boat. Their efforts paid off. The Onrust, crude and rough, although much smaller than the Tijger, served as a sturdy vessel with which to explore the lower reaches around the Eylandt of the Manahata and beyond that, due east, the Long Eylandt. Starting off was a feat. The boat maneuvered through swirling waters.

"It is as if a gate is opening from hell. Name it Hell's Gate," commanded Block as the boat tossed and turned. Further on, he gave an order.

"Mark this in our memories, men. It is a long sound of water that lies beside this Long Eylandt."

Next in the bay, he landed on a tiny island. When his feet touched the soil, he was assailed with inspiration! Let's name it, he thought, surveying the bucolic spot.

"That's it then. We name it Block Island."

With a stiff wind whipping up white caps, Block and his men set out in their little boat each day that spring. The Onrust, only a tad bit longer than forty feet, was not seaworthy. But each evening, Block and his men held a newfound respect for this land.

"Who sails this zee?" he asked one day as they sailed north on the river twenty lengths.

"The Tappans," answered his mates.

"Then it shall be the Tappan's Zee," he replied.

The information they gathered was valuable for mapmaking, and the new mission helped to pass the time. While he gloried in his discoveries, and even re-visited the island named in his honor, there was no mistaking one fact. Block did not care to repeat another year, cold and faced with a hunger that could never be eased, anxiously awaiting another ship from the Old World to rescue him while all the time, day in and endless day out, wondering if he was going to die or if he would ever feel the comfort of a warm bed again.

He anxiously anticipated whether the Indians, though up to this point not barbaric, would turn on him and his men. They had often heard suspicious noises in the woods around them, which told them the Indians were close, possibly spying on them. They waited, knowing they were defenseless, but breathed in deep relief when no attack occurred.

"Praise God," were his words to start and finish the day. "Kneel

THE SAVAGE RIVER VALLEY

men," he commanded. "God is speaking to the hearts of the Red Men in our favor."

Perhaps recognizing the white men's inability to do them harm, the Indians simply let them go on day after day. Still, the thought of death lingered on their minds.

A cough broke through the vivid memories that had detached him from the scene.

"Captain, sir, will we not be aiding the Black Bear's men, sir?" His first mate, clearing his throat, hovered at his side. The man was drenched in sweat, his face a ghostly pale.

Block was shaken from his reverie.

The Black Bear was raising the anchor. Block heard the straining rub of the chain against the wood and could see the figures still scurrying over the boat. The lowering of every sail signaled desperation to flee. There was certainly enough of a wind to accomplish an abrupt exodus.

He gave one last glance around. Once the Black Bear left, and indeed it soon would be gone, his ship would be unaccompanied.

"Alone?" He could feel fear rise within his body.

Suddenly, he made a decision.

"Turn ship, raise sail!" he yelled to his men, giving full swing to the captain's wheel. "And bring my long gun ... loaded!" he ordered his first mate. The first mate quickly turned and disappeared below decks while all hands set to sail. He returned in less than three minutes bearing the weapon, a heavy dark musket and a powder horn. From that distance, Block, under normal conditions an expert shot, would, with one eye shut and the other narrowed, take careful aim, resting the long gun on the shoulder of the first mate. It was time to put those poor bastards out of their howling misery as the ship made its turn, by a shot through the heart or head for an instant death, instant relief. The distance for the bullet to reach the men in agony was, in his estimation, too far, but at least he would make the attempt. Who knows, it might travel farther than he thought. After all, Block would want the same if it were him. He pitied the men. Already he caught a tiny whiff of burning flesh.

What a horrendous smell!

He had to hurry.

He sighted the target down the long barrel.

He took a shot. And he missed.

One minute to reload. He let off still another shot, this time miraculously hitting the mark. A single shot bearing through each man's head. Block, unaware that he held his breath while shooting, exhaled in relief. He could hear the resounding high pitched hooting calls of the Mohawks as they looked about in fury. There was no mistaking that sound. They were angry.

Block sighed.

Indeed, there would be no more trading that summer.

As the ships departed downriver and out of sight, and the peaceful Mohicans deliberately backed away from the angry Mohawks whose intent feverishly centered on the burning corpses, the heavy rain promised by the oncoming storm clouds rushing over the mountains vanished in thin air. There was no sudden clap of thunder, no distant rumbling, and no streaks of jagged lighting piercing the land.

Manito, the Great Spirit, was pleased, or maybe appeased.

As the clouds broke apart, the sky opened up. A wide ray of sunlight filtered down in a brilliant shaft, warming the camp where the newborn babe lay nestled in the arms of Light of the Sun that Speaks Softly. In days to come, all would remark on the remarkable clarity of the babe's eyes, a bright sparkling blue.

The wind gently whispered over the land, a lingering whisper of something that once was and was no longer.

Chapter Seventeen

1624

"Madame, may I walk with you?"

Most of the women, once on deck, moved cautiously. The handful of children, pale from a lack of sun and needing the fresh air, were not allowed to roam freely. One never knew when a rogue wave would sweep them away or when a loosely hanging block from a sail would swing wide and knock them off their feet.

Perhaps it was not simply by chance that he happened to be on deck when she was walking the babe. He had watched for her, curious to see her, to talk with her. It had been on their third day at sea that he noticed the young woman keeping to herself. Apparently, she preferred the company of the women below, for seldom did he see her after that. But what he saw, he liked; the curve of her cheek, the gentle look in her eye, the quiet way she walked with a lightness that he admired immediately. Not to mention her comely face and shapely form, topped with a mass of yellow hair. She was, in his shrewd estimation, a masterpiece.

The very thought of her lit and warmed the long days at sea. Now it was near three months later. The ship was close to land. He knew of the tragic accident some weeks back. But no one spoke of it now. Her loss, unfortunate for her, was his gain, and much to his advantage. It was time for the conquest.

He smiled at her.

She smiled back; a sweet docile vision for his starved eyes. The babe was nestled in the crook of her one arm. The striped skirt she wore billowed in folds from her waist. Under it were other layers of material, woolly stockings, and stout black shoes. Her bodice was of linen, the finest one could imagine, and her cape was of heavy wool, providing a nest of warmth on this day in April.

She extended the other hand shyly in greeting.

Her demeanor with this stranger now showed nothing of the behavior she displayed in front of the women down in the womb-like cabin weeks before. And it seemed that all had forgotten her screams of agony resounding throughout the ship and out over the vast ocean.

"I am strong." At that, he raised his arm, bending it to better display his natural strength. Grabbing her hand, he placed it on a hard muscle. She felt his strength.

"You will need a husband, a place to live," he went on, nodding and smiling at her.

She looked at him carefully, with narrowed eye.

"My name is Isaac. Isaac Raseers."

Seconds passed while she summed him up. His dress spoke of apparel that was finer than the other men on board. How was it that she had not noticed him before? Although scruffy from months at sea, there was nothing frayed or worn about his breeches, stockings, buckled shoes, or top felt hat. He was of medium height, but had shoulders that looked capable of carrying a heavy weight—perhaps the weight of a woman and child. And his hands, wide and strong looking, brushing her arm, appeared ready to tackle whatever came in his path.

He took a step closer.

"I travel with my companions. Among them are Pieter Van Vechten, a farmer, and Robert of Glasco, a stocking-weaver. We will do well in the New World."

He saw a spark of added interest flame in her eyes. His instincts had proved him right. She was smart enough to see the wisdom of his ways. She glanced out to sea. The sky was soft, but cloudy, and

THE SAVAGE RIVER VALLEY

the air was chilly. The weather acted as if on cue, a few faint snow-
flakes falling about them. A long, dark, gray strip of land lay ahead.
She knew the way of the world. A woman must have the protection
of a man. It would be quite difficult, if not impossible, to survive
alone, even with the help of the women below.

A great surge of life burned in her veins.

I hope I am pardoned for all the bad I have done, she thought.

Perhaps the angels her sister always spoke of would see that she
was not a bad person.

Maybe I can live a life of an angel now.

How strange that sounded, but it instilled her with hope, blind
hope. What awaited her was a faith in a God that would flourish in
the New World with plenty of hard but honest work.

There was also the matter of her sister and her whereabouts,
neither of less importance. But there was something else. She had
been robbed of a blessed childhood, snuggled in beauty and gentle
ways. While it had been cruel to live the life she led in Amsterdam,
in perpetual contact with men at their worst, perhaps now she could
lift the veil on life itself and partake of a better portion to render
a spirit like hers free—a spirit that had called on God and was
rewarded with this babe.

∿

Yes, she thought, *whatever awaits me, here I can sprout my wings. I
have come far but I can go farther. To the Nieuw Wereldt.*

She turned back to the young man.

"And mine, Aniline. And this is my daughter, Sarah Claire."

Chapter Eighteen

They called it Nieuw Nederlandt, coincidentally like the ship bearing the first official load of colonists. It was a sprawling, enormous tract of land claimed by the Dutch, stretching from what would be the Delaware River in the south to the Connecticut River in the north. Included was the entire River Valley. The valley of the Great River Hudson: the prospect of which the explorer, in whose memory it would in time be officially named, had taken profound delight. The territory belonged, unequivocally in their prejudiced estimation, to the Dutch Netherlands to be governed by the monopoly of the West India Company—by today's standards, a mega-powerful corporation, in those days the great wealth in the hands of a few. But, all in all, this was a mere portion of what they owned around the globe. Far-reaching was the hand of the Dutch.

But all of that was yet to come.

~~~

The Island of the Manahattoes was a perfect spot. How glorious it seemed upon approach! The verdant shoreline of spring met the eye in a pleasing manner. The air was fresh and invigorating, as to send waves of joy over a person. Surely the land was meant for them! It was deemed the way God wanted it to be. Their newly claimed bit of patria in another land awaited them.

Initially there was much to get done.

They chose the idyllic island whose rugged and slim tip ended at the head of the bay; one whose land mass connected all points

THE SAVAGE RIVER VALLEY

one complete answer that fit and left her satisfied. Since the day in the clearing when she took hold of White Feather's hand, she had never looked back. Was it reincarnation? She wasn't sure. But since the moment that Clara and Klarinda collided that day on the ridge, they were as one, sharing the same life.

Whatever the explanation, she had found a new happiness and wholeness, a sense of having found a home within a home. She thanked God for bringing her here. There was one thing, however, that haunted her, leaving her surrounded by a vague aura of sorrow. She knew her journey had not ended. There was more to come. The words spoken by the Old One had been prophetic. "Your journey will be long, during which time you will live the lives of others, however you will come back to this day." Clara shivered. That day, in September 2001 had been a day in her past and seemed so long ago. But if she reasoned clearly, that day now loomed many years in the future for she had gone back in time. If this was a journey, she had only begun.

It was a strange riddle, a puzzle, a jumble of words that Clara had yet to understand fully.

For now, she was living a life meshed with that of a Dutch girl: the memories were the same—which brought to mind the sister Aniline.

Six months, the older sister had said, six months and they would be together again. Meet in England, divvy up the diamonds to pay off the English merchant, and then disappear to live quietly, far from the reach of the Merchant Rensallear.

That had been the plan. Only it hadn't worked out that way. A plan perfectly laid and executed but with surprising outcomes.

Now it was five years later. Peace was an Indian woman, the woman of White Feather. He often called her his Manitoueeskwa, a female Manito with magical powers, who melted his days into nights, who placed stars around the moon, and who wove clouds of soft material upon which to lay his head and tired body—a woman who refreshed his soul with unlimited love and passion. Each night

341

he came to the creek and knelt in prayer, remembering his Uncle Creek, his mother Tah-neh-wa, and thanking his Manito for sending him his woman.

So much had happened, yet she was excited by the strange dream of her sister and the sound of her voice from far away. What could it mean?

Clara, now named Peace, smiled as White Feather returned to her side. She placed her hands over her abdomen. There was something she had been meaning to tell him. Now was the perfect moment.

∿∿

That night, other Indians heard the same cry.

One of them was a Mohican squaw named Minnah, who lifted her head in surprise.

The other was a Mohawk named Wanaque Wolf, running hard and fast on a trail south, heading straight for a village named Wachachkeek. He was not alone.

∿∿

That night, one angel, a blessed spirit of the Great Manito, heard it also.

The Old One.

The call had awakened all spirits of good and bad, the light and dark sides of the land and its people. Her journey had been long but there was still much work to be done, for the Old One must see to the bestowal of good gifts on the earth. Ancient spirits of her ancestors were gathering about her. It was time to bring another daughter home.

There was silence on the tall mountain peak, with its glittering cover of snow. Far below, the vast dark forests swept on to a distant horizon. The descending slopes jutted from beneath ice and mist.

THE SAVAGE RIVER VALLEY

Off to the north of the long valley, the Great River began, and off to the south, close to the shores where a ship would soon dock, the Great River ended. The flow was not deterred by the waning days and nights of winter. The Great Water, dark and gloomy, ran full and swift.

Should the time arrive when the land awakens from the profound depths of winter and, as of old, basks in the delights of spring?

Ah yes, but until then the Great River awaits the morrow, for then it shall reflect the colors of the changing landscape. And winter's death will pass away.

Was there a low moan of the breeze over the wood or among the mountain crevices and hollows? Did it smell vaguely of balsam, or were there faint whiffs of far off places that spoke of spices, canals, windmills, and the existence of the ageless soul?

The angel became alert.

She looked, from where she stood on a ledge in the Onteoras, to the light in the sky that flashed among millions of sparkling stars, the tips of her feathered wings swaying with the breeze that gently slid over the land. Spring might be a hundred years off, and then again, it might be a hundred years the same.

～⌇

The sacred historian never fails to spark the imagination, to refresh our souls, and to strengthen our hearts. To know who we are, we must know where we have been. Farewell observer, for now you must return to the present day world and leave this one behind. At least for now...

listen|imagine|view|experience

AUDIO BOOK DOWNLOAD INCLUDED WITH THIS BOOK!

In your hands you hold a complete digital entertainment package. Besides purchasing the paper version of this book, this book includes a free download of the audio version of this book. Simply use the code listed below when visiting our website. Once downloaded to your computer, you can listen to the book through your computer's speakers, burn it to an audio CD or save the file to your portable music device (such as Apple's popular iPod) and listen on the go!

How to get your free audio book digital download:

1. Visit www.tatepublishing.com and click on the e|LIVE logo on the home page.
2. Enter the following coupon code:
   090b-5206-ddd0-3ef2-e617-b8d4-1bf2-7a6f
3. Download the audio book from your e|LIVE digital locker and begin enjoying your new digital entertainment package today!